FREEZE FRAMES

FREEZE FRAMES

KATHARINE KERR

A TOM DOHERTY ASSOCIATES BOOK/NEW YORK

FREEZE FRAMES

Copyright © 1995 by Katharine Kerr

This book is printed on acid-free paper.

A Tor Book
Published by Tom Doherty Associates, Inc.
175 Fifth Avenue
New York, N.Y. 10010

Tor® is a registered trademark of Tom Doherty Associates, Inc.

Library of Congress Cataloging-in-Publication Data

Kerr, Katharine.
　　Freeze frames / Katharine Kerr.
　　　　p.　　cm
　　"A Tom Doherty Associates Book."
　　ISBN 0–312–89044–3 (hardcover)
　　I. Title.
　　PS3561.E642F74　　1995
　　813′.54—dc20　　　　　　　　　　　　　　　　　　95-5212
　　　　　　　　　　　　　　　　　　　　　　　　　　　　CIP

First edition: May 1995

Printed in the United States of America

0 9 8 7 6 5 4 3 2 1

For Susan Shwartz

Acknowledgments

A thousand thanks to Eleta Malewitz, who came up with the title when I couldn't think of one.

Contents

Descendants of

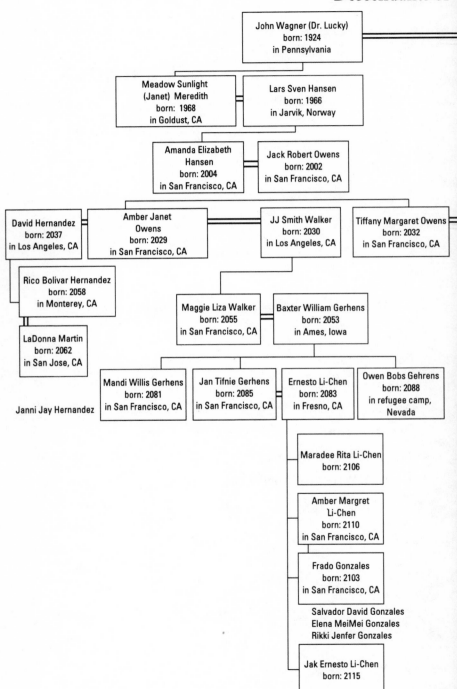

Maggie Cory

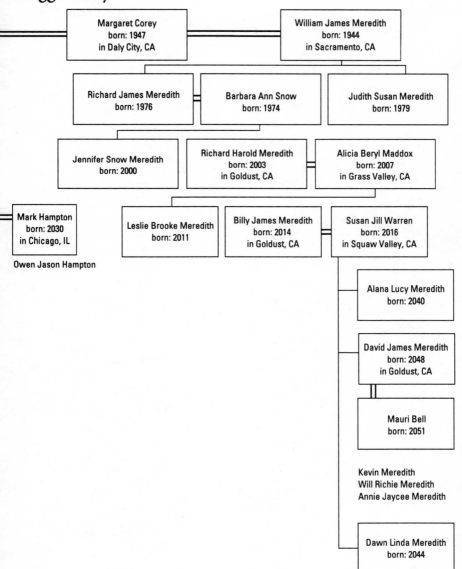

MEPHISTO: *Ir wiβt, wie wir in tiefverruchten Stunden,*
   Vernichtung sannen menschlichem Geschlecht...
                                          Goethe, *Faust, Part II*

(You know, you who were with me in the darkest hour, how we
planned to destroy the whole human race ...)

Dr. Lucky

Prologue in Iowa

$\mathcal{E}$NGLISH OAKS, IMPORTED TO THE PRAIRIE at great expense by some long-forgotten alumnus, edge the green lawn in the center of the campus. Since they were planted to memorialize students who died in the First World War, some morbid wag of the twenties named them Belleau Wood, and the joke has stuck, even though the students sitting under them now assume that the donor's name was Mr. Belleau. Some of these young men, dressed in white shirts open at the neck and khaki-colored chinos, are destined to die in places with exotic names like Vietnam and Cambodia, but at the moment, in the early sixties, those countries lie far away from a small private college in the heartland of America. The oaks, grown to a respectable size, nod in a summer wind that makes the heat just bearable. Flies circle ham sandwiches and bottles of Coke; students wave them away with a slow hand and wonder why they bothered to sign up for summer school.

Dr. John Wagner is beginning to wonder the same thing. He

has just left a faculty meeting, or perhaps it was a council of war, in which he and his fellows in the College of Sciences made hopeless noises about gaining a bigger share of the school budget for the autumn semester. Realizing that pharmaceutical chemistry, his own subject, falls very low on the administration's list of priorities, well below agricultural science and certainly as far south as Hades compared to the football team, has ruined his day. Hell is in a way very much on his mind; he orders the faculty dress code to take up residence there as he pulls off his tie, crams it into the pocket of his tweed jacket, then takes the jacket off as well and slings it over one shoulder.

As he strides across the green, he can feel the sun pounding down on his bald spot. On the edge of the shade sit coeds, plaid skirts decorously tucked over knees, white socks pulled up high over ankles and calves, white blouses buttoned up to round collars. One girl wears a string of pearls. Blue jeans and black leather boots, miniskirts and tie-dyed tank tops are only distant rumors to these girls. As he looks at their gleaming helmets of sprayed hair, Wagner can summon not the barest trace of lust. He does wonder if all those things you read about "free love," the supposed goings-on in places like New York and London and San Francisco, are true. He doubts it.

The faculty office building lies on the far side of Belleau Wood, three stories of fake Gothic, topped with a belltower, approached through a courtyard with an arched ambulatory. Inside, the warren of tiny rooms sports mullioned windows and diamond-paned glass. In spite of the thick stone walls—there is no air-conditioning—Wagner's cubicle swelters. He moves a stack of books from the sill and opens the one window to lean out. Far down below he can see students ambling toward the shiny new dorms at the edge of campus. They seem to be laughing, and he hates them. As he remembers his own college years, back in the 1940s, it seems to him that he never laughed unless he was dutifully acknowledging a professor's joke. The memory must be wrong. He hopes so.

Off among the shrubbery toward the faculty parking lot he notices an animal moving, heading toward the office building. Some student's dog, he supposes, a big black animal, a poodle, maybe, trotting purposefully along, as if it's escaped from a back-yard somewhere and come hunting its master. For a moment Wagner watches it sniffing a hedge, then leaves the window.

He flops down onto the swivel chair with a puff of dust from the cracking leather cushions and wonders if he should put his feet up on his desk in a raffish gesture. If he tries, he'll only dislodge and scatter heaps of books. Facing him like an enemy sits a pile of student exams, waiting for his grade. If he were a professor in some large college or university, such as Yale or Harvard, schools that he can only dream about, or even Caltech and Western Reserve, schools where he applied only to be turned down, he would have graduate students to grade these measly multiple choice quizzes and laboratory notebooks. As it is, he picks up a red pencil and scoots his chair to the desk.

Scattered on the pile by an indifferent secretary lies his mail, three advertisements and a letter from some college in California. The advertisements he tosses into the wastebasket, the letter he reads, skimming at first, then backing up to read more slowly, to savor, to doubt, to read again and confirm. Yes, a small college just outside of San Francisco, not a famous school, but certainly superior to this miserable hole where he teaches, is asking him, John Honus Wagner, to read a paper at a special conference in August, the theme of which is "Methodology in the Synthesis of Organic Compounds," his actual specialty, his island in the vast sea of modern chemistry. How did they even get his name? A scrawled note on the back of the letter explains. An old student of his, his best student—Hell, his one and only good student ever—has just received his doctorate from the University of California, is doing the scut-work of organizing a conference like this, and has dared to broach his mentor's name to the committee. Not only was Roger his one good student, but he's grateful. Wagner's eyes fill with tears, which he brushes away fast and hard.

The problem, of course, is money. The conference pays an honorarium, barely enough for a one-way ticket to San Francisco, if that. Not only is Wagner's salary small, but a large chunk of it goes every month to his ex-wife. The college has made it quite clear that "advances" happen only in science, never in the Accounting Department.

"God damn it all to Hell!"

He's screamed the words, not merely spoken them. At that precise moment, someone knocks on the door. Wagner swallows hard, reaches up to straighten the tie that's no longer there, shoves the chair back, and stands, wondering why he's standing.

"Who is it?"

"Nick Harrison. From Chem 10. I need to get you to sign something, sir."

"Come on in."

Although Wagner doesn't remember the name, he does recognize the student who enters, a tall young man, rather than a boy, with blond hair cropped close to his skull and pale grey eyes. He wears his short-sleeved blue shirt and chinos with some authority—a G.I. Bill student, or so Wagner remembers. In one hand Nick carries an official-looking stack of forms.

"Sorry to bother you, sir, but I've got to leave summer school. I need to have you sign the drop slip for your class."

"Sure." He waves at the other chair beside the desk. "Sit down. I hope nothing's wrong?"

"Well, yeah. Family emergency. In San Francisco."

"That's too bad. San Francisco, huh?"

"Yeah. It's a long drive, and I'm hoping to get all this stuff finished up today, so I can hit the road tomorrow morning."

Wagner merely nods, sitting down, searching for his pen among the books and papers, but he feels his heart start to pound, feels his face turn hot as if blood is rising there. He looks up to find Nick staring at him. His eyes are such a pale grey that they seem almost colorless, and he stares without blinking for such a long time that Wagner rubs his own eyes in sympathy, at which point Nick does, finally, blink.

"Say, Professor? You okay?"

"Uh, yeah, what makes you ask?"

"You look flushed. Real hot in here, but well, I just wanted to make sure you were okay. I mean, not having a heart attack or something."

"My dear young man! I am not old enough to worry about having a goddamn heart attack."

"Sorry." Nick shrinks back in his chair.

Wagner cannot find his pen. He begins lifting stacks of books, shoving stacks of papers, gives that up and begins opening drawers, finally looks up to find Nick holding out a ballpoint. The student's smiling a little, but his pale eyes never blink. Wagner grabs the pen and begins riffling through the stack of forms. At the moment he hates this self-assured young man, all blond and muscled, who survived the Army or maybe even the Marines, who endured some rite of manhood, anyway, while he, John Honus Wagner, was declared 4-F by his local draft board for a large number of small reasons.

"Tell me something," Wagner snaps. "Do you really have a family emergency, or are you just sick of summer school and want out?"

Nick blushes and squirms, looks away out the window fast. Wagner grins.

"Now listen here, I'm not sure I'm going to sign this, then. The regulations are pretty clear, you know. Once you're past the second week of summer school, you've got to have a damn good reason to drop."

"I've got one." Nick looks back. "And it really is a family emergency, kind of. Just not the usual kind. I mean, my old man isn't dead or dying, but this whole thing concerns him, yeah."

"Your father, you mean?"

Nick grins, slouching back in his chair, and all at once Wagner senses a predatory edge in his unblinking stare, as if perhaps he's used to knifing men who get in his way, who throw official reasons and official forms at his feet for stumbling blocks.

"Look," Nick says at last. "I'll try to explain. I'm really

thinking about dropping out of school. It all seems so meaning-less, you know? Like studying all this stuff, trying to get a liberal arts degree, taking courses like Chem 10, I mean, it just seems part of the—well, the absurdity."

"You've been reading Sartre, haven't you?"

Nick goggles.

"How'd you know?"

Wagner laughs, but he manages to make it sound kindly.

"Well, it's kind of a fad, yeah," Nick goes on. "But jeez louise, that stuff gets you. And so I signed up for summer school, just to—well, I don't know. See if I could make my myself believe in the usual things. And now I can't, and I want out."

"Yeah? But you want to leave the door open to come back, nice and legally?"

Nick smiles, suddenly rueful, with a shake of his head. He'd be a charming kid, Wagner thinks, if only he'd blink his goddamn eyes.

"Well, they say there's all this stuff going on in San Francisco, and I kind of wanted to go look around, find myself maybe."

"You've been reading Kerouac, too."

"Yeah, 'fraid so. But that does make sense. Getting out in the real world, living life and experiencing everything it has to offer. I've never done that."

"I thought you were in the service."

"Fort Lawrence, Kansas."

"Oh."

"I'm a world lit major, and I've always wanted to be a writer, and jeez, I don't have anything to say. I'm sick and tired of reading other people's books and pawing over the past."

"Ah, I see. And where does your father come into this?"

"Well, I made a kind of bargain with him. Well, more of a bet, actually, that I couldn't do what I want to do even in San Francisco, even if I tried going there."

"And then he thinks you'll come back and settle down?"

"Something like that." Nick leans forward, all earnestness.

"Haven't you ever felt like this, Professor? Like if you stay here you're going to suffocate? Just sort of dry up and blow away in one of the damn tornadoes? Sometimes when you were lecturing, I'd watch you and think, hell, I bet that here's a guy who understands. You know? Who feels what I do, stuck here in this two-bit college."

Wagner tries to remind himself that Nick is only working on him to wheedle a favor, that at this point he should come down firmly on the side of law and order and announce that he's not signing a drop slip for such a ridiculous reason, but he cannot find words. His tongue seems stuck to his mouth by some enormous thirst.

"Haven't you ever wanted to just break loose and go somewhere, hit the road, end up in a town like San Francisco?" Nick goes on. "They say all kinds of stuff is happening, out west."

"Well, maybe once I would have." Wagner finds his voice at last. "But I'm too old for that now. When you start pushing fifty, you start thinking about security, you know, things like tenure, a good pension plan."

"Ah come on! Are you telling me that the only reason you're staying here is because you feel old?"

"Look, pal, if you want me to sign that slip, you might try being a little less blunt."

"Well, yeah, I'm sorry. But it just seems kind of sad, you know. There's life out there, just waiting to be lived, like a bottle of wine on a shelf. You could just take it down and drink it, drink it right down and really live."

"Huh! And then what? You wake up with a hangover?"

"Maybe. But wouldn't it be worth it?"

"Would it? That's the rub. You wouldn't know until it was too late. But it's all a moot point, anyway. I'm not young, and I never will be again."

"Oh yeah? It could maybe be arranged."

"What in hell are you talking about?"

"What in hell, indeed?"

Nick grins, leaning so far forward that he can rest his elbows on the desktop. His eyes seem swirls of mist, not eyes at all. Wagner suddenly remembers the black poodle.

"Just who are you?" Wagner whispers.

"Names don't much matter, do they? I think you know. What if you were young again? Just what if?"

"Ah come on, even if you're who I think you are, you can't turn back Time."

"Who's talking about turning back Time? I'm talking about making you personally young."

"Ridiculous!"

"Oh yeah? Try me."

Nick rises, shoving back the chair, sweeping one hand toward the ceiling. When Wagner tries to stand, he reels, catching the edge of the desk with both hands to steady himself. The room spins in a golden cloud, slows, stops at last. He cannot quite remember what he's doing here, standing behind some professor's desk, wearing a pair of trousers from some dull suit and a white shirt, both too big for him. Without thinking he runs a hand through his sweaty hair, his thick hair, slightly curly, long enough to cover the tops of his ears. At that point he remembers.

"Jesus God!"

"Never say that name again!" Nick snaps. "I mean, hey, it's pretty damn rude if nothing else."

"Uh, yeah, sorry." Wagner looks down and finds his pot belly gone, finds his hands strong, smooth, muscled again, finds also that he's holding a pen. "Uh, hey? Where do I sign?"

The
House
on
the
Hill

$\mathcal{A}$ T THE TURN OF THE CENTURY the house stood in some glory behind a wrought-iron fence that marks off half a city block. Once there were gardens, and stables, an ornamental fish pond and flowering trees, instead of the current weeds and windblown trash around a pile of lumber, a cracked tile basin rusty with polluted rain. In the midst of ruin rise three stories of elaborate wooden architecture, a couple of turrets, a widow's walk, peaked roofs and bay windows, little porches and scroll work, painted flat grey and peeling. In the windows hang cotton print bedspreads from India, or old sheets tie-dyed purple and red in bull's-eyes and streaks. A wide veranda runs halfway around the ground floor, scattered with live dogs and the corpses of white wicker furniture. It leads away from the street to a massive set of double doors studded with art nouveau stained glass in streaky lavenders and greens, which piece together a wood nymph by a fountain, a satyr in a grove, chastely separated, each on their separate window.

It was once the embassy of some obscure Eastern European country, but the property has lived in the limbo of litigation since 1949. On one side the People's Republic demands the full value in hard western currency while on the other the heirs of a long-dead archduke insist the house is theirs. To pay taxes a real estate agent leased the house out a long time ago to someone who no longer lives there, but the sublets endure in monthly frenzies of rent collection.

Lately this job has fallen to Nick Harrison, who starts up in the warren of cubicles under the roof (servants' quarters once upon a time), where he extorts five dollars here and there from hookers, pill freaks, and one would-be poet. He then trots down the marble staircase to the slightly more prosperous college students and speed freaks, would-be musicians, and small-time dope dealers, who inhabit various portions of the ambassador's old quarters and the once-official offices, waiting rooms, and parlors. Here among the mattresses scattered on the floor, the stereos blaring out the Beatles and Stones, he can collect twenties and tens from middle-class kids come to experience life.

Anything left over he makes up in the basement. Once it was a ballroom, and a vast sweep of chipped and pitted parquet floor remains, as does an actual stage where a local rock band, the Wizards, comes most evenings to practice. Off to one side lies a narrow kitchen, originally built to provide refreshments for the embassy balls, no doubt, with the sinks and stoves that Wagner needs for his lab work. LSD is remarkably easy to synthesize, if you don't worry too much about quality, but Wagner's found his calling at last in manufacturing the best, the purest, the most potent hallucinogens that the Haight-Ashbury has ever seen. His white lightning, purple mist, and the brand-new red thunder have earned him a lot of cold cash and a new name as well. Most people know him only as Dr. Lucky.

When Nick comes whistling in, counting a wad of cash, John is finishing up for the day, writing test results in a stained spiral-back red notebook. He frowns a little, marking columns of numbers in his tiny handwriting. Shoulder-length hair curls round his neck and frames his face.

"Would you shut up?"

Nick stops whistling, waits until John shuts the notebook and slips it into a drawer.

"Having a good day?" Nick says. "Happy, are we?"

"Ah shut up. This is all okay, and it's sure better than the university, but I dunno." John pulls up a stool and perches on it. "There's still something missing."

"You need a little excitement, man. There are all these cool chicks all over the Haight, and what do you do? Close yourself up in here in this damned lab. Live a little, man. They're right out there, and they all got The Pill."

"Better living through chemistry."

They look at each other and laugh.

The Wizards started life as a jug band by another name, and their name will doubtless change again when their style does, but at the moment they play rock and roll very well but prosaically. Four or five guys—the number varies from night to night—straggle into the ballroom and set up speakers and drums, unpack electric guitars and a Fender bass. At that magical invocation, "The band's here," young women appear, trooping downstairs to sit on the floor and watch, passing joints back and forth while they wonder if maybe the band will make it someday and if so, should they start sleeping with it now before the line forms. The core of the band, Jimmy G and Hog and Billy, the good-looking one, concentrate on their music at these rehearsals, but afterwards is another matter.

Dr. Lucky and Nick sit as far as possible from the speakers. Even though his eardrums are young again, John finds the blare of electric music painful. Not far from them, a good distance from the other women, sits a chubby girl in tight jeans and a dirty red turtleneck. Her brown hair, too wavy, really, to be as long as it is, hangs in tendrils round her face. No one knows her name, but she lives in the house and cleans the upstairs kitchen and bathrooms for want of rent. In a brotherly way Hog looks out for her. Every night, round midnight, she takes the five dollars Hog gives her and goes out barefooted to buy doughnuts up on Stanyan Street and bring them back for the band. Once some guy tried to call her Sow, but the enormous Hog picked him up by the shirt and banged his head repeatedly against the wall until Jimmy G made him stop. The name did not stick.

Tonight Nameless Girl has dropped a hit from John's latest batch, to try it out at his request. She sits very silently now, smiling a little, watching many things that no one else can see. Every now and then, while the band plays "Turn on Your Love Light" over and over, trying to get the break just right, John turns to watch Nameless Girl and make sure that her breathing stays regular and her color, good. He prides himself on making clean drugs, not bummers that will send his clients off to the nearest all-night psychiatric intake. At one point the music stops to let the band squabble with the new rhythm guitarist they're trying out. Nameless Girl turns her head and focuses her stare upon Nick.

"Far out," she says. "You don't have an aura, man."

"Huh?" Nick says.

"You don't have an aura. Everyone else has auras. This is good stuff, Dr. Lucky. I can see everyone's aura as clear as anything, 'cept for Nick. He doesn't have one. Can't be the acid. He just plain must not have one."

John laughs.

"Well, shit," Nick snarls. "Then don't go looking at me, if I bug you so much."

"You don't bug me, man. You just don't have an aura."

When Nick growls like a dog, Nameless Girl stands up and moves back, but she continues to consider Nick with a remarkably focused stare. John notices Hog walking toward them. Somewhere inside his tangle of bushy black beard he seems to be frowning.

"Cool it, Nick," John whispers.

"A poodle?" Nameless Girl says, then shrugs. "Weird."

She wanders off toward Hog, who smiles and escorts her to a seat among the other women. The band picks up their instruments again, the drummer settles in, the music starts. Nick sits stiffly, his face pale with rage.

"What's bugging you, man?" John has to shout over the music.

"Nothing. Oh shut up!"

John shrugs and gets up, stretching.

"I'm going upstairs," he bellows. "Too loud for me."

Nick says nothing, merely slouches against the wall and growls to himself.

Weaving through the lounging girls, waving smoke away from his face, John gains the staircase and hurries up. The stairs debouch into the wide entrance hall; he pushes open the double doors and steps outside into twilight for fresh air. Although the shadows are gathering along the street, the sky above still shines pale blue. The unkempt trees in the garden rustle in the evening wind. From behind him he can hear the band, but mellowed by distance and a ceiling.

Out on the sidewalk a girl strolls past. Tall, slender, with golden-blonde hair parted in the middle and falling straight to her waist, she wears jeans and a flowing shirt made of tie-dyed velvet, crushed, glimmering, all purple and blue and red in the street-lights, a barrage and flash of color as she strides by, silver highlights swirling round her sleeves.

"Hey, baby," John calls out. "Don't be in such a hurry."

She slows down, glances his way with a grin, then walks on, crossing the street between parked cars. All at once Nick appears in a waft of smoke, the scent of marijuana drifting on the evening air. The porch creaks under his sudden weight.

"Who's that girl?" John says. "You know?"

"The blonde? I've seen her, yeah. She's got a friend who lives upstairs, one of those college girls."

"That's the one I want. The blonde I mean."

"Maggie? You're nuts, man. She is one tough chick. A drop-out from State, and she's studying karate now or something."

"I don't give a shit about her educational career. She's gorgeous."

"But she's into Zen, man."

"Who cares?"

Across the street Maggie has disappeared, but in his mind John can still see her smile. For a moment he finds it hard to breathe.

"You got it bad," Nick says. "Look, there's all those girls downstairs who would love to spread their little legs for you."

"Don't want them. Nick, you get that girl for me or the deal's off."

Nick squalls, catlike this time.

"I mean it," John goes on. "And I want her now."

"Tough shit. I can't work miracles. Out of my department."

"Oh yeah? Then—"

"Give me a week." Nick rolls his eyes upward and waves his hands in a hopeless little motion. "I'll see what I can do, but it ain't gonna be overnight."

"They make my tits hurt, and I'm not going to take them. They're just not natural."

"Maggie!"

"I'm using a diaphragm."

"A diaphragm. Oh wow, far out—like hell. They're not safe."

Maggie merely scowls for an answer. She and her best friend Rosie, a small and delicate woman with an amazing frizz of jet-black hair, are sitting on the mattress in Rosie's room, once the embassy parlor, with its big bay window, a high ceiling decorated with stucco fruit round the central boss of the light fixture, and wood panelling, cracked vertically from years of dry air and neglect. Books—Rosie is a classics major at San Francisco State—lie spread like seawrack across the floor. On one wall pushpins hold up two Fillmore posters, an enlargement of a sepia photograph of Oscar Wilde as a young man, and a big print of a Renaissance engraving, where a pilgrim, his back to a rural landscape, sticks his head through a starry sky and sees the machinery, all gears and wheels, of the universe. The herbal scent of rope incense hangs in musty air.

"Ah well," Maggie says at last. "I'm not sleeping with anyone right now anyway. So it doesn't matter."

"Oh? How long is that gonna last?"

"Maybe forever. I'm sick of men."

"Oh yeah sure."

"Well, I'm sick of crummy guys, anyway."

"Progress!" Rosie lays a dramatic hand on her chest. "Can my heart take this?"

"Oh shut up. If I get involved with a guy again, he better have some class. That reminds me. I was walking by here last night, you know? And there was this guy standing out on the porch. Kind of tall, with a lot of curly brown hair, and pretty good looking, and he was wearing this cool shirt of some kind of Guatemalan hand-weaving. You know him?"

"Dr. Lucky himself." Rosie pauses for a groan. "Class, she says! The biggest dealer in the Haight, that's what he is. Well, that's not fair. He's the chemist. It's that Nick dude who does the dealing."

"What's he like? Lucky, I mean, not Nick. I've met him, and he creeps me out."

"He never blinks, yeah. But Lucky was asking me about you, actually. Just this morning."

"Oh yeah?"

"Yeah. He's a nice enough guy, I guess, for a druggie. But he's setting himself up, they both are, for a big bust, with the chances they take. I can't believe they haven't been busted already, they're so damn open about it."

"But are they righteous dealers?"

"Real righteous." Rosie sounds as if she hates admitting it. "Fair prices and they give away stuff on the street, too, like at the park concerts. But that's what I mean. The pigs aren't blind."

"How come you still live here, then?"

"Inertia, what else? But I'm thinking of moving. Some of the hookers upstairs are shooting smack, and I don't want to come home one night and find my stereo gone." Rosie cocks one eyebrow. "Maybe we could get a place together?"

"That sounds cool, yeah. I'm getting kind of sick of where I'm living."

Where Maggie lives is one narrow room in a railroad flat over on Waller Street. She owns one mattress, neatly made up with blankets and a huge American flag for a bedspread, one orange-crate of books, mostly about Japanese religion, one duffel bag with four changes of clothing, a pair of sandals and a pair of boots, two towels, and a plastic bucket holding soap, shampoo, a washcloth, and other such things. The bag and the bucket go into the closet, the orange crate stands at the head of the bed. The walls are bare.

"Not a lot of trippy hippie clutter, is there?" Nick remarks. "Cool. Some of these chicks are so messy it makes me sick."

"Yeah, well." John stands in the doorway and looks round. His heart is pounding so hard, just from seeing her room, that he decides he'd better sit on the floor. "Jeez, I never felt like this before. Not with my wife, that's for sure."

Nick makes a sour face and opens the closet door with one hand. In the other he's carrying a wooden cigar box.

"Well," he says doubtfully. "I guess I'll just stick it in here. Things aren't exactly the way they used to be, huh?"

"What do you mean by that?"

"Nothing. You sure you don't want to leave a note?"

"Nah, let her guess. Where'd you get that necklace, anyway?"

"Around." Nick lays the cigar box on the floor next to the bucket. "Well, that'll have to do, huh? Come on, Lothario. If you want her to guess, you better be gone when she gets back."

Maggie finds the box late that night when she puts her boots away. As she picks it up, she's thinking that one of her crummy roommates has left his stash in her closet for safekeeping and without having the decency to ask her, either. Idly she flips it open and stares for a long moment at a silver necklace, Navajo Indian work, a length of silver beads alternated with tiny silver squash blossoms. In the middle hangs a silver crescent set with an enormous chunk of turquoise. Maggie whistles under her breath, drops the box, and holds the necklace up to catch the dim light from an overhead bulb.

"That is really cool," she says aloud.

On a whim she takes it down the hall to the communal bathroom and puts it on in front of the cracked mirror over the sink. It's a heavy piece, but it feels snug and right, lying over her collarbone, the crescent hanging just between her breasts. She turns this way and that way, smiling at her reflection, suddenly so grand with silver to set off her dappled blue and green T-shirt. She wears the necklace back to her room, then returns it to the box. It must have come from Dr. Lucky, she decides, since he's the only man she knows with the kind of money to buy this kind of gift for a girl.

The question is, should she keep it?

"I can't believe it," Nick howls. "I fucking cannot believe it, man! She gave the damn thing to the Zen Center."

"She what?" John swivels round on his lab chair. "The necklace, you mean?"

"Yeah, the fucking necklace, man! She gave it to Suzuki Roshi down at the Zen Center. Sell it for the poor, she says. And of course the old man took it, the sanctimonious little bastard."

"Can't blame him, I guess."

"I can too!" Nick begins pacing back and forth. "This whole thing is getting weird."

"It's going to get weirder, man, if you can't deliver. You've got four days left."

Yet later that afternoon John himself finds Maggie, as he's walking down Page on his way to the Panhandle, that narrow strip of park, mostly battered grass and trees, that runs between Oak and Fell streets. The Jefferson Airplane are giving a free concert on a stage improvised from old lumber and a pickup truck, driven up next to a swing set and a slide. The crowd mills round and spills down the grassy strip as the band struggles to get their equipment running on the truck's generator. Every now and then a guitar squeals; the crowd cheers; the power dies again to a long groan from the would-be audience.

Way off to one side, Maggie is standing on a big cube of concrete installed by the city to replace vulnerable park benches. With her hands in her back pockets she watches the band work, smiles a little. Over a calico patchwork shirt she wears a torn and peeling black leather jacket. When she shakes her head, her hair ripples round her hips. *With the money I've got now, I could dress her like a queen.* As he walks over he feels himself turn first shivery cold, then so hot he's sure he must be blushing scarlet. She hears him coming, turns round and smiles down at him.

"Hi," she says. "Dr. Lucky, I presume."

"Hi yourself. Get any presents lately?"

"So it was you, huh? Who gave me the necklace, I mean."

"Yeah. Nick told me you gave it away. Why?"

"It pays to travel light, that's all."

John can think of absolutely nothing to say to that. Laughing, she jumps downs with a shake and ripple of her hair.

"You like to dance?" she says.

"I don't know how."

"Oh come on, man. Anyone can dance. It's not like the fox-trot anymore, you know."

Although John doesn't know, he soon finds out, when the band gets the music under way. First he learns to dance, then discovers he likes to dance, especially here in the open air in the cool of a foggy day, in the middle of a crowd of people who are too busy dancing to care what he looks like. The music pounds on and on, the dancing ebbs and flows, the crowd changes like a wave as some drop out to catch their breath and others sway into their places.

Maggie never agrees to sit one out; she pauses briefly between songs, panting for breath, running both hands through her sweaty hair, then swirling into dance the moment the music begins again. Every now and then John is forced to rest, forced to watch her dancing with some other man, someone she doesn't even know, just a man the music brings her. Partners change mindlessly; many people dance alone. As the fog grows thicker, colder, the light turns silver and leaches the shadows away until he feels as if they are dancing in a movie, an old movie, in black and white.

Sirens cut through the music, which stops. The police arrive in squad cars and on motorcycles, parking their vehicles randomly out in the street and sprinting for the stage with batons at the ready. The crowd freezes, parts only reluctantly when the officers insist, moves back only when ordered. Bad cop: the neighbors have complained, the band has no permit. Good cop: but there's no problem, no one's gonna get arrested, if only the band stops now, if only the crowd disperses. Things hover on the edge of ugliness. John grabs Maggie's hand and pulls her back, eases her away to the fringe of the crowd and relative safety. The band confers, surrenders.

"The show's over, folks. Maybe another day."

Good cop grins. Bad cop scowls. The crowd breaks up, muttering, streaming away in all directions, shaking its collective head in disbelief, that someone would complain about free music. John and Maggie start walking across the Panhandle, heading west and uphill to Haight. She allows her hand to remain in his.

"Want some coffee?" John says. "Or we could get something to eat."

She considers, drops his hand, stops walking to consider him from a few steps' distance. His mouth turns as dry as chalk as he waits.

"Sorry, but can I have a raincheck?" Maggie turns to him with a smile that clutches his heart. "I've got to get to the dojo by five. What about tomorrow?"

"Sure. Let's go out to dinner and a flick."

*   *   *

These days, when Romance (in the older meaning of that term) has turned into something called a "sex scene," what is there to say? Maggie and John take the N streetcar all the way out Judah to the beach and the Surf Theater, where they watch an Alain Resnais movie. They walk for a few minutes beside an ocean far too foggy and cold to be picturesque, then take the streetcar back to her apartment house. When she invites him into her room to talk, they sit down on the edge of the bed. He kisses her, she responds, much later they fall asleep.

Since he has his work to consider, John leaves Maggie's place about noon, but not before she promises to see him again that night. When he returns to the house, he finds Nick waiting for him, pacing back and forth in the ground floor room that they use as an office.

"Where the hell you been?" Nick snaps.

"Over at Maggie's. I spent the night with her."

"You did what?"

"I'm not the kind of guy who brags." John pauses for a grin. "But let's just say she liked the offer I made her."

Nick stares, his mouth slack enough so that John can notice his most definitely pointed tongue.

"You mean she just went to bed with you?" Nick says at last.

"Well, yeah. What's your problem?"

Nick frowns at the floor, then shakes his head.

"This is weird, that's what. I've been scheming my ass off, trying to find a go-between. That Rosie's a real bitch, man, wouldn't give me the time of day. Work work work, that's all I do, and here you just go and ask Maggie, and she does it with you."

"Go-between? Kind of old-fashioned, aren't you?"

"Well, yeah, so what? I mean, shit, some seduction! Pretty low-class, man."

"Ah come off it! It worked. That's all I care about." John grins, suddenly expansive. "We're going dancing tonight. Down at the Fillmore."

When Nick looks profoundly sour, John laughs; then a sudden thought hits him.

"Hey, man, you weren't interested in her yourself, were you?"

"What? Hell, no! I hate that kind of girl, all clean living and new ideas."

"It's not her ideas I'm interested in."

"Yeah, I know. Good."

Nick turns on his heel and stalks out, leaving John puzzled behind him. With a shrug he puts the matter out of his mind, collects his batch notebook, and heads downstairs to the lab. On the way down he meets Nameless Girl, coming up.

"Morning," he says. "Swell day, huh?"

She stops walking and considers him for a long moment before she speaks.

"Is it? I haven't been out yet."

"Ah. Well, it's a swell day."

"Cool. Maybe I'll go to the park."

"Good idea. Say, I've been meaning to ask you. Don't you have a name?"

"Not when I can help it."

Unsmiling she steps round him and goes up past.

"Are you still interested in sharing a place?" Rosie asks.

"Well, gee, yeah, I guess," Maggie says. "Uh, why?"

"I just wondered if you were going to move in with Lucky."

"What makes you think that?"

"The way you guys have been going at it. What is it, a couple weeks now? If you're not sleeping over at the house then he's at your place."

Maggie grins and leans back onto one elbow. They are lounging in the sun on the grassy slope in Golden Gate Park, not far from the children's playground, that the local press has dubbed Hippie Hill. Close by, three young black men, African print shirts open to the waist, play African-style drums in American rhythms. The sound blends oddly well with the carillon music from the nearby merry-go-round. Scattered across the hillside lie women sunning themselves, guarded by large dogs, and young men sitting in groups, including one small circle passing an obvious joint.

"Well, look," Maggie says at last. "I promised you we'd get a place together. I know you can't afford one on your own, and I've started teaching the beginners down at the dojo, so I'm getting paid now. I don't want to back out."

"Well, it wouldn't bring me down or anything. There's a couple of people at school that are looking for places, too."

"Really?"

"Really. I just need to get out of that house, that's all. It's too damn noisy to get any work done."

"Well, yeah, it is that." Maggie watches a pair of blackbirds strutting through daisies. "I don't know if I should move in with him or not."

"He's asked you, huh? I thought so."

"Yeah. I'd move in with him in a minute if it weren't for that Nick dude. Why do all the cool guys have jerky friends?"

"I dunno. It's one of life's great mysteries."

When they return to the house, Nick is sitting on the porch with a couple of dogs lounging at his feet. Every time Maggie comes over, it seems that there are more dogs, and that they all gather round Nick. *At least he likes animals*—she supposes that this is a point in his favor. She only wishes that he'd pick up after them. Lately it seems that the yard is full of flies. As much as she dislikes her current roommates, she decides that she should just keep her own place, or maybe find a flat with Rosie after all.

Yet that evening, lying naked and entwined in John's arms, she says yes without a moment's thought when, for a second time, he asks her to move in.

Walpurgisnacht

$\mathcal{H}$APPY, ARE WE?" NICK SAYS. "YOU'VE got a beautiful lady, you're rich, you're someone in this scene, man. You got it all, don't you?"

"No," John says. "I'm bored."

"You're what?"

"Bored. You know, like, nothing's interesting or fun anymore."

"You gotta be kidding. You and Maggie have only been together, what? about three months now?"

"Doesn't matter. She bores me, too."

"But she's one cool chick. I've seen all the other dudes looking at her, envying you. Don't tell me she's frigid or something? There are potions for that kind of thing, you know. I could fetch you one."

"No, no, no. It's nothing like that."

"Okay. Then what?"

John considers. They are sitting in the room he shares with Maggie, once the ambassador's grand reception hall and big enough for a full bedroom at one end and a leather sofa and chairs round a coffee table at the other. On the plain white walls hang two natural-dyed Navajo rugs in greys and greens; on the floor lies a beige and grey rug of beaten felt from Central Asia. Maggie's taste does not run to the bright profusion of the current style.

"Well, you know," John says at last. "She's such a kid. She's only twenty."

"Yeah, so?"

"So I'm not a kid." He runs his right hand over his smoothly muscled left arm. "You made my body young, sure, but in here I'm still Professor Wagner and—and well, a grown-up." He pauses for a twisted smile. "I never realized what that meant, before. All she wants to do is go dancing. She doesn't even read much. Dancing and karate and long walks in the park or on the beach. Jeez, I asked her if maybe she didn't want to improve her mind or something and what does she do? She takes up tarot cards."

"Well, hey," Nick says, grinning. "I can give you a young mind, too. It'll involve losing your memory, but—"

"Ah, shut up! That's not what I mean."

"Okay. How about some distraction? There's plenty of other women in the scene, man."

"Yeah, but next to Maggie, none of them are much to look at."

"Bet I could find you one that put her in the shade."

"Yeah?" John snorts in scorn. "Bet you can't."

"You just wait," Nick says. "I heard Maggie say she's going to visit her mother this weekend, right? Let's you and me go on a little trip."

"Where?"

"Just up Haight Street, or at least, that's where we'll start."

"And where are we gonna end up?"

"Back on Haight Street. Don't worry. It's not time for me to call in our bargain."

* * *

Maggie's mother lives in a split-level ranch style house in Daly City, a suburb just south of San Francisco. Her picture window looks across a small lawn, a wide street, and another small lawn, into the picture window of the house opposite, so the blinds are always drawn in the front room. Shirley dislikes letting the sun in, anyway, because it bleaches her forest green sofa and the matching recliner chair. The sofa is Shirley's preserve, while, in those brief intervals when he's home from his salesman's job, Maggie's dad generally occupies the chair, with his feet up and newspapers scattered round him.

At the moment Maggie sits there and watches her mother, sitting on the sofa and knitting a fuzzy pink sweater. Maggie fervently hopes that the sweater's for her sister and not for her. The TV flickers with the sound off; the circular needle clicks; Shirley hums tunelessly under her breath. When she finishes a row, she looks up.

"Your Aunt Linda's coming for dinner tonight. I thought we'd go to that smorgasbord place she likes."

"Sounds good to me, Mom."

"You want to drive?"

"Sure, if you don't mind."

"I thought you might like to try out the new car."

Maggie smiles. Shirley smiles and begins to count out another row of the pattern. Maggie picks up a copy of the *National Geographic* and leafs through brightly colored pictures of Mexico and Turkey, Aztec temples and the site of fallen Ilium.

"Margie?" Shirley says. "When we go out to eat, put your hair back, will you?"

"Back where, Mom? Where it came from?"

"You know what I mean. Braid it or put it up or something. It's just not sanitary, all that hair flying around when people are trying to eat."

Maggie considers starting a fight about her name in order to deflect the one coming about her hair, but she is, at root, too tired to trudge down angry roads. *Been tired a lot lately, she thinks. I've got to take more vitamins.* Shirley waits, her lips pursed for battle.

"Sure, Mom," Maggie says. "If I braid it will you help me wind the braids round my head? I can't reach the back to get the pins in."

Shirley stares, then finds her voice.

"Why sure, honey, that'll be fun."

Back when every neighborhood in America had a movie theater, the Haight had one, too; no fantastic picture palace, this white stucco cube, but serviceable enough. Since its death by television some years back, it has stood empty, rented out now and again for lectures and political meetings. Tonight a somewhat different group has taken it over. On the marquee black plastic letters spell out on one side EQUINOX OF THE GODS, and on the other, ALEISTER CROWLEY.

"I thought Crowley was dead," John says.

"He is, yeah." Nick folds his hands piously. "His work lives on. Not that I ever really had much to do with it, you understand."

"I thought he was a Satanist."

"Oh shit no! He was *not* the kind of guy I want in my camp. A real weird dude. You never knew what he was going to do next."

Under the marquee stands a glass kiosk, where a young woman with roses ringing around her black hair sells them tickets. Since no one's at the door to take them, they walk into a red velvet lobby, where flowered incense strives to cover the stink of mildew. Nick stops to admire himself in the rank of mirrors behind the now-defunct candy counter. For the occasion he's sporting a pair of black bell-bottomed trousers and a red silk shirt with enormously full sleeves; into his hair, now long enough to reach his collar, he's braided a pair of rooster feathers.

"Real cool, man," John says, grinning. "Real hip."

"Ah shut up! I have my public to think of."

At that precise moment someone starts a tape of the Stones,

blaring out "Sympathy for the Devil." With a smile Nick bows to his own image, then opens the doors into the theatre. Waves of scent, charcoal-broiled frankincense and sandalwood, roll out.

"Shall we go in?" Nick says.

John hesitates, glancing round. When he looks back the street doors are closed; night seems to have fallen outside, much too suddenly for the time of day.

"Ah come on," Nick says. "You only live once."

With a shrug John follows him through the swinging doors. The auditorium looks normal enough: a steep sloped floor, narrow aisles, rank after rank of tattered maroon plush chairs, all leading down to a dimly-lit stage. An audience crowds the front rows. Some whisper to each other; some sway back and forth in time to the tape; some pass joints. A few watch the stage.

On the movie screen, oily blobs of blue and purple ooze behind and over an ever-changing flow of images, mostly of naked women. In front of the light show an androgyne is dancing, or so he seems from their distance. A slender fellow dressed in silver lamé and crowned with a mop of dark hair, he writhes and gyrates to the pound of the Stones' song looping endlessly. In each hand he holds lengths of silk, striped purple and silver. With little cries he waves the silks like banners, floating up and around and curling down round him.

"What the hell?" John says.

"Ah, he's just warming up the crowd. They're gonna hold a ritual here tonight." But Nick sounds suddenly doubtful. "I hope they do it right."

"Who is that guy?"

"You don't recognize him? He travels with one of the big groups." Nick frowns, considering the stage. "He's a jerk, actually. He's got a shrine to Flash Gordon in his bedroom, and you know what? It's bigger than the one he built for me."

"You gotta be kidding. Flash Gordon?"

"I told you he was a jerk. Too many drugs. You know, I'm beginning to wonder if that was the right move."

"What?"

"Getting into dealing, bringing you here, all that shit. Well, hell, I had to do something, didn't I? All this peace and love crap! Shit, what if it caught on?"

John takes a sudden step back.

"What's wrong?" Nick says.

"Run that by me again, man. You brought me here to make drugs to do what?"

"Blow the whole scene. You just figure that out?"

John turns on his heel and strides up the aisle. He hears Nick calling him, keeps walking, staggering forward over flowered carpet, turned endless underfoot. No more than ten feet ahead of him he sees door and the red flash of a WAY OUT sign, but it never comes closer. He feels himself turn hot, feels sweat run down his back, and all at once he's panting for breath, rushing hard on the acid he dropped earlier, leaning back gasping in a wave of something very much like lust. When Nick grabs his arm from behind, nails dig into his flesh. The pain swings him round and briefly steadies his head.

"You can't get out until the show's over," Nick says, grinning. "That's the way it works, pal. Come on. Let's go backstage."

"Nick, I want to go home."

"Ah come off it!"

"Won't. You're supposed to be my servant, man. Take me home."

"Ah come on, come on." Nick turns unctuous, all smiles. "You don't wanna leave yet. You haven't even seen the chick."

"What chick?"

"The one I told you about. The one that's gonna put Maggie in the shade. You should see her, man. Tits out to here."

John hesitates, feeling the rush swelling in his crotch. Nick grins.

"Just come meet her. If you want to go home after you meet her, I'll take you there. You're right. You're the boss. But if you miss meeting Helen of Troy, you'll be kicking yourself the rest of your life."

"What is she? Some kind of groupie?"

Nick stares for a long moment.

"You never heard of her?"

"No. Why? Was she written up in that *Rolling Stone* article?"

Nick sighs and shakes his head.

"The two cultures," Nick says at last. "C.P. Snow was right. I keep forgetting you were a chem major."

"What the hell are you talking about?"

"Never mind. Just come on."

John allows himself to be led down the aisle. Up on the stage the androgyne has given way to three women, struggling to set up and light charcoal braziers. With a stench of lighter fluid blue flames spurt, sending waves of silver across his troubled sight. The women, dressed in gauzy white robes that are probably meant to look Greek, jump back fast. The audience laughs and claps. The taped music changes to flutes, bongos, and the whine of an electric guitar.

"Is that safe?" John says. "Having fires in here?"

"Probably not. But there's a sprinkler system." Nick waves a vague hand at the ceiling. "I think, anyway."

They duck through an emergency exit to find themselves in a dusty concrete hallway. Up three steps stands the stage door, but sitting on the steps are a pair of Hell's Angels, a squat dude, his face half acne, and a tall skinny guy fiddling with a switchblade. The squat dude picks up a clipboard from the floor.

"You on the guest list?" When he speaks, a spider dances, tattooed upon on his chin.

"Nick Harrison," Nick says. "And Dr. Lucky."

"Oh yeah." The guard is frowning at a list of names. "Cool, man. Go on through."

Through the door a long corridor leads straight back into darkness. The walls tremble and dance in radiating pulses of colored light.

"Wait a minute," Nick snaps. "Something's weird. The theater's not that big, man. We should be out the back by now."

"Yeah?" John quite frankly has lost track of things like distance and relative space. "Well, whatever."

"Damn that little bastard!" Nick hesitates, chewing on his lower lip. "He's probably too stoned to remember the right words."

Nick turns and leads the way back through the stage door. The Hell's Angels move aside to let them walk back down the steps.

"Something wrong?" says the skinny guy.

"Not exactly. Come on, Lucky."

When Nick turns and walks back up the steps again, John follows, mostly because he can't figure out what else to do. This time they step through the door into a comprehensible chaos. A very short corridor leads back to what seem to be dressing rooms; a big door opens on to the actual backstage. Girls dressed in more pseudo-Greek gauze rush round fine-tuning each other's makeup or stand and stretch out muscles as if they are preparing for a dance. Actors in animal costumes, or in half an animal in the case of the horses, huddle together near a pile of cardboard swords. Through the curtain comes the sound of someone chanting. Gongs ring, drums thud. Nick grabs a man in a leopard suit by the arm.

"Who are you?" Nick says. "What are you doing here?"

"Part of the troupe. Don't be so uptight, man. Hey, Kenneth said to come on down, they were gonna do something trippy, and so we came on down. There's a couple of bands on the way, too, and some comedians."

"Comedians? I hate comedians! I don't want any stinking comedians here."

"Yeah? So what?" The leopard pulls his paw free and hisses with a show of fang. His eyes flash green behind his spotted mask. "Who do you think you are, pal? God?"

With a snarl Nick turns away. John finds a place to stand out of the way between two cardboard columns; in the fluting, electricity pulses twixt the parallel lines. Nick trots back and forth, asking each girl in turn if she's seen Helen, but no one seems to have the slightest idea who Helen might be. By the time he fetches John again, Nick's face is scarlet.

"Never should have trusted that little bastard," Nick mutters. "Come on. Maybe she's materialized out in the audience."

John grins, starts to speak, looks past him, and finds that all words fail. Walking between two columns comes a young woman, her blonde hair piled high above her perfect oval face. Gold shimmers at her throat and dangles from each ear. Although she wears the same Greek costume as the dancers, hers is made not of gauze but real linen, thick-woven and well-worn. Nick sighs in sharp relief.

"There she is," he whispers. "Now what did I tell you? Tits out to here."

"Shut up!" John snarls. "Just introduce us, okay?"

The gongs sound again. A man's voice wails, rising and falling upon ancient words. Helen turns to listen, her head tilted, one delicate hand raised as she pauses, half-smiling until she glances their way and sees Nick. For a moment she goes rigid, her head back, her cornflower-blue eyes narrowed.

"You could at least act glad to see me," Nick says. "Come over here, sweetheart. Someone I want you to meet."

Helen smacks him back-handed across the face with a much-ringed hand. When Nick jumps back, swearing under his breath, John strides forward to catch her hand and kiss it. For a moment she seems to be about to strike him in turn; then she smiles. She inclines her head in his direction and allows a second kiss upon her wrist.

"Why don't you guys get acquainted?" Nick says. "See that door right there? Walk on through and get out of the noise."

A door that John has somehow overlooked before stands open among the stage machinery and flats. Sunlight streams through, and the scent of roses.

Aunt Linda arrives at six o'clock, sweeping into the living room in a cloud of White Shoulders cologne. She's a little too stout for the blue striped minidress she's wearing, her lipstick is way too red for anyone, but when she sees Shirley's moue of disapproval, she laughs like bells ringing.

"Live a little, Shirl," she says. "Margie! It's time you taught your mom how to live a little."

Maggie grins and hugs her.

"I'm trying."

"Good, good." Linda disengages from the hug and holds her at arm's length. "God, what have you done to your hair? You look like you should be wearing one of those Bavarian boob-pushers, those weskit things, y'know? With those braids all wound round your head like that. You look better with it down, honey."

Shirley makes a sound very much like a growl.

"Let it all hang down," Linda says. "Isn't that what you kids say, let it all hang down?"

"Let it all hang out." Maggie finds herself laughing. "Well, Mom likes it better this way."

"Okay. For the sake of peace in the family I'll shut up," Linda says, grinning Shirley's way. "Let's go eat. I'm starved."

Inside the smorgasbord, a narrow place with white walls and painted scenes of Sweden, the warm air hangs thick with tobacco smoke and the scent of brown gravies, one congealing over the sliced turkey and cornbread stuffing, the other drowning meatballs. Maggie takes neither, loading her blue and white plate with salad and bread. By the time the three women sit down in a blue vinyl booth and lay their food upon a grey formica table, Maggie feels oddly dizzy. The area round her mouth has turned cold, but at the same time she feels sweat drops forming on her forehead. Fortunately, neither Linda and Shirley notice, busy squabbling as they are over the length of Linda's dress. Eventually Linda dismisses the subject with a laugh.

"Hey, kid," she says to Maggie. "You okay? You look a little pale."

"It's stuffy in here," Maggie says. "Don't you think so?"

Linda does not, Shirley does, and the discussion reminds them of their teen years, when during World War II Linda volunteered at the local USO canteen, handing out sandwiches and coffee to sailors in rooms much stuffier than the present one. Shirley was not allowed to join her until she turned eighteen, near the war's end. While they squabble over which of them might have flirted with whom, Maggie attacks her salad. Lately she's found herself ravenously hungry at every meal, even though she's begun to worry about her weight—she seems to be putting on water, mostly, round her middle. She assumes that she's just got the munchies, but in truth, she stopped smoking marijuana some weeks past, when suddenly and for no reason the drug began to taste like insects had died in the stash.

A reason which had never occurred to her presents itself at the end of the meal, when she and Linda troop off together to use the tiny ladies' room. As she washes her hands, Maggie notices her aunt studying her. She glances at the reflection of her hair in the mirror, finds it reasonably tidy.

"Hey, kid?" Linda says. "You're not pregnant, are you?"

"Oh shit! Uh sorry."

"It's okay. I'd say the same thing if I was in your place. When did you have your last period?"

Maggie thinks, counting in a growing panic.

"A long time ago," she says at last. "Like, maybe I should have had one, well, oh no, really, ah shit, I guess I've skipped a month. Like, uh, at least."

Linda sighs, leans against the white tiled wall, and contemplates the roller towel.

"Don't tell your mother just yet. We'll get you the test first, okay? Sometimes it's just nerves, being late."

"Okay, yeah." For a long moment Maggie stares at her reflection in the mirror, then begins to pull the hairpins out of her braids. "I'm getting a headache from all this weight."

"Take it down, yeah. You look better with it down, anyway. Uh, look. Think the guy will marry you?"

Maggie stops with one braid drooping and a handful of pins.

"I don't want to marry him. I never realized it before, but I don't want to marry this guy."

"Oh jeez, kid, be sensible. Why not?"

Maggie hesitates, but she knows that she's speaking to the one person in the world who would never betray her.

"He's a drug dealer."

"Well, goddamn!" Linda sags against the wall with a shake of her head. "Pardon my French, but yeah, you're in a real mess, aren't you? You can get rid of it, y'know, and don't worry about the cost. I'll take care of that. I can ask around at work to see if I can turn up the right kind of doctor. And there's always Mexico."

"Thanks. Aunt Linda, I don't know what I'd do without you. I mean, like, thanks, really thanks."

Who would buy a cow if the milk were free? Tramp, slut, cheap, chippie, fallen woman. They're only after one thing, you know. They get it and then they drop you. Talk about you in the locker room. Ruin your reputation. A bun in the oven. Never hold your head up again. What decent man would want you now? Knocked up.

"You gonna faint?" Linda says.

Maggie considers, but what she feels building is rage.

"No," she says. "I was just thinking."

"Good. Too bad you didn't do that earlier, huh, but oh hell, we women never do, do we? Not when it's love."

During the trip home Maggie lets her mother drive the new car while she sits in the back, watching her mother's and her aunt's heads, as she so often has on little drives like these, to restaurants and shopping centers, to the homes of other relatives. She wonders what her mother will say if she finds out, when she finds out. Shirley always does find things like this out. She will cry, Maggie supposes, cry and carry on and rage that Maggie is killing her, that she'll just die, never be able to hold her head up again if anyone ever finds out. After some hours of this she will blow her nose and listen when Linda tells her to shut up and be sensible.

Besides, Maggie reminds herself, there's no use in worrying until she's had the test, which will take a while, anyway. *They in-*

ject rabbits, don't they? And then see if they act pregnant. Takes days and days. Yet, the more she thinks about it, the more she's sure she's pregnant, sure that she should have listened to Rosie and gone on the Pill, sure that what lies ahead is weeks of either trying to convince some doctor that she's crazy so she can have a legal abortion or of taking Aunt Linda's offer for an illegal one, weeks of whining and snivelling in front of men who will decide her fate.

Unless, of course, she keeps the baby? Some women do, these days, keep their illegitimate babies and raise them. *Bastard. Love child. So what? It's mine.*

The rage grows and blossoms to a grin. Maggie settles back into the seat and crosses her arms over her chest.

With John and his spectral lover tucked into an odd corner of the astral plane, Nick feels that he's finally regained control of this ancient story, which for a while there seemed to have a mind of its own. He leaves the stage area and strolls up a side aisle of the theater. On stage the ritual proceeds in a confusion of girls and fake animals, circling round and round widdershins while the officiant androgyne screams out chunks of Crowley's text and throws handfuls of glitter into the chanting audience. Clouds of incense drift this way and that. Eventually, Nick supposes, he should put in an appearance, a guest spot, as it were, but at the moment he only wants to get away from the rock music pounding out of too many speakers.

From the lobby, stairs lead to the balcony, where the incense hangs thick but the music sounds considerably quieter. Since he seems to be quite alone, Nick sinks into a loge seat, puts his feet up on the seat back in front of him, and spreads out his arms to either side. How long will Dr. Lucky stay occupied, he wonders? Days, most likely, plenty of time for the next act of this little tragedy to play itself out. Once he's danced round the stage a bit, he'll leave Lucky where he is, then go back to the house. Nick checks his watch, which doesn't keep the usual sort of time. Yes, Maggie should be arriving shortly, full of despair, weeping and wringing her hands. He's looking forward to this particular scene. All the way along the little bitch has been threatening to ruin things, to deflect, somehow, the familiar sequence of events, but now he has her, good and proper.

With a sigh he gets up, then notices that a man, his head shaved clean and glittering, is standing at the railing to overlook the crowd. Wrapped in a black cloak, the fellow shakes his head and mutters, "No no no, I mean, really!" Someone with good taste in these matters, then, if not in clothes, and Nick marks him carefully for further acquaintance before he leaves to go downstairs.

Although Maggie has been planning on staying overnight at her mother's house, she knows that if she does, she'll blurt out her newfound secret. On a wave of excuses she gets her overnight bag and takes her aunt's offer of a ride to the bus stop. Linda would drive her all the way home, of course, but Maggie prefers being let off on Mission Street, right where San Francisco ends and Daly City begins, and the 14 Mission electric trolley reaches the end of its line. As she tells Linda, she needs to think.

"Yeah, do that, kid. You find out about the pregnancy test, okay? UC Med Center probably does them, or there's that free clinic."

"Right. I'll call you when I know."

"Do that. Well, it's kind of too bad." Linda pauses for a genuinely sad sigh. "You're turning out just like your old auntie. I guess Shirl was right, all those years. I *am* a bad influence."

"Depends on how you define bad."

"Yeah? Well, take care of yourself, kid, and call me."

"I will. Don't worry."

Maggie scoots out of the car and trots to the corner, where a bus stands waiting, glowing against the night. It's a transfer ride home, and a slow one, jerking along Mission all the way to 18th Street, where she can pick up the 33 Ashbury line. The first part of the route runs bleak, through crumbling art deco buildings and Forties wartime stucco, the bubbled paint turned gruesome by the blue light of street lamps. At 30th Street, Mission turns prosperous. The new Safeway Store glitters in the middle of a full parking lot. People hurry along the sidewalks or stop to talk with friends. Store fronts and paper banners advertise in Spanish, here, and Maggie, hungry again, finds herself thinking more about tacos than the future.

At her transfer point, fortunately, stands an all-night taqueria and doughnut shop. Maggie fishes for change in her pocket, finds enough for a cheese taco and a maple bar, buys and consumes both, licking her fingers, before the Ashbury bus finally arrives. By the time it gets over the hill to the Haight, jerking round sharp corners and climbing only to swoop down fast, Maggie is regretting her meal. She gets off a block early, afraid she's going to heave into the gutter like some wino, but the cool night air clears her head and settles her stomach. Is she really going to be able to go through with this, being pregnant for six or seven more months?

As she walks home, Maggie is considering plans. If she doesn't have an illegal or quasilegal abortion, she's going to have to move out on John, because she refuses to raise a child among so many drugs, and she knows that he'll never give up dealing. The dealing itself has hooked him, far more deeply than any drug could ever do. It's the danger, the adrenaline rush, she supposes. LSD, after all, is chemically speaking a close relative of that natural high—or so the lore of the Haight runs. Maggie wonders at herself, that the danger she's taken for granted for months has now become unacceptable, and all because she thinks she's pregnant. Perhaps she's not? There remains that possibility, of course. She'd better say nothing to John until she knows.

Maggie lets herself in the rusting gate and hurries up the porch steps, where she meets Nameless Girl going out, wrapped in a Navy blue pea-coat that smells of patchouli. For a moment they stand in the spill of light from the open door.

"You're back?" Nameless Girl says.

"Yeah. Is Lucky home?"

"No, he went somewhere. Nick's around."

Involuntarily Maggie grimaces. Nameless Girl leans a little closer, her voice confidential and quiet. Her eyes glaze, out of focus, and a pink flush lies across her cheeks.

"He's the Devil, y'know. Nick I mean."

"Oh, yeah, sure."

"No, really. You can see it when you drop. Mr. Mephistopheles, like in that poem. Or was that a cat? In the poem I mean."

"Oh come on! You're loaded."

"Sure. So what? That's how I know. You can see a lot of things when you're loaded." Nameless Girl cocks her head to one and considers her. "You're pregnant, aren't you?"

"Oh shit! Can you see that too?"

"Yeah. See what I mean? Watch out for Nick. He's a mean motherfucker."

"You think I don't know?"

"Better'n me, probably. I gotta go, man. Catch you later."

Nameless Girl wanders off through the litter and the garden, heading for the gate on Page Street. Maggie watches until she sees Girl get safely onto a level sidewalk, then goes inside. No matter how she tries to talk herself out of it, she finds herself believing in those acid-soaked revelations, both of them.

In the room she shares with John, Maggie tosses her overnight case onto the bed, then sits down beside it and picks up the phone from the floor. She can feel rather than hear the pulse of rock music from the ballroom below. She should call Rosie, she supposes, and arrange for an escape hatch, as it were, when she and John have the inevitable fight over the baby, but she knows that Rosie, secure in her new flat over in Noe Valley, will always take her in. Maggie puts the phone back and gets up, pacing back and forth, wondering where John might be. Making a delivery, maybe? But not if Nick's still at the house.

At the sound of someone opening the door, Maggie turns round to find Nick, in fact, standing in the doorway and smiling at her. *He never blinks, does he?*

"Old Nick," Maggie says aloud. "Old Harry, too. Yeah, I should have seen it before this."

"Ah shit!" Nick stomps into the room and slams the door behind him. "Too damn clever for your own good, aren't you?"

"Or for yours. What happened to the cloven hooves? I guess a pair of cowboy boots will cover anything."

"Mock all you want, but I've won."

"Won what? Are you loaded or something?"

"Oh, shut up." Nick glances round the room. "You sure you don't want to go to a church to pray? The atmosphere would be a whole lot more classy. Dramatic, you know. You could clutch the altar and weep."

Maggie sets her hands on her hips. She decides that Nameless Girl's crazy rap had made her temporarily crazy, too: Nick isn't some kind of devil—he's a nut case.

"What are you talking about, man?" she says.

"Well, you're pregnant, are you? Knocked up. Ruined!"

"Oh give me a break. Yeah, I'm pregnant. So what?"

"What do you mean, so what? He'll never marry you now."

"I don't want to marry John."

"Even if he did marry you," Nick goes on as if he hadn't heard her, "it'll be a bust. Everyone will know. The girls will pull off your veil and the guys will scatter chaff."

"Oh man, you've really gone over the edge. Sampling too much of your own product again? Even if we did decide to get married, we'd just go to Vegas or something."

Nick starts to reply, then stops, letting his grin fade, while he stares at her so long without blinking that her own eyes begin to ache. She rubs them with the back of her hand.

"Well, try this on for size," Nick says at last. "You've been deserted."

"Say what?"

"You wanna know where Lucky is? He's balling another chick, that's where. I saw him pick her up, and he went home with her."

Maggie lets out her breath in a long sigh. Suddenly tired, she walks to the end of the room and flops into a chair, while Nick stands in front of her, grinning like a fiend—unless of course he actually is a fiend. His eyes are so pale, the irises grey, the whites dead white without a trace of vein or blood that she wonders if Nameless Girl might have been right after all.

"I should have seen that coming," she says. "John's been so weird lately. Distant, you know? And he started spending all his time in the damn lab again."

"You bore him, that's what he told me."

"You little bastard! You're enjoying this! What's wrong, you in love with him yourself? Guys like you do that all the time, you know, fall in love with their buddies."

"You bitch!"

"Hah. It's true."

"It is not!"

"Bet it is. You're nothing but a hanger-on anyway, aren't you, Nick? John's little groupie, that's you."

Nick hisses and flings his head back. Rather than let him tower over her, Maggie gets to her feet.

"If it weren't for him cooking in the lab, you'd have nothing to push, would you?" Maggie goes on. "You make me sick."

"Oh yeah? Well, listen here—you're gonna be a lot sicker once you're on your own, all by yourself with your little bastard."

"Who's gonna be on her own? I've got my family."

"Oh yeah sure. They'll kick a piece of dirt like you out into the gutter where you belong."

Maggie laughs. All at once it strikes her as profoundly funny, that she would be standing here exchanging insults with the Devil, and all over a man she's already made up her mind to leave. Nick steps back sharply and flings up one hand, as if protecting his face.

"Well, can't you see the joke?" Maggie says. "Here we are, and there's Lucky off somewhere screwing some dumb chick, and it's like we're fighting over him. You know what, Nick? I don't care anymore. If you want him, you take him."

Nick makes a choking sort of noise deep in his throat and steps back again, toward the door. Automatically she follows.

"You really don't care, do you?" he says. "You really don't give a shit."

"Of course I care. It'll hit me tomorrow, probably. I'll miss him. He could be real sweet when he wanted to be."

"But what about the baby?"

"What about it? It's just not a big deal. I mean, come on, Nick, this is the Revolution, y'know. Nobody's going to get down on me except my mom, and she'll get over it."

"She'll get over it." Nick says each word very slowly.

"Yeah, of course she will. Oh, I know she's gonna chew me out, but it's not the end of the world. The next thing you know she'll be knitting little sweaters and stuff."

"You're kidding me!"

"I am not. It's going to be lousy for a while, but hey, time passes."

Reflexively Nick glances at his watch, a gesture that makes Maggie laugh again. She's hysterical, she supposes. She doesn't particularly care.

"Would you stop laughing?" Nick snarls.

Maggie shakes her head and goes on giggling. The laughter seems to have taken over her entire body, shaking her, rocking her, making her giggle and chuckle and howl with tears in her eyes, while Nick's face flushes a dangerous shade of red.

"Stop it!"

She tosses her head and laughs the louder.

"I said stop it!"

Nick screams the words, then swings at her open-handed. Hysteria gives way to reflex. Maggie grabs his wrist, drops to one knee, and flips him over her head. With a doglike yelp he falls flat on his back on the floor. She spins round and considers him, lying spread-eagled and gasping for breath.

"You're damn lucky that rug was there," she says. "It would have hurt worse if you'd hit the plain old floor."

Nick tries to speak but only gasps.

"Don't you ever mess with me again, man. You hear me?"

"Bitch." He hauls himself up to a sitting position. "I'll get you for this. One day. You just wait."

"Yeah?"

"Yeah. If it takes me a hundred years."

"I won't be alive in a hundred years, you jerk."

He snarls, exposing a long canine, but he looks so pitiful, gasping and choking for breath, barely able to sit, much less stand, that Maggie breaks out laughing again. With a howl that clangs like a bronze gong Nick disappears. He does not melt, he does not vaporize in smoke; he merely disappears, precisely and neatly gone. Maggie stops laughing.

"Oh my God! She was right."

For a long moment Maggie stares at the rug. She would like to believe that she's imagined this entire incident, but her shoulder and elbow still ache from the strain of throwing the Devil over her back. With a shudder she goes over to the bed, sits down, and picks up the phone to call Rosie. She's determined to get out of this house before John comes home from his cheap trick.

It seems to John that years have passed while he dwelt in marble halls and ruled a far kingdom with Helen at his side, but even as he hallucinates vast armies, battling at his command, he knows perfectly well that they spring from his own creation, those two tabs of purple mist that he ingested before leaving the house. It seems to him that he stands on a high hill to watch the battle rage; then he wonders if he's perhaps asleep and dreaming. With that thought the battle disappears. He finds himself lying on a pile of other people's clothing, heaped up in the corner of a theatrical dressing room. Distantly, music sounds, and chanting.

What Helen may be thinking as she lies naked in his arms he cannot begin to guess. Since she doesn't seem to speak English, he can't ask.

"Uh, hey," John says. "You okay?"

She smiles and stretches in his arms, then sits up, pushing her golden hair back from her face. He notices a small tattoo on her breast, fondles her, leans closer for a look, and sees a swastika. She giggles at his touch and kisses him, her mouth wet and eager. He catches her by the shoulders and holds her at arm's length.

"The tattoo," he says. "Hell's Angels lady?"

Those words she seems to know. She laughs, nodding, laying one finger on the mark.

"Oh shit!" John lets her go. "Hey, look, it's been swell, but I'm, uh— I've got to go home."

Zipping up his jeans John ducks out fast. Dr. Lucky he still is—neither security guard, their Angels' colors prominent on broad backs, pays him much attention when he trots through the stage door and down the steps into the auditorium. There's no sign of Nick, but John's not inclined to wait for him, not when he could get beaten into dog meat for screwing an Angel lady. Now that he's coming down he feels sick-tired and shaking, and the world's gone flat, as if it were painted on canvas like a stage set. *Sleep. I've got to sleep, and jeez, I could drink Lake Michigan I'm so damned thirsty.*

Outside a foggy dawn turns the street to painful silver. John shuts his eyes to the sight of magenta and turquoise spirals, drifting across his inner view, opens them fast and walks on home, his hands in his jeans pockets, his head aching, pulsing with each step. Trash swirls across the sidewalk round his feet.

"Young man? Young man? Are you all right?"

John looks up sharply, finds the speaker standing in front of him, a little man, slightly stooped, wearing a black suit over a white shirt and a black vest, and a plump black skullcap of great age. With a tilt of his head he looks John over with bright black eyes.

"Yeah, sure, Rabbi."

"Really all right?"

"Really, yeah."

"But what we might wonder is the real, eh?" The rabbi laughs and waggles one gnarled finger. "It's too early to talk philosophy."

"Sure is."

Chortling under his breath the rabbi hurries off, heading, oddly enough for the movie theater. With a shrug, John walks on. By the time he reaches the house he can think only of sleep. As he staggers into his room, he's already unbuttoning his shirt. He gets all the way to the bed before he realizes that things are missing. Maggie's things—the closet door stands open on an empty rack, a dresser drawer sits empty on the floor, the felt rug gone and the Navajo hangings, too.

Suddenly wide awake, he walks back and forth across the room, looking at the empty places, occasionally picking up one of the items that remain, his things—his boots, his books, his records, still there untouched where he last left them. Swearing, he trots out to the hall, trots downstairs to the lab—everything still there, just where he left it.

"Nick! Hey, Nick!"

Silence, a dead and empty silence, answers him. John walks out into the empty ballroom and stands for a moment looking round at torn carpeting and a pair of old speakers, lying on the bandstand. The room smells bitter with old dope.

"What's she done? Run off with my best friend?"

"No."

With a yelp John spins round to find Nameless Girl standing on the stairs and watching him. She's yawning, pushing her tangle of hair back from her face with one hand. Barefoot, she wears her usual jeans but a man's blue shirt, a couple of sizes too large and buttoned wrong, as if she grabbed the first piece of clothing she found by her bed and threw it on.

"I heard you come in," she says. "Thought I should tell you. Maggie's left you."

"I could figure that out, thanks. Why?"

"I don't know. She didn't tell me."

"Okay. What about Nick?"

"He went back to Hell where he belongs. They can't stand being laughed at, you know. Devils, I mean. Maggie told me what happened before she left."

In utter bewilderment John can only shake his head.

"You better get to bed, man," Nameless Girl says. "You're crashing."

Epilogue in San Francisco

THE YEAR THAT HER DAUGHTER TURNS eight, Maggie comes back to San Francisco. Aunt Linda has died of cancer and left in her will a trust fund for the child's education; there are papers to sign, a lawyer to listen to while Maggie perches on the edge of a wooden chair in an overheated office on Sutter Street. The reek of tobacco in the dark-panelled room threatens her with headache. The lawyer, a round man with thin hair, chews gum as he sits behind his desk, reading terms aloud in a pool of electric light. Behind him a window shows nothing but grey as fog rolls across an afternoon sky.

"Now am I to understand," he says at last, "that the child's legal name is Meadow Sunlight?"

"That's correct."

He pauses with a look of distaste.

"She can always change it when she's older," Maggie says. "If she doesn't like it."

"If she does, I'll have to be notified. You'll need to fill out the proper forms and have them notarized."

"Of course."

He says nothing, his fat lips pursed. Maggie glances at his engraved card, then slips it into her shirt pocket. She has put on her best clothes for this visit, a white shirt, a blue hopsacking blazer, a pair of new jeans.

"If you're sure you understand everything," he says at last. "That will be all."

Dismissed, Maggie hurries out and takes the elevator down into the gold and glass lobby of a building decorated like an Aztec temple. Men in wool suits stride past, talking in low voices of baseball scores. Outside the air is cold, the fog lies thick over sky and roof. She has forgotten how cold San Francisco can be in August. Traffic inches past, blaring. She will be glad to get back to the mountains. Tonight, though, she's staying at her mother's house, where Meadow has spent the day.

Turning downhill Maggie walks fast, heading for the parking garage where she's left her beaten-up Volkswagen van. She can see what seems to be a disturbance on the corner ahead and hear the sound of a bullhorn, though the words tear apart in the traffic noise. Caught in memories of her past she suspects a political rally, stops at the edge of the crowd to listen, and finds an evangelist instead, resplendent in gray polyester, waving scripture in one hand while he bellows through the mike held in the other. Laden with tracts, two men stand to either side.

One of them is John Wagner. Maggie can feel herself gaping like an idiot as she stares, wondering how he could have aged so much in such a few years—well, eight years, really now, and some while past she heard that he'd been busted and sent up to federal prison. Perhaps it's the prison that has streaked his thin hair with so much grey and left his eyes so pouched and lifeless. He wears a blue suit, a white shirt, a narrow tie. She begins to back away, to slip into the stream of pedestrians flowing by, but too late. Tucking his tracts under one arm he bursts through the crowd of hecklers.

"Maggie!" His voice cracks with sadness. "Hey, it *is* you! I saw you walk up, couldn't believe it."

"Well, yeah, it's me. Uh, well, how are you?"

"I've never been better." His mouth twitches to portray a smile. "Did you hear I got busted?"

"Yeah, I did, but no details or anything, just through the grapevine. You know?"

"Oh, yeah. Well, I had this big delivery back east, and God wouldn't let me find a courier. He sent me back to DC myself with it so that his officers of the law could find me and save me."

"Say what?"

"I was arrested," he says. "Arrested and sent to prison, where I found the gospel. I met a man there who'd fallen from a high place. He was one of the president's advisors, but he too was a sinner like me. So we prayed together and found Jesus. He's studying to be a minister now, and I spread the gospel where I can."

Maggie feels suddenly sick to her stomach. John is smiling again, his mouth turned briskly up at the corners, his eyes still dead. It seems he looks past, not at, her.

"Ah well," she says. "That's cool, yeah."

"Maggie?" He steps a little closer. "Maggie, you know I really loved you, don't you?"

"Sure, but hey, that was a long time ago, and I'm, like, married now."

"Wonderful! I hope it was a church wedding, a real wedding. But Maggie, because I loved you once, I've got to ask. Are you saved? If something happened, if you died tomorrow—have you ever thought about what would happen to you?"

Maggie steps back sharply.

"I just wanted to ask." The smile disappears. "I know it's a turn-off. But I just had to ask."

Tears form and run beyond her power to stop them.

"Ah jeez!" She wipes her eyes hard on her sleeve. "Lucky, John, to see you like this!"

"Why are you crying? I've never been happier in my life."

"Really? Are you really happy?"

"Of course." He looks honestly bewildered that she would ask.

The crowd has turned to listen, to stare. The evangelist himself, standing on a blue upturned milk crate, is watching with a benign little smile, holding his Bible in one hand and resting it against his heart.

"I've got to go," Maggie says. "My mom's waiting for me."

"Well, sure. Are you still in the city? Maybe we can have coffee?"

"No, I'm living up in the Sierras now. In a little town call Goldust. With my husband."

"Oh, that's right. Your husband. Well, give him my best. God go with you."

"Thanks. Same to you."

Maggie works her way free of the listeners, dashes across the street on the yellow light, keeps running and dodging other pedestrians till she reaches the parking garage. There, hidden in shadows she stops to pant for breath, to weep a little more, too, for the wreckage of a mind and man that she has just spoken with. *I never told him about the baby, she thinks. I shoulda. Meadow's half his, but ohmigawd, how could I? He'd want to see her. He'd want to see me.* She shudders convulsively with a toss of her head, then fishes in her pocket and finds the car keys, runs her fingers over them for the comfort of cold metal. Before her honor forces her to weaken and tell John the truth, she fetches her car and drives out, turning an extra block out of her way to avoid the evangelists on the corner.

After that day, Maggie and John never meet again. In 1997, John dies of a massive heart attack during a revival meeting just outside of Tupelo, Mississippi. The consensus is that Jesus has taken him at the best possible moment a man can be taken. At his funeral red roses heap his coffin and spill round upon the floor.

The Stargazer

LESLIE GETS BEHIND THE WHEEL OF her two-seater Honda and leaves the door hanging while she turns the engine over. The car starts with a chunk and growl, but it starts. Lights glow on the dash, needles quiver on dials—ethanol just above empty. She turns the key and watches the needles sag back. With one last growl the car falls silent. She bites her lower lip while she does some fast figuring. Maybe a gallon left, enough to get into town and reach the only fuel station, about two miles west of town near the entrance of what used to be a state park before the government stopped paying the rangers. If they've had a delivery, no problem. But if they're out? It doesn't pay to count on ethanol deliveries up here in Goldust. Most of the time, about once a week, the pressurized tankers still chug their way up the highway and turn off onto the two-lane road to make their deliveries; often enough the price per gallon's gone up again. There are times, though, when the trucks haven't come, when Big Rick, the station owner, won't pump any more eth for fear of draining the tanks. Empty tanks rise in the ground, and as they rise, they buckle and crack.

Leslie leans back in the seat and runs her fingers over the splitting plastic of the steering wheel. The car sits in the red dirt driveway that runs up to a dark wood and glass A-frame cabin, her mother's house, once, hers now that Mom has finished drinking herself to death. In the rearview mirror of the car she can just see the house front, a huge triangle of plate glass reflecting pine trees that march away down a long slope to a far valley shrouded in resinous mist. Behind the cabin, the mountains of the High Sierra rise, corrugated with forest. Every now and then a bird calls; otherwise, not a sound, not even a rustle of wind. She leans out, grabs the door handle, hesitates. She should just stay home. If she goes into town, she can check the post office box. If she's lucky, she might have a letter from her father, who's teaching in England at the moment, too far for regular phone calls. But if she's stranded? What's she going to do, sleep in the damn car all night?

Pressure starts building behind her eyes. She can think of no other label for this peculiar sensation, a heat that seems to center in the front lobe of her brain and push outward, as if some small warm-blooded animal were burrowing toward the surface from deep in her mind in order to look out of her eyes. Yet she feels no physical pain, merely this ghost of pressure as if from a memory of a migraine, and with it an emotion that does not belong to her, a very faint sense of apology. Without a thought she screams aloud. The sensation vanishes, the pressure, heat, apology—all utterly gone.

"Not in the daytime, damn you! That's not fair."

She slams the door shut, buckles on the frayed shoulder harness, and starts the car. As she drives off, the engine noise seems to hang round her like a bubble, sealing her away from the hills.

Although he'd rather drive the truck, Richie (or Little Rick as his family called him till he put his foot down about it) harnesses up the pair of horses and takes the wagon into town to save what ethanol there is for emergency customers. He's only nineteen, but he handles the team a lot better than his dad, Big Rick. Richie started riding when he was three; he learned to drive the old surrey with its single horse when he was twelve, long before he could legally drive the half-ton pickup. A lot of the older men are talking about coming to him for lessons, when they bow to the inevitable and buy themselves a wagon and a team.

Goldust shelters about four thousand people in maybe a thousand buildings, most of them wood with high-peaked roofs, spread along one side of the highway and reaching back into the pine forests of the foothills on a disintegrating grid of side streets. Behind the foothills loom the High Sierra, the peaks covered with thin dirty snow under a sky tinged with yellow. They form a barrier between California and the rest of the country that's almost as hard to cross, now that the highways are falling apart and airfares are climbing higher than the planes, as it was in the pioneer days when the settlers poured through Donner Pass, which isn't far from Richie's house and the family's ethanol station. The town looks west across the highway where the forests fall lower and lower down the long slopes that lead to the rich farms of the Central Valley, to Sacramento and far beyond to San Francisco on the Pacific coast. Richie has relatives in San Francisco, Aunt Janet and her daughter, Amanda. As he jounces behind his team on the dusty road, he wonders how they'd feel if he showed up on their doorstep, begging to stay awhile.

The Feed and Grain stands on the edge of town, a tin-roofed quonset hut, a roofed yard stacked with galvanized tubs, bales of hay, and cords of firewood. Out on the concrete loading dock Mr. Crawford sits on an upturned crate, hands slack on his massive thighs, his paunch resting on his wrists. He heaves himself to his feet to watch as Richie turns his team and backs them, fighting the buckboard and the ruts, till the wagon bed stands flush with the dock. Red dust plumes around them, then settles.

"You do that like a pro, kid," Crawford says, spitting. "Just like one of them guys in the movies on TV."

"Thanks. Dad said he called ahead about the oats?"

"One dozen fifty-pound sacks. Got 'em ready."

Crawford's young son comes out to hold the horses' bridles and keep them calm. As Crawford shoves the sacks over the edge of the dock and Richie slings them into place, the wagon bed creaks and shudders, making the team prance and snort. By the time they've finished, both men are sweating, and Crawford's face shines a dangerous shade of red. Puffing and blowing, he rubs it on his sleeve while Richie signs the chit.

"Meant to ask you," Crawford says at last. "Tanker been through yet?"

"Nope, not yet. We're expecting it real soon."

"It's been what? Over a week since the last one."

"Close to two weeks, now. But it'll come. Leastways, they haven't called up from Sacramento to say it's not coming."

Crawford merely grunts.

"Well, they got a contract," Richie says. "They can't just go breaking it."

"Yeah, kid? I'll tell you what I think is going on. I think it's like when you catch a lizard by the tail. Tail breaks off in your hand, and the business end of the lizard gets away. The cities—Frisco, LA—they're the lizard. We're the goddamned tail." Crawford laughs in a brief creak. "All us little towns, the farms, too, not counting the damn agribusinesses. They got money to buy votes, thanks to their goddamn ethanol. We don't got the goddamn votes the cities do, and we don't got the money to buy us some pols, and so we get shafted."

"Well, it's the roads that are the problem."

"Yeah? And what pays for the roads? Tax money, that's what, our goddamned tax money. It goes down to Sacramento and that's the last we see of it."

"Yeah, guess so."

"And it's going to get worse. You mark my words, kid. Worse and worse."

When Richie leaves the Feed and Grain, he heads deeper into the crazy-quilt spread of the town. Most houses have big yards, with vegetable gardens and some chickens out in back and a decaying truck or car sitting in front. As he jounces by, Richie sometimes sees a woman or a girl hanging out laundry; when they see him, they wave. In about six blocks the houses back up to the main street of town, a bank, a post office, a straggle of shops, a shoe repair place, the old Safeway supermarket with its new name that no one ever uses. Down at the end stands a coffee shop with a dirt yard round back where Richie can water and tie up his team, out of the way of what automobile traffic there is.

Here in the middle of the afternoon the pale green diner's mostly empty. Two men sit at the beige formica counter and drink coffee while they stare at the TV hanging on the wall between the square red Budweiser sign and the round red Coca-Cola clock. Apparently the satellite dish out back has picked up an East Coast station; in a faint swirl of static an announcer reads the evening news. The waitress, a stout woman with bright hennaed hair, looks up from polishing the counter when Richie shuts the door behind him.

"More riots in New York City," Maureen says. "Sure as hell glad I don't live there."

The two men nod agreement.

"Yeah, guess so," Richie says. "You never hear about riots in San Francisco, though."

"You will, honey. I'm just waiting. Don't see why you're always talking about that awful place, I really don't. All those weirdos and perverts, and that earthquake's on the way, too. Preacher was talking 'bout that just last Sunday. They'll get their due, they will."

Richie nods vaguely. Down at the far end of the counter, a woman's brown suede jacket hangs over the back of one of the red Naugahyde swivel chairs. Looking at it makes Richie's heart tremble in his throat.

"Leslie around?" He keeps his voice as casual as he can.

"Just in the ladies'. You want some coffee? And there's layer cake today."

"A burger, thanks, with everything. And fries. And coffee, yeah."

Richie lays one hand on the back of a counter chair, then hesitates, struck by an idea so bold that he can't resist it. He walks down, picks up Leslie's jacket, and takes it with him to one of the red booths on the window side of the diner, puts it on one seat and sits in the other. His heart pounds so badly that he leans back against the cool vinyl and gulps once for air, but he's sure that she'll prefer sitting in a booth to the counter. Maureen enforces her at-least-two-to-a-booth rule with an iron hand, even when the place is empty. Sure enough, in another minute Leslie emerges from the back, sees him and smiles, strolling over to slide into her side of the booth as casually as if they'd planned the entire thing.

"Now that's real nice of you. I hate the counter."

"Yeah. Kind of thought you did."

While she arranges her purse and jacket beside her, he can only grin and hope he doesn't look like a fool. Leslie's a tall girl (or woman, really, since she's three years older than he), willowy slender with a heart-shaped face dominated by enormous blue eyes. She has a quirky smile—a twist of perfect lips, always glossed a soft red. Her blonde hair curls in the latest fashion around her cheeks, which are fashionably pale, a milky white that speaks of the best in sunscreens and a city life protected from rising UV levels and winter winds both. Even her hands are pale, perfectly smooth, the nails unchipped and polished the same red as her lips. Her clothes, too, the artificial silk shirt, the blue jeans worn skintight rather than baggy for working in, could only come from a city, from the world outside.

"Whatcha doing down in town?" she says.

"Picking up oats from the Feed and Grain. What about you?"

"Hoping to get some eth."

Richie makes a sour face.

"Well, we're real low. Dad says emergency vehicles only. Supposed to get a delivery tomorrow."

Leslie bites her lower lip hard.

"Don't you have enough to get home?" Richie says.

"No, 'fraid not."

Maureen bustles up, plops a plate with a grilled cheese sand-wich and a dome of slaw down in front of Leslie, then scowls Richie's way.

"Yours ain't done yet. I'll bring the coffee."

She heads back for the counter, returns with two mugs and a full glass pot with a wooden handle.

"Milk?"

"None for me, thanks," Leslie says.

"I know Little Rick don't take none." Maureen smiles in his direction and pours the coffee.

Once the waitress is gone, Leslie leans forward and whispers over her sandwich.

"You must hate it when they call you that."

"I do, yeah. Habits, just old habits, Dad says, but it gripes me anyway."

"I'll bet."

Her sympathy keeps him bold.

"Well, say, I could give you a ride home in the buckboard. Tanker really is supposed to come tomorrow, and if it does, well, I'll give you a call, come pick you up."

"Could you? I'd love a ride home." She smiles, all the reward he needs. "But I've got a bike out in the garage. I can ride it into town tomorrow. I mean, it's all downhill coming into town. I don't think I could peddle all the way back, but one way would be easy."

"Okay, then, whatever you want."

His burger arrives, and a bottle of ketchup. As he starts eating, Richie realizes that he should have pressed the ride of next morning upon her, said something like "No, no, no, can't have you biking all the way into town," but the moment's passed.

"How's your grandmother doing?" Leslie says once he's had a few bites. "Maggie, I mean."

"Real good. She blows me away, she really does, how together she is. I sure hope I'm as healthy when I'm her age."

"What is she now, seventy-something?"

"Seventy-three, yeah. Still chopping her own kindling, though she lets me split the big logs."

"That's really something."

"You bet. Say, she mentioned wanting to have you over for lunch one of these days. She's got those snapshots to show you, the ones she told you about. You should give her a call."

"I'll do that. I'd like to see her, too, talk to her about the stuff. Mom's papers, I mean. I've kind of gotten into this habit, calling them The Stuff."

"How's that going, sorting them out?"

"Oh God." Leslie looks away, her mouth drooping. "It's weird, Richie, really really weird. It's like there were two moms. My father says she came down with what he calls OSS—old scientist syndrome—but then, he's still mad at her, because of the divorce. But I guess this syndrome thing happens a lot. A scientist does something really great in their field, but then they go off on some weird tangent. There was this guy a long time ago who was a physicist, and then he went off the deep end and started a sperm bank to preserve superior genes, and then there was another dude who believed vitamins would cure anything. My dad told me about them. And here's my mom, loaded with all those prizes she won, and then. Well."

"Your mom was a physicist?" At that moment Richie bitterly resents the limits of Goldust High School. "I thought she was an astronomer."

"Sort of both. She did research in spectral analysis and the distribution of star types."

Leslie might as well have intoned a magical spell for all that Richie understands what she means. He nods in the best thoughtful manner he can muster and lays the remains of his burger onto the plate.

"There's a lot of unpublished research notes on her computer," Leslie goes on. "It has to do with testing for the presence of iron and carbon in old stars. I don't understand it, but I can see it's important, and I'm making copies and collating it and all that kind of thing. This old friend of hers down in Berkeley is going to help me with it. He's a prof there, I mean. But it's the other stuff that bothers me."

"What's it about?"

"Well." She hesitates for a long moment. "Telepathy. And contacting alien races. She spent the last few years doing research—well, she thought it was research—into something she called xenopsionics. And she wrote it all out by hand in green ink into these notebooks with fancy paper on the covers."

"Uh, well, jeez, Les. I didn't know your mom well or anything, but she was drinking pretty heavy there toward the end. Everyone knew that."

"Oh yeah." She picks up her paper napkin and begins wiping her fingers, very carefully and slowly, one at a time. "I guess it's the drinking that's responsible for the stuff. I know it's crazy, her ideas I mean. But I started keyboarding it, and it's weird, but it kind of gets you after a while. Like a good sci-fi flick does. You start thinking, well, it *could* be true, because it all hangs together so well." She looks up, straight into his eyes. "You know?"

Richie can only stare in return. After a moment he smiles and shrugs.

"Well, if you say so."

Leslie looks down at her shredded napkin. All at once Richie is oppressed by the feeling that he's somehow failed her.

In the chill twilight Leslie stands in the front of her cabin and listens to the rattling, jingling, clopping sounds of the team and buckboard moving away. In the trees birds call, a sleepy warding against the night. For a moment she wants to run screaming after Richie and beg him to stay for dinner, to stay the night in her bed, even, if that's what he wants, if that's what it'll take to keep him there. She spins round, looking up at the mountains. Snow on the peaks catches the last sunset and gleams, streaks and patches of gold among black rocks that haven't felt the sun for millennia. The sound of the buckboard passes away beyond recall. She goes inside.

One long room with a kitchen and bathroom partitioned off

at the back and a sleeping loft in an open mezzanine, the cabin stretches grey and heaped with shadows from the twilight oozing in through dusty windows. Leslie reaches for the light switch, misses, feels her heart pounding until at last her fingers brush plastic. White light floods the heaps of books, the flowered furniture, the long wooden desk with the computer, nestled in stacks of papers and notebooks, disks and cartridges. Shadows flee to the loft and hover around the sandstone fireplace. Leslie weaves her way through the clutter, flicking on lamps until the room blazes with painfully bright light. Although she would like to leave them all on, her eyes begin to water. She returns to the door, flicks off the overhead, and watches shadows spread round pools of gold.

She should, she supposes, eat dinner, a salad or maybe some yogurt, something low-calorie anyway, to make up for that grilled sandwich at lunch. What she really wants is chocolate, but there's none in the house, and her car is far away, parked behind the fuel station. She can't possibly go off her diet tonight, she tells herself smugly. Maybe she should just fast? The sandwich was thick and pretty greasy, she ate some of Richie's fries, well, just three, but they were greasy, too. Bad girl. *Eating too much, flirting with that poor kid. If you can call it flirting when I kind of really do like him. Bad bad girl.* Fasting sounds like a good idea, the more she thinks about it. She can have the yogurt in the morning or maybe if she's good before she goes to bed.

The long, crowded desk faces a wall and a plasma screen, opalescent in lamp light. Leslie sits down at the computer, flips it on, and watches the little icons arrange themselves into a menu as the system boots.

"Please choose a work area." This particular machine's voice is soft, almost syrupy.

Leslie hesitates. She should tell the computer to bring up the archive program storing her mother's statistical studies. She should bury herself in the struggle to understand mathematical data and processes at a level years beyond what she's had so far in college, to analyze at least enough of a given note to place it on the correct branch of the data tree she's so painfully building. She should.

"Please choose a work area or tell me to wait."

"Text."

The screen changes, dissolving to the pale blue start-up of her mother's word processor. The computer's voice becomes brisk and masculine.

"Which directory should I load?"

Leslie hesitates again. She could write to her father. She could in fact exit this session and call her father to wake him in the middle of a British night. *No, wait till it's morning there, then call him and beg him for the plane fare to leave this cabin behind and join him. He might send it.* More likely he'll tell her that she needs to develop a more mature attitude and finish what she starts.

"Which directory should I load?"

"Notebooks."

A list of files appears on the screen, each named for the design on the cover of a given book, Balloons, Cats (one, two, and three), Fractals, HappyFace, Moons, OldCars, Puppies, Roses (one and two), Spirals, Stars, VenusViews. The computer clicks and purrs, waiting for commands.

"Open file Moons. Go to end."

Text pops up on a designated page unit of the screen.

"Keyboard mode."

A keyboard rises, tilting to the correct angle, from the desktop. Soon after she started transcribing the notebooks, Leslie quit trying to read her mother's crabbed and twisted writing out loud. She was hesitating and stammering so much that the computer beeped continual error messages at her. She could, she supposes, read each section of a notebook to herself first, just to figure it out, then read it to the computer. She could even read them all first. If she does so, she can find out what happened in the painfully absorbing narrative of her mother's last year, come at last to the climax of the story.

Considering, Leslie picks up a narrow spiral-bound notebook

whose cover gleams with embossed silver crescent moons, each with eyes and a smile. She's already looked ahead. In order to sort the notebooks out into chronological order, she had to glance through each one and get some idea of the overall shape of her mother's story. Everyone in Goldust knows how it came out, death by alcohol poisoning in a Medevac helicopter as it churned toward a hospital in Sacramento. Knowing so much Leslie doubts if she's in any hurry to reach the story's end. She turns to the slip of paper that marks where she left off typing, but cannot quite remember how far down she'd got.

"Read last page."

The brisk voice, so unlike her mother's, begins.

"The technique worked again tonight. Wrapped in a blanket like a TB patient in Mann's book. Cold out here in the mountains at night, but it seems you must be outside. Stars are necessary. Well, feel necessary. Maybe just using them to focus? Must try this when it's overcast, won't be long now it being almost winter. Had a long wait, checked time at 2150 2212 2234. Just after last check when I felt accompanied."

Accompanied. All through the notebooks Leslie's mother used this awkwardness to signify the touch of another mind on hers. Until this point, the Moon notebook, which must have been written a year and eight months ago, the touch came only rarely.

"Search full directory indexes. Term equals accompanied. Give file location."

The short list gleams on the data window beside the page on screen. Until the Moon notebook, three instances, one unclear. In the Moon notebook, four so far with some twenty pages still to keyboard.

"Give context of search results. Each instance. Two lines plus or minus."

The window expands to allow for the new data. Words spring to Leslie's attention as if they'd been highlighted: pressing, pressure, fullness, warm, warmth, pushing out.

"Clear screen."

The computer beeps twice: recognition error. Leslie breathes deep, twists her hands together, and steadies her voice.

"Clear screen."

The screen wipes itself into clean blue.

"Exit work area."

Icons appear.

"Off."

A square of pearly darkness hangs on the wall. For a moment Leslie thinks she sees an alien face forming in that shadow. When she twists back, half-rising, the face disappears. It was her own reflection.

She gets up and begins pacing through the long living room. She had to check it out, had to know, and now she does know, though she would prefer to believe that she knows nothing. Her experience in the car must simply be some coincidence, perhaps the beginnings of a headache which she simply described to herself in her mother's terms. Most likely her mother's drinking had given her headaches, which she then misinterpreted. Most likely some kind of neurological weakness runs in the family.

When her stomach growls and twists, Leslie walks into the kitchen, then hesitates in front of the tiny green refrigerator. Just because she's upset is no reason to eat like a pig, she reminds herself. Reflexively she runs a hand down her thigh and feels the lumps that she believes are fat deposits under the skin. It would be better to go for a walk, get some fresh air and work off some of the flab instead of adding to it. She heads for the back door, grabbing a pink sweatshirt from the kitchen table.

Outside the stars hang low and glitter in a night abnormally warm for May. She stumbles across the dark redwood deck to the steps that lead down to the yard, but there she hesitates. Her day has left her tired. Walking her usual couple of miles looms like torture. If she stays on the deck, she'll at least be away from the refrigerator and the treacheries of food. She finds a padded chair and sinks into it, leaning back to look up at the arch of the Milky Way. Seeing how close it seems to float makes her wonder if her mother's delusions stemmed in part from feeling like part of the sky. Up in the high mountains it does seem that you could reach up a hand and touch the stars, or that they could indeed reach down and touch you.

All at once Leslie finds herself on her feet without really being aware that she's stood. She knows, however, that she no longer wants to be out under the inquisitive stars. She wanders back into the living room, still golden with the light of lamps, finds the remote, and flops down on the sofa in front of the TV. All night she flips channels, picking a careful path between Fundamentalist preachers and movies filled with gunfire to find cartoons and news, until at last, round midnight, she falls asleep to a tape of the day's session of the California legislature, debating something called the "Christian anti-crime bill." The videocam provides an insert of the opposition, stately men in gray suits from some liberal organization or other, a Catholic priest with his dog-collar shirt, and an Orthodox rabbi, his long gray sidelocks and beard bristling, his black eyes snapping, ready for a fight. As Leslie nods off, she thinks for a moment that the rabbi looks straight out of the screen, and that somehow he can see her.

The tanker arrives round 5:30 in the morning, rumbling into the station, stopping with a squeal and hiss of pneumatic brakes. Richie throws on a pair of jeans and a sweater, grabs his socks and boots, and runs outside carrying them to find his father there ahead of him in the chilly grey light. Richie sits down on an upturned crate by the Coke machine to put the boots on. Yawning and stretching the driver climbs down from the cab, a tall man and as grizzled and paunchy as Big Rick himself. The shirt of his blue uniform hangs wrinkled over his belt.

"Hey, Earl," Big Rick says. "Damn glad to see you."

"Bet you are, yeah. Well, they sent you a full load to make up for the delay. Enough eth here to fill both tanks right up to the top and any of them little transporter cans you got, too." He glances at Richie. "Better round up all the empty pop bottles."

All three of them laugh, just softly under their breaths.

"Good to hear," Big Rick says. "With summer coming on, think the delivery schedule's going to get on track?"

"Up to the front office. I put in my two cents' worth for you, hell, for all my regular customers, but damned if I know what's going to happen. I figure I'll be lucky to have a job five years from now."

"Things that bad?"

"Well, if the legislature keeps talking about phasing eth out. Goddamn eco radicals and Greens, yapping about pollution all the time! Never think about people's jobs."

"Nope, they sure don't. But I dunno. Lot of talk against eth, when they first come up with it." Big Rick shakes his head. "It's that damn agribusiness. Just about damn all owns this state."

"Well, they make a lot of money off corn for the refineries, yeah."

"You hear things, how they rammed the eth bills through."

Earl sighs and rubs both eyes with the heels of his hands, so thick with callus it looks like he's wearing tan gloves.

"I dunno," Earl says. "Little late now to be worrying about that."

"Maybe so. But you wonder."

Richie gets up and goes into the office to fetch the keys that open the hatch over the tanks' input valve. They're locked into a drawer of the gunmetal desk, scattered with papers, tools, and his dad's old computer. Next to the computer sits a shortwave radio, so Big Rick can keep track of emergencies out on the roads. Just outside the four-paned window stands an old pine. Some of its lowest branches hang bare; on others, halfway up the trunk, brown needles cluster. Only the top, high above the station roof where the wind takes the fumes away, grows green.

Filling the tanks takes hours. While the men finish up, Richie's mother, Barbara, gets on the telephone, calling friends and customers with the news. The line forms fast, stretching out of the station and down the dirt shoulder of the highway for a couple of hundred yards. All morning Richie and Big Rick pump eth, watching the gallons tick off, taking cash, taking credit, taking vague promises to pay in a few cases, like Jack Dougherty whose wife just had premature twins. By noon they've sold enough to make the effort of unsealing the tanks worthwhile. Since Barb has fixed him lunch as well as breakfast, Earl's glad enough to hang around and pump a refill.

"Do that after we eat," Big Rick says. "Rich, you better call Leslie."

"Good idea. Thanks, Dad. I nearly forgot."

Big Rick raises a bushy eyebrow as if he doesn't believe a word of it. Richie flees into the office before he blushes.

Although Richie lets the phone ring nineteen carefully counted times, Leslie never answers. He hangs up, calls again in case he punched in a wrong number, gets the same result. He hangs up, spends a minute staring out the window and chewing on his lower lip. No real reason to be afraid, he tells himself. *She goes out walking all the time, or riding her bike. She was expecting his call, wasn't she? But she could be in the shower washing her hair or down the road visiting neighbors for a minute or two.* No need for this sudden flood of cold down his spine, this clench in his stomach as he wonders why in hell she didn't answer her phone. He throws the feeling off with a toss of his head and goes back outside.

"Leslie coming down for her car?" Big Rick says.

"Dunno. She didn't answer the phone."

"Ah. Probably out for one of her walks. She's kind of a strange kid, Leslie. But I like her, mind. She's a real nice girl."

Richie finds himself smiling, a slow smile that refuses to go away. Big Rick laughs and punches him on the shoulder.

"Let's go eat. I'm starving."

And in the end, Richie's fear does come to nothing when Leslie rides in on her multi-gear bicycle, all gleaming chrome and a flash of red enamel. She heard about the delivery from old Arthur down the road, it turns out, just before Richie called, and headed on down.

"Oh, and I called your grandmother like you said. I'm going over tomorrow afternoon."

"Great. She'll like that."

Leslie smiles, takes off her wraparound sunglasses, and wipes them off on the hem of her blue polo shirt. Richie watches, thinking that he's never been so happy in his life, that she'd take his advice about something.

Maggie lives three miles up the hill from her son's fuel station in a rambling grey house that was built back in the 1920s, about a hundred years ago now. Pine trees stand dark round the gravelled path that leads to the back door, standing open. Leslie peers through the screen door into a laundry room with an ancient washer and dryer. On scuffed linoleum stand bags of dry cat food, boxes of soap, winter boots, a bucket and a mop. Even though she's met Maggie several times before, she feels awkward about simply opening the door and going in, even though Richie told her to do just that.

"Hello?" she calls out.

"Come on in, honey." Maggie's voice answers from some distance away. "Just shut the screen behind you. I hate flies."

Leslie does so, carefully. On the other side of the laundry room lies the kitchen, the floor tiled in warm terracotta. Sunlight winks on white appliances and the blue and white tile round the sink. Dressed in jeans and a red bandanna print shirt, Maggie stands smiling at the counter by the sink. Her years of hard work have left her erect and slender, but her face is a web of lines and folds, a network of years hard-wired round her blue eyes. She wears her white hair cropped off, just above her collar.

"Coffee or tea?" Maggie says.

"I'd love coffee, if there is some. I mean, I don't want to use it up or something."

"I wouldn't have offered if I didn't have plenty. Have a seat while I get it started."

Leslie sits down at the round oak table by the big window. She can see out to the vegetable garden, where a tortoiseshell cat is taking the sun between rows of carrots. On the table lie a photo album and a manila envelope that looks like it might contain some papers. Maggie brings over dark blue mugs and sets them down.

"Take milk?"

"No thanks. I like it black. It's got no calories that way."

Maggie hesitates on the edge of a smile. Leslie braces herself against the usual "but you're not fat." Instead Maggie sits down, considers her for a moment.

"Well," Maggie says at last. "Whatever."

They drink for a moment in silence, savoring the coffee, which has suddenly become a rare commodity, thanks to the latest revolutions in South America. Leslie finds herself watching Maggie's hands, the skin wrinkled like a pair of loose gloves over strong tendons. The hands set down her mug, then reach for and open a maroon leather photo printout album.

"Too much trouble to use the computer," Maggie says, flipping pages. "These are clear enough for me, anyway. I do remember, you know, much as I hate to admit it, when all photos came on paper. Here, Les. Here's your mom the first week she moved up here. We had a barbecue and invited her over to be neighborly."

In the photo Laurel leans back laughing in a lawn chair, shades her eyes with one hand while the other holds a glass of orange soda. In the sun her soft grey hair gleams like two wings on either side of her face.

"She sure looks good." Leslie feels the familiar tears rise, chokes them back. "Was she drinking already?"

"Good God, no! She never really drank much before she started writing in those notebooks. A beer or two, maybe, if there was a barbecue, or she liked a glass of wine with her dinner, when she could get the real nice kind, but nothing you'd call real drinking."

"Oh. Did she tell you about the notebooks?"

"Well, a little. Psychic research, she said. After we got to know each other, she used to drop by in the afternoons, just now and then, and we'd sit here and talk about all sorts of things. She didn't mention the notebooks until she'd been up here for a long time."

Leslie has a sip of her coffee and considers. Maggie seems perfectly at ease; when she said the words, psychic research, her voice had none of the twist or sarcasm that Leslie would have expected from her mother's other friends, the ones back at the university. On the same page lies another photo, this one a little too dark, taken in this kitchen. In the chair Leslie is occupying now sits a handsome dark-haired woman in a tailored shirt; across the table sits Laurel, who is talking to a blonde girl in her teens standing nearby.

"That's my daughter, Janet." Maggie points to the dark-haired woman, then to the girl. "And her daughter, Mandi. They were up for the weekend from San Francisco."

"Richie's aunt, then."

"She is, but she's only Big Rick's half sister." Maggie suddenly grins. "I had what they used to call a wild youth, down in San Francisco. I named the baby Meadow Sunlight, but she changed it to Janet, as soon as she was old enough. I can't say I blame her."

Leslie laughs, nods in agreement, goes on staring at her mother's face. Laurel's mouth is half open, caught in the moment of speaking to someone else's daughter.

"She looks so happy."

"She was then, yeah."

Maggie turns a page in the album. Among pictures of Richie and his sister lies another of Laurel, standing, this time, wearing jeans and a baggy sweatshirt and holding a grey kitten while she smiles at the camera.

"That was taken a couple of months later," Maggie says. "I found that kitten in the parking lot down at the Safeway, and I was trying to talk your mom into taking him home."

"She loved cats, yeah."

"Well, I couldn't palm that one off on her." Maggie hesitates for a long minute. "She said the damnedest thing. I can't remember it exactly now, of course, but it was something like she was afraid something would happen to him, something bad, I mean, because of her research. And I said something like, what are you doing up there, inventing a new kind of bug spray? And she laughed and just kind of changed the subject."

Leslie sets her coffee cup down very carefully. She remembers her mother's notebook entry about the grey kitten. It came just after the second time Laurel felt "accompanied."

"She didn't want anyone in the house with her," Leslie says. "She thought something was going to just show up. Some kind of being, I mean. She thought someone had told her psychically that it wanted to visit. Or something. She was real vague about the message. Well, if it was a message. Did she say anything to you about that?"

"Not then. A lot later she mentioned something about aliens from outer space. That's when I started to worry." Maggie flips pages in the album. "It must have been about the time Richie took this one."

In the photo Maggie and Laurel stand to either side of a Christmas tree. Since it's a full-length shot, Laurel's face is small and hard to read, but she stands slumped, her head turned as if she's refusing to look into the camera, her hands clenched into fists at her sides.

"Was she angry?" Leslie says.

"Frightened. And she wouldn't even tell me about what."

Leslie looks away. Outside a grey cat—that kitten, now grown—strolls over to join the tortoiseshell in the sunlight.

"Do you want to look at the rest of these?" Maggie says. "Do you want to hear this stuff, or should I just shut up?"

"I want to hear it. It's just kind of hard."

"Well, sure. Here, let me get us some lunch. We've got all afternoon. I've got some ham."

"Oh, no thank you. I don't eat meat."

"Cheese?"

"Sure, thanks. I'm sorry to be so fussy, but—"

"You don't have to apologize."

"Well, I'm being so much trouble—"

"No, you're not." Maggie holds up one hand. "Really."

All at once Leslie realizes that she's perfectly sincere, that she really doesn't mind, that she's not about to make some nasty comment about vegetarians. Leslie smiles, wondering why she feels like crying.

Over cheese sandwiches on homemade bread, salad from the garden, then brownies and more coffee, Maggie talks, hesitating often to get words just right, hedging more than a little, Leslie suspects, to spare the feelings of Laurel's daughter, forced to hear about her mother's slide into madness. Leslie finds herself eating too much—a whole sandwich, (the salad doesn't count, according to her rules), two brownies—while she listens, fitting each incident into the story outlined by the notebooks.

"Well, it seems pretty clear," Leslie says finally. "She really thought she was talking with aliens from some planet or something. And the more she thought that, the more she drank."

"I've been thinking about that," Maggie says. "She was a scientist. She'd always believed that stuff like psychism and aliens and all that was a lot of crap. When she first moved up here, she used to tease me about my tarot cards all the time. And then all of a sudden she found herself wondering—well, no, she really believed—if it was true after all. She told me once she felt like the earth was moving underneath her. She'd always thought it was solid, and here it was, bucking like a horse. Everything she'd ever believed had gotten itself changed around. If that had happened to me, I'd drink, too."

Leslie giggles, then chokes it back. Maggie hands her the manila envelope.

"Richie copied me that disk of photos, the ones with your mom in them. Before you look at it, I'll warn you about something. Richie thought we should just give you the nice ones, the early ones, I mean, when she looked like she'd want you to remember her. But I said no, we'd better give you all of them."

"The whole truth."

"Well, yeah. Now if you want the first disk he made, the nice one, I mean, I'll give it to you instead."

"No, no, you were right. I want them all."

"Well, I thought you would." Maggie smiles and nods. "And there's a letter in the envelope, too, one she wrote me just before she, well, just before she died."

Leslie starts to open the envelope, hesitates, closes the flap again.

"I'll read it later."

"Good idea. There's only so much of this you can handle at one time. No reason you have to do it all at once."

"Thanks. I just feel I should, you know. My dad always says I put things off too long."

"Laurel talked to me some about your dad." Maggie hesitates, obviously considering how much to say. "I wouldn't let him get under your skin if I were you."

Leslie smiles and looks away. On the wall next to the window hangs a battered and faded print of a Renaissance engraving, within which a pilgrim, his back to a landscape, sticks his head through a starry sky and sees the machinery, all gears and wheels, of the universe.

When Leslie gets home, she opens the manila envelope. The disk she puts down on the desk near the computer. For a moment she looks at the letter, folded so that she can see only the blank side, then slips it into her shirt pocket. She goes out to the deck and flops into a chair, takes the letter out of her pocket and merely holds it, still folded. In the late afternoon sun the hills drowse. Every now and then a jay flies by, cawing insults to the world; otherwise, silence hangs as warm as the sunlight. Perhaps she doesn't even need to read the letter. It was written, after all, to someone else. Laurel left no letter for Leslie, her only child, only this note to her neighbor, a woman she'd met a year or so ago. And yet, why would she have left a letter at all, since her death was an accident?

Leslie opens the letter and reads.

"I'm sorry to dump this on you but if I don't come back,

would you please lock up the house? I suppose they'll call my Ex from the hospital. His name and address are on the magstrip on my ID bracelet. They made me put someone down when they made the bracelet up, in case I went into a coma. Diabetes will do that, you know. But anyway, I want the house to stay nice for Leslie. Thanks for everything. Laurel."

"Diabetes?" Leslie speaks out loud, then stands, feeling herself shaking.

Until this moment she had no idea that her mother suffered from diabetes, a disease stubbornly uncured despite millions of dollars' worth of nanotech research. Although Leslie knows little about it, she does know that diabetics should never drink, much less binge the way everyone said her mother was doing, right before the end. What was Laurel trying to do, kill herself? Leslie trembles so hard that she drops the letter. She stoops and grabs it from the ground. Inside the house the phone begins to ring. Standing where she is, Leslie counts the rings. At nineteen the phone stops. Only then does she go inside.

The computer holds various medical records. Leslie saw them there some weeks ago, when she first came to take over the house, but she never opened those files, which seemed to have little to do with anything. Now, sitting in the shadowed room, safely away from the sunlight, she calls them up and reads them. No doubt about it—her mother was diagnosed with diabetes mellitus just before she moved to Goldust. The files contain reports of insulin implants and regular checkups, though toward the end it records two missed appointments. Laurel must have started drinking at just that time.

"Oh, Mama!"

Leslie rubs her eyes hard with the palms of both hands. Once the tears are dammed, she loads the photodisk, then calls up the viewer utility.

"Display contents of video drive."

One at a time the images of her mother that she has just seen on paper appear on screen, but no longer flat and dull. Although

Maggie's camera must have been a very old model, the computer manages to resolve the images into some semblance of 3-D. Floating upon the monitor the pictures taken outside glow with captured sunlight, while the snapshot in the kitchen loses its shadows and reveals Maggie's sink off to one side and a cat, lying on the floor. Since she has the screen set for fade transitions, as the picture changes, those shadows return before it vanishes. The screen brightens again to display the snap of Maggie and Laurel by the Christmas tree.

"Freeze!" Leslie barks.

Much clearer here on screen, of course, but the picture seems to have changed in another way as well. Standing behind Laurel and off to her left, between her and the tree itself, is a strangely shaped shadow. Neither Laurel nor Maggie could have thrown it.

"Magnify."

Up close the shadow seems more solid than a shadow. Leslie thinks, "Gray jello," then giggles. The objects across which the shadow falls are strangely blurred, not merely darkened. She gets up and steps sideways, just in case she's seeing a reflection of her face, but the grey thing doesn't change.

Someone knocks on the door. Leslie screams.

"Les, Les!" Richie's voice, suddenly urgent. "Les, are you okay?"

Her hand at her throat, her mouth open, she stares at the door and sees the handle turn with a click. Richie shoves it open and steps in.

"I'm sorry," she blurts. "You startled me. When you knocked, I mean. I must have been half-asleep or something."

He grins, walks in, turns to shut the door behind him. He's a tall kid, Richie, broad in the shoulders, narrow-hipped now, but in time, she figures, he'll end up with a beer belly like his dad's. He walks over, smiling, so decent-looking, attractive, really, with his thick brown hair and wide mouth, that she finds herself wishing he were older, just a few years, just her own age instead of still nineteen and fresh out of high school. All at once his smile disappears.

"What the hell is that?"

He has seen the picture, still frozen on the monitor.

"I was just trying to figure that out."

Richie walks over, leans onto the back of the chair, and studies the screen.

"Your grandmother said you took it, so I thought maybe you'd know. Someone's shadow?"

"There was nobody else in the room, and the light wasn't behind me or anything. I've never seen it blown up like that before." He sits down, picks up the mouse, and clicks on the shape. "Isolate."

The computer wipes away the rest of the photo, leaving the grey shape sprawled on the screen. It reminds Leslie of a chalk outline, left on the sidewalk after a street shooting.

"Couldn't be a person's shadow," Richie says. "It's not a human shape. I mighta left the tripod standing in front of the light. I don't think I was using it for this shot."

"It's too thick for the tripod."

"Maybe it was dust on the lens? Or cat hair? Nah, that would've shown up on all of them, all the Christmas snaps, I mean."

"A disk glitch?"

"Now that's an idea." Richie considers for a moment. "Some scrambled bits or something. These are pretty cheap disks. All you can get up here these days."

For a moment longer they stare at the shape. It's sort of human-like, Leslie decides, even if Richie doesn't think so. At least, it has a blob at the top that might be the shadow of a head, and two shadow-tendrils lower down that could have been thrown by arms.

"Restore," she says to the computer.

The original photograph appears in its original size. The grey shape remains visible, but only barely, more like a stain upon the air than an object.

"Weird." Richie stands up and shrugs in dismissal. "Anyway, I dropped by to invite you for dinner down at our house."

"I can't. I ate too much at your grandmother's."

Richie looks sharply away, stares at the floor. Leslie realizes he thinks that she's making excuses.

"No, really," she says. "I can't just sit at the table and not eat, it'd hurt your mom's feelings, and I'm way over for today."

"Way over what?"

"My diet."

"Les." Richie grins, shaking his head. "You're damn near skin and bones."

His phrasing is too insulting to dismiss as mere politeness. Leslie automatically glances down at her body and for a brief moment sees the truth, that indeed, she is not fat at all. Her panic hits as suddenly as some stranger, rising out of underbrush to attack.

"I still need to watch it. How am I gonna stay thin if I eat like a pig?"

He cocks his head a little to one side and frowns, searching for words, a gesture that makes him look a lot like his grandmother.

"Maybe some other time," Leslie says hurriedly. "I mean, thank your mother for me. I mean, I really do appreciate it. But I can't tonight. I just can't."

"Well, okay, if you say so."

For a long moment they stare at each other in the failing light. Leslie concentrates on smiling, on looking perfectly normal, smiles and smiles until suddenly he looks away, turns away.

"Call you real soon," he says. "See ya."

She watches him open the door, walk out the door. Only when the door is nearly shut can she speak.

"Bye. See ya."

The door closes with a snap. She sits down on the floor and begins to cry.

Over the next few days Leslie concentrates on organizing her mother's scientific files, on arranging her days, as well, to leave no room for the notebooks. Every morning she gets up at dawn, works out with her videotape of stretches, then runs for an hour before she sits down in front of the computer. She runs at noon, too, as a break from work, and sometimes at the end of the day. If it's growing dark by the time she quits, she substitutes her aerobics tape for a run. She hates to be outside in the sight of the stars.

She's tackling the big job, going through the backup disks of the stellar analysis data, collating files and transferring them to new, properly ordered disks. There are graphs, screen after screen of equations, most labelled, but some few not, and then paper files, too, pages of scribbled notes laced with statistical constructs and analyses. Leslie can understand little of these. Since her mother jotted a date at the top of each sheet, she can at least put the notes into chronological order and hope that Professor Juarez, back at the university, will be able to figure out what they mean.

Every night, she falls asleep exhausted after her last workout. The pile of untranscribed notebooks, Cats Three, Moons, Roses Two, and AntiqueCars, lies untouched on the computer desk. On the fifth day Leslie considers getting rid of them. Toward evening she stands by the desk in a shaft of dust-flecked sunlight and looks at the pile. She might find an empty drawer or even a cardboard box to collect them, hide them, leave them untranscribed and unknown forever. If nothing else, they stain her mother's reputation by their very existence. Leslie would even consider burning them, but unfortunately her mother talked about them, in letters or over the phone, to a number of her colleagues. If Leslie should destroy them, someone might hold her accountable, might blame or indict her for destroying the records of a famous scientist's work— or so she thinks of it. She lays her hand on the pile, just idly, feeling the smooth cool of the plasticized cardboard.

you must read them you must finish reading them

The voice sounds in her mind but as clear as spoken words. Leslie spins round, half-expecting to see someone standing in the doorway. No one there. She waits, hearing only the scrape of her breathing, suddenly fast. The pressure begins to build, warmth spreads and soothes her, as if a soft hand lay on the back of her neck and radiated warmth into her entire body.

"No!" Leslie screams aloud. "No!"

She takes a few steps toward the door, staggers, feels the pressure turn intense, hovering on the edge of pain. Stumbling, screaming, she gropes her way to the sofa and falls onto it, twists over to her back and hauls her feet up until she can lie flat. The pressure lifts, the warmth fades to clammy sweat, rivering down her back and between her breasts. Only a sense of alien remorse remains, as if she were remembering some other person's sincere and grovelling apology for hurting her feelings.

She hovers on the edge of accepting it. If they regret the pain they cause her, can they be such bad sorts, after all? They. For the first time she felt accompanied by more than one mind. Had that ever happened to her mother? In the gathering twilight the covers of the notebooks seem to gleam with significance, just like in the movies. Laurel would have recorded it, if it had happened to her. Leslie hesitates on the edge of getting up to fetch the books, then grabs the remote control from the floor. Flicking on the TV floods the room with music and colored light. She forces herself to watch the screen, to think of nothing but making sense of a game show, half-over, summoned randomly by the remote, until at last the temptation vanishes.

Yet that night Leslie dreams of the notebooks, and in the morning, of course, they are still there, lying on the desk. Her headache lingers, too. She feels it as a tenderness, apparently centered over her left eye, though that, no doubt, is some kind of neurological ghost. Very carefully she rubs the sore spot, trying to ease the cramp with her fingertips. After a few moments the soreness does lessen. She realizes that she should go to the doctor, who brings his medi-van into Goldust for two days every week, or even drive down to Auburn to get her eyes checked. What if she needs her eyes adjusted? She's never had the surgery or any need for new lenses before, but she's been spending a lot of time staring at the screen, staring at the paper files and the notebooks. The headaches most likely are eyestrain and nothing else.

While she eats, standing up, the last carton of yogurt in the house, Leslie finds herself thinking of that feeling, that surety that at least two beings were capturing her mind. In the sunshine and fresh air of a mountain day, with birds calling outside the open door, the idea of alien mind-reading beings seems so ridiculous, so impossible, that she can sit down and open Cats Three, the next notebook in line to be transcribed. While she eats raw carrots, she flips the pages and finds about halfway through more evidence of her mother's madness.

"Two minds. Tonight the accompanying ones resolved into two, like focusing a scope. Two minds, one's the master, one's a slave, and it's the slave who always feels sorry. Like the master's making him contact other minds, using him like a tool to search out sentient beings, psychic beings, whether he wants to or not. Well, I say he, but who knows what sex he is, they may not even have gender like we do."

"Oh, that's too weird." Leslie speaks aloud.

She Frisbees the notebook back onto the desk and looks at the disordered stack, Moons and Roses and AntiqueCars. Some alien master race searching for worlds to conquer like in one of those pie-pan flying saucer movies from the old-timey days, and the poor slave mind wishing it didn't have to locate them, locate us, Earth, the home planet, and the human race, our race, like fodder, ripe for the harvest—Leslie giggles with a toss of her head, an ill-advised gesture because the room spins sharply to the left.

She feels minds like fingers clamp on to her consciousness. They have her now, good and proper; she feels them like two sets of hot hands, hears them murmuring words she cannot understand, sees pictures of crystalline shapes flitting past her inner eyes. Never once does she see any of these pictures as being outside of her mind; they are like memory images, recalled by a chance word or scent. None of them make any sense whatsoever. Pear shapes, blob shapes, all shiny and glittering, float in some sort of liquid air. Dimly she's aware of the room around her, of the view of Sierra hills outside the window, dimly she hears the jays calling, dimly sees the shadows changing. A car backfires and growls by on the road—those sounds penetrate.

Leslie screams and wrenches her mind away. She can conceptualize it no other way, that she has physically yanked her mind back from something or someone. She feels cold, realizes that she's drenched with sweat, stands up, grabs the edge of the desk to steady herself. They are not going to let her alone, whoever this they may be, just as they wouldn't leave Laurel alone, once they had her. Again she considers burning the notebooks, then realizes that she needs the information inside them, if she's going to resist. *You got yourself into this, Les, you get yourself out.* This particular voice in her head is only a memory of her father's.

She realizes, then, beyond the possibility of explaining it away, that she believes. Her mother wasn't crazy at all. Her mother was contacted by telepathic aliens. The truth, the whole truth, and nothing but the truth—she's never been so sure of anything in her life. She straightens up, glances out the window to find the light changed, glances at the clock and realizes that it's nearly seven o'clock.

"How long have they had me?"

She thinks, tries to remember when she got up, must have been no later than 8:30. She's always been a morning person, never liked to sleep late. And then she ate the yogurt, read for a while, but they must have taken her round nine at the latest, a whole day ago, unless maybe a night passed and then another day and here she never noticed. Her mouth is dry. She has to go to the bathroom. No, it could only have been one day or she would have needed to go before this.

After the bathroom, she walks into the kitchen, opens the green refrigerator and looks in: nothing but a little bit of milk. Tonight, she feels, she can eat, deserves to eat, even, since she's barely touched food in the last five days. She can drive into town and have dinner at the diner—and then she realizes that she's lost track of time. If it's Sunday, and she rather thinks it might be Sunday, the diner will be closed. So will the Safeway. There will be nothing to eat, not for her, though other people will be eating. She feels herself shaking, feels ready to cry, slams the fridge door and walks back into the living room.

Seven o'clock and still light out. Under the clock sits the telephone. Perhaps she could call the diner and see if it's open, see if Maureen will tell her what day it is? She remembers Maggie telling her to call anytime, to come over anytime, to drop by for a meal, even. She hesitates only briefly, then picks up the phone.

Richie has spent several hours over at Maggie's house. He brought her groceries from town, put them away, chopped firewood, cleaned out the lean-to and checked the emergency generator, played with the cats a while, and had some coffee. He is considering going home, when the phone rings. He watches his grandmother pick it up, sees her smile and wink his way as she listens to whoever it is on the other end of the line.

"Why, sure, Les," Maggie says, emphasizing the name. "I haven't had supper yet. Why don't you come right over?"

Richie feels himself blushing. Maggie hangs up the phone and smiles at him.

"Want to stay for supper?"

"Well, sure, Gram, if it's no trouble."

"Never any trouble, honey. You know that. But we won't have meat, since it's Leslie coming over. I was thinking about macaroni and cheese."

"Sounds good to me. Say, Gram? Why is Les always sure she's fat or something?"

"Beats me." Maggie hesitates, thinking. In the strong light through the window she looks pale, her skin close to translucent with age, the veins like threads in rice paper. "Well, she's got a lot of problems, Les. Her father was a nasty kind of dude, her mother told me, always criticizing, always tearing the poor kid down, still does, I guess."

"Bastard."

"Laurel called him that, too, yeah. You gonna grate the cheese for me?"

"Sure." Richie stands up. "I'll just get me a bowl and the grater."

The cheese sauce is made by the time Leslie arrives, stepping into the kitchen, hovering in the doorway while she glances this way and that as if she expected someone to jump out at her. She looks freshly showered, freshly madeup, and dressed as always to perfection, but no makeup can hide the dark circles under her eyes, all puffy and swollen. Maggie gives her one of what Richie calls her "sharp looks."

"Are you okay, Les?" Maggie says.

"Well, I've been better." Her voice trembles and swoops. "I think I had a flu, the last couple of days. It seems like I've lost track of time or something. Today's Sunday?"

"That's right, yeah. You feverish?"

"Not anymore. I went through this thing this morning where I sweated really bad."

"Sit down." Maggie turns firm. "Sit down and I'll make you some tea."

Maggie's teas are always medicinal and always strong. After one sip Leslie allows hers to be laced with honey, calories or no calories. She drinks it slowly, cradling the warm mug in both hands, and in silence watches Maggie cook. Richie finds himself running through possible ideas for conversation starters and rejecting them all. Cats wander into the kitchen, sit near the stove, and watch Maggie with tails curled round paws.

"Rich?" Maggie says. "You want to feed them?"

"Sure, Gram."

Richie picks up the plates and goes into the laundry room to fill them from the big bags of dry cat food. The cats follow in full chorus. As he scoops out the two different kinds and distributes them onto the plates, the cats lean against his ankles or walk round and round like sharks circling a life raft.

"Almost done, guys, almost done."

Over the cat noise Richie can hear Maggie and Leslie talking in low voices, just a few words here and there, but when he comes back, they fall silent. He sets the plates down for the cats, then glances at the wood box.

"I'd better fill that if you're gonna bake that macaroni."

"I am, yeah," Maggie says. "Thanks."

When Richie returns with the full box, he rests it on top of the washing machine in the laundry room and listens. Through the open door he can just see Leslie, leaning forward a little, listening to something Maggie's saying. It seems that she's about to answer, but even though he hesitates, unseen, to let them finish, she never does speak. He brings the box in and puts it down beside the stove.

"Should be enough there for your breakfast tomorrow, too, Gram."

"Thanks, hon."

Richie sits back down at the table. At last the obvious conversation starter occurs to him.

"How's your work going, Les? Up at the house, I mean."

Leslie's hands spasm and let the mug fall, bouncing unbroken on the linoleum.

"Oh God," she says. "I'm sorry. I'm so damn clumsy."

"No damage, honey." Maggie bends down and fetches the mug. "It's not even chipped. Tough stuff, this stoneware."

"Well, still, I just feel so stupid."

"No problem, Les, really." Maggie sets the mug on the counter. "You want more tea?"

"Oh, no thanks, I feel lots better now, really." Leslie turns to Richie with an arranged smile. "The work's going fine. It's just kind of dull, all those stats, you know?"

Richie doesn't know, but he smiles anyway.

"How's the eth holding out?" Leslie goes on. "Are you gonna get another delivery next week?"

"Sure looks like it. They called my dad to tell him it's on the way."

Under her prompting Richie finds himself talking, telling her this and that about the horses and the town and the local gossip. Once Maggie's got the firebox going and the casserole in the oven, she sits down at the table and joins them, leans on one elbow onto the table and merely listens, but Richie notices her studying Leslie, notices too that whether she says anything or not, his grand-mother is worried about something. He assumes that she thinks Leslie isn't quite over her flu.

Although Maggie owns an old red pickup truck that still runs, thanks to Richie's work on it, she rarely drives it anymore, rarely goes anywhere off her property, for that matter, except when Big Rick drives her down to the Safeway. A couple of days after Leslie's visit, though, Maggie decides that she really has to take a hand in whatever's bothering young Leslie. She puts on a flowered cotton skirt and a blue pullover, finds the keys to the truck, shuts the back door to keep the cats out until she returns, and goes out to the garage. As she's backing the truck out, watching carefully for ambling cats, she wonders if she should call Leslie first. What if Les makes some excuse, tells her not to come? Maggie decides that it's better to risk her not being home.

When she pulls into Leslie's driveway the Honda's there, and so is Leslie's bike, leaning against the side of the house. Reflexively Maggie walks round back to go in the kitchen door, as she always did when Laurel was alive. Gravel and dead leaves crunch under her heavy shoes, and she's jingling the car keys, too, swinging them from one hand as she walks, but still Leslie doesn't hear her.

The girl lies in a chaise longue out on the deck, flopped dead-still with the chair back tipped way back, staring up at something. When Maggie glances up she sees only trees, framing blue sky. Leslie is so pale that Maggie feels cold fear clench her heart—has her intuition dragged her over here to find the child dead? She hurries up the steps, and the sound of her footsteps brings Les round. She sits up and stares at Maggie, her mouth half open, sweat beading on her face.

"Oh Leslie," Maggie says. "You *are* still sick, aren't you, honey?"

"No." Her voice is very high and soft. "I mean, I don't think so." She rubs her face with both hands, pushes damp strands of hair away from her cheeks. "Oh yuck!"

"That's what I mean."

"Yeah. Well. Yeah."

Leslie allows herself to be helped up and led into the house. Maggie sits her down on the sofa in the living room and goes back to the kitchen to make some coffee or tea, only to find that there's barely a stick or scrap or swallow of food or drink in the entire place. One half-eaten container of yogurt, one herbal tea bag, a couple of carrots—that's it. Maggie marches back out again.

"Les, look, you're not one of my kids, and I know I don't have much right to say this, but honey, I'm worried about you. You've got to start eating better."

Leslie merely looks at her, her eyes so glazed that Maggie wonders if she's heard.

"Les? I think you need to go to the doctor."

Leslie shakes her head no, but it's a halfhearted gesture. Maggie sits down on the edge of a nearby chair and waits.

"You're right about the eating," Leslie says at last. "I've been meaning to go to the store. I keep putting it off. I mean, I know better." She tries to smile, fails. "I should have fruit and stuff in the house."

"Well, yeah, and some good cereal. Whole grains are real important for vegetarians."

Leslie smiles, nods, looks away so vacantly that Maggie wonders if her problems all come from starvation. It seems likely.

"By now you're probably too tired to get to the store," Maggie says. "I can call Richie, give him a shopping list, and have him bring the things up here."

"That would be real nice of you." Leslie's voice has turned into a whisper. "I'm real tired, yeah."

Maggie organizes a list on a scrap of paper, calls Richie, and makes him repeat back each item as she says it. He's more than glad to help; she can hear the worry in his voice. Once he's been sent on his way, Maggie goes back to the kitchen, boils water in a saucepan, and makes the cup of tea. When she carries it back into the living room, she finds Leslie sitting cross-legged on the sofa, her eyes a little brighter, her smile a little more genuine as she takes the cup.

"It'll be a start," Maggie says. "Let's see how your system handles that. Some times it can't take a lot of food right away."

"Well, I did eat yesterday. Honest." Leslie tries a sip of the tea. "This tastes pretty good."

"Good. Have you been running a fever every day?"

"No. I only get so sweaty when—" A long pause. "When I exercise too much."

Maggie's raised too many kids not to recognize a lie when she hears one, but she decides to let it go. Gaining Leslie's confidence is not going to be easy.

"Well," Maggie puts some cheer into her voice. "I'm glad to hear you're getting some exercise. Instead of just working at the computer, I mean."

"I've been running a lot, yeah."

Maggie smiles, Leslie smiles, neither speaks. Maggie glances round the room and sees the notebooks lying beside the computer. Laurel would, on occasion, read to her from those notebooks.

"It can't be easy work," Maggie goes on, "going over those. I used to really worry, when your mom would read me her notes."

"Worry about Mom, you mean, or the planet?"

Maggie laughs at the joke.

"Well, yeah," Leslie says. "But didn't you ever wonder, well, what if this stuff was true? What would happen, I mean?"

"Your mom used to say that we were marked for invasion, if it was true."

"I found the place where she said that the first time, in Cats Three, toward the end."

It takes Maggie a moment to understand this statement.

"Oh, the notebooks with cats on it."

"Yeah. Sorry." Leslie smiles briefly. "I keep them straight that way, by what's on the covers. So it was Cats Three where she said we were marked for invasion, and that's why the slave was sorry. His people got taken over, you see, by this other race, and so he doesn't want to help take us over, but they make him do it, you know. He really doesn't have any choice. Sometimes he gets a chance at contacting us when they don't know, the masters, and then he can be more honest, but he can't risk sending for very long."

Maggie's stomach turns cold and knots itself. Innocently Leslie talks on.

"Mom kept such careful records, even toward the end when she was drinking. She began labelling the different voices—well, I shouldn't call them voices—the different minds. And she could always tell which one was accompanying her. I don't think you can lie, talking mind to mind."

"Probably not." Maggie finds her voice at last. "Les, uh, you've started doing it, too, haven't you? I mean, talking to these people."

Leslie freezes into a porcelain figure, one hand raised, a smile caught on her mouth.

"I'm not surprised you'd try it," Maggie goes on, gentling her voice. "After all, you've lost your mother, and this was her work, what you've got left of her. You kind of have to believe in it, don't you?"

The statue shatters. Leslie curls into a ball, twisting sideways on the sofa, and begins to sob. Maggie hurries over, sits next to her, catches her shoulders and unwinds her from herself. She puts her arms round the girl and pulls her closer, lets her sob against her, a heartbroken child, now, sobbing and rocking, while Maggie strokes her hair and makes meaningless soothing noises, "There there, there there." At last Leslie falls silent, sits up, pulls away to wipe her face.

"I'll get you those Kleenex from the kitchen table."

Maggie does so, hands her a couple, lets her blow her nose, hands her a couple more to wipe her face.

"Les, honey, you've got to get some help. You've been up here alone, brooding over all of this, missing your mama, too, I'm sure, and well. . . ."

"You think I'm nuts, don't you?"

"No. I think you've got too much on your mind and no one to share it with."

Leslie wads the Kleenex into a ball and stares at it.

"Putting all this stuff in order's a big job," Maggie goes on. "I think you need a break, hon. A vacation, some time off. It wouldn't hurt to hire someone to do the typing for you."

"Typing? Oh, yeah, keyboarding. But I couldn't let anyone see the notebooks."

"I don't suppose anyone really needs to."

Leslie's eyes narrow, and she squeezes the Kleenex ball hard.

"Anyone but you, I mean," Maggie says.

"Oh. Oh, well, yeah. I should probably ship the other stuff down to Berkeley. My mom's friends need to go over it, anyway. I don't understand all the math."

"I'll bet. There's not a lot of people at your mom's level."

This brings a grin, open and grateful.

"A vacation never hurts anyone," Maggie goes on. "And maybe someone else to talk to, a little counselling, I mean. They have those grief counsellors, don't they, down in the city? It's a real hard thing to lose your mother as young as you have."

"I never thought of it that way. But yeah, you're right, aren't you? Maybe I should think about that."

"I wish you would, honey. I really think it'd help."

Just then they hear a truck coming, slowing down, turning into the driveway.

"That'll be Richie with the groceries," Maggie says, getting up. "We'll talk about this again, honey, real soon, any time you want to. I'm usually home, or if I'm gone, it's not for long, not anymore."

With a long sigh Leslie leans back against the couch, rests her face against a pillow, pale skin against pale upholstery. Her eyes drift out of focus, seem focused elsewhere, very very far away. Maggie wonders if she should call Leslie's father, decides against it. Judging from Laurel's anecdotes about him, he considers any kind of mental illness a moral failing and would tell Leslie so in no uncertain terms.

"I think I'll make some supper, while I'm here," Maggie says. "That all right with you?"

Leslie never answers. When she hears the screen door bang, Maggie goes into the kitchen just as Richie steps in, his arms full of brown paper bags.

"I'll put those away," Maggie says. "Why don't you go keep Les company in the other room? But she's running a fever, so don't sit too close."

Richie blushes and makes his escape. *Of all the girls to fall for! But Les is a nice kid, really, aside from all of this.* As Maggie stores the groceries, she can hear them talking, hesitantly at first, then more naturally, two kids laughing together over the gossip of a small town. Maggie decides to stay in the kitchen a little longer and starts making a big pot of vegetable soup.

When the soup is ready, and fresh-baked cheese muffins to go with it, Leslie cannot stop herself from eating. She tells herself that she's stuffing herself like this—two bowls of soup, three muffins and with butter, too—just to please Maggie, but it seems that her body has swerved out of control, that it's determined to grab food with its hands and stuff food into its mouth, whether she wants it to or not. She does manage to pass on dessert, though she promises Maggie that she'll have pie with her breakfast in the good old-fashioned way.

With dinner over, Leslie finds herself yawning. She hasn't slept much, this past few days.

"Richie," Maggie says. "I think you'd better get on the road. Les, you need to rest. I'll just put this stuff in the fridge, then leave myself."

Richie follows orders, but he does linger long enough to carry the dirty dishes to the washer. Leslie considers walking out to his truck with him, but she cannot force herself to stand up. *It's all that food. It's made me too heavy to think.*

"Thanks, Richie," she says. "I really really appreciate this."

"You're welcome. Hey, any time."

Leslie smiles, keeps smiling as he walks out, stops smiling only when she hears the truck start, then drive away.

"I should help," she says to Maggie.

"No. You're sick. You just sit there."

Maggie scrapes the dishes and puts them in the washer, then wraps up the food, tucking the muffins into the bread keeper, the leftover soup—there isn't much—into a small covered bowl.

"Now, you eat this tomorrow," Maggie says. "I'll call you in the afternoon."

"Okay. Thanks, Maggie. Thanks so much. I don't know how to repay you—"

"You don't need to." All at once Maggie grins. "Just eat some of that pie."

"I will. Promise."

As soon as Maggie's gone, Leslie shuts up the house, then falls into bed. She has just time to pull the sheet over her before she sleeps.

In the dream world they come for her, the Master and the Slave. The Master she has never seen, and this time as well she only hears his mind-voice, muttering incomprehensible words. The Slave has a face of sorts, two eyes high on a cylindrical skull, or it seems at times cylindrical, at others stretched and wavering like a reflection in a pool of water. She sees his head emerging out of robes, or at least, soft sweeps of blue and green that might be fabric wound round a neck. For some time they speak, Master and Slave; then the touch of Master's voice disappears. Slave's view widens to include a greenish sky and large fronds that might be growing from muddy ground. Thick air spreads over the view, the crystalline pear and blob shapes appear—bubbles in the chemical drink that either enhances or produces Slave's psychic abilities.

I am sorry I have no choice

I know that

they have set the beacon they will come

The crystalline shapes spread, fuse, thicken to a pane of opaque glass. Screaming, Leslie is awake, sitting up naked in a disordered bed.

She forces herself under control, stops screaming, stops crying, gets up and staggers into the bathroom. From the mirror two faces look out at her, her own and then, slightly behind and to the left, a cylindrical shape with eyes, the skin pale grey, the eyes pools of black. She twists away, stares at the shower wall, then glances back to find the second face gone.

"You never should have eaten so much, you little pig. It made you dream, all that food."

She starts to cry again, walks back to the bedroom, picks up her dirty jeans from the floor and pulls them on without underwear. Tears blind her so badly that sits down on the edge of the bed, then remembers.

"They've set the beacon."

The tears stop, leaving her cold, icy cold and calm. The Master knows, his entire race knows, where Earth lies in the spangle of their alien sky. She is the only one who knows they know. From the floor she grabs a shirt, slips it over her head, then stands, fumbling in her pocket for car keys. She has to warn the world.

The local TV station seems the obvious place to begin. Barefoot, Leslie runs outside, slides into the Honda, and leaves the door hanging, while for a moment she tries to organize her thoughts, her words, the things she's going to say, the warning she'll deliver. If only her mother were here, if only her mother weren't dead—and she remembers again that her mother drank even though diagnosed diabetic. Did Laurel want to die, she whose world had shattered, she whose beloved stars had turned strange beyond reckoning? Leslie sobs once, then shoves the thought aside.

When she turns the engine over, it starts right up, and she sighs in relief and shuts the door. She backs out of the driveway, then turns onto the main road fast. While she drives, curving down the mountainside and heading for the highway that goes down into Auburn, where the station is, she's planning out what she will say. She's watched the local news enough to know the names of the newscasters. Which one should she ask for? The Hispanic woman, Lupe, seems the most accessible.

Leslie lets the car slow to take a sharp turn at a decent speed. The road here runs narrow, with the mountainside itself rising sharply on her right, and off to the left, dropping down and down into the far distance of a valley. All at once she realizes that she's come away with no shoes. And in dirty clothes. And without combing her hair. They're going to think she's crazy, when she shows up like this talking about aliens from outer space. Is she crazy? She remembers Maggie, saying that the notebooks were all she had left of her mother. Orphaned so young. Grief counselling.

"But I hear them. I know they're there."

Yes, of course she hears them. They have been using her, an unconscious traitor, to track down the human race. For the first time she realizes the enormity of her crime. If she hadn't kept working with the notebooks. If she'd burned them. She should have burned them. She should never have opened them. It's all her fault. Once again yet again she's failed. It's all her fault. She's not seen it until this moment, that the fate of the Earth, the coming subjugation of humanity, are all her fault, her sins, her shames, hanging before her in the sunlight like bubbles, crystalline bubbles.

they use you as a beacon they will find you

In perfect calm she wrenches the wheel to the left. The car spins, skids, bucks on the shoulder, and leaps free of the road and of the earth. For one brief moment Leslie knows how it feels to fly.

When the fire engine screams by, Richie is standing out in front of the eth pumps, his hands in his pockets, watching the road and hoping for a customer. The siren leaps out of nowhere and spins him round to watch as the red rescue unit races toward and then past him, the wail dying and echoing as it heads up the mountain in the direction of Leslie's house. Leslie's house. He feels a trickle of fear down his spine, reminds himself that she was too sick to drive anywhere, feverish and all of that. Yet he takes a few steps out into the road and watches in the direction the engine's gone. Distantly he sees a thin plume of grey smoke rising into the sky.

Richie moves, fast but not too fast, walks into the office and turns on the emergency shortwave radio. He fiddles with dials, picks up a clear signal at last.

"We've found it. A car wreck. Must have gone over the edge up above a ways. Can't really tell. A two-seater car." More squawks, perhaps from the other end of this conversation. "It's burning too bad to tell. But there's someone in there. Ah shit!" A long pause, filled with static and dim voices, far from the mike, a long long pause, too long.

Without thinking Richie turns the radio off and walks back outside. Plenty of people in Goldust drive two-seater cars these days, with eth so expensive. When he looks up at the sky, he finds the smoke dispersing to a flat faint plate against the blue. They must have got the fire out, then. Too late for whoever it was, in there. He looks both ways down the road, sees no one coming, then turns and walks back into the office to turn the radio on.

A lot of chatter, a call for an ambulance. One of the firemen has a burnt hand. The person in the car is dead.

"Looks like a girl. Looks like the car might have been a Honda."

Richie turns off the radio. He knows, then, knows in his very soul as grief stabs like a knife, but he can pretend he does not know, cannot know, for another twenty-odd minutes, until the phone in the office rings. He answers it to find Maggie on the line.

"Richie, honey, close up the station and come up to my house. I talked to your dad. He'll be down to open it again. There's something I have to tell you."

Richie hesitates, wondering if he can pretend he doesn't know for the time it'll take him to ride up to her house. Since Big Rick has the van, he'll have to take one of the horses.

"Richie?"

"Still here. I saw the fire engine. She's dead, isn't she, Gram? Leslie I mean."

"Oh God. How—"

"The radio. The radio in the office."

"Oh God. Just get yourself up here."

As he hangs up it occurs to Richie that his grandmother needs him. He saddles up a horse, swings into the saddle, and heads out without even telling his mother where he's going. That afternoon he discovers an advantage horses have over cars; you can cry and ride at the same time.

That afternoon Maggie spends pacing round her living room, alternately storming and weeping, blaming herself or cursing Leslie's father. She will have to call him, she supposes, better her than the police, after all, even though she's never met him, even though he's nothing but a name and a set of nasty habits to her. He's in England, Leslie told her once, teaching for the summer. She hopes she can find his number over at the house. Eventually she will have to go over there and sort out things for a dead friend once again, just as she did for Laurel.

For these hours Richie sits in a chair and says nothing, barely moves, until she feels like screaming at him to weep, to curse, to do something anything for God's sake. Finally, when the sun hangs low in the sky and shadows fall dark across the windows, Richie gets up, stretches, sits down again.

"You know why she was out driving around?" he says.

"I don't, no. I've been wondering. She could have called me if she'd needed anything."

"Yeah, that's what I thought. She was too sick to handle the car, I guess."

Maggie hesitated, considering whether or not to tell him the truth. Judging from everything she knows about Leslie, put together with the skid marks that the rescue crew found, most likely Leslie killed herself.

"She was real feverish," Maggie says. "I don't know why she was out of her bed, much less out driving. Those curves up there are tricky."

Richie nods, looking away.

"It's getting dark out," Maggie says. "I'm going to go get the cats in."

He nods again, staring at the far wall.

The herd of cats comes not exactly to Maggie's call, more in answer to the sound of food being shaken on a tin plate, but slowly, a few at a time, they wander into the kitchen. By the time the last of them has condescended to come eat, the shadows have turned to twilight on the hills, though far above and to the west the high peaks still gleam gold. Maggie returns to the living room to find Richie sitting on the floor, his back to the sofa, all six feet of him sprawled akimbo, one hand clutching the remote. On the hanging screen of the TV some faded frenzies of Donald Duck play soundlessly while he stares at them without, mostly likely, really seeing them, his face illuminated only by the silver glow in the dark room. For some minutes she stands in the doorway and watches him watch. At last he turns his head to acknowledge her presence.

"I could give Janet a call," Maggie says. "I was wondering if you wanted to get away for a little while. She's got an extra room, you know. You'd be welcome to go down to the city, stay a couple of weeks."

Richie turns his head back to the screen and flicks the remote. The same cartoon starts again from the beginning, still without sound.

"If you think she wouldn't mind," he says at last. "Don't know if I should, though."

"Well, you don't need to decide right away. She's told me a couple of times that you'd always be welcome."

"Thanks. Real nice of her."

This is, Maggie realizes, the first time he's ever mourned anyone. Her husband died in a logging accident when Richie was two and a half. The grandson, that skinny little toddler with sandy hair who was Little Rick back then, did notice Grandpa's absence but found the news that he was in Heaven solace enough.

"Do you want to stay here tonight?" she says. "Not go home?"

He turns to her and manages a smile.

"Yeah. How'd you know?"

"I guessed."

He lets the smile fade, considering something.

"Real nice of Aunt Janet," he says at last. "But I don't think so. But you're right about getting away."

"Well, is there anywhere else you want to go?"

"I was thinking 'bout going down to Grass Valley. I've been thinking, you know, 'bout learning to drive a real team. A four-in-hand, you know? Or even a rig of six. There's a guy there, said he'd teach me."

"Old Tim Wilson?"

"Yeah. He told me he used to drive a stagecoach, back when they had those 'Old Timey Days' for the tourists."

"I remember that, yeah. Him and his brother Jack, but Jack's gone now."

"Yeah. And well, if old Tim dies, there won't be anyone left who knows, will there? He's damn near ninety. No use in me putting it off much longer. I was just thinking about that."

"Yeah, I bet you were."

Richie nods, wipes his eyes on the back of his hand, and turns back to the screen, where the cartoon is ending. A flick of the remote begins it again. Maggie sits down in a chair nearby, where she can see Richie more than the screen. She wishes that she'd taken some snapshots of Leslie, just to put in the album with those of her mother. Someday Richie will want to see her again, a picture of his first love, no matter how badly it ended. Someday Maggie herself will want a picture too, when she stops wishing she had done something more, reached out a little more, asked perhaps the one right question or made the one right comment that would have started Leslie talking about whatever problem it was that drove her first to starving herself, then to suicide. *If only I'd stopped by again this morning early, if only I'd helped her, if only if only*—a requiem in her mind for the dead, even though she knows that she did try, that nothing, probably, would have saved Leslie's life since, it seems, she was determined to kill herself.

"Tim said he'd put me up for a couple weeks, while I learned," Richie says.

"Um? Well, right. It's not something you can learn in an afternoon, handling a four-in-hand. Or a coach rig."

Richie nods, staring at the screen. A different cartoon is playing now, but still he hasn't turned up the sound.

"You better call your dad," Maggie says. "Tell him you're staying here tonight."

"Yeah."

Richie gets up, hands her the remote, and walks into the kitchen for the phone. Maggie lays the wand in her lap. She can only hope that Leslie's found whatever peace she so desperately craved, if indeed something does happen to a person after she dies, if a soul is somehow translated or recycled or given at least a few moments to consider how it lived. For the first time in fifty years she finds herself thinking of Nick Harrison and her odd fantasy that he was the Devil incarnate. Too many drugs, she supposes, we all took too many drugs. *But we had hope, back then, drugs or no drugs, hope that kids like poor Leslie don't have anymore, hope that the future would be good or at least fair somehow, justice for all, or at least damn it all interesting. Strange the way things work out, but well, nothing lasts forever, not even hope.*

Maggie finds herself on the edge of tears. She wipes them away and gets up, then goes into the kitchen to make Richie something to eat.

Asylum

I'VE ALWAYS LOVED BRITAIN SO MUCH," Janet says. "It's going to be wonderful, this couple of weeks. I haven't had a vacation in so long. Jam tomorrow, jam yesterday."

Rosemary smiles. Ever since they met at Oxford, some forty years ago now, they've kept in touch across the Atlantic by phone calls and faxes, e-mail and bulletin boards, the occasional paper letter, the even rarer visit. They have shared their careers, their divorces, and their family news during those years, as well as this long-standing joke about Janet's lack of vacations.

"Well, then." Rosemary supplies the punch line. "I'd say that you've finally got your jam today."

"Finally, yeah," Janet says, grinning. "And the view from here is an extra helping. It makes me feel all John of Gauntish. This sceptered isle and like that."

They are standing at a window on the top floor of the Canary Wharf office building, rising among the ruins of the Docklands.

Since they are facing west, London stretches out before them into the misty distance on either side of the Thames, glittering in the bright sun of a warm autumn day. All along the banks the new retaining walls rise, bleak slabs of concrete, while the river runs fast and high between them. Janet can pick out the complex round the Tower and the new barricades round its ancient walls, protecting them from tides gone mad. Just east of the Tower, near what used to be St. Katharine's Docks, huge concrete pylons, hooded like monks in sheet metal, rise out of the river. Boats swarm round, workmen overrun them, all rushing to finish the new barrier before the winter sets in.

"Well," Janet says. "Maybe not John of Gauntish. Rosemary, this is really pretty awful, the floods, I mean."

"If the new barrier holds . . ." Rosemary lets her voice trail away.

Janet considers her friend for a moment. In the glittering light Rosemary looks exhausted. Her pale blonde and grey-streaked hair, carefully coiffed round a face innocent of makeup, somehow emphasizes the dark circles under her eyes. Along with a handful of other MPs, Rosemary fought long and hard to get the barrier built further east, just upriver from the old one, argued and insisted that the East End should be saved, that millions of people and their homes not be abandoned—but in the end, more powerful interests won. Engineers could guarantee the barrier if built at this location, and of course, it cost much less than her counterproposal. As a sign of social impartiality, the Docklands, an embarrassment to British business for the last forty-odd years, have been left beyond the new barrier as well.

"We'd best go down," Rosemary says.

"Yeah." Janet turns, glancing round the lobby toward elevator doors that hang not quite at a right angle to the floor. "How long do you think this building's going to stand?"

"Well, we don't get earthquakes here, you know, like you do at home." Rosemary smiles briefly. "The Free University will probably be able to use it for some years yet. After all, the predictions are vague—about the warming trend, I mean. No one can pinpoint the rise year by year. It may even have peaked."

"That's true, of course. And if they get the embankment built up along here, well, that'll hold for a while more."

"If they do. If, my dear."

During the ride down neither woman speaks, both listen, rather, to every small creak and rattle that the cage and cables make. Groundwater and shifting terrain have begun to damage the ever-so-delicate array of wires and power conduits upon which Twentieth Century buildings depended. When the doors open smoothly at the ground floor, Janet lets out her breath in a long sigh of relief. She's glad, as well, to get outside to air that needs no artificial circulation.

On the small flagstone plaza students gather, chattering among themselves under the huge canvas banner, lettered in red, announcing the conference at which Janet has just been the featured guest. "Women's Gains: a Century of Progress." A century of crawling forward would be more honest, Janet thinks. Even on this lovely afternoon, the work to be done haunts her. She reminds herself that this is a vacation, that she has left all the files from outstanding cases at home, that her law practice will survive without her for two weeks and her new book will, as well. Besides, her assistant back home has her itinerary, and he can always call if he really needs her.

"It was a good speech, you know," Rosemary says abruptly. "It was one of those that makes me think, my God, I know someone famous!"

Much to her own surprise, Janet blushes.

"Oh now really," Rosemary says. "Sorry."

"No problem. And I have to admit, I wallowed in all that applause. But you should talk! Lately you've been in the media lots more than me."

"Only as a crank, my dear. Another Liberal Party crank, flogging her unpopular ideas."

"Well, don't you think that's what I am? Back in the States, I mean. A small 'l' liberal crank at best. A tool of Satan is more like it."

They look at each other, grimace, shrug, and walk across the plaza. In the shade of the low embankment, near the steps up to the RiverBus dock, someone has set up a table and folding chair. A young woman lounges in the chair; a monitor and set of input tablets lie on the table. Nearby stands a man of about fifty, short and compact, his dark curly hair streaked with grey, his skin the light brown of Thames mud. At the sight of Rosemary he waves vigorously and grins.

"Jonathan, hullo!" Rosemary drifts over. "Have you met Janet? Janet Corey. Jonathan Richards."

They shake hands and smile. Jonathan wears a stubbornly old-fashioned shirt, white and buttoning up the front, with long sleeves rolled up just below his elbows.

"I'm manning the trenches today." Jonathan waves at the table and the monitor. "Petitions."

"Petitions for what?" Janet asks.

"Raising the banks round the Free University. I'm its bursar, you see, and I'm not looking forward to rowing to work every morning."

"Well, yeah, I guess not." Janet glances at the low dirt bank, topped with a thin layer of asphalt. "That won't hold long, if the predictions come true."

Jonathan nods, glancing at Rosemary, who sighs, reaches up to rub her eyes with the back of one hand.

"We keep introducing the special requisition," Rosemary says. "Perhaps if you do get some show of popular support. . . ."

"Just so. Hence, the petitions." He grins at Janet. "I'd ask you to sign, but obviously you vote elsewhere."

From the river drifts the sound of an airhorn—the hovercraft on its way to dock. Muttering good-byes, fumbling in their hand-bags for pass cards, Rosemary and Janet hurry up the steps. Out on the water the hovercraft is pausing, backing, working its way through the crowd of small boats and barges, which are scurrying out of its way in turn. On the dock, down by the gangplank two men in the blue uniforms of the RiverFleet huddle over a portable media link. Janet can just hear the announcer's midget voice say, ". . . deteriorating situation in Detroit . . ." before music carries it away.

"Er, excuse me," Janet says. "Could you tell me what that was about?"

At the sound of her flat American voice the officer nods agreement.

"I hope you're not from Detroit," he says. "There seem to have been more riots. Fuel oil rationing, I believe it was."

"Probably. It usually is. Thanks; thanks very much."

As she follows Rosemary down the gangplank to the boat, Janet wonders at herself, that she would take the news of "just another riot" so calmly.

News, bad news, dogs her holiday. As she leaves London, heading north on the Flying Scotsman, she reads of riots spreading all through the Rust Belt, from Chicago in the west to New Jersey in the east. Pictures of the American National Guard quelling riots scroll past on the media screens that hang from the girders in the Edinburgh train station. By the next morning, British time, the news reports deaths; the waiter in the hotel dining room informs her, his voice grave, as she helps herself to whole grain cereal from a stoneware crock at the buffet. Seven young men, two young women, shot as they tried to loot—food in every case, he thinks it was.

"How dreadful." *I'll never get used to this, at least.* "How awful. Ohmigawd."

He nods, hesitating, glancing round the nearly empty dining room, where a profusion of white linen lies on sunny tables. In a far corner two elderly men eat behind matching newspapers.

"We had an American gentleman in earlier," he says at last. "He joked about it."

"No! Oh God, that's really awful. What did he say?"

Again the glance round.

"He said that in his day, young people had the sense to loot luxury items, like televisions. Said he didn't know what was wrong with them, nowadays."

Janet cannot speak; she merely shakes her head.

"I didn't know what to answer," he says.

"I wouldn't have, either. You know, most Americans who can still afford to travel have, shall we say, rather right-wing leanings these days. The rest of us don't."

He smiles as if relieved, but she feels like a hypocrite, lumping herself in the category of "the rest of us" when she so obviously wears expensive slacks, a silk shirt, when she so undeniably is spending her vacation on expensive foreign soil.

"Shall I bring tea to your table or coffee?" the waiter says.

"Tea, please. Thank you."

For the next few days Janet tries to bury herself in problems of the past in order to ignore those of the present. She climbs up the rock of Din Edin, as she always thinks of it, where the Gododdin built their fortress. She knows too much about Mary, Queen of Scots, to romanticize her, finds herself avoiding the guided tour through the castle, and merely stands, looking down at the fang-sharp grey city below, while white storm clouds pile and build in the blue sky. That night, while she listens to the news on television, it rains. As an aside, almost an afterthought to the real news, the announcer speculates on how long the Holy Isle of Lindisfarne will remain above sealevel. The restored castle on its smaller version of Din Edin's rock is safe, of course, but on the flat, villagers stubbornly cling to ancestral land, which sinks into a rising sea.

On the morrow, guidebook in hand, Janet wanders through the National Museum of Antiquities. She spends much of her time there studying the Pictish standing stones. Across the marble floor of a vast hall, decorated with murals of the Highlands, the newly completed collection stands, tucked away from acid rain as the Highlands themselves cannot be. The present, it seems, cannot be avoided.

In her hotel bedroom that night, while she writes postcards to her only child, Amanda, to her nephew Richie's family up in the Sierra Nevadas, and finally, to friends, she flicks on the news out of habit and lets it rumble half-heard until American voices raised in anger force her to watch. Just a few seconds of footage make it plain that Congress has deadlocked over the question of imposing military law on rioting cities. Janet watches fat senators invoke God's name until at last the screen changes to local news, good news: the child who wandered away from his family last night has been found, chilled to the bone but unharmed.

Janet windows the screen into four, then flips channels, finds at last among the meager sixty-four available on British television an international news feed, which turns out to be devoting itself to the droughts in Central Africa.

"Damn!" She flicks the monitor off. "But really, you know, you *are* supposed to be on vacation?"

Yet, all too soon, America invades her holidays across the bridge of the media. At first the troubles at home appear toward the end of a broadcast and only in the evening program, but slowly they pull ahead and begin appearing on the morning feed as well. By her fourth night in Scotland, they've taken precedence over the Parliamentary debates about preserving British farmland. On the night that she reaches York, American news—the spreading of riots into Sunbelt cities, where fuel oil shortages provide no excuse—has inched in front of the ongoing discussion of whether King William should abdicate. By the time she reaches the Lake Country, the lead story and the headline in the newspapers as well have become REGULAR ARMY UNITS SUPPLEMENT NATIONAL GUARD IN AMERICAN CITIES.

Military law declared, generals replace mayors all across the nation—and in many pulpits, though not all, preachers and priests announce that God is punishing America for pride and sin. The *Times* runs a special feature on the situation, which Janet reads, twice, sitting in the lounge of a small hotel, at a diamond-paned window, under a wood ceiling certified as Tudor. Janet stares at the pictures of torn streets, impassive soldiers, smug preachers, for a very long time. All at once, she finds herself afraid.

The outcome reaches her in Cardiff. She has just emerged from the National Museum and crossed to the park where Iolo Morgannwg's gorsedd circle stands, a miniature henge of reddish stone. The morning's rain has stopped, leaving the pale grey civic buildings clean and gleaming, the sky a parade of sun and cloud, the grass between the slabs of Iolo's fancy bejewelled with drops. By the curb a small electric truck dispenses whipped ice cream, and Janet debates buying a cone, setting her ever-present fear of cholesterol levels against the girlishness of this day. Not far away a group of teenagers huddle round a media kiosk—a newsstand, she suddenly realizes, not a video viewer, and without really thinking she drifts closer, hears the announcer mentioning Washington, D.C., and drifts closer still. One of the boys looks up; she sees a familiar face, dark bangs, blue eyes, the busboy from her small hotel.

"You're the American, aren't you?"

"Yes, as a matter of fact."

Silently he steps to one side to let her have his place in the huddle. The announcer, mercifully, is speaking English.

". . . riots feared in San Francisco. Units of the National Guard, as it is called in America, are moving into the city's center in spite of scattered resistance."

Earthquake. Her first thought is natural disaster, the quake hit at last, the waiting over, and looters in the street. The announcer drones on.

"Although news lines are down all across the nation, it would seem that the only resistance to the coup does lie in California. Leaders of the junta report that the control of other major cities passed peacefully into their hands early this morning."

Nightmare, not earthquake.

"How well those reports may be trusted remains to be seen. An emergency session of the European Parliament has been called for later today. Earlier, the prime minister made this announcement outside Number Ten, Downing street. . . ."

"Ohmigawd." Janet hears her voice tremble and skip. "Oh-migawd."

The young men are watching her, she realizes. One steps forward and touches her elbow.

"I'll flag you down a cab."

She can only nod, not speak, merely stands and trembles until at last the compu-cab pulls up to the curb.

Back at her hotel room the telephone blinks, signalling messages. Janet hits the button, stands in the middle of the room and listens, merely stands and looks at striped wallpaper while Rosemary's voice, harsh with unfamiliar urgency, asks if she'd heard the news. A second call, from her daughter, Mandi, left behind in San Francisco—for this Janet watches the phonevid. Mandi's face is dead-pale, her hands shake, even as she assures her mother that she's all right. When Mandi begs her to call as soon as she can, Janet finds herself speaking aloud, "of course, dear," in answer. A third message—this from her assistant, a terrible connection, Eddie's voice chattering fast over the sound of traffic. The phonevid shows only static.

"I'm calling from a pay phone. I hope to God you get this. Don't come home. They ransacked the office this morning. It's *Seven Days in May*. They took the files. Don't come home. Stay where you are."

Other voices break into the background of the call. Eddie curses. A click, the message over. Janet sits down in a blue-flowered chair next to the telephone, rewinds the tape, and listens to all three messages again. Clever of Eddie, to use the name of an old video to tell her everything she needs to know. The army's been in her office. Half her discrimination cases are pending against various military bureaucracies. There is no doubt now who will win them.

Her mouth is dry, her hands shake, and she feels abruptly cold, gets up to find a sweater, stares numbly round the room while she tries to remember what made her stand up, sits down again. She should call Mandi, reaches for the phone, stops herself.

Doubtless they, this vast, suddenly ominous "they," will have tapped Mandi's phone by now. Will they go to Mandi's flat and take her away like the files?

"Her engagement will save her." Janet hears her own voice tremble, continues speaking aloud just to hear a voice in the room. "She's Army now herself, really. She's going to marry an officer. He'll take care of her. Jack's a good guy."

Unless he has chosen to honor his sworn oath to the Constitution and refused to go along with the coup? Jack's stationed in California, after all, named by the announcer as the one place offering any resistance. But who's resisting? Military units? Street gangs? Libertarian and survivalist fighter packs? All of these in some patched-together coalition?

"I've got to call my daughter."

Janet reaches for the phone, pulls her hand back. If she calls, she might implicate Mandi in . . . in what? Something, anything, being the daughter of a liberal, who knows now what the word, *crime*, may mean. *They've taken my files. They know all about me. They know about my daughter.* When the phone rings, Janet screams. She gulps a deep breath and picks it up on the third pair of rings.

"Janet? Thank God." Rosemary's voice, slightly breathless, precedes her image, irising onto the phonevid. "You've heard?"

"Sure have."

"Well, look, the maglev train runs from Cardiff to London every hour up until seven o'clock tonight. Call me once you've bought your ticket and I'll arrange to have you met at Euston. It's going to take a while, so we have to start the process as soon as possible, and of course you'll have to declare, so you'll need to be at my office tomorrow morning."

"Declare? Rosemary, wait, slow down. What process?"

"Applying for political asylum, of course. Janet, my dear friend! I've just been briefed by the Foreign Office. You can't go back. You'll be arrested the moment you step off the plane. They're rounding up anyone who might oppose them. It's horrid."

Janet stares at the stripes, blue and white and grey.

"Janet? Janet, look at the camera. Are you all right?"

"Yeah, sure, sorry."

"Well, this has all been a bit of a shock, I'm sure."

Janet restrains the urge to laugh like a madwoman.

"At any rate," Rosemary goes on. "Do get packed up and get yourself down to the station. Wait, someone's talking. . . ." A long pause while Rosemary chews on her lower lip. "Good God! Janet, listen. I'll have a ticket waiting for you there. They might have taken over your accounts. Your cards might not work. I'll contact your hotel, too."

"Already? They might have cut people's cards off already? Oh God, they must have been planning this thing for years!"

"Yes, it would certainly seem so. The Foreign Office are shocked, really shocked. They've been keeping an eye on something called the Eagle Brotherhood, but they had no idea of just how high it reached. Well. I'll brief you later. Just get to London, so you can declare."

"Of course. Should I keep an eye out for assassins?"

"Good God, don't joke!"

"Okay. Sorry. I'm on my way. Oh, Rosemary, wait!"

"Yes, still here."

"Don't worry about the train ticket. I've got a BritTravel pass. They couldn't have touched that."

"Right. I'll just ring up your hotel, then."

Janet crams clothes and her bedtime book into her suitcases, checks the bathroom and finds her various toiletries, crams them into plastic bags and stuffs them into a side pocket of the biggest case. She carries the luggage down herself, reaches the hotel desk to find the clerk talking to Rosemary, writing down her charge numbers to settle the bill. The clerk pauses, her dark eyes narrow with worry, with sympathy.

"It's all been taken care of, ma'am."

"Thank you. Could you call a cab for me? Or wait, will they take a BritTravel card?"

"They will, yes. Best of luck to you, ma'am."

"Thanks."

Janet restrains the urge to add "I'll need it" like a character in an old video.

On the maglev, the trip to London takes a bare hour. Through polarized glass Janet sees the countryside shoot by, clear in the far distance, blurred close to the train. Although she's used to thinking on her feet, having practiced for years in front of hostile judges, today she cannot think, can only worry about her daughter, her assistant, her sometime lover and closest friend, Robert, and all the other friends in their politically active circle, all left behind in San Francisco. *I alone have escaped to tell you.* She leans her face against the cool glass and trembles, too tormented to weep.

At Euston she hauls her bags off the train, finds a luggage cart and ladles them in, then trudges down the long platform, leaning on the cart handle for support like some bag lady, drifting through the streets with all she owns before her. As she emerges into the cavernous station hall, she sees two things: the enormous media screen on the far wall, and Jonathan Richards, wearing an old-fashioned tweed jacket flung over an old-fashioned blue shirt, hurrying to meet her. On the screen a man in uniform stands in the Oval Office next to a pale and shaking president. Across the boom and bustle of the hall the general's words die before they reach her.

"Hullo," Jonathan says. "I'd hoped to see you again on a better day than this."

"Yeah, really."

"Rosemary rang me up and pressed me into service. She's afraid that sending an official car would attract too much attention."

Janet starts to answer, but her mouth seems to have frozen into place. Attract too much attention? From whom? Does the coup have the power to pluck its enemies from the streets of foreign cities?

"Rather a nasty situation all round," Jonathan says. "Here, I'll push that cart. The wheels always stick on these beasts."

Nodding, Janet relinquishes the handle. As she follows him through the crowd she is trying to convince herself that she's simply too unimportant to be a target, but her new book rises in her memory, and its brisk sales—*Christian Fascism: The Politics of Righteousness. You saw this coming, you've seen it for years, why are you so surprised?*

Jonathan has spoken to her.

"I'm sorry," Janet says. "I missed that."

He smiles, his eyes weary.

"Quite understandable. I'm just abandoning the cart. We go down the steps here."

Books and papers heap the back seat of Jonathan's small electric Morris. He slings the luggage in on top of them, hands Janet into the front seat, then hurries round behind the wheel. As they pull out, Janet realizes that night's fallen. Street lamps halo out bright in a rising mist.

"Where are we going?"

"Rosemary's flat."

"Ah. Thank you. I mean, really, thanks for coming down like this."

"Quite all right."

During the drive out to Kew, where Rosemary lives in a huge walled complex of townhouses and gardens, Janet says very little. Her mind searches for its old humor, tries to find some quip or irony, fails, trails away into wonderings about Mandi and Robert. Suddenly she remembers that Robert talked about leaving the city during her vacation, about going up to her mother's old house in the mountains. If he has, he will be safe; up in Goldust her family knows him, and they will take him in if he needs it. If he left. Will she ever know?

"Jonathan? Have you heard if the phone lines to the States are down?"

"It seems to depend on where you want to call. The various media have their own links, of course. The news program that I was listening to on the radio implied that private calls are difficult, and the farther west you want to call to, the worse it is."

"I was thinking that might be the case, yeah."

"We'll get some sort of underground news network set up down at the university as soon as we can. Hackers." He glances her way briefly. "For a respectable sort of person I happen to know a remarkable number of hackers."

"They'll see it as the best game in the world."

When they reach the flat, Rosemary's housekeeper lets them in, takes the luggage from Jonathan and takes it away. They wander into Rosemary's yellow and white parlor, all slender Eurostil furniture and wall paintings. Rosemary loves florals, and on the display screens glow Renoirs and Monets, each garden blooming for some minutes, then fading to allow the next to appear. Jonathan heads straight for a white wooden cabinet.

"Drink?" he says.

"Gin and tonic, please. I bet Rosemary's on the phone."

"She'll be hoarse before the night's out, yes."

Janet sinks into the corner of the pale leather sofa only to find herself confronted with a picture of her daughter, a snapshot she herself took on the day that Mandi graduated from college. Rosemary has had it enlarged and printed out, then framed in a yellow acrylic oval. In her dark red robes and mortar board Mandi looks overwhelmed, no matter how brightly she smiles for her mother's camera. She is pale and blue-eyed, like her grandmother, and her long blonde hair streams over her shoulders. All at once Janet's eyes fill with tears. She shakes them away and looks up to find Jonathan holding out a glass.

"I'm so sorry," he says.

She nods and takes the drink.

"You must be worried sick about your daughter."

"I am, yeah." She takes a sip before she goes on. "But actually, I was thinking of my mother. I'm really glad she didn't live to see this."

Jonathan sighs and flops into an armchair opposite. He is drinking something golden-brown, Scotch most likely, sips it and seems to be searching for something to say. Wearing a crumpled blue suit, Rosemary steps in to the room. Her red scarf slides from her shoulder and falls without her noticing.

"Hullo!" She smiles at Janet. "It is *so* good to see you safe."

"Thanks. Really, thank you for all the help. I don't know what I'd have done without it."

"I'm sure you'd have thought of something, but I'm glad I'm placed as I am. Sorry I was on the phone when you arrived. I've been being courted. Rather nice, really."

"By the party whip, I assume?" Jonathan hands her a drink.

"Exactly." Rosemary sinks down into the other corner of the sofa. "Thank you, darling." She pauses for a long sip. "This is the situation. Emergency session tonight in a few hours. Labour want to threaten an immediate boycott of all American goods and services and to call for immediate restoration of democracy. The Tories, of course, do not. Enough Labour members may bolt to make our votes important. The Labour leaders are willing to be accommodating. I pretended to have doubts about the boycott for the sake of the British middle class." Rosemary smiles briefly. "And so you'll get the embankment, Jonathan, to protect the Free University."

"Brilliant!"

"Tremendous!"

Jonathan and Janet raise their glasses and salute her.

"Corrupt, actually," Rosemary says. "But there we are." She turns Janet's way. "I'm having some information transmitted to my terminal for you. About applying for asylum. We'd best get that underway tomorrow. They're setting up a board to handle the applications, you see."

"Do you think there'll be a crush?" Jonathan said. "Most of the Yanks I've met lately will be overjoyed at the developments."

Rosemary shrugs.

"The coup wouldn't have struck without being sure of having a broad base of support," Janet says. "They've been building it for years. Mostly by playing on the crime issue—you know, the need for order in our embattled streets. And of course, moral values. The so-called family values."

"It's always order, isn't it?" Jonathan says. "The excuse, I mean, for military governments. We must have order. Keep the people in line."

Janet nods agreement.

"Anyway, we'll have dinner before I go," Rosemary says. "Have you remembered to eat today?"

"No." Janet allows herself a smile. "Not since breakfast. Kind of a long time ago now."

"Thompson will be serving soon, I should think. You know, I have no idea what sort of questions the Board will want answered during the asylum proceedings. Your books and career should be enough to satisfy them you're in danger. I hope they don't want an actual threat or your presence on some sort of list. How long do you have left on your tourist visa?"

"Close to two months."

"Splendid! Surely that should be enough, even for a bureaucracy."

"Even for a British bureaucracy?" Jonathan puts in, grinning.

Rosemary groans and holds out her glass for a refill.

"It's a good question, though," Janet says. "I'll have to have some visible means of support, won't I?"

"Oh here." Jonathan pauses on his way to the liquor cabinet. "Surely that won't be a factor in the Board's decision."

"It might," Rosemary breaks in. "The junta are bound to put pressure on our government in turn. They do have all the bombs, you know. I imagine they'll be able to force a very strict adherence to the rules and regulations for this sort of thing."

Jonathan thinks, chewing on his lower lip.

"Well, here," he says at last. "The Free University sponsors lecture series. There's no doubt that you'd be a major attraction, Janet. First, a series of public lectures featuring your book: Christian fascism—its roots and rise. Then a proper course for the student body: American fascism, the historical background. I foresee no difficulty in getting the Committee to approve it."

"No doubt they'll thank you." Rosemary turns a good bit brighter. "And of course, the book! It's only just come out here, and my God, what a publicity event!"

Janet tries to laugh and fails.

"But what about the money from that?" Rosemary goes on. "Does it go to your agent in America?"

"No, fortunately. She has a coagent here in London, and David gets all monies received and converts them to pounds before he sends them on. I'll call him tomorrow. He can just send my agent her cut and let me have the rest. Oh my God. My agent!"

"Oh now here," Rosemary says. "You don't think she'll be arrested?"

Janet shrugs helplessly. She has absolutely no idea which of her acquaintances might be endangered by the simple act of knowing her.

"It sounds to me," Jonathan says, "that one way or another you'll do very well for yourself."

"Yeah, it does, doesn't it? If I don't mind being a professional exile."

Although Janet meant the phrase as irony, it cracks out of her mouth like a pistol shot. Rosemary sighs and watches her, worried. Jonathan busies himself with refilling glasses.

"Well, sorry," Janet says. "It's not like I have a lot of choice."

"Just so, darling. Do you want to try to ring Mandi? It can't put her into any worse danger than she's already in."

"Just from having a mother like me? Oh God. But yeah, I do. I'll just go into the other room."

"The green guest room. The one you had before."

Janet sits on the edge of a narrow bed in a pool of yellow light and punches code into the handset. Halfway through, at the code for the San Francisco Bay Area, a string of whistles and shrieks interrupt.

"I'm sorry, but we cannot complete your call as dialed. Please attempt to ring through at a later time."

"Damn!"

Later that night, when Rosemary has gone off to the Houses of

Parliament and Jonathan to his home, Janet lies on the bed in her green-and-white guest room and watches the late news. Footage of tanks rolling down American streets, soldiers standing on guard in front of banks, here and there the ruins of a shelled building—and yet it seems clear that the coup has faced little resistance, except out in the American west. The east, the south, and the capital belong, heart and soul, to the coup and the Christian right. Utah as well has declared for the new government, as have the southern counties of California, but up in the mountains, the Rockies, the Sierra Nevada, the rain forests of the Cascades—in the high places even the spokesmen for the junta admit that a campaign of "pacification" lies ahead of them. There are no reports at all from Alaska. All network links seem to be down. Since the Native Americans there have been sabotaging government installations for the past fifteen years, Janet can guess that they've found sudden allies among the whites.

It doesn't matter, Janet knows. In the end the coup will win, because the areas that resist matter little to the economic life of the country. They can be cut off and starved out until their cities fall to the neo-fascists. Perhaps Alaska will stay free, an instant republic. Down in the continental United States, up in the mountains, a guerrilla war may continue for years, an annoyance but no threat to the new government, fought by a patchwork army of libertarians, survivalists, and honorable men.

The newscast changes to a parade through Washington, rank after rank of soldiers, Army and Marines marching through the rain. Past the Lincoln Memorial—Janet lays down the remote to wipe tears from her eyes. Yet she cannot stop watching, finds herself staring at the screen, puzzling over some small detail. She finds the close-up function, slides it on, zeroes her little white square over one soldier, clicks—and sees upon his shoulder the new patch added to his dress uniform, a white cross on a blue ground. She punches the screen back to normal so hard that the remote squalls in protest.

The end of the newscast shows the Senate voting extraordinary powers to the new chief of government security, that is, to the head of the coup, an Air Force general named James Rogers, and, almost as an afterthought, establishing a new office of public security, to be headed by a certain Colonel Nicholas Harrison. One picture catches Janet by surprise—she hadn't expected Rogers to be black, just somehow hadn't expected it.

Janet flicks off the terminal. For a long time she lies on the bed, staring at the blank screen, until at last she falls asleep with the lights on.

Morning brings coffee (real coffee served in a big mug by the ever-efficient Thompson), the sound of rain pounding on the windows, and memories. On the nightstand lies a telephone, its little screen a green gleam of temptation. *Call my daughter. Don't dare.* Thompson opens one pair of curtains to grey light, smiles, and leaves again.

Janet gets up, flicks on the news, and dresses, gulping down the coffee in the intervals between zipping up her jeans and pulling a sweater over her head. The American coup has taken over the television as well as the United States. Janet windows the screen into four, finds a silent feed station for one, mutes the sound on two other programs, and lets the BBC announcer drone at low volume while she unpacks her suitcases.

Except for Seattle the coup now controls every city in the continental United States. The BBC expect Seattle to surrender at any moment, guarded as it is by only two regiments of National Guard and some armed citizens. Since Russia and Japan have both offered their protection to the new Republic of Alaska, it will probably stand. In all three program windows video rolls endlessly, tanks, Congress, dead bodies, fighter planes, refugees streaming north into Canada from Seattle and Detroit. On the silent feed maps flash; Janet takes a moment to click on the western states and freeze their image upon the screen. She zeroes in on San Francisco, clicks to magnify, sees a street map covered in a thin wash of red, too cheerfully raspberry for even metaphorical blood. The junta holds the city, the bridges are secured.

The search function throws a box on to the screen.

"Do you wish to see a news feed from the city you have selected?"

"Yes."

The BBC disappears, and an ITV reporter pops into focus, standing in the Civic Center. Behind her rises City Hall, grey and domed in a foggy morning, but the high steps are strewn with corpses. Janet begins to tremble. She sits down on the edge of the bed and clasps her mug in both hands while the reporter, pale and dishevelled, speaks in a low voice of a night of horror, of teenagers firing handguns at tanks, of teenagers shot down by those who were once their countrymen. The camera starts to pan through the pollarded trees of the skimpy plaza. A siren breaks into the feed; the reporter shouts something into her microphone; the feed goes dead.

Janet raises the remote and clicks the monitor off. She cannot watch any more of those pictures. Yet she must see more, she must know more. She raises the remote again, then hurls it onto the carpet. *You'll feel better if you cry. Why can't you cry?*

She cannot answer.

"More coffee?"

Thompson at the door, holding a tray—a silver pot, a pitcher of milk, a plate of something covered by a napkin.

"Yes, thanks. Is Mrs. White at home?"

"No, ma'am. She's gone to her office."

"Ah. I thought so."

Thompson sets the tray on the dresser, then stoops and picks up the remote. Janet takes it from him and without thinking, flips the monitor on again. An ITV executive stands before a studio camera, speaking very fast and very high while sweat beads on his high forehead. As far as he can determine, his crew in San Francisco have been arrested, hauled away like common criminals despite every provision of the UNESCO media pact signed just last year in Nairobi. Janet changes the station out from under his indignation. This time a search on the strings "San Francisco" and "northern California" turn up nothing, not on one of the sixty-four channels.

Janet makes the BBC and the silent feed into insets at the top of the screen, punches up the terminal program, then glances round for a more convenient input device than the TV wand. On the dresser, next to the silver tray, lies a remote keyboard. She picks it up, looks under the napkin—croissants, which normally she loves. Today they look disgusting. She sits on the floor with her back against the foot of the bed and rests the keyboard in her lap while she runs a quick search on documents filed under her name. She finds two directories created and set aside, coded for use, ASYLUM and JANETSWORK. Once again, Rosemary proves herself the hostess who thinks of everything.

When Janet brings up the first directory, she finds more than a meg of docs listed, including the full text of the Special Circumstances Immigration Act of 2028 and a subdirectory of material pertaining to the famous Singh case that triggered the writing of said legislation.

"It's a good thing I'm a lawyer. Hey, I better get used to saying solicitor."

Janet cannot laugh, wishes she could cry. In her mind sound the words, "Call your daughter." All morning, as she studies the government-supplied infofiles and readies her application on the official forms, she pauses every ten minutes to try Mandi's number, but the phone lines stay stubbornly down. While she works, she glances often at the two inset windows, where footage of the States in chaos silently rolls by. Finally, toward noon, she transmits the completed application to the office LOC number listed on the form. As an afterthought, she prints out a copy, wondering if perhaps she should go down and apply in person as well. When she calls Rosemary's office, she gets Rosemary herself. Even on the tiny phonevid Janet can see dark smudges under her friend's eyes.

"I'm surprised you're there."

"I just popped in to the office for a minute," Rosemary says, yawning. "Have you transmitted the application?"

"I did, yeah. Yesterday you said something about going down to New Whitehall. Do you think I—"

"No, don't! I've heard that pictures are being taken of Americans entering the building."

"Taken? By whom? Wait, no, of course you can't tell me."

Rosemary's image smiles, very faintly.

"I'll just check to make sure the transmission's been received, then," Janet says. "And stay here."

"Yes. That would be best. I'll be back for dinner. If you'd just tell Thompson?"

"Of course."

Rosemary smiles again and rings off.

Janet returns the monitor screen to four windows of news. When she runs the search program, she finds one station with taped video from San Francisco, looping while serious voices discuss the news blackout. Colonel Harrison has issued a statement assuring the world media that the blackout is both regretted and temporary, that the telephone service has been disrupted by rebel sabotage and that it will be restored as soon as possible. No one believes him. As the video reels by, about an hour's worth all told, Janet watches like a huntress, her eyes moving back and forth, studying details, searching desperately for the images of people she knows, seeing none, even though she stays in front of the monitor all day, watching the same loop, over and over.

"Rosemary was quite right," Jonathan says. "The committee are beside themselves with joy. How soon can you give the first lecture? That was their only question."

"Wonderful," Janet says. "In a couple of days, I guess. I'll have to call Eleanor—that's my editor—and see if she can send me a copy of the book. I didn't have one with me, and I don't have any cash, and I can't stand asking Rosemary for pocket money. She's done too much for me already, feeding me and like that. Maybe I can squeeze an advance out of HCM. God knows the book's been selling like crazy over here."

"HCM?"

"HarperCollinsMitsubishi. My British publisher."

Jonathan nods his understanding. On a day streaked with sun and shadow they are walking through the gardens in the center of the condominium complex. Although the trees have dropped their leaves, the grass thrives, stubbornly green. All round the open space rise white buildings, staggered like drunken ziggurats.

"No word from the immigration people yet?" Jonathan says.

"None. But it's only been a couple of days since I filed the application."

"They probably haven't even looked at it, then. The morning news said that over two thousand Americans have applied for political asylum in various countries. Quite a few businesspeople were caught in Europe, I gather. A lot of them have come here."

"Yeah. I heard that three times that number are just going home." Janet hears her voice growl with bitterness. "Happy as clams with their new theocracy."

"Um, well, yes." Jonathan sighs, hesitates before continuing. "At any rate, I've got the University's contracts for the public series and then for the course of study. I'll transmit them to you tonight, so you can look them over. We'll need to get handbills out for the lectures, by the way, and some notice to the media. We'd best start thinking of a general title."

"That's true. I wonder if I'll get hecklers? Oh well, they'll be easier to handle than the ones back home."

"Rosemary told me once that you'd—well, had some trouble with thugs."

"Oh yeah. They beat the hell out of me. It was after an abortion rights rally, maybe what? Thirty years ago now. I had bruises for weeks. And a broken arm."

"Horrible, absolutely horrible! It's lucky you weren't killed."

"A lot of people were, back in those days. Doctors, nurses. Doctor's wives, even." Janet shudders reflexively. She can still remember images of fists swinging toward her face and hear voices shrieking with rage, chanting, "Jesus Jesus Jesus." "All in the name of God. No, that's not fair. In the name of the warped little conception of God that these people have."

"The history of an illusion. Living history, unfortunately."

"Yeah, very much alive and well in the US of A. I suppose abortion's the first thing the new government's going to outlaw."

"They have already. The *Times* had a list, this morning, of the various acts they've pushed through your Congress. Quite a lot for just a few days' work. The junta released the list, you see. They're holding press conferences for official news as well."

"I should look that over." Janet tries to muster an ironic laugh, can't. "Well, there goes my life's work, right down the drain. What do you bet that I've been on the wrong side of every law they've just passed?"

"Doesn't sound like my idea of a fair wager at all." He hesitates, frowning down at the gravelled walk. "Rosemary said there's been no word of your daughter."

"That's right, yeah. Well, no news is good news. The Red Cross doesn't have her name on any of the casualty lists. It hasn't appeared on any of the lists of political prisoners, either."

"That's something, then. Some of my young friends are working on getting a network pieced together. Perhaps they'll run across something."

"How can they even reach the States with the phone lines down?"

"Satellite feeds of some sort. Military, probably. I've asked them not to tell me more. And then they can maybe get in through Canada. Somehow. As I say, I don't really want to know."

That evening Janet goes over the contracts from the Free University, finds them fair and the proposed payment generous. Since the money will come from a special fund, the check will no doubt be slow in coming. She decides to call her agent tomorrow and ask him to see about an advance from the publishers.

"But who knows when we'll get it?" Janet says. "Rosemary, I hate sponging on you like this."

"Oh please!" Rosemary rolls her eyes heavenward. "Who was it who fed and housed my wretched son when he was going through his loathsome phase? He leeched for absolutely months."

"Oh, he was no trouble, really, since I wasn't his mother."

They share a laugh at the now-respectable Adrian's expense.

"Well, you're not any trouble, either," Rosemary goes on. "In fact, that reminds me. I had a phonecard made up for you—on my account, that is. It'll be weeks before you can open your own, and you'll need access."

"Well, I will, yeah. Thanks. I wonder when I'll be able to phone home."

They both find themselves turning in their chairs, glancing toward Mandi's picture on the end table.

"Sometimes I'm sorry that I waited so long to have a child," Janet says. "Here I am in my sixties, and she's just getting married. God, I hope she's still getting married. Jack means the world to her."

"She's not like us, no."

In the photo Mandi smiles, tremulous under her mortarboard, the English literature major with no desire to go to graduate school.

"I just hope she's happy." Janet's voice shakes in her throat. "I just hope she's all right. You know what the worst thing is? Wondering if she hates me, wondering if she hates what I am."

"Oh, surely not!"

"If they won't let her marry Jack? If they call her a security risk?"

"Oh God, they wouldn't!"

"Who knows? Look at the things that happened back in the fifties, with that McCarthy creature. Witch hunts. It could happen again. I won't know how she feels until I get through."

Rosemary is watching her carefully, patiently. Janet concentrates upon the changing gardens on the display screen, view after view of Giverny fading one into the other.

"They'll have to restore the telephones soon," Rosemary remarks at last. "Businesspeople are howling worldwide. The more centrist Tories are coming round, even. Imagine! Tories actually entertaining thoughts of a commercial boycott! I hear the European Parliament is considering a strong resolution to embargo. It's supposed to come to a head tonight. Then we'll take it up tomorrow here, if it passes. Of course, it's just a call for embargo, not a binding act."

"The junta won't care."

"What? Half of America's wealth is in trade!"

"I know these people. They'll be willing to plunge the country into poverty, if that's what it takes to keep it isolated and under control. Of course, if they do that, they'll lose a lot of their support among the middle class and the corporate types. So what? It's a little late for those people to be changing their damn minds now."

"Yes. Rather."

"Well, I mean, that's just my opinion."

"It's one of the best we have, isn't it?"

"What?"

"Well, you *have* lived there." Rosemary shakes her head. "It's so odd—I read your book, and yet I thought you were being something of an alarmist. I suppose I didn't want, I suppose no one wanted to believe it possible, like that ancient novel, what was it called, the Wells?"

"*1984?*"

"No, that's Orwell. Sinclair Lewis. *It Can't Happen Here.* That was it. I think."

"Well, it hasn't happened here, just there."

"Yes." Rosemary hesitates for a long moment, then sighs. "Yes, but that's quite bad enough."

WAITING

Janet has always been good at waiting. In discrimination cases waiting served as a weapon, asking the court for a postponement here, a recess there, playing a hard game with powerful opponents who knew that every day they waited without settling was another day for her team to gather evidence, to sway public opinion, to demand another investigation, to serve another writ. But none of those waits ever involved her daughter.

Over that first fortnight of exile, Janet evolves a ritual. Every morning she scans the news, both media and hard copy, for information about the American telephone shutdown, as the papers have taken to calling it. Then, on the off-chance that she missed something, she calls Mandi's number four times a day, mid-morning, mid-afternoon, dinner hour, late night. She never gets through. Since the junta has stopped all outgoing calls, Mandi cannot call her. Janet assumes her daughter knows where she is, that she must realize, by now, that her mother will be sheltering with the woman Mandi's always considered her aunt. Every now and then some military spokesman announces that service will be restored soon, very soon. Oddly enough, the infamous Colonel Harrison has disappeared, and a new chief of public security appears now and again on the news. Janet assumes that Harrison has fallen victim to some sort of internal purge; fascists always do fall out among themselves, sooner or later.

Some news does get released: the names of casualties, the names of those imprisoned. Unlike South American dictatorships, which at least realize their crimes to be unspeakable, this junta sees no reason to conceal their victims in silences and mass graves, not when they believe themselves the agents of God on earth. Amanda Elizabeth Hansen-Corey never appears among the names, not on either list. Janet reads each three times through, very slowly, to be absolutely certain of it. By doing so she finally spots Eddie's name, spelled out formally as José Eduardo Rodriguez, who has been sentenced to six months' imprisonment for assisting an enemy of the state.

"Oh, Eddie! How horrible, how unfair!"

Only much later does Janet realize the full significance of the charge. She herself, of course, is the enemy of the state to whom they referred. She has now been publicly branded as a criminal.

HACKING

The students at the Free University call their building Major's Last Erection, a name that's been handed down for the last forty years or so, even though few people remember who the major in question was. A prime minister, Janet tells them, not an army officer at all. Few seem to care. Several times a week she goes down to Canary Wharf, ostensibly to meet with Jonathan and the Curriculum Committee, but in reality to sit around and drink tea with a group of women students. Like most of the students at the university, Rachel, Mary, Vi, and Sherry come from working-class backgrounds; indeed, they all work, waitressing part-time, mostly, to keep themselves in school.

Vi—small, skinny, and very pale, with ash-blonde hair and watery blue eyes—always wears black, black jeans, black shirts, black cloth jackets, since she can't afford leather. Unlike the rest, she knows computers from the inside rather than merely being able to use what BritLink offers the average citizen. Her father was a repairman for the computer end of the Underground; he helped his daughter put together her own system from obsolete parts when she was seven years old.

"It was for my birthday, like," Vi tells Janet. "I was ever so pleased with it, too, all those lovely games it could play. Course, I'd never seen a real system then, mind." She grins with a flash of gold tooth. "But it was a good time, anyway, and it got me off to a good start."

Good start, indeed. When the other girls leave for their jobs, Vi takes Janet up to the thirteenth floor of the office building and a room officially labelled, "Computer Laboratory." They march through the ranks of official students learning programming and pass through a door into a smaller room, where Vi's boyfriend, Harry, has put together another system from spare parts—but these, state of art and pilfered, probably. Janet never asks. Vi is installing a remote feed to a satellite hookup in the pub where Rachel works over in Southwark, just a few blocks from the cathedral. This particular pub features sports on television and thus owns its weak linkup quite legitimately, but it's also close to various corporate offices with strong links and remote feeds to other satellite systems.

"Piece of cake," Vi says. "Once we link up to the Goal Posts' feed, we can bleed into anything within a couple of kills."

"Kills?"

"Sorry. Kilometers. And then." Vi smiles with a flash of gold. "And then we'll see. You don't want to know any more."

"That's very true." Janet grins at her. "I don't."

PARANOIA

At Janet's first public lecture so many people turn up to buy tickets that the University Audio/Visual crew set up a video link to a second auditorium to accommodate the overflow. At the second lecture, scheduled for the largest hall available, two unobtrusive men in dark blue suits appear upon the platform as Janet arranges her notes. Jonathan introduces them as Sergeant Ford, Officer Patel.

"The Foreign Office thought you'd best have some protection," Ford remarks. "You never know these days, do you now?"

"Ah, well, no, I suppose not." Janet is annoyed to find her hands shaking. She shoves them into the pockets of her blue blazer. "You're from the Foreign Office?"

"No, ma'am. Scotland Yard. They just had a word with us, like."

"I see. Well, thank you."

During the lecture Ford sits on the platform while Patel stands at the back of the hall. After the lecture they follow, staying close but not too close, as she goes to lunch with Jonathan and several students. When she returns to the condominium, Patel escorts her while Ford follows in an unmarked car. At the gate to the complex, Patel has a few murmured words with a new security guard. Janet has never seen security guards at the gate before. From then on, she sees guards every day.

CATCH 22

On the seventeenth day of her exile Janet receives a telephone call from the Immigration Office. Her application for political asylum is being processed. If her application is accepted, she will be issued a "red card", a visa allowing employment, good for a two years' stay in Britain, at which point her case will need to be reviewed. Janet, who knows all this, senses trouble.

"Is something missing on the application?"

"Well, not exactly." The blonde and pink-cheeked girl on the phonevid looks sorrowful. "It would be a good thing, you see, if you had a bank account or some sort of financial arrangement. We can't legally require this, but. . . ."

Janet has heard many such "buts," fading with a dying fall, in her career.

"I understand. Thank you very much. I'll attend to it."

"Fine. Just transmit a one oh oh four seven, will you?"

"A what?"

"A change or correction to an application form. The parameters should have been transmitted with your packet."

"Yes, of course. I do remember seeing the file now."

On the high street in Kew stands an imposing Eurostil building, all glass front and slender columns, a branch of Barclay-Shanghai-Consolidated. Armed with several large checks, one from her publisher, another from the Free University's public affairs fund, Janet walks in one sunny afternoon to open a checking account. Does she have references? Well, she can give them. But does she have the references with her, signed and ready? By British citizens, please. With the situation in America so dodgy, they are worried about money transfers and suchlike. Surely she understands? No, she does not understand. She has checks drawn upon British banks in her possession, paper checks, stamped and validated for instant deposit. Ah. Another manager must be called.

This manager, tall and grey, sports incredibly refined vowels. Janet tells her story once again, waves the checks about, mentions Rosemary's name several times. He understands, he tells her, but with the situation in America so dodgy, they would prefer to have a British co-signer. Janet tells him, with some vehemence, that she is not a minor child or a half-wit. The manager bows several times in an oddly Japanese manner and apologizes as well. He drops his voice, leans forward in a waft of lemon-drop scent.

"The real problem is that you've not got your red card."

"If I don't have a bank reference, I won't get one."

He blinks rapidly several times and looks round the cream-colored lobby. Janet does, as well, and spots a large brightly-colored poster.

"It says there that anyone can open a Christmas Savings Club account. 'From nine to ninety years of age, all are welcome.' It must be a special deal, huh?"

The manager blinks again and stares.

"I want to open a Christmas Club account," Janet says, as calmly as she can manage. "According to your own advertising, I may do so anytime before fifteenth November. It is November eleventh today."

"Ah, why, so it is." He sighs in a long drawn-out gush of defeat. "If you'll just step up to this counter?"

Janet deposits over a thousand pounds in her Christmas Savings Club account and receives in return a bank number, an electronic access number, and a passbook with a picture of Father Christmas on the front. Later that day, she brings up the bank's public information files on her terminal and spends several hours studying them. As she suspected, holders of one account may open another electronically. She opens herself a checking account, transfers most of her Christmas Club monies into it at a mere one per cent penalty, and has two numbers to transmit to Immigration on Form 10047.

On the twenty-seventh day after the junta killed the United States of America, their underlings restore full international telephone service to the corpse. Thompson brings Janet the news with her breakfast.

"They say the service isn't at top quality yet, Ma'am."

"As long as I can get through, I don't care."

Janet checks the time: seven o'clock here, minus eight makes damn! eleven at night there. Mandi will most likely be asleep, but Janet cannot wait. Even reaching her daughter's answering machine will be better than nothing.

Picking up the handset gives her a moment of doubt. Will this call bring Rosemary trouble? For a moment she considers the shiny plastic oblong, studded with buttons. Somewhere inside it lies the white strip of encoded optics that sum up Rosemary's identity as a communicating being. Somewhere in a vast computer is the Platonic ideal of this actual number, the electronic archetype which gives this physical object its true meaning, its *being*. Frail things, these archetypes, and so easy to destroy with one electric pulse, one change of code. What if the junta is automatically wiping codes that dial certain numbers? Could they do that?

Not to a British citizen's account, surely. Janet punches in Mandi's familiar number. Although the call seems to go through smoothly, after two rings a long beep interrupts. A switch of some sort—Janet can hear a different ring, oddly faint. Her hands turn sweaty—FBI? Military police? At last a voice, a taped voice:

"I'm sorry. The number you have reached is no longer in service. Please access the directory files for the area which you have attempted to call."

A click. A pause. The message begins again. Janet hangs up with a fierce curse.

Gulping coffee, she throws on a pair of jeans and a striped rugby shirt, then sits on the floor cross-legged with the keyboard and the remote wand in her lap. Switching the terminal over to remote phone mode takes a few irritating minutes, but at last she can dial on-screen and start the long process of accessing the international directory number. The British memory banks still show Mandi's numbers as functioning. She should have expected that, she supposes. When would they have had time to update? If indeed the junta will ever allow them to update.

On her next pass Janet tries the normal directory number for San Francisco. Much to her shock she reaches it. For all their talk of rebel sabotage, obviously the junta had disabled the phone system at some central source, some master switch or whatever it might be, so that it could be restored cleanly and all at once when they had need of it again. In this directory she finds Mandi's old number clearly marked as out of service.

When Janet tries a search on Mandi's name, she turns up nothing. A moment of panic—then it occurs to her to try Amanda Elizabeth Hansen-Owens, Mrs. Sure enough, such a name appears, cross-referenced to John Kennedy Owens, Captain. *My daughter is married. I wasn't there.* In the next column, however, where a telephone number should appear, Janet finds only code: UNL-M. She windows the screen in half, leaving Mandi's entry visible, and in the Help utility finds at last the decipherment of codes. UNL-M. Unlisted, military. For a long time Janet stares at the screen. She wipes it clear and turns it off, lays the keyboard and the wand down on the carpet beside her.

At least Mandi has been allowed to marry her officer. At least. Even if the little bastard has hidden her away from her mother. *Don't be ridiculous! She'll call you. She's not dumb. She knows you're at Rosemary's. Or that Rosemary will know where you are.*

Or, Janet supposes, she herself could call friends in California and see if they know Mandi's new number. Mandi had a job in a bookshop—perhaps she could call there? But she was going to quit when she married, because she would be living on base, too far away. Perhaps her old employer will have her new number? The thought of Eddie's prison sentence stops Janet from calling him. She should wait until the situation settles down, until the normal traffic on the telephone lines picks up. Surely the junta won't be able to tap every call, surely they wouldn't bother, not just on the off-chance that she and all those other enemies of the state might say something subversive in a casual conversation.

At lunch, in a little Italian restaurant near the Houses of Parliament, Janet tells Rosemary of her morning's frustrations.

"I'm honestly afraid to put people at risk by calling them," Janet finishes up. "Or am I just being paranoid?"

"I don't know. You're quite possibly being realistic. A

dreadful thought, that, but there we are." Rosemary contemplates her wine glass with a vague look of distaste. "Poor Eddie. I only met him briefly, of course, during that last flying visit, but he was such a nice fellow. It's so awful, thinking of him in prison."

"I'd hate to have the same thing happen to Mandi's boss or any of my friends."

"Well, of course. Or your nephew. What was his name? The one who's so good with horses."

"Richie. Although, you know, he's probably the safest person I could call. He lives way the hell up in the Sierras, and I can't imagine anyone suspecting him of subversion, up in that tiny little town."

"True. What about Robert?"

"Yeah. What about Robert?" Janet lays down her fork. "I went back later and looked for his number on the directory. It's been taken out of service, too. But I've never found his name on the lists. Of the prisoners, I mean." Janet's voice breaks. "Or the casualties."

Her mouth full, Rosemary nods in the best sympathy she can muster. Janet leans back in her chair, turns a little, too, to look over the crowded restaurant, and sees Patel standing at the door.

"It must be time for me to head out to the Free You," Janet says. "There's my bodyguard."

"Well, he can wait while you finish."

"I'm not hungry anymore. I don't know who I'm more worried about, Mandi or Robert. Robert, I guess. At least I know now she's married."

"And she'll call. She must know that I'd provide for you, one way or another."

"Yeah. You're right. She'll call."

But Mandi never does call, not that day, not the next, not for the entire week after service is restored. Janet wakes every morning to a winter come at last, stands by her window and looks out on slate grey skies, afraid to leave the flat and miss her daughter's call, which never comes.

* * *

"I suppose she's just afraid," Rosemary says.

"I hope she doesn't hate me."

"Why should she? She's been allowed to marry Jack."

"Well, maybe so. Do you know what I really think? She's disowned me. They may even have made her do it, for all I know. But I do know she's got too much to lose by associating with me."

"Oh my God! No!"

Janet shrugs, finding no words.

"I'm so sorry," Rosemary says at last. "But I think you're right."

"Yeah? So do I."

With Officer Patel trailing behind, they are walking across the plaza in front of the Free University. Around them students in long hair and American blue jeans drift by. Some wear crumbling leather jackets; others, bulging canvas coats decorated mostly with pockets. A few carry books as well as the standard terminal units.

"It's very odd, this place," Rosemary says. "Do you suppose they actually learn anything?"

"I'm about to find out. It's not exactly a new idea, though, a free university. The ones back home have been around for a long while, anyway. Well, I suppose the junta's closed them now."

"I suppose so, yes." Rosemary pauses, watching a particularly grubby couple saunter by. "Better to give them this than to have them rioting again, anyway. Not that they were real riots, compared to yours."

"Um. Maybe so." Janet stops walking and points to a small crowd, standing by the steps up to the RiverBus dock. "There's your photo op."

"Right. I see Jonathan. I suppose I'll have to wear that silly hard hat he's carrying, even though nothing's been built yet."

Today the work starts on the new flood barrier round the university. Wearing plastic hard hats, men in suits stand uneasily next to men in work clothes wearing solid metal ones. Sandbags, the first, temporary line of defense against the river, lie scattered about and rather randomly. The media, Minicams and mikes at the ready, cluster near a van serving tea in foam cups. When Rosemary trots over, Jonathan does indeed hand her the yellow hat. She puts it on as the cameras close in.

In the middle of the night Janet wakes from a dream of San Francisco in late afternoon, when light as gold and thick as honey pours down the hills and dances on the trees. There is no light in the world like the muted sun of Northern California. Sitting up in bed she weeps, knowing that she will never see it again. She will never see her daughter again, either. She knows it at that moment with a cold hard twist of sickness in the pit of her stomach.

And she weeps the more.

The phone call from Immigration comes some ten days before Christmas. Janet's application has gone through. Would she please pick up her red card in person? They require a witnessed signature and a look at her old passport. For the occasion Janet puts on a grey suit that she's just bought at Harrod's—severe trousers, a softened jacket with pleats—and wears it with a peach-colored silk shirt suitable for a woman her age. As she combs her hair, she looks in the mirror and sees her face as a map: all the roads she's taken are engraved on her cheeks and round her eyes. For the first time in her life she feels old. *There's nothing for me to do in Britain but die here.* The image in the mirror saddens and droops. What can she do against the men who taken over her homeland? She can write and lecture, yes, but it's so little, so weak, so futile. Perhaps she should just give up, live out her last years as an exile, write poetry, maybe, teach for a pittance at the Free University and keep her mouth shut. *My big mouth. Look at all the trouble it's gotten me into.*

She turns and hurls the comb across the room. It bounces on the bed, then slides to the floor with a rattle.

"I will not give up. I'm only a mosquito, maybe, on their ugly hide, but goddamn it, I'll draw what blood I can."

During the cab ride down to the Immigration offices, Janet begins planning her next book. Since her research material has no doubt been confiscated by the junta, she will have to write a personal memoir, hazy on hard facts, but if she works on the prose, she can make it sting. She will dedicate it to Mandi, she thinks, then changes her mind. She refuses to make danger be her last gift to her daughter.

Picking up her red card turns out to be easy and anticlimactic. Two clerks look at her passport, one asks her to sign various documents. In front of the pair Janet promises, quite sincerely, that she will refrain from attempting to overthrow the British government. The first clerk hands her a packet of paper documents and the small red card, laminated in plastic.

"Keep this with you at all times," he says. "And your passport, I suppose. We've not had any guidelines on that, but you might as well."

"Thanks, then, I will."

When she leaves the building, Janet finds herself thinking of her mother, of her mother's house up in Goldust, her nephew's house, now. It was a wonderful place to be a child, that house, with the mountains hanging so close and the big trees all round. She remembers hunting for lizards in rock walls and rescuing birds from her mother's cats, remembers thunderstorms bursting and booming over the high mountains as well as drowsy days of sun and the scent of pine. What if she had never left the mountains? What if she'd married Jimmy, the boy in high school who loved her, married him and settled down to get pregnant the way most girls did up in the mountains, or maybe taken a job in the drugstore till the babies came? She wouldn't be an exile now, drifting down the streets of a city that will never be hers, no matter how much she loves it. She would have gone crazy, probably. She reminds herself sharply of that. She always knew that she would have to leave Goldust from day she learned to read and found a wider world beyond the hills.

But Mandi would have been happy in that house. She loved

visiting her grandmother. Mandi might have been happy living in Goldust, too, safe and tucked away from the world.

Driven by her memories, Janet finds herself drifting to the nearest card phone, built into a red plastic slab inside a red plastic kiosk, sheltered from the sound of traffic plunging past. While she fumbles through her wallet, out the door she sees long lawns behind wrought iron fences. It should be safe to call Richie, it really should. Why would the authorities bother her nephew, a rural teamster? But he might know where Mandi is, he really just might know.

When Janet slides the card through the slot, she can feel her shoulders tense and hunch. With shaking fingers she punches in the code, hears other beeps, and then rings. The phone is ringing. By the most slender of all links she's connected again, for this brief moment, to the Sierra, to Goldust, to what was once her mother's house. She can picture the yellow telephone, sitting on Richie's old-fashioned wood slab desk, right next to the pictures of his family in their red acrylic frames. Three rings, four—a click, and the room changes. She can think of it no other way, that the piece of space at the other end of the line has changed, grown larger, as if she could see the shabby wicker furniture, scattered with cats.

"Hello." The sound of Richie's voice brings tears to her eyes. "You have reached 555-5252. Richie, Allie, and Robert aren't home right now. Please leave us a message, and we'll call you back."

Another click, a long tone. Janet hesitates, then hangs up fast. She cannot risk leaving a message, tangible evidence to some kangaroo court, perhaps, that Richie knows a traitor. As she takes her card out of the slot, the names she heard finally register. And Robert. Not just Richie's name, not just his wife's name, but Robert's name as well.

"He made it to the mountains. Oh thank God."

Janet reaches for her wallet to put the card away, but her fingers slip on the vinyl, and she nearly drops her purse. She glances round: two people have queued up to use the phone. Her paranoia stands at the head of the line. What are they really, this Pakistani woman in the pale grey suit, this Englishman in pinstripes? Agents, maybe? She pretends to drop her purse to gain a little time, squats, cooing unheard apologies, collects her things, shoves the card away along with the wallet and the handkerchief, her stylus and her notebook, her U.S. passport that used to mean so much. With a gulp of breath she stands, settles the purse on her shoulder, and lays a hand on the door. The Englishman is looking at his watch. The Pakistani woman is studying a tiny address book.

Janet gulps again, then swings the door wide and steps out. The Pakistani woman slips into the booth; the Englishman drifts closer to the door; neither so much as look her way as she strides off, heading blindly toward the gate into the park, searching for the safety of green and growing things. In the rising wind leafless trees rustle. Out on the ponds ducks glide. Janet smiles at them all like an idiot child. Robert is free, will most likely stay that way, because indeed, the junta has no reason to hunt him down, the apolitical artist, the popular teacher of the least political subject in the world.

But no news of Mandi. She watches the ducks glide back and forth, the midges hovering at the water's edge, while she tries to make up her mind once and for all. Will she dare call Richie again? It was stupid of her to endanger him at all, stupid and selfish. At least if the military police do try to trace that call, all they'll get is the number of a public phone near Green Park. *My daughter. I don't dare call my daughter. She doesn't want me to.* She feels her joy at Robert's safety crumple like a piece of paper in a fist. She sobs, staring at an alien lawn, at the roots of alien trees. Overhead white clouds pile and glide as the wind picks up strong.

Rain falls in curtains, twisting across the Thames. In yellow slickers men bend and haul, throw and pile sandbags in a levee six bags across and as high as they can make it. The thin yellow line, Janet thinks to herself. In a slicker of her own she stands on the

RiverBus dock and watches a red lorry, heaped with sandbags, drive down the grey street toward the workers. Struggling with a bent umbrella Vi scurries to join her. Drops gleam in her pale blonde hair.

"Dr. Richards tells me you got your red card."

"Yesterday morning, yeah. There apparently wasn't any problem. Just the usual bureaucracy stuff. The guy who needed to sign the red card was on vacation. That's all."

"That's super."

"Well, yeah. I'm glad, of course." Janet turns away to watch the men unloading the lorry. "I wasn't looking forward to being deported and thrown in prison."

"We wouldn't a let that happen. Me and the girls, we'd a thought of something. Hidden you out, y'know? here and there. There's a lot of us, y'know, all over this bleeding island. Girls like me and Rach and Mary and the lot. We think you're super, y'know, we really do, and we're networked."

"Do you?" For a moment Janet cannot speak. She recovers herself with a long swallow. "Thanks. I'm kind of glad I don't have to take you up on that."

"Course not. It wouldn't a been any fun." Vi grins, a twisted little smile. "But you've got the asylum, so it doesn't matter, right?"

"Right. But tell everyone I really appreciate it."

"I will, don't worry. Look." Vi pauses for a glance round. "We've got the feed working. Is there anything you want us to search for?"

I could ask them to get Mandi's number. I bet they could. Piece of cake, breaking into a military phone book. Yet she cannot ask, her mouth seems paralyzed. What if they find the number, what if she calls only to have Mandi cut her off, what if Mandi makes it clear, undeniably once and for finally all that she never ever wants her mother to call again? Vi is waiting, smiling a little. Janet could ask her. They'd find the number, she and Harry.

"Well, actually," Janet says. "What I really need is my notes and stuff, all my research banks. But the military confiscated my computer, I'm sure of that. If it's not even plugged in, you won't be able to reach it."

"Oh, I dunno. What if they downloaded everything to some central bank, like? I'll bet they're like the Inquisition was, filing everything away, keeping all the heresies nice and tidy."

"I never thought of that."

"But now, that'll take us a while to figure out. I know, you start writing down everything you can remember, file names, codes, anything at all. That'll give us something to match, like, if we find their central banks." Vi grins again. "And that's what we'll want, anyway, their central banks."

"Yeah, I just bet it is."

"And if you think of anything else, you just tell me, and we'll see what we can do."

"I will, Vi. Thanks. Thanks a whole lot."

But she knows now that she'll never ask for Mandi's number, knows that having it would be too great a temptation to call, to late one night break down and punch code only to hear her daughter hang up the handset as fast as she can.

"Bleeding cold out here," Vi says. "Coming inside?"

"In a minute."

She hears the umbrella rustle, hears Vi walk a few steps off. The girl will wait, she supposes, until she decides to go in. Yellow slickers flapping, the workmen turn and swing, heaving the sandbags onto the levee. The Thames slides by, brown under a grey sky.

"Riverrun," Janet says. "These fragments I have shored against my ruins."

She turns and follows Vi inside.

Resurrection

For Diane Hendriksen

Who overcame something
too much like this.

ONE

Except for the clammy feel of electrodes pasted to her forehead and the nape of her neck, and the weight of the monitors and boosters slung over her shoulders, Tiffany enjoys the repatterning drills of neuro rehab, a string of video games, especially now that she's advanced to Stage Two. Stage One got old fast, staring at the holo screen while she tried to slide the red arrow inside the green ring or drop the yellow ball into the blue cup. Here in Stage Two a little purple alien pops in and out of a three-dimensional maze while an assortment of monsters tries to eat him. Every now and then he finds rocks to throw, and every hit scores big points. She has been promised various refinements in this scenario if she can get him out of the maze and into the next section of the game world. So far, he's been eaten at the exit every time.

While he runs and finds and throws, the boosters gleam with red numbers or hum to themselves as they fire bursts of electricity into her nervous system; the monitors beep and click, chasing her neural responses down endless mazes and cornering the booster pulses at all the dead ends left in her brain by the crash, or rather, the ground impaction event, as the Air Force prefers to call it. The purple alien runs straight into the mouth of a green dragon-ish thing as Tiffany's mind skips and shies. *A hot, still day over the Mediterranean, a hot still day over the desert. She was on patrol. Not ferrying. Patrol. All at once, at seven o'clock high, screaming out of the sun on a suicide mission over Israel, hostiles.* The monitor produces a cascade of beeps and tinny shrieks as her fingers lie still on the console. *Crashed, shot down, failed, burning, spiralling, failed.*

No matter what anyone tells her, she sees herself as a loser, though how she could have possibly won a dogfight in a half-armed plane she cannot say. She's been told repeatedly that she had no missiles on board and only enough ammunition for a couple of warning shots; she was never supposed to fight, not her, a woman, not her, a mere ferryman, flying a new F-47D to a base behind the lines for the men to take into combat. A perfectly reasonable excuse, this, except that she remembers testing her missile activation codes when she was preparing for takeoff. Remembers testing her cannon, too. Remembers them all checking out just fine. Remembers being a combat pilot, not a ferryman. And then remembers—not defeat, no, not exactly. This part of the story she can never quite explain, not even to herself. She remembers only lying on the ground dying while seeing the power plant she was trying to guard—not exploding, no, but in a state of having already exploded. *The white pillar. Blazing light blinding. Blind.*

"Captain." Someone has grabbed her arm, someone is shaking her arm. "Captain, you're here now. You are *here* now."

The monitors are shrieking, the voice is sharp but concerned. Tiffany sees a beige face, black eyes, black bangs, swimming in front of hers. A therapist. With a name of some kind. A manicured hand reaches out and shuts the monitor blessedly up. The silence brings Tiffany's mind back.

"Sorry, Hazel."

Hazel Weng-Chang smiles but does not release her patient's arm.

"Come sit down, Captain. Come have some juice. Time for a rest."

Free of the monitors Tiffany limps into the lounge, all restful blues and lavenders, plus two walls of windows with a view that any realtor would drool over. Down at the bottom of a steep wooded slope the San Francisco Bay spreads out blue in the sunlight to the golden hills of Marin County; close by to her left lies the Pacific Ocean, and, turning back to the right, toward the City itself, she can see the rusty-orange bridge, gleaming and glinting with windshields as the maglev trains rush back and forth. As she watches, a white-and-red grain ship slides under and through, headed out to sea, loaded with California's new gold, rice for a rich but always hungry Japan.

Inside the lounge, slumped on one of the blue sofas, the two Jasons are talking about the Forty-Niner game. By the window, wired into his electro-chair sits Pedro, staring at nothing again. Thanks to the chair he can use both arms, as well as breathe, spit, think, and perform a few other basic functions. Chair or no he'll never talk again, but the set of his shoulders tells Tiffany to stay away. They all know each other very well here in the rehab lounge, better than the doctors and the therapists (both physical and neuro) ever will. The two Jasons, one black, one white, look up, study her face for a brief moment, smile, then leave her alone. For that gesture she loves them.

In the corner stands the pale blue juice machine, dispensing three flavors, apple, orange, lemon-lime, but the real juice of course is the mixture of liquid vitamins and drugs that the computer plops into each pre-measured glass. When Tiffany presses her thumb onto the ID panel, the machine mixes up her personal formula, dumps it in, then opens the little door. As she takes the paper cup, the machine clears its mechanical throat.

"Please take a stickette and stir your juice. Please drink slowly. Please dispose of your stickette properly."

The more advanced patients, like Tiffany, have come to hate the scrape and echo of this perpetual message, but plenty of people in therapy here at Veterans' Hospital need to be reminded every single time. Steadying the cup in her good hand, she limps over to an armchair by the other window, to leave Pedro his space, and sits down with a sigh. Automatically she glances at the clock: 1430 hours. In another half an hour she can leave and go home. She's one of the lucky ones, Tiffany, an outpatient with a home here in San Francisco. She's one of the very lucky ones. Two months ago she would have looked at the numbers on the clock readout and found them utterly meaningless. She could name the numbers: one four three oh. She merely could not connect them with an idea as abstract as time. Now they have regained their alchemical power of transforming a moment of time into a point of the virtual space known as a day. Of course, everyone at this rehab center, the Zombie Ward as they call it, is lucky. All of them have died at least once, have lain dead for at least a few minutes until frantic doctors could pummel their hearts back alive and force their blood to start circulating the drugs that jump-started their brains. Tiffany, in fact, is a twofer, dying once in the desert near the wreckage of her plane and once again on the operating table of the field hospital. Two termination incidents, two resurrection events. It gives her a certain status.

As she drinks her juice, she is thinking about her book. That's what she calls it, "her book," though in fact the science fiction novel in question, *Hunter's Night,* was written by a man named Albert Allonsby. Over a year ago now she picked it out of a bin of paper-books in the Athens USO officers' lounge and carried it round with her for another month, reading a few pages whenever she got a few minutes. A good book, well-written, set in a vastly important and meaningful war on some other planet in some other era far far away from the tedious peace maintenance campaign that she was stuck fighting, and in it there were a couple of really solid alien races and some finely designed starships that even a pilot like herself could believe in—but she never had the chance to finish the damn thing.

"Only sixty-five lousy pages from the end."

Tiffany often speaks aloud without realizing it these days.

Here in the lounge it doesn't matter; on the street, people do turn and stare. White Jason grins at her.

"You thinking 'bout that fucking book again?"

"Well, jeez, I was just gonna find out who the traitor was, the one who blew up the AI unit, y'know?"

Black Jason rolls his eyes skyward, but there's no malice in his gesture, merely the shared comfort of a long-standing joke.

"Maybe they gonna make a movie out of it one day. Then you find out."

"Rather find the damn book. They always change stuff for the movies."

The two Jasons nod in unison. Tiffany hauls herself up, judging with a fine ear the creak in her bad leg, broken in six different places during the ground impaction event. She is one of the lucky ones. She bailed out in time—well, nearly in time. *Spiralling downward. White chute popping, so slow, so late. Black smoke. Failure. Black smoke, desert, white light in a blinding burst. Failure.*

"Captain." Hazel Weng-Chang stands in the doorway. "Doctor has a few extra minutes. Want to check out early?"

"Yeah, I do, thanks. Gotta stop at a bookstore on the way home."

Doctor Rosas's office has walls of forest green and restful blue, blank expanses of color, not a picture, clock, bookshelf, knick-knack, not one thing that might confuse the eyes and agitate the torn neurons of her patients. Her desk, too, spreads out bare, not one thing on it except for the chart or file that she might need for the appointment at hand. The light filters through diffusion panels near the ceiling. Her grey hair is short, her doctor's smock pale blue and utterly unadorned; she speaks quietly, she moves her hands slowly or not at all. When Tiffany comes in, Rosas smiles but sits tombstone still, leaning back in her chair unmoving until her patient has taken the chair opposite and come to a complete stop herself. Tiffany sees the white shapes on the polished desk and recognizes them instantly as printout from her last few neuro sessions. Just two months ago they would have been white shapes and nothing more.

"You keep on doing very very well, Captain. I'm so glad. Don't worry. You'll get the purple guy out of the maze yet."

Tiffany smiles. Rosas opens a drawer, pulls out a green tennis ball, and tosses it over. Tiffany grabs with her bad hand and manages to make contact, but, claw-like, her fingers refuse to close. The ball totters on her palm, then falls, rolling across the floor.

"It still kinda leaves a streak behind it, when it's rolling, I mean," Tiffany says.

"Kinda?"

"Well, the afterimage is faint, you know? It used to look solid."

Rosas nods and makes a note on one of the sheets.

"The hand still hurt where they reconnected it?"

"Only when it's cold and damp."

Another nod, another note, a pause while she consults the pieces of paper. Tiffany realizes that she's trying to decipher every gesture the doctor makes as if it were a word, some holy word delivered by a priest.

"Captain," this said very casually. "What nationality are you, again?"

"Californian. Shit. I mean, American."

"So California's not a sovereign nation."

"Course not. That was weird, when I thought there was a Republic, I mean. I could see how I'd forget stuff, lots of stuff, but it was just weird to find out I was remembering something that never happened."

"I hear blame in your voice. You cannot blame yourself for the weird things." The doctor smiles, putting the word weird in invisible quotes. "It's in your wiring. So your memory glitched. Big deal. We've all seen 'California Republic' written on flags thousands of times, haven't we? It has its own logic, when you think about it. A reasonable mistake."

"Yeah, I know, but. . ."

"But it's hard not to blame yourself. I know that too. And then you blame yourself for the blame. A vicious circle. But we'll get you free of it yet. Remember: almost ten minutes total without oxygen to the brain. Remind yourself of that. Over nine minutes total. Of course you've got problems, but we'll teach you how to wire around them."

A joke, of course, an often-repeated joke at rehab, this business of "wiring around" various problems. Tiffany grins, but even as she shares this moment of good humor, she feels like a liar. Caught in her memory—no, created by the wiring, or so she tells herself—is a mental image, as sharp and clear as any photo, of a tiny booklet covered in forest-green leatherette and stamped with the California seal in gold leaf. Along the edge lies gold lettering, illegible in the memory image, yet the entire booklet seems so ominous in the root sense, as well as charged with anxiety, (a thing that she was always groping for in her shoulder bag or patting her pockets to confirm its presence) that she knows it must be something crucial, her passport, perhaps, her officer's identification papers, maybe, something that marked her officially and legally a California citizen and a member of its Air Services. She feels nothing for the word, American, except a faint whisper of connotation: foreigner. That such a concrete picture, so charged with emotion, could emerge out of a glitch, out of an accident and death and chaos, turns her stomach cold simply because it's such an irrelevant detail, such a trivial stupid fiction. If she'd forgotten her own name, say, or what her fiancé looked like, she would have been able to accept such lapses more easily, perhaps and maybe only because those are the things most often forgotten by resurrected war casualties in the made-for-TV movies, or maybe because it's the problem she doesn't have. She isn't sure which.

"Tomorrow's Saturday, but the workout room's going to be open from ten till four," Rosas says. "Gonna come in?"

"Oh yeah, but I promised my mom I'd take Sunday off. My sister's coming up from San Luis Obispo, and who knows when they'll get another chance at train tickets."

"Right. You can't miss that, for sure. Okay, come in tomorrow, skip Sunday, and I'll see you on Monday, round 'bout this time. Any questions you want to ask me?"

There is always a question, but one that Tiffany has yet to get up her nerve to ask. *Will I fly again? Will I ever ever be able to fly again, to do the one thing in life, the only thing in life that I wanted to do badly enough to risk my life for?*

"No questions, no. Thanks, Doc. See you Monday."

From her locker in the rehab room Tiffany gets her red and tan Forty-Niner jacket, puts it on, then uses her good hand to slip her bad hand into a side-pocket, because people on the street do tend to stare at it. Then comes the big step, forcing herself to leave. In the Zombie Ward proper all the corridors are painted bluish-grey in a matte finish, and all the lights hidden behind diffusion panels, except for the last hundred yards or so, designed as a transition to the noise and shattered light of the outside world. First the blue-grey turns shiny; chrome strips appear along the mouldings; the lights brighten; the walls change to glaring yellow. Then on one wall hangs the crucifix, all bronze and gleam, Jesus twisted on a cross, his mouth open, his eyes rolled back in his head. Tiffany cannot bear to look at it for more than a moment.

In the big foyer, the world glitters behind double glass doors. Tiffany hesitates just out of range of the electric eye and takes a deep breath. Going out reminds her of the scuba diving she used to love so much, a plunge, a dropping down, an immersing into a peculiar world of shattered light and immeasurable shadow. When she takes a step forward, the doors slide open with a blare of sunlike trumpets. She steps through onto grey walkway. Green spreads out and menaces while white flames rise in pillars and swell. A fanged mouth gleams in the green.

"Let your eyes adjust. It be just your eyes. And the light."

A passing orderly ignores her comment. She reminds herself, no more talking out loud, and begins her walk down to the bus shelter at the bottom of the hill. The green resolves itself into ice plant, tufted with purple flowers, each water-conserving spike somewhat tooth-shaped, and trees, rather typical cypresses, not twisted vampire forms writhing in sun fire. The white and bloated towers become hospital buildings. The view makes sense again. It takes a few seconds, at times, for her recently grown axons, the neurons firing in a new order, to cross-connect and control sensory overload. Names, which swarmed round her brain like so many tiny flies circling above fruit, have all settled down again, each in its proper place. She glances back, savoring labels, rejoicing in the ability to label. Enclosed lawn. Door. Window. And distantly, in the blueness of the bay, water. And nearer by, her own head. She touches the back of her head. Hand. Takes out the bad hand and looks at it. Palm of her hand, crisscrossed though it be by scars, paper-cut-thin scars, where the surgeons sliced in to reattach major nerves. Puts the bad hand back in the pocket of the Forty-Niner jacket.

"My hand." Damn. Speaking again.

But no one hears. The bus shelter, an open hut of plexipanel and chrome, stands empty beside an empty street under the overhead wires for the electric buses. By leaving early, she's beaten the change of shift from the hospital; she'll get a seat on the bus, here near the end of its long run from downtown. It will trundle a few blocks to the ocean, pause, turn, and then head back along Geary Boulevard, but Tiffany will transfer off long before it reaches the concrete and glass jumble that used to be the heart of the City. Across the street the long row of pastel stucco houses, stuck together cheek by jowl, gleam in the warm November sun. House. Window. Door. About half the houses have their windows boarded up, doors nailed shut, roofs peeling and crumbling. The rest, judging from the improvised curtains, flowered bedsheets or the red-and-yellow stripes that the Brazilians like so much, shelter refugees. On the tiny porches, behind rusting grates, sit stacks of baskets and cardboard boxes, flowing with things, unrecognizable piles of cloth and packets. On a couple of the porches toddlers, dressed only in dirty diapers or a little shirt, clutch the safety gates and stare out like prisoners. Tiffany yawns. The sun is too warm, deadly warm. She can remember cold Novembers, when the fog lay thick on the Bay and the hills, or it would rain, sometimes even three days in a row. She remembers her mother picking her up at day care, and how they would run giggling through the cold rain to their warm house with light glowing in the windows. Her sister would be home before them, because she was old enough to have her own front door key and let herself in after school, but not old enough to pick Tiffany up from day care. Water. Hand. The palm of her hand, stiff and reluctant to move. She was never left alone to curl her hands round metal bars and stare down empty streets. Her mother, an Army widow, was never forced to work for near-slave wages as these Brazilian mothers are.

Orange and white, the electric bus glides up to the stop. Blue sparks flash as its connector rods tremble, sway then slip from the overhead wires and fall, bouncing and flaring, onto the roof. Tiffany boards, sliding her FastPass into the computerized slot, squeezing out of the stout operator's way as she clatters down the stairs to get the rods back up and power back on. Tiffany spots her favorite seat, a single jammed in across from the back door, where no one can sit directly beside her, and heads for it. As the bus shudders and sparks appear outside the back window, the handful of passengers all mutter to themselves or their companions.

"Jeez, they can put a man on Mars, but they can't build a decent trolley."

Spoken aloud again, but fortunately she's passing a plump old woman, laden with shopping bags, who smiles and nods agreement, just as if Tiffany had in fact been speaking to her. Tiffany smiles in return, hurries to her chosen seat, scrunches down in it, stretching her long legs into the aisle, pulling them back, stretching them out again since the trolley's mostly empty. Being inside a small metal space can be very difficult, and today she feels the walls shrinking . . . or do they swell? They move somehow, at any rate, and eat up the space around her. She takes a deep breath and stares across the aisle to the door. And the window. And hospital hill outside the window. Swearing under her breath the operator hurries up the front steps and into her tiny compartment. The computer beeps once, announces that the next stop will be Land's End, and signals the operator to begin. Just as the bus swings out into the street, Tiffany sees a man running, or rather trotting, for the bus. The operator ignores him, the bus pulls away, he stands waving his arms and calling down half-heard imprecations.

Tiffany turns in her seat to keep him in view a moment longer. A little man, slightly stooped, wearing a black suit over a white shirt and a black vest, and a plump black hat of great age, he raises one fist and shakes it in the direction of the fleeing trolley. She cannot see clearly, but she thinks she noticed a long sidelock of grey hair dangling at either side of a bushy grey beard, and a mass of grey hair spouting from under his hat. Since she spent nearly two years stationed in Israel, she can guess that he's one of the last of the Orthodox, clinging to a way of dress already old-fashioned when his great-grandfather's generation brought it to the Promised Land. But what, of course, is he doing here in San Francisco, home of all the world's gentiles, refugees from a hundred countries, gathered over hundreds of years, where nothing could be less pure, where the very land itself partakes of two mingled natures, water and earth blending inexorably as the tides rise day by day and chew at the shore, and water and air mix into fog. Somewhere, no doubt, he has found a place selling kosher food, or at least food that he can convince himself to be pure enough to eat. She would shrug the problem away, remind herself that it's none of her business, if his image would only unstick itself from her mind. Yet for a long time, as the bus lumbers beside the seawall that once was Ocean Beach, she can see him in her memory, dressed in black and yelling curses upon all things too impatient to wait for one old man, his thin arms waving, his hands curled into fists.

Just at the end of the line, the bus breaks down. In mid-announcement the computer dies, the lights go off, the rods fall with a thump and pronounced lack of sparks onto the roof. The other passengers sigh and mutter remarks, thankful that they're transferring to another bus, rise and gather parcels, clatter off behind the operator, who trots to the rear and begins working the wires again. Tiffany scrunches down farther in her seat and watches the wires twitch and flutter outside the rear window as the operator raises the connecting rods, makes contact, settles them onto the wires. Nothing happens. No hum, no lights, no computerized voice apologizing for the interruption to service. A sudden flash of orange-and-green uniform, the operator appears in the back doorway.

"Might's well get on off. 'Nother bus waiting just ahead anyhow."

Tiffany goes out the back door and steps into the long cold sweep of shadow cast by the seawall. Out across the Pacific the sun is dropping fast toward the horizon, but thanks to the forty-foot-high reinforced-concrete wall that runs all the way down San Francisco's western border (continuing on south, as well, to protect Daly City, Pacifica, Half Moon Bay, those little towns long since swallowed up by Bay City sprawl), no one will ever stand on Ocean Beach and watch it set again. The beach lies under ten feet of water, anyway. Shivering a little she passes the other ex-passengers, walks up the line of buses, neatly arranged in a half-moon of a turnaround, and finds the other Geary bus at the head of the line. Its door, though, is shut, and its operator stands conferring with a little clot of Muni people back by the newly-dead bus. Termination incident. Soon a mechanic will arrive, and there will be a resurrection event. Wiring. All in the wiring.

The seawall makes Tiffany nervous, it looms so high and cold, splattered with red graffiti, black obscenities, green and purple tags from one gang or another. How they get up so high to scribble and paint amazes her, as does their determination. As she studies the wall, she thinks she might see a couple of cracks in it, down near the bottom where it counts. When she looks at the ground immediately below the cracks, she finds depressions, as if the asphalt were just starting to sink, as if a rift were just starting to develop. She steps to one side, squints: the depressions exist, all right, still shallow but an inexorable sign that the sea is eating away at the base of the wall. No doubt it can be patched or propped to give this boulevard and the public housing on its far side a stay of execution. For how long? She prefers not to think of that.

She walks a little way forward out of the shadow, but the sun hurts her eyes; she paces back, scowling at the clot of trolley operators, wishing someone would open the door and let her sit down, paces into the sun again and turns to look up the boulevard. The old man in black is heading toward them, trotting along all stoop-shouldered, one arm crooked so he can keep one hand firmly on his hat. A short block away he stops, stares at the bus, does a visible double take at the clot of operators and the grumbling passengers. She can see him abruptly hunch his thin shoulders, waggle his head, then turn and hurry off, dashing up a side-street and disappearing into the public housing, a sprawl of beige stucco ziggurats, brindled with graffiti.

"Almost like he ripped something off or something." Damn. Did it again.

No one notices. The operators have progressed to waving their hands and swearing over the dead bus; the ex-passengers have migrated closer to listen. Tiffany shifts her weight from one foot to another, breathes slowly and deeply, wonders if she's too warm, decides against taking the jacket off, shifts her weight again. She feels the rage starting, a sliver of glass deep in her mind, pushing and slicing its way toward the surface, forcing the long tendons in her neck to tighten and her jaw to clench. She refuses to give in. It's all in the wiring. She is not truly angry. She turns and strides back along the line of buses, walks fast, whips around and strides down the street on the outside of the line, where no one can see her fighting the rage. All in the wiring. Not their fault. All in the . . .

Suddenly she realizes that her bad hand is clenching. The rage vanishes in a whoop of delight that she turns into a cough. For a long moment she stands in the middle of the empty street and smiles, merely grins at the sunlight, at the sky, the asphalt, the beige ziggurats, the dead bus. The hand aches, the fingers straighten; she ignores the ache, clenches her fist again. Hurts, a stab of fire along the nerves, a tingling. She laughs and strides back to the sidewalk, where the operator is opening the doors of the bus at the head of the line. The passengers are staring at her. She gives them all a brilliant, impartial smile and takes her place at the end of the line. Door. Window. Behind her, wall. In her pocket, hand. Clenched fist. Palm of the hand. Pain. Who cares?

She finds her favorite seat, scrunches down into it, and makes an effort to stop smiling, to assume the polite mask of indrawn attention that people wear, sitting on buses. The hand tingles, then subsides into an ache. She remembers the last cup of juice that she drank at the hospital, realizes that in the random way they have, the drugs have finally blasted through the blocked connections or knit up the ravelled sleeve of neural tissue or whatever it is, exactly, that they do do. Months ago Dr. Rosas explained the drugs, drew little pictures, brought better pictures up on screen from video files, spent a patient hour repeating her explanations, but although Tiffany heard the words, although they even at that moment made a kind of sense, especially associated with the pictures, she cannot remember the information now. Only the words, "protein sheath," dangle in her mind, disconnected yet profoundly meaningful. She will ask again on Monday, she decides. If, of course, she can remember.

Even though other passengers pile on at every stop, even though people soon crowd in front of her and close to her, the wave of good feeling carries Tiffany all the way through the trolley ride, sweeps her off the bus at Sixth Avenue and in a warm mental foam floats her down the cross street, one long block, to the bookstore just around the corner on Clement. As she lingers in front of the bins of cheap used paper-books, though, the wave recedes. This bookstore has existed longer than she has; her mother shopped for storybooks here when she herself was a little girl.

That, Tiffany knows. But in her memories from before the war, the store stands right on the corner, not several doors down. It looks much the same as this store does now; the memory-store is merely a corner store, not a flush-to-the-sidewalk store. The discrepancy makes her shake her head hard. She turns and looks back at the broad street, crammed with pedestrians hurrying along between the bus lanes, and at the sidewalks, packed with the bins and barrows of the various peddlers—a woman selling *shao mai* here, a man with sausage rolls there, a table of cheap clothes, wooden crates of spatulas and ladles. Overhead the sky is darkening to the velvet blue that means sunset and night, when white lights will stab and shatter the world. She should take her transfer to the stop on Sixth and get the streetcar for home. On the other hand, the bookstore seems to invite her in with its yellow light and a quilt of colors beyond the windows: the shelves inside, all stacked with book cartridges and paper-books, red and blue and yellow. She walks through the door.

In this particular store the science fiction section lies all the way to the back. As she makes her way through the narrow aisles, past heaped and jumbled sensations of bright covers, holograph scenes of far places, the shiny 3-D portraits of authors, the occasional poster talking at her in a tinny voice, and as other customers cross her path or block her way, women burdened with shopping bags and one precious novel to take them to some better place in their minds, children clutching shiny comics to their chests, old men holding news cartridges that need refilling, she begins to breathe a little fast, to feel sweat form and bead on her back and upper lip, but she forces herself to walk slowly, to breathe slowly, to concentrate on keeping her bad hand in its pocket and the good hand from knocking stacks of cartridges to the floor, until she reaches a relatively open space in front of the correct shelves, where she can let the tension ease.

The nearby posters start talking as soon as they sense a warm organic presence in front of them. Although she automatically ignores the babble of tinkling blurbs, Tiffany stares at the pictures for a long time. Starships against dark galactic skies, aliens holding beautiful artifacts, landscapes never seen, washed by strangely-colored seas, stretching out to jagged mountains, dotted with trees that never grew—they all glow with fascinations that swarming Earth and the barren dullness of Mars and Moon will never match. If she cannot find *Hunter's Night,* she decides, she will buy a new book and see how well she can follow it. Since she's always loved reading, every few weeks she buys a new book, takes it home, spends an hour or so making slow sense out of letters that used to form words automatically, trying to make the words once deciphered form into mental pictures and meanings and sounds, the way they always used to before, easily and magically. So far she's always given up after two or three pages or two or three screens. Dr. Rosas suggests that she buy kids' books, but the doings of clothed animals and small children have not yet been able to hold the interest of a woman come back from four years of war. If she could only find *Hunter's Night.* She's sure that it would be different, reading again the one book that she can remember reading, and this time she would find out how the damn thing ended.

Since she cannot just remember and match the name she carries in her head with the names she finds on the cartridge labels or the spines of paper-books, she fishes in the cargo pocket of her pants for the slip of paper she always carries. Some weeks ago she printed out Allonsby's name and the book title in big blocky letters with black ink, a template of sorts. She finds the slots allotted to the 'A's' on the shelves and goes through them slowly, hesitantly, dreading the disappointment which does indeed come. A-D, A-L-L, A-L-L-E, A-N. She holds the paper up, squints back and forth between her own printing and the long line of names on label and spine. No A-L-L-O's at all. Not one. No Allonsby, no nobody.

"Damn!"

"Help you, Miz?"

Tiffany yelps, spins, sees a young man, slender, black, hands up over his face as he steps back fast. With a gulp for air she catches herself, stands still, gulps again, feels sweat run down the small of her back, lowers her good hand.

"Jesus God I'm sorry. Dint see you come up, dint see you at all, kid."

"You a vet, right?"

"Yeah."

"It's cool. My brother he's a vet. I understand. Sorry I startled you. You dunt have to feel bad. Really."

She takes a last deep breath, lets it out very slowly, tosses her head once, shoves her bad hand deeper into one jacket pocket and puts her piece of paper away in the other. The boy—he's maybe seventeen—manages a tentative smile. She sees then the name tag pinned to his shirt: J-O-S-H. Josh. An employee.

"You looking for something?" he says. "Be glad to help you find it."

"Yeah, actually. A book called *Hunter's Night*. By Albert Allonsby."

Josh frowns, considering, unsnaps a transmit from his belt, frowns at the tiny keyboard, then one letter at a time with a careful forefinger types in the name of the book. A beep: he turns the unit so that she can see the thin stripe of screen, flashing "unknown."

"Sure you got that right?" Josh says. "Hey, lemme try the author. Can't be a lot of dudes with a name like that."

He types again; again the screen flashes. Unknown.

"Come on up to the counter, and we go ask the boss. She maybe look it up in *Books in Print* or something."

The boss, a grey-haired white woman in jeans and a T-shirt that says "What's the good word?" does just that, talking the author and title into the main ROM comp behind the cluttered counter. While the unit searches, Tiffany studies the piles of dollar postcards and free bookmarks that lie every which way, so jumbled that she loses track of where the edges of one stack end and the next begins. Fortunately, before this contour meltdown can spread and disorganize her entire view, the boss speaks.

"No such book in print, sorry, not for the last ten years anyway."

"Weird. The copy I lost was new. I mean, I'm pretty sure it was new."

"Where'd you buy it?"

"Got it at a USO in Greece."

"Oh!" The boss grins, painted red mouth in a wrinkled face. "Well, you know, I bet it's a Euro edition, then. It was probably never picked up by a publisher over here. Happens all the time, and Albert Allonsby sounds like a Euro name to me. Lessee, there's a couple of import bookstores in town. I probably have a card for one of them lying around here. Or you can try a used bookstore. They get all sorts of odd things."

She rummages through the heaps on the counter and the stacks behind it, finally pounces in triumph and hands over a business card.

"Give these people a call. If anyone's got it, they do."

"Thanks, thanks a lot. Never dawned on me, that it just plain might not be a California I mean American book."

Neither the boss nor young Josh notices the slip. They merely nod and smile as Tiffany thanks them again and leaves, slipping the card into the breast pocket of the Forty-Niners jacket where she won't lose it. She'll never call the store, of course; using the vuphone terrifies her for one of those obscure reasons beyond her discussing, even with herself. But she just might go over and drop in one morning, on her way to the hospital, maybe, or on one of her rare afternoons off. Surely she'll be able to work through a mere sixty-five pages of reading, and maybe, with those sixty-five under her belt, she'll be able to tackle a completely new book.

Outside, night. Caught off-guard she stops, staring, seeing dark sky, night shadows, stripes of white slashing through dark as trolley after trolley clangs its ways through rush hour. Up and down the streets mercury-vapor pole lamps radiate solid spheres of light. People rush, people crowd round, people push by. Tiffany feels her mouth opening for a scream, chokes it back, shuts her mouth, feels her bad hand stab with pain as the fingers clench, feels her good hand balling into a fist, shoving into its own pocket. She never should have stopped, should have gone straight home, can't remember which way home lies, can't see her streetcar stop, can see nothing, in fact, but striped light, spherical light, and the faces and shoulders of women dashing home from work, women lugging heavy shopping bags, women dragging kids behind them or carrying kids in backpacks, a perfumed sea of women, dotted with the occasional islands of men and boys. And a boy's face at her elbow: Josh from the store.

"You need help, doncha. Which bus you take?"

She would like to scream at him to leave her alone, would like to lie and swear or state calmly that she's fine, that she needs no help, but the lights shatter into a thousand swords and the faces swirl by on a perfumed tide.

"The D-car. And thanks."

A strong hand on her good elbow steers her through the raging sea of faces, past the exploding lights and the crates of cabbages, the tables spread with bolts of cloth, the kids racing and playing tag out in the street. Josh leads her round the corner and down half a block to the dark and shuttered post office, where some twenty people stand, their backs to the street, reading the news-loop on the bright red digital strip above the door. Chinese ideograms flash on and crawl past, a steady parade.

"Don't look at them words," Josh snaps. "You look at them red words moving and you be *gone.*"

"You're right. Your brother, he a zombie like me?"

"Yeah, but we sure glad to have him back anyway. Here's the streetcar stop, and look, here it comes."

"Thanks, Josh. Thanks a lot."

"No problem, miz. No problem at all."

The kindness of strangers. The phrase echoes in her mind as she climbs the steps, slides her FastPass through the slot, and makes her trembling way down the aisle. *I'm dependent on the kindness of strangers. Where the hell is that line from?* She can't remember, knows she'll never remember, finds a seat and slides in, turning to press her face against the window as the trolley groans and moves, clanging wildly at the women crossing back and forth. The conductor leans out and screams at sudden children, pressing alongside, raising cupped hands to open windows, begging for a coin or a piece of candy, Brazilian kids, barefoot and shivering, dressed in baggy shorts, thin shirts, those that have shirts at all. At last the streetcar sways across the intersection, stops, clangs, moves again, stops. On the Geary corner, another crowd streams through littered banks of fruit stands, sausage sellers, tables strewn with cheap merchandise. She sees one display clearly, notebooks and calculators, boxes of scribers, kids' school supplies, before the car lurches into the middle of the wide boulevard. On a concrete island two men stand under a deathly glare of mercury vapor light.

"Whattha hell? No, can't be."

But it *is* the old man in the black suit, the rabbi, as she finds herself thinking of him, with his flood of grey hair escaping from his pudding-shaped black hat and his beard and his sidelocks, his skinny arms upraised as he argues with a young man, a very flash young man, his blond hair slicked back into moussed forks, wearing a bright red shirt of some shiny cloth, a pair of very tight black pants, and a wide belt, encrusted with buckles and studs. He struts back and forth with his arms folded over his chest and a sneer on his face as the old man waves one bony finger under his nose. The streetcar clangs, glides, clangs again and picks up speed, darting into the silence and safety of residential streets, leaving the old man and the flash dude far behind on their island of light and concrete.

Tiffany slews round in her seat to sit facing forward and lets out her breath in one long sigh. It's been a peculiar trip, getting home, a weird day, but then all her days fall into these disconnected chunks and oddities. It's the wiring. Nine, almost ten, minutes without oxygen total. Two termination incidents. Two resurrection events. Wired weird wired. Weird. Outside the window Golden Gate Park slips past, trees dark mounds strange shapes flowers, a distant tower picked out by floodlight, streetcars clanging by in the opposite direction, fast, too fast. She looks away, concentrating on the brightly-lit car and the passengers nearby, but she has to keep track of where she is, out of the corner of her eye: Lincoln Avenue, by now, free of the park. The streetcar groans as it loops round to Seventh Avenue. Time to count. If she forgets to count the cross streets, she will lose her place in the complex book of the city. Two blocks, three. Sirens wailing, an ambulance darts past; the flash of lights and a roaring, a fire engine howls nearer and nearer. The streetcar lurches, quivering, to a stop. Her count is broken, and she feels the rage, rising on a sharp slivered tide of exhaustion, pounding in her ears and making her eyes fill with mist.

Deep breaths, clenching fists. Cold window touching the side of the head. Breathe slowly, count your breaths. Count count count, and the streetcar moving again, a sigh of metal wheels on metal tracks, a sigh of breath, releasing the rage. Tiffany sits upright, seeing the lights and the gleaming tracks of the N-car line on Judah Street, where she can start her count again and find a new point on the grid, her place in the story, her stop, her cross street as she rises, gives the cord a smart pull, and slides her way through the crowded aisle to the back door. The last stage of the journey is the easiest: almost home, trotting in the cool night air down a blessedly dark street, houses, yellow windows, tiny patches of ivy and ice plant out front, or the defeated patches of concrete painted green, and the stairways rising up to doors. Door. A grey door, scabbing paint, beside a small window, covered with rusty iron bars, light gleaming through the window. Key, lock, two steps down. Home.

Inside, soft light on a blue rug, stained but clean, a dark green sofa, sagging into hollows, a coffee table, chipped along one edge, but there are no pictures, no clock, no heaped magazines or shining comp monitors, no TV set in the wall, though distantly she hears electronic voices mutter. Her family followed doctor's orders when they set up this room. Nothing moves but a grey cat, rising from the sofa to hump its back and stretch one front paw at a time, yawning, all pink mouth and fangs. The smell of chicken and cabbage, rice steam, ginger and garlic, drifts on warm air.

"Hi Meebles. Daddy's home, huh?"

"Tiff?" Mark calls from the kitchen, a hint of worry.

"Yeah, it's me. Am I late?"

"Nah, not very." Relief shimmers in his voice. "You hungry?"

"Sure am. Smells good."

She takes off the Forty-Niner jacket, drops it on the floor, means to pick it up, forgets it and walks down the narrow hall, past the door to their bedroom, which was once the other half of a two-car garage, and into the kitchen, a bright gold pool of light over green linoleum and dark-wood cabinets and walls. Mark stands by the stove. A pillar—that's how she thinks of him—her pillar of strength, her tower, tall and heavyset, dark skin, dark hair, safe and steady. Her Mark. She lets him enfold her with one massive arm, pull her tight, catch her good hand in one of his huge hands, hers slender and pale against his brown skin. He understands about the wiring and the bad hand and the lacing of scars, Mark who slogged through twelve years in the Marines, Mark who made it through the entire Brazilian war and another year in Israel. The bad hand. She pulls away, grinning.

"Got something to show you."

When she holds up the bad hand and clenches the fingers, he whoops and laughs and does a few quick steps of a war dance.

"All right! Wish we had champagne."

"Wish I could drink it."

They laugh together. At times they both resent that her neuro drugs keep her from drinking, at those odd moments when she'd really like to join him in a beer during a game on TV or in a bar with friends, but now, seeing the scarred fingers move, neither of them mind the side effects. While he turns the food out of the work onto plates she squeezes herself into the chair between the tiny table and the blue-tiled wall. An ancient box TV sits on the opposite counter; a talking head mutters on-screen.

"Want that off?"

"No, it's okay. Oh hell, sounds like the Yemen treaty's breaking down."

"Yeah. You surprised?"

She shakes her head no. She has grown up with war flaring and dying back in the Middle East, year after tedious year. News commentators speak images of brush fires and the waves of the sea; Tiffany thinks of it as a case of acne. You can scrub and scrub all you want, and maybe for a week your face looks fine, but one bite of chocolate and you're a goner again. On the TV, tiny images of planes flit inside a box of sky. Mark reaches over and turns it off.

"It was okay," Tiffany says.

He merely shrugs and sets full plates on the table.

"How was your day?"

"Okay." He sits down carefully on the rocky chair. "Put in a lot more applications. Something's bound to open up soon for a vet with my record. That's what they all say, anyhow. Sure as hell hope so. Can't see myself working a farm. Sure dunt want to re-up."

They eat in silence. Tiffany finds the food tasteless, but she's used to that by now. The centers of her brain that control taste were hard hit, harder, perhaps, than those controlling any other sense, an odd glitch, difficult for the doctors to explain, since she can smell things clearly. Still, the warmth of the stir-fry comforts her, as does the spicy scent, the bright colors on the plate, neatly arranged—Mark is an excellent cook, or so those who can taste food tell her. She needs the comfort and the warmth because she feels sick and cold at the very thought of his re-enlisting, but aside, of course, from food, the rice and wheat that feed Europe and most of Asia, America's mercenary armies are its biggest export, and their weapons its last true industry. In the cities, jobs for men are few and far between, even for twice-wounded vets with a long list of commendations and medals. She herself will never fly to war again; she has lost all the high economic value her fine-tuned reflexes and steady hands once gave her. They cannot live forever on their combined benefits, hers of course much higher than his. Since he was only an enlisted man, his checks will stop soon. She has a lot of mustering-out benefits left, years' and years' worth.

"Not like I need much of a job," he remarks. "Maybe two thousand a month would do it."

"We could scrape by on less. Wish you'd just marry me, and then we'd get another allotment for a dependent."

"Damned if I'm gonna leech off of your rank."

"Well, if you're gonna keep seeing it that way, you stubborn bastard."

They glare at each other across steaming plates in over-familiar anger. At length Mark sighs and begins shovelling food.

"Sorry," Tiffany says.

"Ah well y'know." A pause. "What's happening tomorrow?"

"The clinic's gonna be open. I've got to go in for physical rehab. Oh yeah. Did my mom call about Sunday?"

"She did, yeah. Amber and the kids are coming in on the morning train. So we'll go over to your mom's place in the afternoon, give the kids a chance to settle down after the trip. We're invited for dinner."

"Well, I'd like to stay, talk to Amber."

"Maybe we can bring a bottle of wine. And something for the kids. Chocolate if we can find some."

"Good idea."

Mark smiles, relieved that he can shore up some small thing against the constant tide of her mother's generosity. Tiffany chases a slice of carrot round her plate, spears it, eats it, remembering how carrots once tasted. The silence hangs over the table like the pool of light from the overhead lamp. Mark leans back and turns on the TV, letting the drone of bad news fill the space between them. A consortium of Korean investors is already negotiating with the president for thirty-three fighter squadrons and two divisions of infantry to guard their Yemenite refineries, one of the last lucrative installations in the Middle East. Pictures flash by, a holo scene of the haggling: serious American women in suits argue over the cost of lives with serious Korean men in suits.

"Those dudes sure look nervous 'bout something, don't they?" Mark turns the box off again. "If I had me all that oil, I wouldn't be pinching the yen over the cost of GAMs."

"Makes you wonder, don't it? What they've found out there, past Jupiter, I mean."

"Oh hey, those big moons, they could be drowning in methane, but the Euros, they still gotta get it back here, don't they? And down to the surface. That stuff catches fire real easy."

"I wouldn't want to be flying the shuttles down, no. I suppose they could freeze it somehow. Guess it is frozen, from what you hear on the news. Titan is *cold,* man. Long way away from the sun."

"Yeah, but gas expands when you warm it up. Bringing it down in tanks or something, all that friction warming them up, it could be real dangerous."

"Yeah, but if they work it all out, those Euro dudes won't be taking anyone's orders anymore, will they? Could change a lot of things, man."

They both nod in the same rhythm, lean back in their chairs, smile, the brief gap bridged again. Mark gets up, takes the plates away, stacking them in the sink, where they will sit until the non-potable wash water gets turned on, round about 2100 hours. Although Tiffany lets him bring her the collection of pill bottles—too many and too slippery for her to manage—from the cupboard in the bathroom, she insists on getting up and fetching herself a glass of drinking water from the tank in the corner. She can set the glass on the little stand under the tap, turn the tap on with her good hand, turn it off again, then pick the glass back up without having to use the semi-bad hand at all. After Mark opens the vials, she shakes one or two of each kind of pill out, red and yellow and green on the tabletop, takes them one variety at a time, while Mark checks them off on the printed list from the clinic. Some she takes every day, others go in descending sequences, (seven one day, six the next, and so on), others still are occasional, every fourth day, twice a week, whatever Dr. Rosas and the pharmaceutical therapist have decided. She needs three glasses of water to get them all down.

Mark is just putting the bottles and the list away again when the vuphone rings, a harsh claw of noise ripping the kitchen. Both of Tiffany's hands clench tight as Mark rushes for it, hits the console, answering the call and turning off the screen all in one smooth smack of his hand.

"You want to see, I'll go in the living room."

"No, it's okay."

But she leaves anyway, limping into the green and blue refuge of the living room so he can see the person he's trying to talk to like normal people do. As she listens to his end of the call—a series of okays, mostly, though he certainly sounds happy about something—she wonders why she hates watching a vuphone so much. It's the wiring again, or so the doctor says, a glitch like the irrational rage and the memory lapses, a mere misfiring of neurons that make her detest the sight of a familiar face on a screen, surrounded by a harsh black line to set it off from the various message fields. She can watch the number-called-from blinking on the screen with no problem, just as she can copy off any words or graphics transmitted; it's just the face, seeing the face and knowing that the face can see her, that fills her with a flood of ridiculous anger, a sheerly chemical rage. Yawning and stretching again, Meebles pads over to climb into her lap and sniff at her mouth, checking out just what she's been eating for dinner. Gently she pushes him away.

"Rude critter." But she smiles, stroking his soft back, rubbing his chin.

Meebles has just settled down in her lap when Mark trots in, moving as gracefully as a dancer in spite of his bulk. He has arranged his expression into a careful indifference.

"Okay, what is it, poker face?"

The grin breaks out, a flash of white.

"Got a callback on a job. The one I liked the best. The warehouse dispatcher one." He holds up an enormous hand flat for silence. "It's just a callback, not a promise. Another interview, the woman said, but hey, it sure sounds good."

"All right! Wish we had some champagne."

"Wish you could drink it."

And they laugh, so wild, so happy, both of them, that Meebles leaps up and stalks indignantly away.

Two

When Tiffany arrives, the rehab clinic is just getting started for the day. At the check-in desk the computer is updating files, the comp-op is finishing her coffee, the physical therapist is leaning against the wall and talking about imported shoes with her respiratory counterpart. Tiffany takes her clinic card out of her shirt pocket and holds it out with the good hand.

"I knew you'd be here the minute we opened that door," the comp-op heaves a fake sigh. "No rest for the wicked."

"Tiff, I'll be right with you." The physical therapist's name is Gina. "They're bringing some new guys down from the hospital any minute now, and I want to get them started on the diagnostics."

New guys. More people who have died and come back to life. Tiffany feels her sympathy as an electric shudder, racing down her spine.

"Sure, of course. I'll just go in and start stretching out."

"Good, good. Be right there."

Although the workout room sports an entire wall of mirrors, Tiffany has grown quite skilled at avoiding looking into them. She knows by heart each of the scars that lace her once-beautiful face. Plastic surgery has reduced their number and smoothed out the pink ridges pushed up by shrapnel shoving into flesh, but military surgery will only do so much cosmetic work, even for an officer, and she can't afford a private clinic for the rest. The scars on her bad leg she has to confront, because she must use the mirrors to check her posture and position throughout the session. Most of the feeling has returned to her shoulders, but her bad leg still seems to belong to someone else. If she forgets to keep watch over it, it drifts, and she ends up standing at an awkward and unbalanced angle. At least she does have both hands back again. Stretching and pointing with an arm that ends in sentient fingers turns out to be a much easier proposition than flapping a dead hand at a wall, so much so that she's humming along with the taped music by the time Gina comes in.

"Ohmigawd, look at those fingers! When?"

"Yesterday on the way home. I had my juice up in neuro, and they just started clenching up."

"That's so wonderful, it's super!" Dancing automatically to the music, Gina comes over. "All that hard work! See, told you it'd pay off."

Rather than hurt Gina's feelings, Tiffany allows herself to be hugged.

"Let's get you a squeezer for that hand. Oh, this is just so tremendous!"

The squeezer turns out to be a tennis ball with a chip tucked inside. Every time that Tiffany clenches her fingers around it, the chip records the amount of pressure she can generate and keeps a running total of the number of times she grips it.

"We'll download it into your file once a day and reset it. Once you get to a certain level, we'll upgrade and give you one that's harder to squish." Gina always uses words like squish. "Let me have your card so I can check this one out to you. I want you to keep it in your pocket all the time. Whenever you've got a moment, squish squish squish! The more you can do, the better. But if your hand aches, stop for a while and like rub it. The hand I mean, not the squeezer."

Getting to take the ball home with her, having therapy that she can do by herself, makes Tiffany happier than she's been in a long while. Her good mood, however, lasts only a few minutes. She's just getting into her rhythm on the push'n'pedal bike when

Gina reappears in the doorway, stands there watching, merely watching, except she's chewing on the side of her hand as she always does when she's anxious. Tiffany lets the bike slow and stop.

"Uh, yeah?"

"We need a favor from you. I mean, like, only if you feel you can. Y'know? One of the new guys, his morale is down. I mean, way down. Like, running on empty. Can I show you off?"

It takes Tiffany a long moment's struggle with herself before she agrees, nodding a yes rather than speaking it, swinging her bad leg carefully off the bike.

"I mean, if you really really don't mind. I don't want to bring you down, but God, Tiff, you're our big success, you know. And it does the other guys so much good when they see you."

She cannot begrudge Gina her pride in her work, cannot begrudge the possible good, either, that her own recovery, so successful beyond the first diagnosis, might do for this human being who, like her, has seen death only to be wrenched back to some semblance, some altered and limited version, of life. She follows Gina down the pale blue hall to the diagnostic room, painted pink, the corners carefully rounded, the shiny machinery hidden away behind blue screens except for the inevitable cables and connections. The new patient sits in an ordinary powered wheelchair rather than an electro-chair—a good sign in itself, as is the tilt of his head, and his defiant scowl. His hands, too, clasp the ends of the chair arms in white-knuckled rage.

"Bob . . . Major Wong, I mean. This is Captain Owens."

He swivels slightly to glance at her, forces a smile, nods at her answering smile. His face—the dark bangs of hair, the dark eyes, thin mouth, strong jaw—look perfectly normal, untouched, but the back of his head puffs out hairless, bright pink and engraved with the scars of old sutures, as if, perhaps his skull had got itself crushed, and the hunks and splinters pounded into the vulnerable brain lying just below.

"Hello, sir," Tiffany says. "If you can't answer don't worry about it. I couldn't talk when I got here."

His head jerks up a little, and he stares full into her face, searches her face, really, as if he were reading a text written on her mouth.

"It's true," Gina says. "She couldn't even say yes and no like you can. Honest cross my heart."

His mouth twitches in a smile.

"Can you stand, sir?"

The noise he makes sounds more like the moo of a cow, cut short, than a no, but Tiffany can understand it. Even if Gina hadn't prompted her, she still would have understood—another good sign.

"Neither could I."

Tears fill his eyes, spill helplessly as he jerks one arm, can't make it reach his face, mutters a noise that might be "God almighty," wrenches the arm up somehow almost to his chin. Gina darts forward to help, to wipe the tears away on one of her omnipresent kleenexes. Although Tiffany turns and walks out fast, she know she's done the right thing. *When you cry, it means you care, and when you care, you want to live.* Her hand finds the squeezer in her pocket and clenches. Hand. Back of the head. *God almighty. Fat lot of good he can do. Uh God.* She does not want to remember the back of his head, the reconstituted bone, the pink puff, scraped clean of the ever-so-thin layer of cells that carry whatever coloring a person's skin might have. She makes herself think of other things, repeats words that fill the blank screen of her memory with other pictures. *Don't think of a white horse.* Her sister would say those words and giggle, sitting on the edge of the top bunk and swinging stockinged feet. White horses. Green fields, fenced. Here now, you are here now, in the workout room. See the metal arms and levers of the equipment, hear the music rocking out from hidden speakers. Don't look at the mirrors.

After long hours on the push'n'pedal bike, the flat boards and the pull-up bar, after more juice in the rehab lounge and a fastidiously nutritional lunch as well, Tiffany puts her new squeezer in the pocket of the Forty-Niner jacket and slides the semi-bad hand in after it. She has plenty of room to grab the ball and clench her fingers, but she stops at the mirror by the check-in desk and watches herself for a moment.

"That look funny?" Tiffany says to the receptionist. "Seeing my fingers move in there like that?"

"Well, I wouldn't do it in a crowded place or anything, no."

"Okay. That's why I asked."

The receptionist smiles, hands her card back, hesitates.

"Gina tells me you went down to see Major Wong," she says at last.

"Yeah. Sure did."

"Real nice of you. He's a hero, they tell me. Saved all kinds of lives. Guess we'll find out how sooner or later. A real hero, Doctor says."

Tiffany smiles, nods, turns and leaves as fast as she can manage. *A real hero. Not like me. The plant going up, tower of white light. Shoulda stopped them.* How? In a half-armed plane? She shakes her head until she trembles and can forget.

Outside the world lies wrapped in fog, the sunlight blessedly gone, all bright colors blurred, all sounds muted. In the fog the firestorm in Tiffany's brain dies fast, leaving her confident enough to decide to stop at a bookstore and look for *Hunter's Night.* As she walks downhill she fishes in her pocket, finds the card for the import store and checks the address: too far away. She'll save that one for next week. On the other hand, she does remember a large used bookstore just off her usual streetcar line, just a couple of blocks on the far side of Golden Gate Park. She can even remember the cross street and the stores that lie on either side of it. Not that she trusts the memory, of course. The wiring may well have betrayed her again, and she braces herself for the shock, the disappointment.

Which come. The bookstore indeed exists, a narrow aisle of a building, and indeed, on one side a delicatessen still displays rows of hanging ducks and trays of pork buns in its window, but on the other side stands a dry cleaner, a dusty faded store smelling of chemicals and old cloth, that must have been there for years and years. The drugstore she's remembering is gone, obviously never existed except as a ghost or hallucination in the wiring. Somehow her torn brain built colored images of that drugstore, added the smell of perfumes and hair sprays, shrimp chips and cheap candy, fleshed out the scene with a crabby clerk and her pimply daughter. *Betrayed by the mind's eye. Again. Eye. That will not see. That sees what does not exist. Pluck it out.* For a long time Tiffany stands on the sidewalk and stares at the dry cleaner, until the elderly Chinese man behind the counter notices her and looks up, peering through the philodendron leaves that ring round the window.

Tiffany flees into the used bookstore, a gap-toothed cavern in the earth, glowing with phosphorescence, filled with boulders and stalactites. The smell of dusty paper and humid plastic reassures her, soothes the neurons firing in disordered clumps, stanches the flow of adrenaline pouring into her system, until she can focus her eyes in the dim electric light and realize that what she is really seeing is the merchandise. Near the window stands a counter, with a clerk perched on a stool behind the computer. Down the length of the shop run shelves, piled high, sagging, blocked by stacks and cartons of books and paper-books. The clerk looks up, smiles, returns to reading her news cartridge. Tiffany turns sideways, inches herself down the length of the store between piles of cartons, past the shelves of Bibles, the tacks of tracts, and finds the science fiction section exactly where she remembered it. For a moment her eyes well tears of relief. She wipes them dry, finds her piece of paper, and begins trying to match titles.

No *Hunter's Night*, but she feels only resigned. She is beginning to consider that her memories of this book might be as illusory as those of the drugstore. Why her mind would bother to create imaginary novels and places she cannot explain, any more than Dr. Rosas can offer any reasons that make sense. For the first time in her year's fight back, she begins to wonder if her doctors really do know all the answers. That comforting catch phrase, the prayer or litany that's kept her going, her lifeline, even, "it's in the wiring" suddenly rings empty and dead.

"Why is it in the wiring? That's what counts."

She's spoken aloud, and the clerk has heard her, or at least, heard sound drifting from the aisle. A young woman caped in uncombed black hair, she slips off her stool and hurries down.

"Can I help you?"

"Well, uh, maybe. I'm looking for a book by a dude named Albert Allonsby. *Hunter's Night.*"

"Ess Eff?"

Tiffany thinks for a moment before she can decipher the abbreviation.

"Yeah, that's right."

"I really like that stuff. You do, too, huh? I never woulda thought . . . well, I mean."

"Yeah, why wouldn't I?"

"Well, sorry, I don't wanna be rude, but you're a vet, right? I mean, you musta done stuff that was real exciting on your own. A lot flashier than just reading books."

"I guess. I was a pilot, and I loved flying. That was flash. But you know something? Sitting around, waiting to fly? That was boring, superboring. We all read a lot, while we were waiting. To pretend we were somewhere else."

"You dint watch TV?"

"The hostiles woulda picked it up, homed missiles on it."

"Oh." Her lips part, and she stares, just for a moment, before she catches herself. "But Allonsby. Wait. I know him. I've even read some of his stuff, but I never knew he wrote novels. I mean, like, I've read short stories of his, just not a whole book."

"Well, I picked it up when I was overseas."

"Oh. I getcha, a Euro edition or something. Say, if you find it, and if you're over this way, let me know, okay? I sure did like his stories."

Her relief at finding out that at least Allonsby himself exists is so strong that Tiffany would do the clerk a lot bigger favor than that if the chance presented itself. As she walks down to the streetcar stop, she pieces together the small fragments that repair another bit of her shattered mind. A real Albert Allonsby writes science fiction stories; he most likely lives in the European States; his novel, *Hunter's Night*, most likely exists as well, simply in a hard-to-find edition that was never imported into America. By concentrating on this syllogism, by repeating it over and over, she can make herself forget the missing drugstore.

At the streetcar stop a crowd stands and mills, women with shopping bags, women with kids in backpacks, women clutching the hands of larger children or hissing orders in their direction. Tiffany walks a few paces away, where she can stay by the curb and build herself a small booth of privacy. When she shoves her hands into her jacket pockets she finds the squeezer and smiles. Hand. Her hand, and working again. She has a prize to take home, a tangible proof of her progress.

"Tiff! Hey, how are you?"

The voice strikes her as utterly unfamiliar: male, but soft; soft, but scratchy. She looks up to find a young man, ever so barely familiar, smiling at her. Tall, with blond hair greased back, wearing black leather pants, a red silk shirt—very flash, this young man, and, she supposes, handsome in a way, but she dislikes his eyes. They are so pale that she can't tell if they're blue or grey, and they stare, glitter, never blink, never waver, until her own eyes seem to itch in sympathy. When she does blink a couple of times, then, at last, so does he.

"It's me," he says. "Don't you remember? Nick, ol' Nick Harrison. Hey, heard you were, uh, wounded in the war. Sure sorry 'bout that. Uh, say, *do* you remember me?"

"No, sure dunt. I'm real sorry." By now Tiffany has grown used to this bleak routine, of running across acquaintances only to find that the wiring has wiped itself clean of their memory. "Nick, honest, it's nothing personal. Okay? I'm afraid I got shot up pretty bad, and there's just a hell of a lot of people I don't remember."

"Well, sure, I mean, you hear about stuff like that on TV. I understand, yeah."

He tilts his head a little to one side and watches her unblinking while she tries to follow down the memory trail leading back to the part of her history that includes him. Behind her, a streetcar clangs, hissing with brakes as it glides to a stop.

"I better go," Tiffany says, turning.

"No, wait! Hey, can't I buy you a cup of coffee? How long you been home?"

Although she hesitates, taking his offer—no doubt intended kindly—would mean telling the story once again, remembering the story all over again. *Black smoke rising. Missiles screaming down.* She keeps turning, keeps walking toward the streetcar, but she is seeing the wing of her plane fall away, then a flare of white light and a sound shattering her life and mind.

"Whoops! Young lady, watch out!"

"Oh God! I'm sorry."

She has walked straight into someone climbing down from the streetcar. For a moment she can only stammer and blush as the old man picks up his round black hat, brushes it off, and settles it on his mass of grey hair. Sidelocks and a long beard, a black suit—the rabbi, smiling at her, clasping his hands in front of him, bowing at her.

"Jeez, I am so sorry, mister."

"No problem. At least you had the good sense to run away from the Devil, huh? I've been looking all over for you."

The streetcar clangs a warning of imminent departure.

"Let it go. We've got to talk." The rabbi takes her arm and swings her around. "We'll go have a nice cup of coffee in one of these cafés."

All at once she remembers where she last saw Nick, out on the streetcar island, arguing with this same old man. His arms crossed over his chest, Nick stands glowering at them, his pale pale eyes unblinking, his mouth twisted into the ugliest scowl she's ever seen on a human face. If indeed he is human. *What did the old man say? Run away from the Devil?* Just as if he knew her thoughts, Nick smiles, and draped in that smile he looks nothing but human, and a good-looking guy at that.

"Hey, I take it I'm invited to this kaffeeklatsch?"

"You'll take it whether you're invited or not, won't you?" the rabbi says. "I know you. Tiffany, come along, my dear. Oh, and by the way, my name is Akiba."

Picking up speed the streetcar runs past. Since here on a Saturday it'll be a long time before the next car, Tiffany decides that she might as well go along. If nothing else, she is curious as all hell. . . . She hears herself use that image, feels her mind shy away out of some brute instinct, some impulse that seems to come from the deepest level of her mind, as if the neurons and the axions themselves recognize Mr. Nick Harrison, as if her very DNA fears him and his bleached unblinking stare.

Yet the café they find is so ordinary, so normal in every detail, that Tiffany feels that sudden insight slip away and fade. Scented with steam and peanut oil, the narrow little place sports pale green walls, hung with pictures of Mexican scenery and calendars of girls holding bottles of beer. Neo-samba music pounds out of the speaker panel hanging over the back door. Behind the counter a old woman is twisting won ton; a young one polishes an espresso machine with a spotless white rag. She turns and smiles, tossing the rag down, as Tiffany and the two men come in. The three of them slip into a bright red poly-foam booth while she brings menus, which the rabbi waves away.

"You got any coffee today?" Tiffany says.

"Sure do. Hawaiian, the dealer told me. Maybe it is. Wasn't gonna ask too many questions."

"Well, as long as it's coffee." The rabbi seems honestly puzzled by this exchange. "Coffee all round, then, with milk for them, but not for me, and I suppose, pastries?"

"*Pan dulce* or pork buns?" the waitress says. "All we got left."

Nick snickers with a twist of lip.

"Just the sweet bread, miz. Though I dunno." This last to the rabbi. "You can't be keeping kosher if you'd eat here. And with me."

The rabbi ignores him, struggles with a coat pocket, then brings out a wad of dollar bills, which he tosses onto the table. The waitress stares, wrinkling her nose against a smell of mould and damp earth.

"Cash? I dunno bout that. Lot of paperwork for three coffees."

"It's not good?" The rabbi sits up straight and glares. "It's old, yes, but they said it should still be good."

Nick covers his mouth with a paper napkin and chokes back laughter. Tiffany uses her good hand to sweep the wad back to the old man.

"I'll pay," she announces. "Just bring the coffee, okay? And I'll get out my card."

Her turn for the struggle, with her wallet stuck deep in a pants pocket, but at last she frees it from her keys and pulls it out. When she looks up, her prize in hand, the girl is back behind the counter, fiddling with the machine. Her head reflects, a stretched balloon-shape, on the copper cylinder. Nick leans forward and jerks a thumb at the rabbi.

"Where you get those bills? The earth spirits dig them up for you?"

"Of course. A tin box that someone buried during those riots they had in New York. So the spirits can't keep track of currency laws! What do you expect from them, anyway?"

Nick snorts. It is at this point that Tiffany begins to wonder if she's hallucinating the entire scene. The café, of course, is real— she's passed it and looked in many times—but these two men might be elaborate constructions of her own mind, as detailed and solid as those memories of the drugstore. Never before has she hallucinated an event in the present moment rather than the past, although, she reflects, for all she knows she has indeed done so and simply never caught herself at it. This hallucination theory pleases her much more than the idea that she might be having a snack with the Devil and Rabbi Akiba, the great Talmudic scholar, or was he a Kabbalist? Both, Tiffany thinks. It seems to her that she has two sets of memories, broken shards dating back to her time in Israel, when she felt obliged to learn a little something about the history and great men of the place that she just might die defending. Which was he again? She knows she read it somewhere, can't remember, only sees in her mind words that tell of men in black sitting under trees and discussing holy things. Whether those things were the sobrieties of earthly law or ecstatic visions of the throne of God she no longer knows.

Doubtless it doesn't matter, either, because she wants to believe that this elderly man in black does not exist, no matter what name he might attach to himself. Unfortunately, the waitress returns with three cups of coffee, one black, on a flowered tray and a chipped plate of *pan dulce,* smelling of cinnamon and oranges. Tiffany cannot make herself believe that she's hallucinating the waitress, especially when the girl takes her debit card in warm fingers, or that the waitress hallucinated the order. Tiffany turns her head away to avoid looking at the row of red numbers that blink on the transmit box hanging from the girl's belt. She does, however, remember to take her card back.

"Three cups 'spresso, thirty bucks. Plate a *pan dulce,* three-fifty," the waitress says. "That be all?"

"Thirty?" Reb Akiba snaps. "Tiffany my dear, I can't let you pay for this. I meant this to be my treat."

The waitress seems to be about to speak, then shrugs away a problem that's not hers to solve. She heads back to the counter and picks up her polishing rag again.

"Look," Nick whispers. "Tiffany can use that cash on the street. Plenty of places that'll take it, no questions asked."

"Paying a debt isn't breaking the law, no matter what the tax-collectors here think of paper currency." Akiba flashes him a surprisingly youthful grin. "I know what you were trying to do, creature, but what's that phrase? No dominoes."

"No dice." Scowling, Nick shoves the wad of bills back in Tiffany's direction. "Take it, kid. Won't do him any good."

With a glance in the waitress's direction—she is studiously ignoring them all—Tiffany pockets the bills. At this point it occurs to her that she might indeed be having real coffee with real men while hallucinating or distorting their words.

"Uh, look," she says. "It's hard for me to really understand you guys, okay? It's the wiring. When you been dead a couple of times, you kinda lose parts of your brain."

"Oh, I know, my dear, I know. I've died, too."

"Long time ago now," Nick puts in. "What? Couple thousand years?"

"Something like that. You lose track. It was before the Romans took the Temple, wasn't it?"

"How could you forget that? Jeez."

"Wait a minute," Tiffany says. "I thought Rabbi Akiba lived in the thirteenth century."

"No, my dear, you're confusing the real me with the fictional version in those books by that sephardic weirdo. The *Zohar*. And Moses something."

"De Leon," Nick says. "But I don't get it. How you could lose a piece of big data like the year you died?"

"You do forget those things. Dates, names, details."

"Details? When the Temple went down is a *detail?*"

"It's become one now, yes. Besides, how would you know? You've never even been alive to die."

"Uh, excuse me?" Tiffany breaks in. "I'm not understanding you. I can kinda tell."

"You're understanding us perfectly well, my dear. You simply don't want to believe you are, and I can't say I blame you." Akiba frowns into his coffee cup. "I think I'll let this cool a little."

Automatically Tiffany drinks some of her own coffee, not, of course, that she can taste it. She can, however, feel the heat and register a certain sharp sensation which, she supposes, once would have been bitterness.

"But anyway," Nick says. "We don't have a lot of time. You going to start, old man, or should I?"

"I will. You'll only interrupt soon enough." The rabbi picks up a circle of pan dulce, blesses it under his breath, and breaks it in two. When he hands half to Tiffany, the suddenly warm bread smells of roses. "Tell me, my dear. Do you find yourself getting confused these days? Are you suffering from bouts of disorientation?"

He sounds so much like a TV commercial that Tiffany nearly laughs. To cover she takes a bite of the bread: still tasteless. Somehow, she realizes, she'd been expecting it would be otherwise after his blessing.

"If I could simply cure you, believe me, I would," the rabbi says with his mouth full. "Can't." He swallows quickly. "No, I wasn't reading your mind. You spoke aloud."

"Damn."

"Don't say that here, please." Nick is grinning. "It gives me ideas."

"Shut up, you. But Tiffany, my question?"

"Well, yeah, I do. It's the brain damage."

"Do you ever feel that you should be somewhere else? Or that you're in the right place, but things are wrong around you?"

"At least once a day. My doctor says . . ."

Nick is grinning; Reb Akiba is smiling but in a sad sort of way; all at once Tiffany can't remember what she was going to tell them. She is possessed by a sudden idea, that everything Dr. Rosas has told her is not so much wrong as irrelevant.

"I don't suppose you know much about physics?" Reb Akiba goes on. "Quantum physics. The interrelationship of waves and discrete particles. How God created the universe with the letters of the alphabet."

"You're mixing metaphors again, old man." Nick winks at Tiffany. "You gotta watch him, you know. He does it all the time."

"Shut up, wretched creature! Let me start again. Tiffany, you must have read some Moses de Leon. How?"

"I ran across him when I was stationed in Israel. I was there for a real long time, you know. I decided I wanted to learn Hebrew, so I could talk to the Israeli pilots and support people. In their own language, I mean. Like, a lot of people spoke English, but not real well. And so, I took this class, and I made some friends, and one of them belonged to this Kabbalistic study group. She didn't tell me much—"

"Not to one of the *goyim*," Nick mutters.

"That old secret knowledge slur? The lore's all been published in books, English books." Reb Akiba fixes him with a nasty look. "So don't overdramatize, will you? Her friend probably just didn't want to bore the poor girl stiff. Tiffany, you must have read de Leon in English."

"Yeah, I did, just some selections. My friend gave me some books. I mean, when you're just sitting around, waiting to fly, you'll read anything, you know? Just to kinda keep your mind alive. But what's *goyim*? That's not a Hebrew word, is it?"

"No, dear, it's Yiddish. A dead language now. But—"

"It means," Nick interrupts, "people who aren't Jewish. I mean, it meant that when the language was—"

"Will you shut up?" The rabbi's voice growls like penned thunder. "As long as you keep interrupting we'll get nowhere." He glances Tiffany's way. "He can't help confusing things, you know. It's in his nature."

Much to her surprise, Nick winces and pouts.

"It's not like I want to. It's not fair." He looks at Tiffany with watery eyes. "Part of my punishment. It has a rotten sense of humor, if you ask me."

"It?"

"He means the Godhead. He can't say the name, you know."

" 'It' suits It better, anyway," Nick snaps. "It can't be a he or a she or even a they. It's beyond all that—dualities, categories, all that stuff. And jeez, It never lets you forget it, either. It stinks smug, I tell you. So what's It doing with a name, anyway? I mean, look, if It's transcendent It's transcendent, and there's no two ways about it."

When Tiffany laughs at the joke, Nick grins; he would seem charming if only he would blink his eyes.

"You've disrupted the line of thought again," the rabbi says quietly. "Now where were we?"

"Moses de Leon and quantum physics," Tiffany says. "You asked me what I knew about quantum physics, and somehow or other we got into Kabbalism."

"Perfectly logical connection," Nick mutters.

The Rabbi waggles a hand at him for silence.

"Well, I don't know much about either," Tiffany says. "I read just a little bit when I was in Israel, about Kabbalism, I mean, 'cause Miriam was into it. I took a lot of science in school, because I was on the Air Service track, but I don't remember it now."

"What's the diff between Air Force and Air Services?" Nick says.

"None."

"Oh yeah?"

They stare at each other for a long moment. *He knows. Oh God, he knows.* Suddenly she remembers a detail, no, not a detail: the crux, the all-important thing, the one overwhelming difference. Air Services planes always go fully armed. *Lots of women pilots in the Service. Combat pilots. All of us. Failure? Oh no. I shot them down. Oh my God, I shot them down. No way that power plant shoulda gone up like that.*

"Come on, Tiff." The Devil is smiling at her. "Level with me. You know—"

Tiffany cannot speak, cannot stop him, cannot save herself.

"Shut up, creature!"

Nick bites his lip hard and falls silent.

"That's better." Reb Akiba gives him a brief, approving smile. "Parallel worlds, Tiffany. What about those? Alternate universes. Ever hear of them?"

"Well, yeah, but they're not real, are they? I mean, it's just one of those ideas math makes you get. Logical necessities? Oh, hell, I used to know the right name. Something like, null-content concepts? No, that's not it, either."

Akiba sighs.

"Let's try the alphabet instead. Twenty-two letters, well, twenty-six here in your country. Right? Yet hundreds of thousands of words. It's all in the way you mix them up, all in the pattern they make. Rabbi, rabbit. If you had an infinite number of letters, wouldn't you have an infinite number of words? Worlds, words. Not a lot of difference there, either. Well, It, the Transcendent One, created an infinite set of letters. So the words It spoke became infinite. Sometimes these names shift back and forth, or they split into new words, because It is pure possibility. And because It is It, what It speaks as possible becomes actual. Likewise the quantum equations. They shift, open possibilities, possible events, possible objects. But they can't all be actual—not in the same world. Somewhere they have to be actual, mind, but not all in same world." He pauses, taken with a thought. "I don't suppose there'd be room."

Tiffany stares in complete and utter incomprehension. In her mind she sees a picture of the rabbi carrying a rabbit; nothing more.

"On the other hand," the rabbi goes on, "not all possibilities do become actual. Words, worlds, all created out of the same pieces, the same letters, but some don't make any sense. When you mix up letters randomly, a lot of the combinations you get won't be real words, right? Rabbi, rabbit, but not rabbo or rebbot. And it's the same for worlds. Now, I don't know why. The Transcendent One never spoke those names, I suppose. I never asked It."

"Messy, that's all it was." Nick's voice drips contempt. "Jeez, a lousy mistake, leaving half-realized possibilities lying all over the universe. Sloppy."

"Hah! And I suppose you could have done half as well?"

"I never said that! I just pointed out Its lousy mistake, and It's been hounding me ever since."

"Poor little snakey-wakey."

Nick starts to make a sound very like a hiss, then chokes it back. Reb Akiba laughs. Tiffany begins to feel that everything she's ever believed or thought, the totality that she calls mind, is shrinking, fading, growing smaller and smaller, turning to a tiny core or kernel, as small as a mustard seed. *Do something. Say something. Take control of this talk. Something.*

"What mistake?"

"When It didn't know Its own strength." Nick jumps right in. "When the vessels broke and the worlds-to-be all shattered. None of this crap woulda happened, you know, if it wasn't for that."

"I wouldn't call that a mistake." The rabbi snaps. "Neither of us are in any position to judge why It does anything."

"Oh bullshit! Or course it was a mistake. There was law, there was order, there was light, waves and waves of wonderful light— and all of a sudden, bang! The vessels shatter! Chaos! All these messy forces! Discrete particles! Messy little souls running around everywhere! Alternate universes! Quanta! Photons!" Nick turns dramatically in the booth toward the aisle.

"Don't spit!" Reb Akiba barks. "We're inside, you know."

"Sorry." Nick collects himself with a cough. "This argument's just so familiar. I keep thinking we're all sitting around under those plane trees again."

Tiffany glances toward the counter to find the two women staring, the stack of wonton skins, the bowl of filling forgotten between them.

"Look, you guys, maybe you could like keep your voices down?"

"Of course, and my dear, you have my apologies." The rabbi glances at the women. "And so do you, dear ladies. I'm afraid that my students here take all these abstract things rather seriously."

The old woman grabs the bowl, slaps the stack on top of it, and heads, with slow dignity, toward the back room. The waitress smiles.

"Padre, you guys be from Berkeley?"

"I've taught there, yes. At the Theological Union."

"Oh, well. That explains it, then." She picks up her rag and goes back to her polishing. "They all nuts, in Berkeley."

Although he makes an effort to hush his voice, Nick is glaring as he leans across the table.

"What makes you think It had a reason?"

"And did I ever say I thought It did? Just the opposite."

"In civilized company the word 'why' generally implies a reason."

"Since when are you civilized company?"

They glare at each other over raised cups of coffee. Tiffany feels pain running from one side of her forehead to the other. She finds the tennis ball in her pocket, wraps the fingers of the bad hand round it, and begins squeezing; oddly enough, the exercise helps her headache as well. Reb Akiba turns to her and frowns in thought.

"Let's go back to the way you keep feeling disoriented. Tell me, do you ever feel like you come from someplace else?"

"No."

"What? Not really?"

"I mean, I grew up here. Of course I belong here. It's just that. Well, sometimes the city's not right. I mean, things are gone. Other things are there."

"Aha! A close match but not exact, eh?"

"Match for what?"

"The other city. The one you've got mapped in your memories."

Again she feels words slip away and shatter like so much dropped china.

"The hell with this." Nick leans across the table. "She don't even need to understand it. Tiff, you're in the wrong world, that's all. You remember that explosion? The missiles, hitting that fusion power plant? Did you realize that it *was* a fusion plant? The Israelis are way ahead of everyone else in this world and yours on that. That's why the Emirate sent the suicide squad in. To take out that particular plant with nuclear warheads. Yeah, that's right, forbidden nuclear warheads. And in this world, the one we're sitting in now, they did it. The force, the energy, that got itself released was . . . was huge, enormous, more than you, more than any of us can understand. If you'd really been in this world when that plant went up, there wouldn't have been enough left of you to find. You got to have wondered how you coulda survived that explosion."

"Well, no, I dint, but—I mean, till now—wait a minute. I didn't survive. Fucking thing killed me, man."

"No, that was the impact when you bailed out too late. Almost death by natural causes, by comparison. That explosion woulda taken your corpse apart molecule by molecule. That's what happened to the other pilot. The one with the unarmed plane. The other Tiffany. The other you, sweetheart."

He sits back, panting a little from the effort of speaking clearly. Her words fail. The rabbi's questions, the Devil's talk of other outcomes to the same battle, seem to run together, to swell inside her mind and grow like some greasy bubble, filling all the available space, smashing even the possibility of other thoughts against her skull, cramming and strangling until they die. In her hand the squeezer beeps in protest. She lets it go.

"Don't bully," Reb Akiba says to Nick. "She has to understand, so she can make her decision."

"Decision, hell!" Nick snaps. "She's got to go back, and that's that! Look, girl. You don't belong here. You're out of place. The other Tiffany, the one who lived here, she was supposed to die, yeah, and she did, blown all to hell. Not enough of her to find. But somehow or other, you got sucked through to take her place, in some kind of backlash after the explosion. That's all wrong."

"Wrong? Hell, it's crazy." The bubble breaks. "Are you talking about two mes?"

"A very large number of yous, but only two are involved in this." The rabbi glares at Nick. "I was trying to build up to the truth gently."

"And getting nowhere, old man. Tiff, you've got to go back. The alternate worlds are always trying to snap back together, anyway. It's like, what? Lemme think. Ever seen a bowl of cake batter, something thick like that? You draw a knife through it, it looks like it's gonna separate into two parts, but they ooze and sort of smoosh themselves back together. Well, the worlds are kinda like that. All you gotta do is go with the flow."

"Now wait just a minute! If you think I'm gonna end up where I was a year ago—I couldn't even stand up, couldn't even take a piss by myself—you crazy, mister. Dunt care who you are."

"Who said anything about that?" Nick snaps. "I can't turn back Time. No one can, not even Akiba. We're going to take you back to right now. Or what's now there. But you won't change any. You'll be exactly the you you are now."

"That's where he comes in." The rabbi flaps a hand in Nick's direction. "We'll have to have some sort of story to explain your return. You've been missing there for over a year."

"The Prince of Lies, that's me, kid. I'll think of something. I don't know what, yet, but once we're there, back in the stinking desert, I'm sure I'll get inspired." He looks down, eyes lowered in creditable modesty. "It's a gift."

"I'm not going anywhere with you, fella." Tiffany stands up. "I mean, like, get stuffed!"

To a babble of protests she slides free of the booth and heads out, forcing the bad leg to move fast by sheer will. Ahead, the door: oblong of grey light, safety. With the good hand she reaches out, grabs the jamb, and pulls herself through, glances back to see Reb Akiba shoving Nick down into his seat while the waitress trots over, frowning and troubled.

"Her choice." The rabbi's last words drift her way. "Has to be her choice."

With a pull Tiffany swings herself out the door and manages, somehow, to run for the first time in over a year. At the intersection the streetcar clangs and trembles, jerks forward, stops, and opens its door. Blessed safety. She stumbles up the steps, slides her FastPass through the slot, and lurches down the car, falling into her favorite seat by the back door just as the car glides forward. On the sidewalk stand Nick and the rabbi. They wave. The car clangs and turns, picking up speed on the open track. They disappear. Tiffany presses her hands to her eyes and wonders why she isn't crying. The bad leg flames pain, her lungs ache, she has just lived through the most vivid hallucination of her entire recovery, a symptom that stands like a warning buoy marking passage into a whole new ocean of disease. Dr. Rosas warned her that there would be stages, periods of change to be endured like storms. This, she supposes, is the beginning of one of them. Yet, deep in her mind, she feels no fear, not even her usual resolve to endure pain as best she can. A clot of rebel neurons keeps firing, keeps sending a message down lines of traitor brain cells, repeating against all reason and all will: *At last, we have answers.*

"Not true. Not answers. They weren't real."

All around her passengers turn to stare, accusing eyes of women peering over books held up to painted faces or over shopping bags balanced on laps. Crammed in beside them children giggle. Tiffany scrunches down in her seat and stares at the slotted view through the doors across from her: green stripe of trees outside, grey strip of insulation on the window, blue stripe of sky, white strip of door. Strip, stripe. She refuses to think of an imaginary rabbi. No white horses. No brown bears, no California bears on flags in other worlds. None of those. Not even her victory. She refuses to—she must—she will sacrifice the knowledge that she won her last dogfight even if in the end they took her down with them. The eye must not see. Only the door. Window. Her hand, clenching on the tennis ball buried in her pocket, warm pocket, rough-napped ball, the pain in cramped tendons as she squeezes the ball over and over, harder and harder. By the time she reaches her streetcar stop, she has managed to forget many things. Not all, no, but many.

At the door she fumbles for her keys, reassures herself that her wallet still lies deep in the cargo pocket, pulls the keys out and allows the bad hand to hold them for a moment, then transfers them back to the good hand and opens the door. As she steps inside she hears from the kitchen voices, Mark and another man, and the electronic roar and mutter of a sport on TV.

"Yo!" she calls out.

The electronic mutter stops, victim to the mute.

"Tiff?" Mark's voice. "We got company."

When Tiffany limps into the kitchen, LoDarryl, one of Mark's old war buddies, slides out from behind the table so she can have her usual chair. Tall, rangy, the elder by some two years, he's much lighter than Mark, almost white-looking, really, except for his tight black hair, which he wears in dreadlocks. He also has a perpetual limp, courtesy of a land mine during the Brazilian War, which left him with an artificial left foot. There wasn't enough left of the original to reattach. *Not enough of her to find.* Tiffany shakes her head hard.

"Mark, you butthole, turn that box off," LoDarryl says. "It's bothering Tiff."

"No, it's not." Tiffany says. "It's okay. Really."

"It's only jai alai." Mark leans back dangerously in his chair and flips the muted TV off. "Sit down, hon. Almost time for your pills."

"Is it that late? Jeez."

"Yeah, it is. I was starting to get worried."

"I'm sorry. I ran into this guy at the streetcar stop. I guess we used to know him. Or I did. Nick, his name is, white dude, blond and flash looking. I can't remember his last name. Ring a bell?"

Mark and LoDarryl share a blank look and a shrug.

"Someone from school, maybe," Tiffany goes on. "And I had coffee with another friend, an old man, a rabbi, actually, is what he is. Then I hit a bookstore, but no *Hunter's Night.*"

"Well, one day maybe." LoDarryl pulls a rickety stool over to the table and perches on it. "I just stopped by for a minute. Wanted to talk to this man of yours about this idea of mine."

"Another weird scheme," Mark breaks in, grinning. "From the World Renowned LoDarryl Think-Tank. You know what that means."

LoDarryl makes an obscene gesture in his direction, but he too smiles.

"No, this one's real, Tiff. Honest. I applied for the license and everything. Dump running."

"Oh God! Mark, you're not gonna—"

"I already told him no. Dunt worry."

"Well, hell, you gotta do something, man." LoDarryl leans forward, the smile gone. "It's real good money. Nowhere near as dangerous as Brazil."

"You dunt see me going back to Brazil, neither."

LoDarryl ignores the comment.

"Not dangerous at all so long as I get the license and stick to the legal areas. Lot of good stuff, man, sitting in them old dumps. They threw away all kindsa good stuff, back in the old days. You get a lot of cash for aluminum. Enough to pay your expenses, and then all the rest is gravy."

"To cook all them rats they got out there, huh?" Mark lets his grin fade. "I know you, man. Just how long is it gonna be before the restricted areas start calling to you?"

LoDarryl manages, barely, an injured look.

"Nothing like that, man. All on the up and up."

Yeah sure, Tiffany thinks, *oh yeah I just bet.*

"Look," LoDarryl goes on. "I may be greedy but I ain't dumb. I ain't gonna go burn bits off myself with toxics, and I ain't gonna get myself rad poisoning, neither. I dint live through Brazil to die up in Altamont running junk."

"Not on purpose, no." Mark's grin is gone. "You never step in dog shit on purpose, neither."

LoDarryl sighs and looks away.

"Well, hell," he says after a moment. "Man's gotta do something, dunt he? I can't sign up for the Valley and work the agribiz, not with this foot. I ain't real keen on living in a barracks again, anyway, even if they ain't nobody shooting at me this time. What else is there, man? You go to the Army, or you go to the Valley, and if you stay in the city 'cause you can't do either, well, hell, you gotta do something. I been looking for a job a lot longer'n you have, man. I'm giving up. Gonna make my own damn job."

Unspoken the thought hangs there: like you'll have to, one of these days. Mark merely looks at him for an answer.

"Ah well." LoDarryl gets up, shoving the stool back. "Gonna

be running 'long home. Let Tiff take her pills in peace. Tuesday night, now, you guys coming over? We gonna watch the big game on the big screen. Manny Mike, he got it running again."

"Yeah? Cool. Well, we'll see, buddy. Depends on how late Tiff gets home, how she feels."

While Mark walks LoDarryl to the door, Tiffany watches Meebles hunkering over his plate of dry chow. The little crunching sounds he makes as he eats drive into her head like nails, but she refuses to disturb him. *No ox in the manger,* she tells herself. *No, it was the dog in the manger. Ox trying to eat. Ox. Aleph. No imaginary rabbits. Rabbis.*

"Tiff?"

Mark is standing in front of her. She has not heard or seen him come back.

"Sorry. I'm just real tired. Long workout, and now the bad leg hurts. I tried running, just a little, but it was too soon."

"Oh. Well, lemme get you your pills."

"You dunt mind, do you? I mean, I feel so goddamn guilty, you waiting on me like this."

"Better me waiting on you than not having you here at all to wait on. Dunt you worry. It gets to be a drag, I'll tell you."

"Okay. I just . . ." She lets the words trail away.

"Something bothering you? LoDarryl? Dunt you worry about that. Even if it wasn't for you, I ain't going off dump-running with LoDarryl and his crazy ideas and his crazier friends. Manny Mike—shit! A genius, yeah, sure, the guy can build anything, fix anything. 'Cepting his own brain. A real space case, that dude. Jeez, I just hope to God LoDarryl dunt get himself killed. Lot of guys scrounging for the same damn junk."

"That's why he wanted you, ain't it? For a rifleman."

Mark winces sharply.

"Yep. All them medals, he says. Let's put 'em back to work. huh? No way. No fucking way."

Mark gets the bottles, begins arranging on the table in tidy rows blue pills, red, green, white, and the big clear capsules that she always gets out of the way first. Merely looking at the array makes her throat tighten, her stomach churn.

"You need to eat something first?"

"Maybe so, yeah. Mark, I been thinking. If it wasn't for me you could get your own farm. You been decorated, you made it up to master sergeant, you got the record they're looking for. They'd give you one, somewhere out in the Heartland. You wouldn't end up working the agribiz in the Valley at all. I'm the one who's holding you back. Me and my damn wreck of a body. I could never work a farm with you."

"What?" Mark spins on her in honest rage. "Who you been talking to? Where this come from?"

She can only shake her head in numb misery.

"I dunt wanna hear it. You understand me? I dunt wanna hear it." He grabs her shoulders. "Tiff, I ain't going nowhere without you. I dunt even want to go nowhere without you. Understand me?"

Tears slide, burn in manic relief. He clutches her close, so hard, so tight, that she can barely breathe between his grasp and her own crying.

"Oh jeezuz God," Mark says. "Tiff, Tiff, why you work yourself up into these things! Come on, honey, come on. Let's go sit on the sofa, okay? And I'll bring you some soup or something in there. Where it's comfortable."

Still sobbing she lets him lead her to the soft cushions and the calm of blue and green walls, lets him sit her down like a child and wipe her face like one, too, while Meebles watches, his ears pricked forward to catch a sound he's never heard before: Tiffany crying.

"Besides," Mark says at last. "What the fuck would I want with some damn farm? All that mud and way the hell out in Hicksville. I'm a city man, honey. Last thing I want is pigs and a bunch of plants."

And that she can believe, and believing, laugh.

THREE

Grey dawn comes in slits round the one window in the bedroom. Tiffany has been dreaming of flying, a precise pilot's dream of taking off in an old F39C and climbing in wide spirals over the eastern Mediterranean. In the dream she radioed a flight plan back to some unnamed base, then headed for Tel Aviv to keep a dinner date with Mark, on guard at the embassy there, (as he indeed was when she first met him) as casually as if she were taking the bus back in the real world, but long before her scanner showed the familiar Israeli coastline, the hostiles appeared, screaming out of the sun at seven o'clock, to fight a dream-battle over open sea. She wakes, drenched in sweat, knowing that she shot them down, knowing that she couldn't possibly have shot them down. She breathes slowly, deeply, concentrates on the throbbing of her bad leg, the ache in the formerly bad hand, watches the room surface from the sea of night, each object dripping darkness as it rises into silver—a lump of clothes on the floor here, a behemoth of a dresser there, the movement of the cat washing himself on the wooden chair, a glint of light in the mirror. For a long time she tries to ignore the pain in the bad leg. Running was a stupid idea, and why did she run, anyway? For a mercifully long time she cannot remember. When that memory breaks through, when she sees with the inner eye Nick sitting in a bright red booth and the rabbi leaning earnestly across a red table, when she hears with the inner ear fragments of their talk, she is wide awake beyond all hope of sleep. *An infinite set of letters. Poor little snakey-wakey.* Beside her Mark snores, gurgles, and flops over onto his stomach with a sigh. *Snakes dunt have to blink. They got an extra eyelid or something.* She sits up, using both hands to swing the bad leg over the side of the bed. The dawn is brightening, and the lump of clothes on the floor reveals itself as hers. She scoops it up and hobbles into the bathroom.

Moving around eases the ache in her leg, eases the pain of shoving forbidden memories away from her mind, too, so much so that she decides to walk down to the store and buy a surprise for Mark. At eight o'clock, which it almost is, the neighborhood catch-all will open, and by nine, the line for everything but actual food will stretch halfway around the block, too long a wait for her to manage. When she opens the door, fog greets her. She grabs the Forty-Niner jacket, shoves the spent news cartridge into one pocket and her string bag into the other, and slips out fast before Meebles can escape to the dangerous outside world. Without a shred of evidence, everyone in San Francisco is convinced that the Brazilians eat dogs and cats when they can catch them. On the sidewalk she pauses, blinking hard, struggling to get the jacket on as the formerly bad hand stiffens in the cool damp. The wind strikes chill, even though off to the south, the fog is already breaking up in long streamers. Through the scattering mist she can see Mt. Davidson, with its crumbling concrete cross rising from the last few trees at its very crest, and on its lower flanks the dazzling-white walled compounds of the rich.

The store stands some six blocks to the west, down the long slope that eventually falls all the way to the ocean. A couple of vets run it, stocking the things they know that the neighborhood, mostly vets like themselves or Mark and Tiffany, both will want and can afford to buy. As Tiffany limps up, Ger Chong is just raising the American flag that hangs over the front window. In the brightening sun, the brand-new Stars and Stripes and Maple Leaves snaps and sways: an ugly design, really, with too many elements all jumbled together, but it's only temporary, until the National Committee comes up with something better.

"News yet?" she says.

"Not the local. That'll be any minute. But we got the overseas cartridges already. And the bread truck's been."

Getting a bottle of milk, a couple of cinnamon rolls, and a loaf of raisin bread into the bag takes Tiffany a while. She has to hang the handles over her left arm, set the bottom of the bag on a pile of boxed noodles to make the top open, then slip the objects in, one at a time, with her good hand. All the while she is aware of Ger not looking, of exerting his willpower to keep from insulting her by offering to help. Finally she's done, adds a stick of butter—only half the price of real margarine—and limps to the counter to find two other customers ahead of her. Or rather, one customer, a tall blond dude wearing an Army fatigue jacket over a pair of cammo pants, is buying a pack of gum, while an old man dressed all in black stands beside a bushel basket of apples. Her heart wrenches; she thinks of dropping the bag and running for the door; too late. Nick turns round with a smile and moves out of her way.

"Fancy meeting you here."

"Oh get stuffed." She flops the bag onto the counter. "And the news, too, Ger."

The Devil and the rabbi wait for her on the sidewalk outside while she pays. Although the store does have a second exit near the dairy case, she decides that sneaking out that way would be cowardly. Besides, try as she might to shut them up, her memories are demanding answers. As she walks out the front, Nick reaches for the string bag with a small bow.

"I'll haul it myself, fella. What are you guys doing here?"

"Seeing how you feel this morning, my dear, nothing more." The rabbi raises his hat to her. "You're well, I hope?"

With a shrug she starts walking toward home, but with the weight of the bag to balance, the bad leg slows her down to a hobble. Nick and the rabbi stroll along, one on either side of her, as she makes her painful way up the long slope. She decides that her only safety lies in silence. It seems to her that she can physically feel the rebel neurons firing, the questions forming, racing down the nerves toward her mouth, burning in her mouth. She refuses to speak one word.

"Well, yes, of course, there's another Mark," the rabbi says. "A large number of Marks, really, but I'm sure you only mean the one back in the California Republic."

"Damn! Did I say it?"

"What?" The rabbi looks briefly puzzled. "You asked me a question, yes, if that's what you mean."

"Shit! Well, sorry, Reb Akiba. But I dint want. Oh hell." Rebel eyes burn with tears. She wipes them on the sleeve of the Forty-Niner jacket.

"You believe us, don't you?" Nick laughs, crowing victory. "Half the battle, right there! You believe us."

"Dunt! Just a what if. Just a what if question, just taking your damn crazy theory for argument's sake. That's all."

"Yeah, sure. You're bullshitting and you know it."

"Will you shut up?" Reb Akiba intervenes. "But, Tiffany my dear, that Mark is indeed alive and well. He mourned you, of course, and rather bitterly. I don't suppose he's over you, yet, though he does seem more his old self these days."

"Now you shut up," Nick says. "When Tiff comes back, he'll be the happiest man alive. Not like he forgot her or anything."

"And this Mark here?" Despite all her intentions, she cannot take refuge in silence, cannot let this conversation go on without her. "If I leave?"

Neither man says anything. Nick glances absently at the clearing sky; the rabbi frowns at the sidewalk. Giggling and elbowing each other, a group of young girls runs by, heading for the store with their parents' cards clutched tight in their fingers.

"You know, Tiff," Nick says. "Back home you're a hero. California's naming an air base after you."

"You lie."

"Nope." He glances at the rabbi. "Do I?"

"Not this time, no." Reb Akiba admits it reluctantly. "Down in the desert, in that part of Los Angeles that's been cleared away."

"Owens Air Services Base. The president herself's gonna open it. 'Bout six more weeks now. Sure beats the crummy little citation you got here, doesn't it? What's it say? Thanks for trying, you and your lousy unarmed plane? Here's a piece of paper with eagles on it. Cheap gold ink, too. But back home, jeez, just think what would happen if you, hum, if you, lemme see, if you got released by the Emirate. Yeah, that's it! One of the anti-shah terrorist groups, they've been keeping you a secret hostage, waiting for their chance to trade you in for something big! I knew I'd think of something, and I've got just the group lined up. Kind of on retainer, you could call it. Okay, so, they hand you over to the California Embassy as a goodwill gesture, trying to get some of their prisoners back from Israel, and you get back home just in time for the opening of that base. Hero's welcome. Parades, TV interviews, marching bands, flowers. Your fellow officers lining up to salute. Hell, bet you could run for the senate. Be president yourself, someday."

"The prince of lies, that's you, fella," Tiffany snaps. "You said it yourself."

"So I did. But it's the old Cretan paradox. If I say I always lie, well, hell, sometimes I gotta tell the truth. And besides, all I did was say you could *maybe* be president someday. No guarantees. Just a possibility. It'd be up to you."

"Yeah? Dunt worry 'bout it. Last thing I wanna be, some stinking pol."

The rabbi is scowling, his lips set in a thin line, as if he's forcing himself to stay silent. In her mind Tiffany is seeing not cheering crowds and the television appearances, but a line of her fellow officers saluting as someone hands her a folded flag and antique rifles fire. The most seductive image of all, however, is a simple green and white railway sign: Owens Air Force Base, next station. In that world, back in the California that Nick persists in calling her home, everyone knows that she's one of the best damn pilots that ever flew.

"Ah get out of here! Get stuffed! None of this crap's true anyway. Who the hell are you guys, talking all this crazy bull?" Her voice shakes in her throat like a living thing. "Leave me alone!"

Hauling her bag she wrenches herself forward and strides off, as fast as she can, so pitifully slow.

"Tiffany, my dear, don't hurt yourself! We won't follow you."

She glances back to see the rabbi grabbing Nick's arm and making good his word with surprising strength, but still she strides on, gasping for breath, dragging the bad leg, until she turns a corner and can no longer see them standing, far behind her. *Get thee behind me, Satan. Ohmigawd. I dunt believe this. Can't believe this. Can't.* And yet, of course, she does believe it, finds her traitor of a mind's eye picturing the green and white sign and, as she pants up the last block to home, the cheering crowds as well. In that world the power plant still stands, in that world a hundred thousand people still live who died in this one, and all because Captain Tiffany Owens pulled off a miracle, shooting down solo three enemy planes before they could arm and fire a single missile.

When she gets back to the apartment, Mark is awake, half-dressed, shaving, his baritone booming in the tiny bathroom.

"Run to the stars! Stars they be a-fallin! All on that day!" A gasp for breath at verse's end, then the next one. "Oh sinner man, where you gonna run to? Oh sinner man, where you gonna— Hey Tiff, that you?"

"Sure is. Why the hell you singing a morbid fucking ugly song like that one, anyway?"

Half-bearded in white soap Mark's face appears round the doorjamb.

"You okay?" he says mildly. "Oh hey, you been to the store! Great! Thanks, hon."

"Oh shut up." She slings the bag, dangerously hard, onto the kitchen table. "I been to the store, yeah, and on the way back I met the Devil. Whaddya think of that?"

"I think maybe you gone and taken too many pills. Doctor warned me 'bout this. Want me to call the hospital?"

"No. Just shut up and shave. Just making a joke, man. You and your lousy hymns."

The face retreats, and she hears wash water running. Apparently, though, he believes that indeed, she was merely joking in a bad-tempered way, because when he comes out, wiping his face on a torn towel, he's taken the time to finish shaving.

"Well, that ain't the most cheerful number from my days in the choir, no." He is grinning at her. "Wanna hear 'Let the Sun Shine In'?"

"Ah shut up." But she finds herself smiling in return. "I'm sorry. Kinda tired me out, walking all that way."

"Yeah, I bet. And we got to go to your mom's next. I mean, I'll be real glad to see Amber and the kids. They ain't seen you since you started walking."

"Hey, that's right. That'll be cool, yeah."

Tiffany sits down and takes the bread out of the bag, sets the milk bottle upright and just so while Mark gets out a pair of plates and a couple of mugs. He's brewed up Postum in a glass carafe, dark, steaming, foaming as he swirls it round to pour. Tiffany puts an inch of milk in each mug just ahead of him.

"We need to leave early," she says. "Buy some wine to take with us. Think we can find some chocolate for the kids?"

"On the street, maybe."

"Oh, hey, right. I've got cash. I think." She starts patting her pockets, half-expecting the wad of bills to have vanished like elf-gold. "Yeah, here it is, all right. Smells a little musty, huh?"

"Where you get that?"

"From that guy I told you about. Nick whatever his name is. He said he owed it to me. I sure dunt remember loaning it to him, but he said I did. Maybe he was in Basic with me. Jeez, wish I could remember."

Mark nods, believing her lie so easily that the guilt stabs like another pulled muscle. But what is she supposed to tell him? The truth? She cannot bear to repeat that even to herself.

"Better stop in Braziltown, then," Mark says. "Never know what you gonna find for sale there."

Even though the refugees have settled all over the city, everyone calls the old Mission District "Braziltown." The neighborhood was Irish way back in the Twentieth Century, then Hispanic, then a mixed bag of Asian cultures, then Rumanian, and now finally Brazilian as waves of refugees broke on the San Francisco docks and flowed down this flat and sunny valley at the city's heart. Even though it suffered perhaps the least of any neighborhood in the Great Quake, it was a barrio for so long than none of the dispossessed rich even thought of settling there. Now, sixteen years later, with the city rebuilt, more or less, Mission Street crawls along through a welter of old wooden buildings, patched and propped, and new poured stucco-crete "temporary" structures, the kind that always, somehow or another, become permanent once the emergency that spawned them ends. The cubes and blocks of stucco-crete have flowered, though, into purples and reds and blues; huge murals cover every windowless wall, graffiti sprawl across doorways and overrun the commercial signs plastered on storefronts. For Tiffany, all these colors, the jumbled blocks of buildings, the crowds oozing their way down the street, men standing on street corners, gossiping and smoking tobacco, women crouched over blankets strewn with contraband, children racing through, shouting and pushing—the entire scene disintegrates into blots and splotches, streaks of movement, glints of light, all pulsing, throbbing, heaving like the chest of some vast and terrified animal, while the pitiless sun pounds down and robs the world of shadow. As the trolley bus lurches and hoots its way down the middle of the street, she slumps down in her seat and clutches the string bag, clanking with wine bottles, to her chest. Mark watches, frowning a little.

"Tiff, if you dunt wanna get off and shop, we dunt have to."

"I wanna get something for the kids. I know you do, too. Besides, I might be better off, outside and off this goddamn bus."

"Well, I dunno bout that."

In two more blocks the decision's made for them. On the corner where 30th Street dead-ends into Mission stands an enormous stucco-crete structure, a heap of cubes, one square tower, thrown together in an old parking lot to replace the big Catholic church on Dolores Street that went down in the quake. Over the years the devout have paid artists to cover the bleak flat walls with trompe l'oeil paintings of fluted columns, baroque arches, swags of fruit and flowers, bas-relief angels, and scalloped niches complete with faux marble portrayals of various saints, all this decoration earthquake proof, now, frescoed deep into the walls beyond

the power of St. Andrew and his fault to shake it loose. Just past
29th the bus stops with a squeal of brakes and a lurch. Out in
front of the church, spilling down the street and across the street,
a crowd sways in place to music and waits, faces upturned to the
pink tower with its painted bells in painted niches. The bus driver
can lay on her airhorn all she wants, can lean out the window and
scream her lungs out, too: the crowd will not part.

"Hell," Mark says. "Well, might's well get out and shop,
then."

Swearing, muttering, scowling at the Brazilians crouched at
the back of the bus, the rest of the passengers are getting up and
filing for the doors. The Brazilians—two young men in khaki
pants and sweat-stained tank tops, and then, some seats away, a
family, father in a white suit, mother in a flowered dress, four
daughters in starched ruffled dresses—wait until most are out and
off. The family cowers against the blame they're taking for this
crowd of their countrymen; the young men swagger down the
aisle, waiting, perhaps hoping, for someone to insult them openly.
Tiffany would like to say something reassuring to the family, but
she knows no Portuguese, an infuriating language, or so the average bilingual San Franciscan thinks of it. It looks so much like
Spanish that it seems you should be able to understand what these
people are saying, that you should be able to speak to them without effort, but of course, you can't, and they can't reply, either,
can only stare with miserable eyes as people shout at them in Español or speak Pocho very very slowly as if the Brazilians could—
if they really wanted to, if they only wouldn't be so stubborn—understand at last. As Tiffany steps off the bus in the
shelter of Mark's broad back, she feels as if she's diving into a sea
of Portuguese, the soft waves of voices she cannot decipher lap-
ping her round.

"We're getting 'cross this street now." Mark has been changed
back into a Marine sergeant by the alchemy of danger. "Tiff, come
on." He grabs her shoulder with one broad hand. "Move!"

At that moment music breaks out in a blare of brass, thunders with a hundred snare drums, jogs and jigs and syncopates as the crowd yells and sways. By peering through the packed dancers Tiffany can see that up on the church steps stand two huge box speakers. A fat priest wearing a black soutane and a pair of headphones huddles over a quadro off to one side. Swearing, glaring, shoving when he has to, Mark gets them around the back of the bus. The crowd, smelling of sweat and tobacco and rum, presses close, turns solid, one impenetrable body swaying back and forth on the dance floor of the street, but somehow Mark snakes and wiggles and slides their way across, yelling the few words of Portuguese he picked up during the war, snarling at someone here, smiling thanks at someone else there. At last they reach the far sidewalk, but making it to the bus stop, their transfer point, only two blocks but a universe away, lies beyond even Mark. By sheer Marine arrogance he manages to shove their way to a block of old wooden flats with a sheltered doorway, a tiny porch. He pushes a place clear for Tiffany to stand, two steps up and behind him, safe from the crowd, at a tolerable distance from the samba music bellowing out of the speakers.

"Well hell," Mark screams. "Guess we're going to see what's goin' on whether we want to or not. Good thing we left home early."

Tiffany nods and rests her hands on his shoulders. The crowd is clapping to the rhythm, rocking back and forth, but no one sings, no one yells, no one even smiles, really. The faces that Tiffany can see are solemn, wide-eyed, expectant but never gleeful. She remembers, suddenly, that religion has something to do with this festival, that most likely the gathering celebrates the special day of one of their saints, beings as alien and innumerable to her as the stars. She looks back to the church just as the doors swing open from inside. The crowd does yell, one sharp wordless bark as a procession spills down the steps. How the crowd manages to move back and out of the way Tiffany cannot see; she's only aware of a streaming, a sea of discrete particles forming a wave of motion, parting like ebb tide around rock, flowing down the street and spreading out onto sidewalks blocks and blocks away to leave the middle of Mission Street clear.

While music pounds and pulses, painted wooden statues, each about ten feet high, ride this river down on little boats—litters draped in flowers, swaying and jerking on the shoulders of men dressed in white. Each figure wears real clothes, sewn, no doubt, by the ladies of this parish, according to some mixed iconography of Mexican Catholicism and Brazilian Candomblé. A few Tiffany recognizes: the Virgin Mary in her long blue cloak, spangled with stars, stands on the crescent moon; Jesus sails by, wearing a black top hat, his frock coat open to reveal a crucifix in the midst of the starched white ruffles of his tuxedo shirt; just behind them comes a tall, white-robed figure, wearing a triple crown and carrying a crook, who most likely represents the current pope. Others she cannot label, but each carries a palm frond in one hand. Before, behind, around each saint dance troupes of women, their loins and breasts wrapped in twists of bright cloth, yellow and orange, blue and purple, their skin glittering with spangles, their heads plumed with dyed feathers or bound round with strings of glass jewels; like birds flitting from branch to branch they twirl and kick and bob along from curb to curb. Too poor to buy their church electric generators or seats on the city council, they give dancing instead, their own flesh the offering to the word made flesh. In and among them snare drummers march in precise cadres; entire mariachi bands, their guitars and trumpets gleaming, ride by in carts pulled by teenage boys wearing white shirts and garlands of flowers round their necks. Everyone goes barefoot on the hot asphalt, all pitted, pocked, bristling with gravel. By the end of the route, their feet will be bleeding, the pain another offering to their Jesus.

Every now and then the procession crawls to a stop. The dancers sway sideways, the drummers march in place, the trumpeters tuck their instruments under one arm and catch their breath. Girls with water bottles and wet towels rush out of the crowd to wipe the faces of the men carrying the saints and give them drinks.

One of these intervals leaves a saint floating right in front of Tiffany. A towering woman, slender, with blonde hair but black skin, she carries a sword instead of a palm leaf. Her dress is white, and all around her on the street dance young women, their arms bare, their bodies encased in yards and yards of muslin, bleached bone-white, pleated and starched as stiff as cardboard, lashed down with ribbons at the bodice, tied down at the waist, but billowing out in enormous skirts almost to the ground. Barefoot, they solemnly jog in place, swaying a little with a rustle of skirts like the beating wings of giant insects. Tiffany leans down to bellow into Mark's ear.

"Who's this?"

"Santa Barbara," he calls back.

The woman next to him laughs.

"Yansen," she says. "The priests, they call her Santa Barbara, but her name be Yansen. She be one of the *orixas.*"

Tiffany hears this name as "yan san," as Mr. Yan, and she goggles at the vast image floating above her. Her mind simply cannot reconcile this figure that the priests call a saint with an Asian male name. The huge head, crowned in gold; the full mouth, smiling with a tight and secretive curve of lips; the huge blue eyes that should jar against black skin but that, somehow, fit; the sword, gleaming with salvaged aluminum foil, smoothed out and pressed over cardboard by devout hands—at that moment Tiffany feels that she should know this figure's real name, just as she feels that knowing Pocho she should understand Portuguese. If she only knew the real name, everything would be at long last clear; if she could only speak this name, all her long years of combat, first in Israel, now with her own body, would at last have meaning—she believes it suddenly, fiercely. Further down the route, the music picks up; the speakers on the church steps blare in answer; the parade moves on. As her litter-bearers break into their slow trot, the *orixa* bobs her head Tiffany's way in silent blessing.

Behind her the parade thins to one last cadre of drummers, young and a little off the beat, one last swirl of dancers, glittering green and turquoise, and then, at the very end, a press of crowd, sucked into the vacuum left by the procession, drawn inexorably after their saints and gods, dragging with them the worshippers on the sidewalk as they pass. In a few minutes Tiffany can step down from her shelter and reach Mark, who automatically catches her hand.

"Superstitious bull," he remarks. "Pretty flash, though. Makes a great parade. But jeez, they believe it all, poor bastards. Damn priests sucking them dry. The things I saw in Brazil, Tiff." He shakes his head hard. "Anyway, it be 1300 hours. We're gonna be late if we dunt hurry."

"Damn. I did want to bring the kids something."

Right near the transfer point, however, where three different bus routes meet, lies an unofficial market, a spread of blankets and old sacks, each with a vendor crouched behind it on the sidewalk. A few meters up the narrow hill of Cortland Avenue, an old woman, wrapped in a gathered striped skirt and draped in a once-white blouse, trailing torn lace, sits cross-legged behind a big basket of Mexican chocolate, kilo chunks wrapped in glazed paper, each sealed and stamped with a red and green eagle. While Mark haggles, waving a handful of the rabbi's moldy bills to show he's serious, Tiffany kneels and unwraps one packet to check for worms and rat dirt—you never know with this semilegal kind of provender, the brand passed for sale in America, yes, in the abstract, but this actual cache of chocolate has no doubt been smuggled across the border without inspection. Even though the smell of crushed almonds and sugar makes her mouth water, she won't be able to taste anything if she succumbs to the temptation of nibbling. Save it for the kids, she tells herself. Amber will doubtless ration this kilo block out for weeks to come. The haggling over, Tiffany slips the block inside her bag with the wine. The old woman counts the bills, rolls them, and tucks them into her blouse with a toothless smile.

"Did you like the procession?" she remarks in Español. "I thought the music was very pretty."

"It certainly was, yes." Tiffany struggles with the verbs, which are much more formal in the old woman's mouth than in the Pocho she knows. "I didn't know who all those saints were, though."

"Some of them weren't saints, that's why." The old woman turns suddenly sour. "Those Brazilians! Oh well, they'll learn American ways sooner or later, I suppose."

When the bus finally comes, it disgorges a flood of chattering passengers, all miffed that they've missed the procession, then stays empty except for Mark and Tiffany. Later the church will be sponsoring a carnival of sorts, with music and bingo, a major event here in the barrio. No one's going to leave until the celebrating's all over.

"We better take the long route home," Mark remarks. "Tonight this bus gonna be packed to the roof."

"Uh lord, you're right. Say, Mark? What are those *orixa* guys anyway, if they ain't saints?"

"Old African gods, come over with the slave trade, or that's what I heard, anyway, when I was in Rio. The captain of my company, he was kinda keen on all this old stuff, folklore, he called it. The church took the *orixas* right in and made them saints, because the people were gonna pray to them whether they did or not." He grins. "You could say the church baptized them, I guess. They don't miss a trick, them priests."

"Kinda like *voudoun,* then."

"Yeah, a lot like that. Some of the women, they go into trances, after dancing for hours, I think, something like that, and then the *orixas* take them over and make them say things, prophecies I guess, I dunno."

"Take them over?"

"Yeah. Lemme think. It's like the *orixas,* they live in some other world, and they need a body to get into this world, and so the women let them use theirs. A lot of crap, if you ask me, but old Captain Connors, he went and watched some ceremony, and he came back real impressed." He looks suddenly sad. "But he was a good man. And a good officer. Too damn bad, losing him like we did."

To the same Argentinean land mine that maimed LoDarryl, Tiffany thinks it was, but she cannot quite remember the story and she doesn't want to depress Mark by having him repeat it. As the bus groans its way uphill, she is thinking about Nick and the rabbi. They drank coffee, they ate bread with her. They have bodies, then. Or rather, the figures she saw seemed to have bodies. Maybe they never really ate and drank; it might have been some kind of trick. Or a neurologic hallucination. All at once she doubts the reality of what she saw or seemed to see. *But the waitress served them coffee. Could have imagined that, too.* How could they be in her world, the Devil and a holy man dead for hundreds of years? *Ger Chong sold the Devil a pack of gum.* Couldn't be. Impossible. Unless they took over someone's body like an *orixa,* an idea that strikes her as so ridiculous that she laughs aloud. Mark, wrapped in some brooding about the war, does not notice.

Tiffany's mother lives in a condominium up on University Mound, a middle-class village within the city. Although the entire complex stands inside high walls, studded with long blades of broken glass, the security there is a good bit more lax than it would be in one of the fortresses that cater to the rich. Although video cameras record their entry, and the uniformed guard does ask their names and make a show of looking them up on the list of approved visitors, he doesn't bother to call up to the flat, merely waves them through the gates. Just beyond his kiosk stands a shuttle, an electric surrey with a flat bed, wood and wrought-iron benches, and a pink-and-white ruffled roof. In the back stands a Compu-drive unit. When Mark punches in the address, the surrey starts with a hum of batteries and whines off, making its way down the middle of the lanes between white buildings roofed in black solar collection panels. Although the units sport rustic shingled entranceways, canvas awnings over wooden decks, wooden shutters over the windows, and little picket fences round real lawns, they are at root the same stucco-crete cubes as the projects lining Mission Street.

Tiffany's mother, Mandi, lives in a flat on the top floor of the southernmost building, two cubes piled up with a third cube nestled next to them to break the stark lines. When the shuttle sighs to a stop at its door, Tiffany looks up and sees her niece and nephew leaning dangerously out of a window to wave and yell.

"Aunt Tiff, Aunt Tiff! You can walk! You can walk!"

"Sure can!" she calls back. "I can do lots of stuff now."

By the time that she and Mark have gotten off the shuttle and sent it on its way back to the gate, the kids have come pounding out the front door to surround them with the illusion of an entire pack of children. As is the case with most families these days, with so many men gone off either to war or the corporate farms of the Central Valley, Amber's kids have different fathers, so that Rico, just four, is blond and blue-eyed like his mother and his aunt, while Maggie, seven and getting close to eight, has raven-dark hair, black eyes, and skin the color of teak veneer. They grab Tiffany for hugs, then dance around her as she makes her slow way across the entrance way and up the stairs. Mark brings up the rear, grinning and carrying the string bag.

"We got new games," Maggie announces. "Gramma got us new games."

"For the comp wall?" Tiffany says.

"You betski," Rico chimes in. "Space dock revels."

"Rebels, you dope. Not revels."

"You betski. And trains on fire."

"Say what?" Tiffany says.

"It's a routing game." Maggie favors her brother with a look of massive contempt. "And if you blow it the trains crash."

"Gotcha."

At the top of the stairs, Amber and Mandi stand together, Amber's honey-colored hair long and wild, Mandi's chemical blonde nipped short, turned under in a tidy wave, but they are both slender women, immaculately dressed in pressed shorts, tucked shirts. In the dim light Mandi does realize her often-expressed wish and seem as young as her daughters—if not, in fact, a little younger than Tiffany with her scars and the permanent dark circles under her eyes from the medication. They smile, hug, pull everyone into the cool refuge of a white room with tan drapes, tan furniture, and artwork in muted pastels, including the portrait of Christ obligatory these days. Mandi has stripped the walls of her collection of painted china plates, probably to spare Tiffany's fractured sight as well as sparing the plates the attentions of the kids. The empty black plastic racks hang like blank staves of music. On the long coffee table in front of the fake fireplace lie plates of food: sensible vegetables, dips, rice cakes.

"Aunt Tiff got something in that bag," Rico announces. "Smells good."

"Chocolate," Tiffany says. "But your mom be the one who gonna ration it out."

"Oh no! She mean!" Maggie is grinning even as she wails. "Ain't you, Mom?"

"As mean as I gotta be, yeah." Amber takes the bag from Mark. "And wine? Wow. You guys do it up right, huh? Thanks!"

"You really shouldn't have." Mandi grins, just a little too broadly, and her voice is just a little too light. "You really should have left all that to me."

Everyone smiles, vaguely, glancing round the room with its tangible evidence that Mandi alone makes more money than a pair of vets bring in together.

"Uh well," Mark says at last. "Wanted to chip in something."

"Of course, dear. And thank you. It was very nice. We could sit down?"

But everyone stands, hovering by the door, waiting for someone else to make the first move toward the sofas, smiling, everyone smiling while Mandi searches her younger daughter's face, studying her every scar, checking the one shoulder that's a little lower, maybe, or estimating how she's doing with the bad hand, until Tiffany feels that she once again is ten years old, running off the soccer field after school to find a mother waiting who will comment on every slop of mud, every grass stain, every bruise, every indication that her daughter cares more for sports than she ever will for her studies. Rico saves her, saves everybody, from the growing silence.

"Well, Mom, please? You gonna cut it up? Gramma, please?"

"What, love?" Mandi wrenches her gaze away, turns a little pink as if she's embarrassed herself more than anyone. "Please what?"

"Chocolate. We can smell it, you know."

Everyone laughs, grins, moves, turns this way or that.

"I'll get you some," Amber says. "You said please real nice. Why dunt you show Uncle Mark the new comp wall?"

"Oh yes, he'll like that," Mandi chirps. "Gramma will come turn it on."

Mark and Mandi collect kids and stroll across the living room toward the door leading into Mandi's office, where during the week she reviews disputed claims for the Veterans Administration. Tiffany trails behind her sister as Amber carries the bag into the tiny kitchen, all beige and black, each treasured appliance so shiny-clean that Tiffany has to blink hard against the fractured light. For a moment she sees faces grinning with silver teeth on every door and control panel.

"You okay?" Amber says.

"Sure." She leans back against the microwave's polarized glass door and watches Amber to avoid the glints and reflections that crowd upon her. "So, how was the trip up?"

"Fine. The kids are getting pretty civilized these days. Only four fights in six hours, and Rico dint even get sick on the curves out of Monterey."

"Cool."

Amber puts the wine bottles into the cooler, sets the chocolate onto the counter, and hands Tiffany the bag.

"You could take that Forty-Niner jacket off. Warm in here."

"Is it? Thanks." Tiffany crams the bag into a pocket, then slips the jacket off, lets it drop automatically onto the floor, mutters, and picks it up again. "How's the university doing? And the aggie lab? Any new projects?"

"No such luck." She wrinkles her nose. "Still the drought-resistant barley. Damn stuff keeps dying on us when we plant it anywhere but the Andes enviro-tank. But I did get a raise. And a new title. Senior geneticist."

"Congratulations. That's great. Look real good on your office door."

"You bet, but we really needed the money. The housing down in San Luis is getting so expensive. Sure wish I could afford to buy a place like this, but it's going to be a while yet."

"Mom dint offer to help?"

"Course she did. But . . . well, you know."

Automatically they both glance at the door to confirm that Mandi's still absent.

"Yeah, I do know," Tiffany says. "Gets on Mark's nerves, but she really means well. I mean, she only wants to know she's still part of our lives."

"There's more ways of paying off a debt than with money, and I just can't afford it. If you get what I mean."

Tiffany considers. As the older sister, Amber has always carried the greater part of the burden of their mother's relentless generosity and, of course, of the unspoken contracts of gratitude that go with it.

"I do get it, yeah. Just kind of sad."

"Oh, I'd never deny that. Well, I sure hope her giving you stuff dunt cause any, well, friction, I guess, between you two. I sure do like Mark."

"So do I."

They share a laugh. Amber brings down an old plastic plate from the cupboard above the sink, rummages in a drawer, finds a knife. From a distant room comes the sound of beeps, squawks, and simulated trains, punctuated by laughter. They can guess that Mark is being shown the new games.

"I'll let the kids have a little candy now," Amber goes on.
"We'll be eating later than usual, Mom says. She found a beef
roast for sale somewhere, and she's getting it cooked in the oven
over in the dining hall."

"Hell, wish I could taste it! Trust Mom to come up with something like that."

They shake their heads, marvelling, as they have for years, at
Mandi's ability to find things, whether for sale or barter, all the
small details of civilian life that were once mundane but are now
exotic, shoved to one side in the production schedules that keep
America's profitable armies supplied. Real vinyl rain ponchos,
clothes for antique Barbie dolls, metal cookie cutters, freeze-dried
coffee, copper pennies for a pair of loafers, a tetherball set for the
Girl Scout camp or metal paper clips for a hospital charity drive,
belt buckles, computer cables, aspirin, and those little rubber tips
for the feet of garden chairs—if such a thing exists somewhere in
the Bay City's vast network of legitimate stores and discount
warehouses, or if it's for sale on the street without being in a
downright black market, Mandi will, eventually, track it down for
a child or a close friend or a good cause, though never, by some
quirk of her own, for profit.

"Mom, Rico's cheating again!" Maggie comes barrelling into
the kitchen. "He is he is he is, and Uncle Mark won't let me hit
him."

Amber gives her a fractured chunk of chocolate. When the
wail stops, plugged at the source, she hands over the plate of splinters and chips she's hacked from the block.

"Take this into the comp room and share. With Uncle Mark,
with Gramma, and with Rico."

"Rico gonna grab his. Dunt worry." Maggie licks her fingers,
balancing the plate precariously in her other hand as she dances
out of the room. "Thanks, Mom."

"What were we saying?" Amber is watching Maggie's progress
across the white carpets in the living room.

"Roast beef. Mom finding stuff."

"Oh yeah." Amber pauses, pushing a long wisp of hair back from her forehead with her little finger. "I guess I am tired, today."

"Long ride on the train, especially when you got kids."

They both nod again; Amber licks her own fingers clean.

"There are towels, sweetie." Mandi appears in the doorway. "In that niche by the blender. Yes, just there. Tiff, your Mark is being an absolute martyr, playing with the kids. They certainly toe the line when he's here."

"You can take a man outta the Marines," Amber remarks. "But you can't take the Marines outta the man."

"I suppose so, yes." Mandi's smile wavers, fades. In the bright overhead light she suddenly looks her age as the wrinkles round her eyes fill with shadows. "Tiff, darling, give me that jacket."

"I can hang it up, Mom. No problem."

Mandi's hand stays outstretched.

"I'll just take it into the bedroom for you. I'm going that way to the necessary."

Tiffany gives her the jacket, which she shakes, smooths, folds over her arm.

"I was just going to do some wash for the kids. I can throw this right in, can't I? No use you having to take it to the laundromat and use up your ration on it."

She is smiling, but Tiffany is suddenly aware that the jacket is dirty, that she really should have washed it last week sometime, that perhaps she never should have worn a sports-team jacket here to her mother's house.

"Mom, I got some stuff in the pockets."

"Of course you do, dear." Automatically her manicured hand goes fishing through them. "What's this? A card for a bookstore I've never heard of? You really have to tell me what it's like when you go, sounds just great. Couple of notes. Put those in your pants pocket, dear, so you don't lose them. And a tennis ball?"

Tiffany snatches the squeezer back, covers the snatch with a grin.

"Something to show you, Mom. Remember the bad hand?"

Amber and Mandi both watch, wide-eyed, as breathless as children entranced by a trapeze artist, as Tiffany squeezes the ball, tosses it into the air, and catches it again.

"All right!" Amber claps, solemnly.

Mandi's eyes fill with tears, wiped quickly on the corner of Tiffany's jacket, but she keeps smiling, a natural grin, now, of pride, pure pride. It is at these moments that Tiffany remembers how much she's always loved her mother.

"That's so wonderful. Oh honey, you've done such a good job. I knew you'd put yourself back together, I always knew it, no matter what that doctor said. I'm so happy. It's just . . ." She sniffs loudly. "Well. Be right back. You girls could even sit down, y'know."

While Mandi trots off to the rear of the flat, the two sisters trail into the living room, stand for a moment at the picture window, looking out and over the white wall, glittering with glass, then down the long slope of tangled streets and houses to the blue and misty bay in the far distance. The two former points, or brand-new islands, Hunter's and Candlestick, rise from the swamps and mudflats of low tide at the edge of the view. From the comp room comes laughter and the sound of electronic music. One of the gamers has reached a new level, most likely.

"Say, Ambi? What's Mom got against Mark, anyway?"

Amber winces, reaches out to straighten the folds of a drape.

"Well, it's something. Dunt lie to me, will you?"

"Never. Dunt worry." With a little sigh Amber goes back to studying the view. "Just that he was enlisted personnel, not an officer. Nothing more than that."

Tiffany lets out her breath in a sharp puff.

"Shoulda guessed that."

The silence again, the things they daren't speak here where they might be overheard at any moment. Across the sky, over the East Bay hills, an airplane writes a line of white.

"Must be a Navy plane, if it's based over there," Tiffany remarks.

"Hum? Oh. Oh yeah, I see it now. You know, something I wanted to ask you. You think you'll ever fly again?"

"I dunt know, but I dunt think so. Not well enough for combat, that's for sure. I mean, ferrying planes into a combat zone. But I dunt think I could even be an instructor. Not the way I am now."

"Oh. That must hurt."

"Yeah. No use pretending it dunt."

"I'm real sorry about that, but Tiff? You're gonna hate me for saying this, but I got to. I'm glad you're not going back. I'm glad nobody's ever going to be shooting at you again."

"Well, hell, I ain't gonna miss that part myself."

The plane disappears into the sun. The vapor trail remains, an arc across the sky. *A lonely impulse of delight drove to this rapture in the clouds.* Another line of poetry whose source she cannot remember. In this world does that poem even exist? The question strikes her like a blow. If the rabbi and Nick should, by some vast stretch of the reality she's always known, be real themselves in the different and terrible reality they have spoken of, if this world is not the actual world into which she was born, then any number of things she's been taking for granted may or may not have changed.

"What's wrong?" Amber says, and sharply.

"Oh, uh, muscles in my arm just cramped up. Just a little." She makes a show of rubbing the bad arm with the good hand. "Say, Ambi? Do you remember where this line comes from? It's a poem, I think, a real old poem. 'A lonely impulse of delight drove to this rapture in the clouds.' "

"This tumult in the clouds." Mandi trots back, a glass of mineral water in her hand.

"Not rapture?"

"Well, I think it's tumult. We can look it up when the kids are done with the comp. Willy Yeats wrote it, darling, and you always loved it so much. The only poem you ever memorized, and you were what? thirteen, that's right, and Miss Rodriguez was so pleased. Do you remember Miss Rodriguez?"

"No, 'fraid not. Long time ago now."

"Such a good teacher. I was amazed at how many poems about airplanes she managed to find. I don't remember how the Yeats starts, I'm afraid, but there's this bit: 'Those that I guard I do not love, those that I fight I do not hate.' Then there's a bit I can't remember. And then 'Nor law nor duty bade me fight, nor public men nor cheering crowds, a lonely impulse of delight' and so on. I think that's how it goes. I can't remember the title, though."

"It sure fits, dunt it? My life, I mean. Weird, how a little kid would sort of know. What was in store for me, I mean. Though I dunno about that line about not loving those you guard. I liked Israel a whole lot."

"Yes, you always said so in your letters."

They stand together, watching the vapor trail turn soft and dissolve. In the bay below red-and-white grain tankers crawl along, heading north toward the channel out and west. Tiffany is so relieved to find her memory confirmed that she could laugh aloud. All at once more returns to her.

"Hey, I remember the title! 'An Irish Airman Foresees his Death.' "

Amber and Mandi turn just a little pale, just a little tight around the mouths.

"Uh, well, sorry, I forgot how that would sound to you guys. It's not like I did die. Not permanently, I mean."

"Close enough, dear. Would you two like something to drink? There's mineral water. And cola for the kids. Amber, do you mind them having all these sweets? No? Well, it is Veterans' Day, after all. I'll just go see if they want something to drink. And Mark. Poor dear Mark, trapped in there all this time. I'm sure he'd like a beer. I'll just go get him one."

And she is gone, gliding across white carpets, one hand automatically touching her hair, tucking under a random curl. Just as automatically Tiffany and Amber drift from the window and sit down on the sofa—just in time, Tiffany realizes. The bad leg is aching, and she can feel her back tightening as well. Amber is watching her closely.

"Want something to drink? I'll get up and get it."

"You know, if you wouldn't mind?"

"No problem. Just sit there and rest."

When her sister goes into the kitchen, their mother's voice greets her. As she listens to them chatter about drinks, Tiffany finds herself thinking of another Mandi, another Amber. Do they really exist, there in that other world which also includes Owens Air Services Base? Is there a Mandi and an Amber sitting in a flat just like this one in that world, remarking to one another that they wished Tiffany were alive to join them while the children route imaginary trains with no Uncle Mark to watch?

"Over a year, now." Tiffany has spoken aloud again. She looks up to find Amber standing in front of her, holding out a glass of mineral water. "Sorry. I dint mean—"

"It's okay, Tiff." Amber hands over the glass and sits down. "You thinking about, well, the accident again?"

Tiffany has a sip of water. The accident. Neither her mother nor her sister have ever been able to face the truth that the crash was no accident, that the Emirate pilots had every conscious intention of blowing her plane out of the sky. The only accidental factor was her unarmed plane happening to be in their way . . . but in that other world, that event was no happenstance. If that world exists, her fully-armed plane was meant to be there, on deliberate patrol. In that world, in some dusty white city in the Emirate, where it's now the middle of the night, there are mothers and sisters lying awake, perhaps, to mourn the sons and brothers she shot down.

"I mean, like," Amber is still talking, picking over each word. "A year, it's not that long. To get over what you've been through."

"Not me I'm thinking 'bout. Can I ask you something? What if I'd died in that crash, really died, I mean, like there wasn't enough left to resurrect? How would you feel now? After a year, I mean? Would it still bug you?"

"What? Damn right we'd still miss you." Amber sounds completely taken aback. "I mean, look at Mom, when you remembered the title. She turned white, dint she?"

"But look, you wouldn't be . . . well, I dunno. You wouldn't be like, crying all the time and stuff, would you? And Mom, either. Especially Mom. I mean, life's gotta go on."

"Of course it does." Amber frowns, thinking. "Everyone loses somebody, sooner or later, everyone, and you can't just stop living."

"Right. I was hoping you'd feel that way."

"Well, it's like when Dad was killed. Do you remember any of that?"

"Only a little." Yet of course Tiffany wonders if she remembers anything at all that happened with this Amber, this Mandi. "I was too young."

"I was afraid Mom was going to die." Amber's voice turns flat and weak. "I really was, she cried so much. And the preacher came twice a day, just to see if we were okay and she was managing. I mean, she was alone and everything, really alone, with her own mom . . . well you know."

Tiffany does not know. She realizes in a kind of panic that her mother's mother, Grandma Janet as she remembers her, has in this world some new story, some unknown shame judging from the drop in Amber's voice, that she has never heard.

"Tiff, what's wrong? Something is."

"Yeah, but I dunt know how to say it. I was just. Ah hell, forget it. I feel so dumb, all of a sudden."

Amber stares over the rim of her glass for a long moment, then finally drinks, looks up with a smile as Mandi comes to join them, perching on a chair nearby. Tiffany feels a sudden need to make amends, to repair the moment that she blames herself for shattering.

"Mom, how's work treating you? Must be pretty good, if you got a new comp."

"Well, yes, I've been pretty busy, and it looks like old Paula Bronowski's going to retire at last. I mean, my dears, she must be eighty if she's a day."

"And you got a chance at a promotion?"

"Oh." Mandi smiles delicately. "I'm working on it."

"In the bag, then," Amber says, grinning. "In the bag."

For some while they talk of work, of Amber's research and Mandi's role as advocate for those denied veterans' benefits on one pretext or another, yet both of them seem on edge, glancing Tiffany's way, speaking in chopped sentences, as if they realize that this talk of their important jobs, the succoring of widows and orphans here at home or developing new sources of food for a teeming, starving Latin America, leaves Tiffany out, moves her to the edge of their lives, where her only job is recovery at taxpayers' expense. Everyone is grateful when a blare of sound interrupts them: Maggie trotting in, the office door left open behind her.

"I be sick of *Space Rebels*," she announces. " 'Sides, this way Uncle Mark gets to play."

"That's nice of you, darling," Mandi murmurs. "Going to sit down with us?"

Grinning, Maggie flops onto the couch between her aunt and her mother. Amber reaches out, only half-thinking, to run her fingers through her daughter's hair, to draw her into the circle of women that has always been the real heart, the real center of their lives, that unmoving point on which they may stand and watch the comings and goings of men temporarily loved. With a sigh Tiffany leans back, listening to the honks and beeps, the bursts of music and simulated voices, the simulated bombs and laser fire coming from the other room. Once she ventured out beyond the circle, but the fortunes of war have thrown her back again, for good this time, she supposes. Eventually she will have to figure out what she will do here. Unless of course she chooses to move on to another world entirely.

"Tiff darling?" Mandi's voice, a slash of worry through her thoughts. "Are you all right? You look so pale, dear."

"Do I? Well, sorry. Just a little tired, that's all. Put in a long week at the clinic."

They are all watching her, even young Maggie, slewing round on the couch in imitation of her mother's concern. Mark appears in the door, Rico trailing behind him, clinging to his hand. He must have overheard Mandi's remark, Tiffany supposes.

"You need to go home, hon?"

For her own sake she would say yes, but Rico looks so heartsick at the thought of losing his uncle's company, the attention of one of the few men he knows well, that she manages a smile.

"Not yet, no. I mean, Mom went and got this dinner, least we can do is eat it, huh?"

"Well, darling, only if you're sure. . . ." Mandi is leaning forward, her eyes searching her daughter's face.

"Tell you what? Think I could lie down for a little while?"

A flurry, a wave breaking, a wave fashioned of concern, of voices, of children's hugs, of standing up and feeling dizzy, the wave sweeping her with Mark's help down the hall to Mandi's own room, where her mother plumps pillows and brings out an afghan—and then, at last, she is alone, the wave spent, lying in the semidark behind a closed door, watching mottled shadows from the curtained window fall across the pink and white afghan, across the peaks and valleys formed by her own body. The land of counterpane, another poem, she thinks, one her mother read them when they were small, if indeed this mother did read poems in this world. *She must've. She knew the Yeats. Yeats not yeets, Keats not kates. Told us that, too.* In other rooms, old flats in those days, with windows that often stuck, and doors that hung all angled to the floor, flats that a widow with two children could afford on her Civil Service salary, small then, before the promotions. But every night, stifling yawns, pausing to rub aching eyes, she would read to them before they went to sleep, read poems and stories of other times, wonder tales, rather than the sad stories that Tiffany can tell herself now.

In another world a mother has put her loss behind her, or, as much behind her as any mother can ever put a daughter's loss, and gone on with her life. In that other world a mother no doubt will go to the opening ceremonies for the base named after her daughter. She will wear a grey suit and sit on a wooden platform near a podium while the Air Services Academy band plays. Right behind her will sit the hero's sister and her two children—her two beautiful children, the newspeople will call them. The mother will receive a folded flag, the Bear Flag of the California Republic, from the commander of her daughter's squadron and hold that flag decorously upon her lap during the speeches. She will bring the flag home and put it away in the cedar chest with the similar flag that came home from Rumania over her husband's coffin. No doubt she will cry while she does so, sob out loud for old grief remembered, then wash her face and take comfort in the presence of her beloved grandchildren.

Unless, of course, this next story becomes true. In that world a dazed mother, still in something like shock from being reunited with the daughter that she'd long given up for dead, will put on a pink suit to sit on the platform, but in a chair slightly behind that of the daughter herself. The Bear Flag will be flying free in the wind, rather than folded in a lap, as the Air Services Academy band plays. There will still be speeches, but the last of them will be delivered by the daughter, standing straight and proud, since she will be able to lean on the podium. Unfortunately, that story has its logical correlate: in this world, in America, a mother does not know that she is on the verge of losing her daughter yet once again, that some mysterious and utterly unforeseen event, engineered by the Prince of Lies, is about to sweep her daughter away forever, the same daughter that was already snatched twice, not once but twice, from the jaws of death by medical science. In this world, no officer will hand her a folded flag. The Air Force Academy band will not play. She will not have the Stars and Stripes and Maple Leaves to lay into the aforementioned cedar chest with the politically outdated, unfoliated Stars and Stripes that came home from Rumania.

The daughter lies on a flowered bedspread and decides that none of these stories can possibly be true. Their truth depends for its existence upon another, even more peculiar story, that the Devil and Reb Akiba have come to earth to tell the daughter tales in the first place. As much as she enjoys the story of Owens Air Services Base and her brilliant performance in her last dogfight, she will have to label it wishful thinking. Or compensation? Not quite that word, but a fancier label, one she heard from the psychotherapist assigned to the resurrected in their first weeks back alive. Compensomething. Compensatory fantasy. Wishful thinking dressed up to go to dinner. If only she'd been given a fully armed plane. If only they'd let her fly combat the way she knew she could fly. If only. And Old Nick came to tell her that it was indeed true. But the rabbi? Why would he come to reinforce a lie? Because he wasn't really there. Neither of them.

As the curtains stir in the window and mottled shadows drift across the bed, she reminds herself that she, however, is here now, in her mother's room, in the only world in which she can truly believe. She makes herself be aware of her body. *Head. Back of the head. Eye. Mouth. Tooth. Hand. Palm of the hand. Nail. Window. Door. House. Sword. Snake. Ox. Camel. Fish. Fishhook. Water. Field. Tent-peg. Tally mark. And the one I can never remember the name for. Lamed? Yeah, Lamed. Something to do with oxen, dunt it? Dunt matter. The twenty-two letters with which God created the universe. The infinite letters with which It created all the universes.*

For a moment Tiffany wonders if she's going to scream. Instead, she falls asleep, with the complete suddenness of a combat veteran who knows what it means to grab sleep whenever she can.

On Monday morning, when Tiffany reaches the clinic, she finds that she's been scheduled for neuro rehab first thing, as Gina's still working with the new arrivals up in diagnostics. Tired as she is from the weekend, she's just as glad to sit down and play video games, once she gets used to the weight of the monitors and the sticky feel of electrodes. At first the game goes badly, and her mind drifts, thinking of her sister. They would like to spend tomorrow evening together, go out to dinner alone, just the two of them, to talk. Mark has already agreed; he'll go to LoDarryl's for the game on TV. Mandi will no doubt feel hurt. When monitors shriek and complain, registering her lack of concentration, she forces herself to pay attention to the small purple alien and his enemies. He seems easier to order around today, moves faster, ducks quicker, dashes through the maze as if he somehow knew that his little electronic life depends on it. All at once she realizes that she has him at the door without a monster in sight. He slams himself against it, the door pops open, the screen changes. The maze lies behind him. What stretches ahead is a long tunnel, grey and cold and seemingly endless, but all along, on either side, there are doors.

"Captain?"

"Damn!"

"Oh no, I'm sorry." Hazel Weng-Chang stands behind her. "What have I done?"

"Nothing." Tiffany hits the save button hard. When the screen freezes, she whistles under her breath and turns to give Hazel a smile. "Sorry. I just got to the next level."

"Wonderful! Doctor's going to be glad to hear that! Which is, by the way, why I'm here. She's got hospital duty this afternoon. She wants to see you now. Okay?"

"Sure, fine with me."

In her office, Dr. Rosas is sitting behind her desk, cluttered with data disks, a stack of papers, a couple of books. Tiffany realizes that this disorder, left for her to see, is a test of some sort. Most likely Rosas changed the time of their appointment on purpose, too; once such a change would have disoriented her. She smiles, sitting down, glancing at the desktop again. It all makes perfect visual sense.

"You look good this morning, Captain," Rosas says. "How was your weekend?"

Here is the moment of truth, the crux, when Tiffany should tell Rosas about her peculiar hallucinations, her vivid mental creations of the Devil and the Rabbi Akiba, her strange delusion that these figures have spoken to her of other worlds.

"Well, pretty good, really," she says instead. "Had a great time with my sister on Sunday. But . . ." she hesitates only briefly. "But I had a lot of pain in the bad leg on Sunday morning. I kinda gave in to temptation and ran about a block, just to find out what it would feel like."

The doctor rolls her eyes to heaven but smiles.

"Well, now you know what it feels like. Still hurt?"

"No, it eased up round noon."

"Good. But before you try running again, let's build up some more muscle mass, okay? Gina will let you know when it's time for track and field."

They share a laugh.

"Anything else?"

"Well, I was doing some thinking. Everyone says I keep making all this progress, doing better than they ever thought I could, right?"

"Yeah, that's sure true. Our star pupil."

"But I started thinking about what I'm gonna do next, when I'm not doing therapy anymore. And I know I could still fly, if only I *could* fly. You know? The data's still there. It's the wiring that's no good." She holds up the formerly bad hand. "And the meat."

"Well, you're making tremendous progress in physical therapy. I wouldn't rule out a complete recovery there, no, I certainly wouldn't."

"But the wiring?"

Rosas sighs, looks down, straightens the edges of the papers.

"I can't promise anything."

"Tell me something—honest, I mean. Think I'll ever be able to fly again?"

"No." Rosas looks up, her eyes sad pools in the shadowed light. "I really don't. I can't see your brain healing enough to take a cybernode, and I can't see your reflexes ever being as fast, as steady, as they used to be. But Captain, you've proved me wrong before, you know. I said you'd never get that hand back, didn't I?"

Tiffany smiles and clenches her fingers, but the smile is a sham to ease Rosas's feelings. When the doctor made her pronouncement about the hand, Tiffany knew, in some deep and wordless way, that the doctor was wrong, that if she fought and clawed her way toward health, she would prove the doctor wrong. Now, she feels only grief for her lost skies.

She has, however, one more authority to consult. Much later, as she's leaving the hospital, she remembers that she told Rosas nothing about her hallucinations. There is something she wants to ask them first, before she tells the doctor the truth, before the doctor powers up her comp unit to access ROM graphics and explain these hallucinations away once and for all as symptoms of her condition, as a particularly irksome and detailed glitch in the wiring. She takes it as a given that once the doctor does explain them away, she herself will believe that they don't exist, no matter how compelling it seems that they do exist, no matter how much sense this story of their existence makes of all her shattered memories, her scattered thoughts. She is, first and foremost, a soldier, and Rosas is now, in this peculiar war of recovery she's fighting, her commanding officer to be implicitly obeyed. Until then, however, she will fall back on another military rule, a very ancient one: what commanding officers don't know about, they can't countermand.

In another world the powers that be are building Owens Air Services Base out of the ruins of Los Angeles; here, in this nonsovereign California, the same base will exist, but with another name: the two bases, the two names, each a different letter in the long chains that speak the universe. And she, one person, not important enough, really, to be called a letter, some small diacritical mark, maybe, a tiny accent, a rough breathing—she, or so they say, must choose where she will fall in the long discourse of the worlds. So they say.

As she waits for the bus, she keeps looking round her, expecting Nick and Akiba to come walking up the long slope of street. Once the bus arrives, and she boards, she expects to see them sitting in the back, waiting for her. All during the ride round by the ocean, the turn and the long journey east, she finds herself tensing every time the bus stops to take on passengers, finds herself craning her neck to peer around the standees and check out new arrivals. Logically, she supposes, if Nick and Akiba are hallucinations, she should be able to call them up by thinking about them, to invoke them with their names and images from whatever dark place in her mind it is that they live, but no matter how hard she concentrates, they never appear. All at once she realizes that what she's managed to conjure up is a missed bus stop, that the trolley is crossing Arguello a good long ways beyond her transfer point. She starts to rise and reach for the cord, remembers *Hunter's Night*, sits down again. She finds the card of the EuroFaire Bookshop, restored to the breast pocket of the newly-washed Forty-Niner jacket, and checks the address: just off Geary on Masonic, only a few blocks farther on.

Since Tiffany hasn't been in this part of town in years, it takes her a while to orient herself after she leaves the bus. She stands at the crest of one hill, looks east along wide grey Geary Boulevard, which runs downhill through a jumble of stucco-crete cubes, cardboard shacks, temporary shelters of all sorts cluttering round the ruins of an old hospital, then hits a valley green with vegetable gardens and small trees sprouting among rubble. She can just pick out a white-and-orange trolley, trundling across to meet the bus she's just left. Far far at the edge of the view another hillside rises, patched green and grey with housing and weeds, shacks and gardens, in equal measure. She can remember being a small child and standing at this same bus stop, watching electric cars rush by on the now silent streets, looking east toward downtown and seeing, peeking over the rise of that distant hill, the tops of tall grey buildings, gleaming with windows. Now she sees blue sky and an empty crest. In that other world, could there be money to rebuild downtown, civilian money for investing in a city that here in this world the military no longer needs and thus refuses to repair? Probably not, if there in that world she flew to defend a foreign country. She cannot imagine a world in which American troops fight for some reason other than cash. In that world, if it exists, she, the combat pilot, took even greater risks than the other Tiffany, the mere ferryman, did in this one, and not for love nor duty, but for only the chance to fly. In both worlds, equally desperate for fuel, civilian airlines must no longer exist.

With a shrug she pulls out the card again, checks the address, turns and walks down Masonic, leaving the Geary view behind for a welter of shops and offices, eking out a marginal business in the stucco-crete cubes left from the downtown relocation after the quake. She finds the bookshop on the top floor of an old wooden house. At the head of a chipped and dusty mahogany staircase she lingers on a landing piled with wooden crates of sale books, glances at the titles while she pants and finally catches her breath. Most of the books are French, German, Italian, or one of the many languages that use the Cyrillic alphabet, which she can't read. Scattered throughout, though, are Euro-English titles, mysteries, cookbooks, romances, serious-looking histories, and even a bird guide. The books look so promising that she's afraid to go in. For so long now she's searched for *Hunter's Night* that finding it would make a rip through the fabric of her daily life.

Before she can turn and head down the stairs, a young black woman, dressed in a blue and green dashiki, her head wrapped in matching cloth, appears in the open door.

"Help you with something, ma'am?"

Tiffany finds herself caught by the demands of civility.

"Well, yeah. I'm looking for a science fiction novel that's probably a Euro book. You guys carry something like that?"

"We got some SF, yeah. Come on in."

Tiffany limps into the store, and for a moment the only open space that she can see is the narrow strip in front of the counter. The rest of the room appears to her sight as solid walls and towers of books, looming and leaning. The clerk shoves a box to one side with her foot, then slips behind the counter.

"What's the name?"

"Oh. Uh, here. I got it written down." Tiffany fishes through the cargo pockets of her pants, finds the slip of paper, and hands it over.

"I'll just run it through ROM. I seen that name, Allonsby, but I dint know he wrote a novel."

The comp unit hums, sighs, throws words onto a screen.

"That's weird," the clerk says. "No book by that name in

print. Not in Europe, not here, not anywhere. We got the global service—everything that's been in print for ten years back shows up right here."

"Damn. Well, look, maybe I'm misremembering. I started reading it over a year ago now, got it from a USO in Greece, and maybe I just got the title wrong."

"Could be, for sure. Lemme run a check on Allonsby for you." She waits, chewing her lower lip, then shakes her head at the screen. "Good news, bad news. Only book by Allonsby listed is *Collected Stories*. Good news is we got a copy. Thirty bucks."

"Swell. I'll take it. That'll be something, anyway."

The clerk sidles out to navigate through the shoals and towers of books while Tiffany searches her cargo pockets and finds her debit card, down at the bottom where she shoved it last Saturday at the cafe. *Collected Stories* turns out to be a fat paper-book bound in slick pressboard. While the clerk transmits the sale, Tiffany stares at the cover. She remembers this picture, a dramatically cropped shot of a silver-grey fighter in the foreground, a golden planet looming in the middle in front of a vast reach of black and starry space. She remembers, however, a very different title embossed in silver over that view. This is the cover for *Hunter's Night*. She knows it, she's sure of it, she can't talk herself out of it. Or it was the cover, back in some other world.

"Ma'am? Your card?"

Tiffany realizes that the clerk's been holding her debit card out to her for some seconds. She takes it with a forced smile.

"Thanks. Sorry. Uh, nice store you got here. Have to come back sometime."

"Thank you, and please do."

Clutching the book in both hands Tiffany hurries out and clatters down the stairs, takes the wrong turn on the sidewalk, keeps walking anyway, away from Geary Boulevard, in the somewhat muddled thought of picking up the Fulton trolley on Fell Street, over by the Panhandle section of the park. After a couple of blocks she slows down and shifts the book to the formerly bad hand, tucking the fingers round, cradling it against her body. Although her fast pace has made her break out into a sweat, when she glances at the sky she sees fog coming, wisping out grey and rolling over the city with a slap of cold wind. She zips the Forty-Niner jacket up and wonders if she should go back, but her panicked dash has left her just about halfway between bus lines. Ahead down the empty street, she can see the dark line of trees marking the Panhandle; a clock in a launderette window tells her that it's only 1533. Mark won't even expect her home for another couple of hours. She might as well go for a walk in the park on the way, she decides, but by the time she reaches the narrow strip of grass and trees, she's exhausted. Next to a children's rusty swing-set and slide stands a concrete bench, painted over with graffiti, speckled with pigeon-white. She finds a reasonably clean spot, sits down, stretches out the bad leg, and sighs in sheer relief.

When she settles the book on her lap, she sees the cover again. For a long time she merely stares at it, then forces herself to pick the book up, open it, hunt through the advertisements in front until she can finally locate the title page, but nowhere does she find one of those usual listings, "By the same author." She does read, however, an introduction that explains the lack. A brilliant author, Allonsby (or so his friend, writing in memorial, describes him) the author of these pitiably few short stories, each one a gem, full of a promise broken. Allonsby was killed by a "tragically senseless and random act of terrorism in London when a street bomb exploded" some four years earlier, long before he could have written the novel Tiffany's been remembering. In fact, the friend goes on to state that when she sorted through his tapes and perma-disk after his death, she found notes, a few scattered pages, of a book he was planning on calling, there in its beginning stages, *Night of the Hunter,* "too few, too brief, too rough, alas, for me to think of publishing them here." She even remarks that of course, if indeed he'd lived to finish the project, Allonsby would have had to revise that title, reminiscent as it is of a tape dating from the so-called Golden Age of Video.

Tiffany slams the book shut and gets to her feet, tucking it back into the formerly bad hand again. Logically she knows that her wiring must have knitted itself together in some random way to produce another set of false memories. She can make up a new story, if she works at it, that will explain everything. Perhaps she was reading this very book, or perhaps one of his stories in a magazine. She could have seen a picture of the cover in an advert in that magazine, too. Later, in the Athens USO she picked up a novel by someone else and attached the now-sinister name of Albert Allonsby to that book, which was the one she never did finish and has been thinking of ever since. Even as she recites the logic of the thing, she knows deep in her heart and mind that she never heard of the little British bastard before she picked up *Hunter's Night*. She can see the cover in her mind, the same cover that graces this book of stories but with the other title embossed right at the top, and in the memory image she's holding an entire paper-book, not looking at an advert in some magazine on a screen. All at once she hates Albert Allonsby and his stupidly random death. Why couldn't he have stayed out of Harrod's, or avoided Hyde Park, or kept away from Buckingham Palace, or restrained himself from going on whatever trivial walk, errand, or adventure it was that had taken him into the arms of exploding flame and steel?

"You butthole, Allonsby!"

She's spoken aloud again. She feels the accusing blood rising in her face and looks round, but no one's near her in the park to hear. At that point she realizes that she's left the Panhandle behind, that quite unconsciously she's been walking, crossing the street without looking, wandering into Golden Gate Park proper and far away from the bus line again.

"Ah shit!"

Eucalyptus rustles in a rising wind, spice in fog scent, silver-green on grey light. A long lawn stretches silent. She pulls the good hand, a balled fist, from her jacket pocket, makes herself open it, finds red lint in her palm and the crushed slip of paper, wipes the lint off on her pants and smooths the paper out. *Hunter's Night,* Albert Allonsby. Her talisman. Spent and broken.

"This sucks, you know. It really does."

She glances round for a trash can, finds none, shoves the paper back into her pocket because it has lived there for so long and she cannot bear another tiny change, another small loss. When she sees two men, one tall and blond, the other short and dressed all in black, hurrying across the lawn toward her, she isn't even surprised. It makes sense, somehow, that they'd show up now, to rub salt in the wound.

"Tiffany, my dear!" The rabbi raises his hat to her. "You left the hospital early, did you not?"

"You guys looking for me there?"

"Yeah," Nick snaps. "Now come on, Tiff, make up your mind. We gotta hurry. The interface isn't going to stay open forever, y'know."

"Tough. I gotta have a little more data before I make up anything, pal."

Nick stares, goggling in disbelief, while Akiba smiles. Together they start walking, drifting aimlessly down an asphalt path through green lawns, past gold and purple clumps of gazanias. Distantly comes music, carillon tapes from the antique carousel hidden behind a low hill, a stand of trees.

"Listen, you guys. I wanna know something before you start yammering on my head with this parallel world crap again. Why are you here? What's it to you what world I'm in?"

"A fair question," Reb Akiba says. "You did die for Israel, you know. Twice, as a matter of fact. You must admit that dying twice is rather remarkable, even in the part of the universe where I'm currently residing. Not exactly a common event, no, not at all, not until very recently, anyway. So it seemed to me that the least I could do was make sure you were happy where you were. So I arranged a small visit. If you weren't happy, I thought, well, we could simply take you back. It's not much, I know, but one feels that one has to show one's gratitude somehow."

"Okay. And thanks. Really, thanks for the thought." She glances at Nick. "You. Explain."

"Don't you order me around!"

"Why not? I been thinking, about some of the Bible stories I heard when I was a kid. Creature. That's what the rabbi calls you, and it's true. You're as much a creature as I am. Created. It made you up, dint It? And you hate to admit it, but there you are, Its creature, and not even human. I got a lot more right to order you around, buddy, than you do me."

Nick's face flames red with rage, the pale eyes filling with blood until they gleam like coals in a fire. When the rabbi whoops aloud in laughter, Nick spins on him. He raises one hand for a blow, and it seems that his fingernails turn long, curve, become claws—then he catches himself, stopping stone-cold before the rabbi's mocking smile.

"And so what are you going to do to me, with me already dead for thousands of years?"

Nick snarls. Slowly he lowers his hand, an ordinary human hand again, and sighs. Slowly the rage drains from his face, leaving him pale, his eyes the palest thing of all, unblinking as he scowls.

"Front and center, mister," Tiffany says. "Why?"

"You're in the wrong place. I told you that. Should be reason enough. You're out of order."

"So what's it to you?"

"I cannot stand it when things get out of order. Why do you think I warned It against you and all your wretched kind? I did, you know. They're just going to cause trouble, I said. Would It listen? Oh no. Told me to mind my own business. And then, the gall of It, when I went to prove my point, there in that stupid garden, and that's all I was doing, too, trying to prove my point, It got furious."

"Totally unfair." Reb Akiba folds his hands in fake piety. "How could It?" He winks at Tiffany. "Don't take him literally, my dear. There wasn't any real garden. He's the one who's mixing his metaphors now."

"Oh stop mocking me, will you?" Nick turns back to Tiffany with a snarl. "Human? Oh yes, you are that. I'd never deny it. Big fucking deal, lady, big fucking deal. All your kind's ever done is mess everything up for everyone else. Making your damn little choices. Worlds dividing off all over the place. Huh, one of your own kind said it best, 'The trouble with organic life is it's so messy.'"

"Beg pardon, but Lewis did put that line in the mouth of a villain," the rabbi breaks in. "That character worshiped you, as a matter of fact, which showed her rather alarmingly bad taste in gods, if nothing else."

Nick growls under his breath.

"All right, next question," Tiffany snaps. "Suppose, just suppose, you guys are telling me the truth. I got a choice to make. Well, okay, won't everything split again when I choose? Won't there be four worlds instead of two? You know, like this one where I stayed, and this one where I left, and that one where I stayed away, and that one where I came back."

"Jeez," Nick mutters. "I never thought of that. Oh crap."

"No no no no," Reb Akiba says. "You see, the worlds have already split. The only question remaining is into which one you fall. Let me see, I'm the one who needs a metaphor this time. Aha. Atomic orbits. That's it. The potential for orbits exist unchanging for each element. Where each individual electron falls, now, well, that's another matter entirely. Like a page from the Torah. The letters must exist in each word in their proper order. Which drop of ink becomes which letter . . . that's not important. It doesn't alter the sense of the word, which molecule of ink the scribe uses to write it out."

"But we don't know what kind of choices this is going to influence down the line," Nick says. "Hey, old man, this is scary. What if . . ."

"No more what ifs!" Tiffany is determined to keep this discussion under her control. "Now, these parallel worlds, they can differ in a lot of small ways at once and still match in a lot of other ways, right?"

"Yeah," Nick says. "Or differ in big ways but match in all kinds of small ones. It just depends. Dunt make any sense. That's why I hate it so much."

"Okay, so tell me something." She appeals to Akiba. "I bet you know this. Just somehow I bet you do. In that other world, am I ever gonna heal enough to fly? I dunt mean ride in some lousy plane. I mean fly."

"No, dear, I'm afraid not. Your nervous system, what you call the wiring . . ." He let his voice trail away. "Well, you could probably fly an antique plane someday. One of those ones with the blade-things on the front end."

"Big deal. If I could find one that could even still get off the ground, huh? Or the gas to put in it."

They stab her to the heart, his words. They burn through her entire body worse than the pain of waking from death upon a field hospital table. Her last hope is gone. She'll never fly again, not in any world. Not that she would want to fly in combat, no. She has drunk her fill of death, could never again inflict death upon another living soul no matter who ordered her to do so, not now, having tasted it herself. But to be an instructor, say, to fly in peaceful skies, to feel again her mind meld with her plane's cybernetics until there is no mind, only flight . . . the lonely impulse. Rapture no more. Never. When both men swivel to look at her, she knows that she is weeping for the second time in a couple of days, for only the second time in a couple of years.

"It means that much?" Reb Akiba says, and softly.

"That much. The one thing I woulda left here for. The only lousy thing I ever wanted." She pulls herself together, wipes her face on the jacket sleeve. "Well, hell, then. Forget it. I ain't going anywhere."

"Yes you are too!" Nick snarls. "I'm not going to stand for this! You can't mess up two whole worlds—"

"Hey, man, chill!" Tiffany uses her best officer's voice. "Nothing's ever going to be perfect, you know. Dunt matter what world you're in."

"It coulda! It coulda been perfect! You've spoiled it, all of you. And I hate you for it! All of you! You won't do what you're supposed to. You never would and you all blame me for it, as if I wouldn't whip you all into shape if only I had the chance! Why won't you go back? You belong there, you should be there, so why the hell won't you go there?"

"Too many people here are gonna miss me too much if I go. Mark, my mother, my sister, the kids. In that other world, they be over it already, losing me, I mean. Here, they never did lose me. If I leave, they will. It'll hurt."

"Oh, that! I should have known. Your little cutesy-pie human sentiments. Love, I suppose you mean? Disgusting! What about the air base, Tiff? What about the honor? They know, back there, that you're the best damn fighter pilot that ever lived."

"Yeah so? If I dunt go back, they'll still know. And I'll know they know. So what?"

Nick's defeat is almost comical. His mouth drops like a cartoon, he closes it with a snap, tries to speak, shakes his head. For a long moment he stares at the ground, then looks up, his eyes running tears to match hers.

"Please?" he says. "Just this one little thing?"

"Ain't a little thing, not to Mark and my family."

The tears stop as suddenly as they started.

"I really wish those old legends were true," Nick snarls. "The ones about the eternal fires and all that hell crap. I would love to drag you kicking and screaming—"

"Then she'd really be out of place, creature," the rabbi breaks in. "You're contradicting yourself."

Nick screams and vanishes. One moment he was there; now he's gone, completely gone. Rabbi Akiba stops walking, considers the spot where once the Devil stood on earth, and shrugs his shoulders.

"He always was a poor loser, you know. Well, my dear, I'm afraid that I have to go now, too, but I really do think you've made the right decision." As he speaks, he seems to be growing thin, stretched out like the fog at its edge, turning first pale, then transparent, wisping away. "And don't worry about that other world. It really won't split again, not because of you, anyway." Only his voice is left. "Farewell. And thank you again, my dear, for guarding my people."

He too is gone. Despite all her reservations, despite the part of her mind that is screaming at her, telling her that she's been hallucinating, that she's making all this up herself, Tiffany regrets his going. She would have liked to have sat at the feet of Rabbi Akiba for a long afternoon, the first woman in history to do so, most likely, to have listened to him talk about the law and the holy books without Nick around to interrupt.

"Neither of them were real, you know," she remarks aloud. "You gotta remember that. It's all in the wiring."

Spoken aloud, and she glances around fast. No one's within earshot, but the long lawn has disappeared, the trees have vanished, she stands on the sidewalk in front of a grey door, scabbing paint, beside a small window, covered with rusty iron bars, light gleaming through the window. Automatically she finds her key, puts it in the lock, walks the two steps down. Home. Shuts the door fast as Meebles gets to his feet on the sofa and stretches, yawning. She whirls round, sees grey light, the last of the foggy day, coming through the window. She's reached home before dark. It cannot still be Friday, as for one panicked moment she was convinced it was. Tonight, as well, she smells no chicken and garlic—smells sausage, rather, and a lot of onions, frying together, and she hears no TV, only Mark singing "Down by the Riverside" in the kitchen. If nothing else, she knows that she did not hallucinate every event for the past three days.

Yet still, she strokes the cat, soft and warm, rubs her hand along the scratchy back of the sofa, touches the smooth painted wall, too, just to reassure herself that she's no longer in the park, that somehow or other she must have kept walking in the company of the rabbi and the Devil to fetch up like a bit of foam thrown by a wave against her door.

"I'm sorry, my dear, to startle you." Akiba's voice sounds just behind her right shoulder. "I was only trying to save your strength, you see, by bringing you home."

She swirls round. No one there.

"Tiff?" Mark calls out. "That you?"

"Sure is." She can feel the blood draining from her face as she hurries toward the kitchen.

"Someone with you?"

"No. Just me."

"Okay. Thought I heard someone else, that's all."

"Yeah? Just some kids outside."

All of a sudden her knees seem made of wet bath towels. By taking one careful step at a time, placing the bad leg just so, moving the good leg ahead of it, dragging the bad one forward again, she manages to get to the kitchen. Mark turns from the stove in some concern.

"Jeez, I'm so glad you're here." She catches the doorjamb and steadies herself. "Just for a minute there I thought—well, I dunno what I thought. Tell me something. We did go to my mom's yesterday, dint we?"

"Sure did."

"And on Saturday LoDarryl, he was here, talking about dump running?"

"Yep. What's wrong? You having trouble with your memory again?"

" 'Fraid so." She's not sure if she's lying or telling the truth. "I'm gonna talk with the doctor 'bout it, tomorrow."

"Good. Hon, you look dead beat out. Come on, sit down."

"I did too much walking. God, I'm thirsty."

She lets him lead her to a chair, lets him sit her down like a child, and fetch her a glass of water, which she drinks fast, in big gulps. He refills it, frowns at the stove, then hands her the glass.

"You better take that jacket off, and I better stir this dinner."

She takes it off, spends a good couple of minutes smoothing it out, folds it neatly in half, then lets it slide unnoticed to the floor.

"How was your day, sweetheart?"

"Oh, pretty good."

His voice, his expression, are so carefully arranged that she knows he's hiding something.

"Oh yeah? Out with it. Something happened."

"Not much, really." All at once the grin breaks through. "Got myself that warehouse job today. Salary starts at fifteen hundred a month, but they's built-in risers."

"All right! Wish we had some champagne."

"Wish you could drink it."

Tired as she is, she manages to laugh, snaps him a salute, laughs again when he returns it. He takes the frying pan off the heat and sets it to one side, then sits down and catches both of her hands in his.

"So I been thinking," he goes on. "You wanna get married?"

"You bet." She can hear her own voice shaking. "I mean, hell, why not, now?"

"Just what I thought. Why the hell not? We can throw ourselves a big old party, hire a band, maybe. Gonna do it up right."

"Sounds good to me, man. And hey, if you want to invite Lo-Darryl and Manny Mike and the guys, that's cool with me."

"Really?"

"Yeah, really. No matter what, they were in the war with you."

"Yeah, they sure were. Thanks, hon." He raises their clasped hands and kisses her fingers. "I think that's one reason I love you so much. You understand 'bout stuff like that, being in the war, and how you feel about the guys you were in the war with."

Tiffany merely smiles, thinking that she understands a great deal more, that she remembers a great deal more, than she can ever tell him.

Afterword

O N A F RIDAY MORNING, SOME TWO weeks after their wedding, Tiffany is just leaving for the hospital when the mail carrier pounds on the door. She accepts a battered parcel, wrapped in torn brown paper and too much tape, starts to toss it onto the couch and leave, then hesitates. In the usual place right above the address, and spilling over the top of the box as well as running down the side are Israeli stamps, postmarked all over with Hebrew letters, far too many stamps for the weight and faded ones at that, a commemorative Golda Meir issue that must be at least twenty years old. Her first thought is to wonder where Reb Akiba dug them up this time. Her second is to decide that for a change she can be a few minutes late. When she finds a knife, back in the kitchen, and slices the parcel open, a big paper-book version of *Hunter's Night* slides onto the table. For a long time she stares at the cover picture, the cropped silver-grey fighter, the golden planet against a backdrop of black sky and stars; at the title, embossed silver; at the author's name in smaller black letters, Albert Allonsby. On top of the vuphone lies the *Collected Stories.*

"Right about that cover picture, wasn't I? Oh jeez!"

The book that doesn't exist, whose author died before he could write it, lies in front of her. She grabs the wrap, turns it this way and that: no return address, just the Israeli postmark, but the stamps convince her that Rabbi Akiba has sent her a wedding present from another world. No one else she knows in Israel would have put six times extra postage on a parcel like this. Anyone else would have sent her a note, even if they had time for only one line, a simple "Write and let us know how you're doing," if nothing else. When she reaches for the book she finds her hands are shaking. Slowly, carefully, as if it just might vanish at her touch, she picks it up, opens it, flips through the pages, reading a word here, a sentence there.

"Same book all right, just like I remembered. Well, I'll be damned."

Curled on a kitchen chair Meebles opens one eye, shuts it again. Tiffany tucks the book under her arm and heads for the door. Book or no book, she refuses to miss therapy, and she can, after all, read a few pages on the bus. As she's locking the door behind her, it occurs to her that she never did tell Doctor Rosas about those hallucinations. As she walks down the street toward the streetcar stop, it also occurs to her that now she never will.

Once she's installed in her favorite seat, she flips through the book, glancing at a scene here, a bit of dialogue there, discovers that these words do lift off from the page and make sense, form pictures and sounds in her mind exactly as they used to. She finds, as well, her old place in the story. She remembers perfectly where she left off, right at the last chapter but one, just as the heroine realizes she can crack the traitor's comp access codes. As the car picks up speed, clanging round onto Seventh Avenue, Tiffany begins to read.

Messengers: ΑΓΓΕΛΟΙ

One

Nothing can travel faster than light.

Suppose for a moment that back in the early years of the twenty-first century, Leslie had been not perfectly sane, no, but as sane as most people ever are; suppose that she indeed had telepathically contacted alien beings; suppose, in short, that thought can travel faster than light though nothing else can—it's an old supposition, after all. If Leslie had unwittingly betrayed the human race, the alien beings that she called the Masters would have had to build a battle fleet and supply it for a journey of over seventy earth-years, staff it with Slaves to do the menial work and tend the Masters onboard, then send it off blind, as it were, with no information about human weaponry and military structure, because Leslie knew nothing about such.

These putative Masters might assume, as we ourselves tend to assume, that a sapient race with advanced technology in one area will develop advanced technology in all areas. That the Masters have learned to sail between the stars might mean that they can easily conquer what they find there—it's possible that they believe this, at any rate. On the other hand, their minds might take a more practical turn and realize that no race advances evenly, that all sapient beings nourish most what they love the best.

Along their way, these aliens would have met television and radio signals, faint, at first, and disrupted by assorted magnetic fields, mere bits of cryptic information scattered through static like raisins in a loaf of speckled bread. It would be ancient information, most likely from the twentieth century, the last dying ghosts of situation comedies and variety shows, pictures of a queen's coronation and the testing of atomic bombs, all jumbled together and spoken in languages as yet unknown. It's likely that the aliens would have made some provision for translating these languages. The mind-contact with Leslie (assuming such existed) would have given them some basic grammar and a beginning vocabulary for American English, as it was spoken in her day.

As the aliens came closer, as they learned to work with human frequencies, the information they would have mined from these veins of electric pulses and waves would first clarify itself, then come pouring into the reception equipment they would have learned to fashion. (We may safely assume that a starfaring race would have a talent for devices. Would the Slaves be trained to do the actual building? Probably.) Imagine the flood of words, music, images, black and white at first, then suddenly brightly colored—if of course these aliens saw color as we do, if of course they even thought to tune their equipment to receive colors—a full spate of sitcoms, banal documentaries, MTV, broadcasts from the House of Commons, cooking shows, sports, news, and preachers, mullahs, priests, all exhorting their various faithful within the range of their local stations. We may assume that it's the news reports that the aliens would treasure the most highly, spending much time in deciphering each gesture, each word, archiving maps and pictures of the endless wars and weapons of humanity.

And then, suddenly, the river would dry up, the flood become a trickle. The aliens would have captured news reports about the invention of focused beam transmission, about the placing of mirror satellites and the conversion of the world to a vast fiber-optic network where expensive signals ran hoarded through cables instead of being flung wholesale into outer space. But would they put those reports together with the sudden dearth? What data would they connect, what would they assume, as their sleek black fleet sailed ever closer to Earth?

Actually, of course, the fleet is neither sleek nor black. The ships, ugly spheres of various alloys and metals, annealed with a grey permacoat of a ceramic-like substance when they left their home skies, have managed to become even uglier, all nicked and battered by debris as they glide, deformed bubbles, through the gaseous drifts of interstellar space. Each ship is wound round with pipe and shielded cable and studded with equipment pods; each carries before it a ramscoop made of bilious green ceramic. A battle-fleet, yes, and bent on conquest, although the largest ship, some three miles in diameter, is a travelling hydroponic farm and little else. Our assumption that they would treasure news broadcasts the most highly has also turned out to be wrong, although they certainly have listened to the news. By the time the fleet passes through the Oort Cloud, its commanders have learned much about humanity, enough to worry about their chances of conquering the planet without reducing it to useless rubble.

As they decelerate, dropping at right angles to the plane of the major planetary orbits, they discover the fuel stations round Titan, pick up the existence of intra-system shuttles and worry the more. By now they can translate English and many other languages as well—after all, have not language lessons been some of the most popular programmes on television for over a hundred years? They have scooped up *Guten Morgen America, Living French, Ingles Hoy* and many like them with the same efficiency as they gathered hydrogen and interstellar matter for their fusion drives.

At this point they are moving far, far below the speed of light. They have plenty of time to play with their devices, plenty of time to discover the radio frequencies bouncing between France, China, and their various interplanetary probes and vessels. As they listen in to one cryptic conversation after another, the aliens discover that one country on Earth, Christian 'Merrka, has if not all then most of the bombs. It possesses, in fact, one of the finest planetary war machines that the Masters have ever come across, enough submarines, fighter planes, cyber-armored ground soldiers, missiles, ships, and various miscellaneous means of killing sapients to give the aliens what the commander calls, proud of its nearly learned 'Merrkan, "a good damn run for our dinero."

They also learn that all over the world, this war machine is hated and feared, that even within its own country, there are those who would bring its rulers down. Alliances. Subversion. The commander rubs all of its hands together, considering. How best to contact these people? The 'Merrkans seem only the most dangerous of a thoroughly dangerous bunch. The commander dislikes putting its own kind at risk, especially since it has Slaves at its disposal.

Oh, and what were the broadcasts that they treasured most? The religious shows.

Two

Now that the global temperatures have stabilized high, the pines are dying in the Sierra foothills. On the slopes that get full sun, grass spreads round and over fallen trees. Live oaks spring up at the meadow edges like black-green bubbles in the pale grass. In the valleys and cañadas poplar and aspen invade the sagging forests. Deep in the shade of the old growth evergreens, orange needles lie thick upon the ground. Dead trunks lean against dying trees in one last desperate attempt to prop up their fellows. Arches form over dells like hidden chapels, while all round sunlight falls in dusty shafts like pillars of smoke.

In such a clearing among the pines Father Kevin is celebrating mass. He wears his white cassock and purple stola over a pair of baggy black pants. The altar, a tailgate from a buckboard, lies across two boulders for support; the salver and the chalice are tin, old National Guard issue dinnerware. The wine—well, as Father Kevin says, Christ will turn the water to wine if we keep the faith. Father Kevin talks a lot about miracles, almost as much as he talks about the early Christians, worshipping in secret. Not that the ancient faith of Rome needs to hide, not even from the grimly Protestant government—Father Kevin openly runs a church down in Goldust—but these particular communicants do.

Every week, it seems, his secret congregation increases. Today fifty-two people sit on the ground in orderly rows. The adults, men and women both, have rifles lying beside them. The children, some dozen of them between the ages of two and thirteen, sit between the adults and the altar; the adults like to think, anyway, that they're safest that way, as if somehow the power of the altar and the tin chalice and salver will protect them should some marauding unit of the National Guard burst out of cover. Father Kevin can remember the days when there were Jews, bravely clinging to their own true faith, and Buddhists, too, hiding out in the hills with pagans and nonbelievers, but since none of the people sitting in front of him were born then, they have turned to the only alternative to the state-sponsored Calvinism that they can conceptualize. The Resistance is becoming Catholic. Every now and then, even while he prays before the altar, Father Kevin hears the distant whistles of the sentries, signalling to one another and to him that all is well. He has served them Mass already, just at dawn.

When the service is over, the communicants pick up their rifles and their children and disappear into the forest, so silently, so efficiently, that Father Kevin feels as St. Francis must have felt, preaching to the animals. For a few moments, while he stands with his hands still raised in benediction, he can hear their moving—twigs snap, leaves rustle, a baby gurgles with laughter—then nothing but the wind moves, sighing through the dying trees.

With a shake of his head Father Kevin turns back to the altar.

In a bucket of river water he washes the salver and the chalice, wraps them in faded purple cloths, then packs them into one side of a pair of saddlebags. His cassock and stola go into the other. He retrieves his shirt of coarse black homespun from the dead tree that serves as his vestry and puts it on, then slides the altar onto the ground and artistically sprinkles it with pine needles. Murmuring prayers aloud in the same archaic English as the Mass, he walks round the clearing, scuffing up needles, blurring his tracks and the traces that his congregation has left behind. Slinging the saddlebags over his shoulder, he heads out of the forest.

In a valley meadow he had left his horse, grazing at tether, and as he steps carefully to the forest edge, he pauses, stopped by some instinct, for a look. The bay gelding stands with its head up high, nostrils flaring, watching something move on the far side of the long meadow. Father Kevin hesitates, hears his heart thump once, decides that caution will only look suspicious and strides right out into the meadow. The bay whickers a greeting.

"Hi!" Father Kevin calls out. "Who's there?"

Across the meadow motion flickers among trees, disappears into shadow. *No good, no, no good at all.* But surely the sentries would have seen, if some spy was there? Father Kevin waits, watching, turning slowly, studying the forest edge all round the meadow, while the sun climbs higher and sweat runs down his back under his shirt. Insects buzz and chirr in the tall grass; otherwise, nothing—a bad sign, that the forest would fall so silent. *May the good Lord guide and keep you. Mary watch over me. No good waiting here.* While Father Kevin saddles his horse, he pauses often to look round, but he never sees his silent watcher again. By the time he mounts, the normal noise of the forest's picked up. During his long ride home, he sees and hears nothing but the occasional squirrel, chittering on a branch.

Goldust shelters a couple of thousand people in less than five hundred buildings, all of them wood, now, with high-peaked roofs. They straggle and spread along one side of the strip of grey rubble that marks the dead highway. More small farms than houses, the compounds reach back into the meadows of the foot-hills on a disintegrating grid of side streets. Most of the actual houses are fenced and barricaded inside big yards, with vegetable gardens and some chickens out in back and a wooden wagon or cart sitting in front with the cows and horses. As he rides by, Father Kevin sees a woman or girl hanging out laundry or a boy tending the stock; when they see him, they wave, even the Protestants, and he raises his hand in impartial blessing. Since the Baptist circuit rider only gets out here every three weeks, Father Kevin does a lot of the funerals and sickbed visits that need doing.

In the middle of town stands the old Safeway supermarket, surrounded by grass, weeds, and shards of asphalt. The windows lost their glass to scavengers a long time ago now, but the walls and roof still stand, sound enough to shelter the farmers' markets that take place every week. Father Kevin's church, Our Lady of the Mountains, sits just down the dirt road in what used to be the bank, a grey stone building with fluted columns on either side the main door and high ceilings inside—a churchly sort of place, in its way.

Father Kevin lives round the back in the old bank offices. After he stables his horse, he carries his saddlebags inside to his grey stone rooms, their veneer panelling, acoustic tiles, and wall-to-wall carpeting long gone, mere stains on the concrete floor or a line of drilled holes down a grey wall. What furniture there is, a wooden table, two chairs, a narrow bed, a desk, are as old and shabby as Father Kevin himself. He pauses for a moment, glancing round, wonders if he heard a footstep, turns round—no one there.

Or is someone in the church? Leaving the saddlebags on the table, Father Kevin walks over to the door that leads from his living quarters into the vestry, hesitates there, listening, hears nothing. He opens the door and steps through into the vestry itself, dim and cool, smelling sharply of homemade pine resin incense. A door on the far wall leads into the chancel. When he listens beside it, he can hear someone moving in the church beyond.

Most likely it's just a parishioner, come to pray or light a candle. Most likely. He turns away, leaves the vestry, shutting the door very carefully and quietly behind him, then walks to the back door and looks out. Nothing moves but a pair of jays, squawking and squabbling by the stable door.

With a grimace for his own suspicions, Father Kevin steps outside. As quietly as he can, sticking to the flagstone path and avoiding the loose gravel, and as quickly, too, he strides round to the front of the church, finds the front door open, and strides in, blinking at the sudden dimming of the light. At the far end, before the altar rail, someone wearing a big blue and green shawl over grey trousers kneels in prayer, gazing up at the enormous wood crucifix hanging behind the altar. Father Kevin smiles—just a parishioner, after all. He offers a quick prayer of his own to the Blessed Virgin, then walks inside, ready to give his blessing if this troubled soul should require it. Someone tall, he notices, and very thin—his eyes are adjusting to the inside light—and when you come right down to it, pretty darn strange. Even though he knows everyone in and around Goldust, Father Kevin certainly doesn't recognize this person, who seems to have pale bluish-grey skin and a long almost cylindrical skull. *Mary, Mother of God, be with me in this hour!* Father Kevin prays as he walks down the aisle between the rough wood benches that serve as pews.

The worshipper at the altar crosses himself, then rises, turning to face him. Very tall indeed—most likely over seven feet, with long spindly arms, covered with pale grey scales, ending in hands with two fingers and two thumbs. It or he or whatever does indeed wear trousers of some baggy grey cloth, held round its waist with a heavy belt from which hang small shiny objects. But the blue and green "shawl" turns out to be a pair of triangular wings, folded neatly over their wearer's back, made not of feathers but of skin and scales. The scaly face has two recognizable blue eyes, set deep inside hollows and pouches of skin, an arrangement of skin folds and slits where a nose ought to be and a longer slit and fold for a mouth. Father Kevin can only stare, goggling. For a moment the blue eyes study him; then the being kneels on the floor. Its wings flutter, then droop.

"Father, don't be afraid," it says. "We come from the stars. We wish to hear more of the word of God."

The voice hisses and slurs from a mouth more rigid than a human one. Father Kevin swallows long and hard, then finds his own voice at last.

"My son, all are welcome to hear God's word and to believe in Him."

"That believing we may have eternal life?"

"Yes, my son."

"Even slaves, Father? Did the Lord come even for slaves?"

No amount of slurring and strange popping sounds can hide the enthusiasm, the hope, the aching aching hope in that voice. The eyes shine, too, looking up at him with the eternal agony of all sapient beings, who see their own death crouching ahead of them, a monster on the road.

"Yes, my son," Father Kevin says. "For slaves, too. Jesus said, other sheep have I that are not of this fold. And I'll bet He was talking about you."

Three

The night lies misty over Salisbury Plain. Every now and then the moon breaks free of scudding clouds and gleams on the fields that lie either side the road up from Bournemouth. Already the sleek grey limousine has glided through the edge of New Forest. When it sped along the bypass around Salisbury, the driver, Sergeant Potter, saw a glimpse of the cathedral spire under the moon as the road turned. Whether his important passengers in the back seat, invisible behind smoked glass, saw the spire or even cared he does not know. They have left the ruins of Roman Sarum behind, too, and now run free through farmland, rolling over the downs. Here the road runs past Bronze Age tumuli and the barely visible scars left by cursi and avenues, but Potter knows little and cares less about the Bronze Age or the Romans either. To him Salisbury

Plain means what's left of Britain's army, the artillery ranges and the infantry base, the airfield that shelters the new StarHarriers.

Although Potter of course knows where they are going, he hasn't the slightest idea of why, in the middle of the night, he is driving the prime minister, two generals, and the Duke of Kent to Stonehenge. The only logical reason he can come up with is that the entire government has gone daft, but he would prefer to think otherwise.

At the crossroad, as he turns right and heads down the last slope, Potter can see the ancient stones, standing behind their new plastiwire barrier, which shimmers and gleams in the moon-shot mist. Not far from the circle, across the access road and just past the refreshment kiosks and souvenir shops, stands a pale structure. In the moonlight it seems to be made of several tea tents clustered together. Potter wonders if he's the one going mad. Behind him, a tap on the glass—the general's aide-de-camp slides open the communication panel.

"Just pull into the regular lot, Sergeant," the lieutenant says. "Down at the far end."

"Very good, sir."

Potter pulls into the last space at the end of the asphalt strip, then slides out of the car to open doors. Out of the circling ditch materialize sentries in field uniform, rifles at the ready. The lieutenant barks a hasty password. The sentries nod, one salutes, they stand waiting while the generals and the Duke get out. The prime minister needs a little help; Potter smells brandy hanging about him like perfume.

"Wait with the car," the lieutenant says.

"Yes, sir."

His cargo delivered, Potter leans against the bonnet and watches the Important People clamber down the side of the wet ditch, re-emerge safely on the other side, and hurry toward the collection of tea tents with two of the sentries trailing behind. This close Potter can see that yes, tea tents are exactly what they are, pink-and-white striped pavilions, lit from within—a cool white light very different than the usual field lanterns and electric torches. The last sentry clambers out of the ditch and strolls over to help him guard the limousine. Potter jerks a thumb at the tents.

"Wotthehell?"

The sentry shrugs. Since clouds have darkened the moon, Potter cannot get a good look at his face, but when the man speaks, his voice shakes badly.

"They called us out of barracks to put the bloody things up," the sentry says. "Emergency, they told us. Only thing they could find were bloody tea tents. Ours weren't big enough, they said. Hurry it up, lads. Then they hauled something in on a couple of lorries. Something big. Looked like a tank, maybe, wrapped in canvas. A couple of squads put up another tent around it. To hide it, like, before the wraps came off."

"Missiles? Something the sodding 'Merrkans don't want us to have?"

The sentry shakes his head no. Potter waits.

"After they had it stowed," the sentry says in a moment, "The captain sends me up there with a message from Field Command to the colonel in charge. He was inside, you see, the colonel. So I handed it over at the door." He falls silent.

"Well now, here, if you're under orders to keep your mouth shut—"

The sentry shakes his head again. Overhead the moon breaks free and floods them with silver light. Even though he's a veteran of the Pakistani Border Wars, Potter has never seen a man so terrified as the sentry is now.

"There's these creatures in there," the sentry says. "With wings. Wearing clothes. Aliens, they must be, from outer space."

Potter would like to laugh, but he restrains himself in the interests of morale.

"Uh, now here, you've had a few, have you? It's cold out here, can't say I blame you, and it's none of my job to report it, anyway."

The sentry laughs, an unpleasant giggle like a teenaged girl's.

"I'm not drunk, and I'm not joking." The sentry's voice turns hard with near-rage. "I saw these things, I tell you, a couple of meters tall, they were, and they had wings. Blue and green wings. And they were walking back and forth and talking to the colonel."

Potter says nothing. The sentry obviously believes that he has seen two-meter-high outer-space monsters with wings. What this may mean will take a bit of thinking about. One of those new VR and hologrammic stress tests would be Potter's guess. Show the men something strange, see how they react. But why bring two generals, the PM, and the Duke of Kent out here in the middle of the night? He starts to speak, thinks better of it, looks up to find the sentry watching him.

"I'm not lying," the fellow snaps.

"All right, then."

The lieutenant emerges from a tent and begins trotting toward them. He pauses at the edge of the ditch, then picks his way down and through. Potter strolls over and gives him a hand up. In the moonlight the lieutenant's face gleams as pale as death. They walk slowly back to the car and the waiting sentry.

"What's wrong, sir?" Potter says.

The lieutenant lets out his breath in a short sigh.

"You'll have to know sooner or later," the lieutenant says. "Something very odd's going on, sergeant. We have, um, visitors."

"Told you," the sentry mutters. "With sodding blue wings."

The lieutenant ignores him and goes on speaking, much too fast.

"There's a radiophone in the limo. Get it for me, Sergeant. And how long will it take someone to drive down from London? Or no, we'd best send a chopper, I think. He'll prefer that. If he comes. Or no, the PM will see to it that he comes."

"Sir?"

The lieutenant sighs again.

"Sorry. Our visitors want to see the Archbishop of Canterbury."

* * *

In Australia the messengers appear at Hanging Rock; in China, at the Great Wall; in India, at the Temple of Kali in Benares; in the Emirate, on top of the mound of Ur; in Egypt, in front of the Sphinx; in Japan, inside the grounds of the Imperial Palace. What do these places have in common? The commander saw them all in movies it particularly liked. They also lie a long way away from any 'Merrkan military base. Since the messengers materialize out of transporter beams on shielded frequencies, the commander hopes the 'Merrkans will know nothing until it's too late. Since the 'Merrkans have grown careless from their long domination, the commander proves right.

Four

A bright sunny day, and on the green lawn stand the big white blocks of plasto-foam, about five feet high and seven long, each marked with a red number scribbled on the side, sixty-four of them drawn up in ranks like a squad of soldiers. Jan Tifnie Gehrens, who was named for a great-grandmother, Janet, and a great-aunt, Tiffany, walks down the line, counting them off on her data tablet, checking for damage to the packaging. The lawn rises to a low hill, and on the crest trees dance in the rising wind. From behind her comes snatches of carousel music, a digital recreation of old tapes. The actual musical mechanism has long resided in a museum in downtown San Francisco with the original wooden horses and the remnants of the gold-trimmed and mirrored panels of the original wood canopy. The brand-new carousel of the recently restored Children's Playground in Golden Gate Park looks exactly like the old one, but it's made of longer-lasting stuff than wood—various forms of soy-derived plastics, extruded, molded, formed, carved, puffed out with air and laid down in thin sheets, each component brightly colored, then resinated with acrylics to last for a hundred years. Jan Tifnie takes a moment to admire the carousel housing, the gilded canopy, the mirror panels, the polished floor, the unmoving chariot seats all bright green and red and gold, the shiny brass-colored poles hanging temporarily free. Thanks to the stuff it's made of, the carousel can stand right out in the sun and glitter. Rain won't be rotting it away or dimming its gaudy rainbow.

Whistling along with the music, Jan's supervisor, Enrico, comes strolling over. He grins at the plastocrete blocks.

"They be okay?" he says.

"Yeah, boss."

"What you say we open one?"

"Bueno, yeah. I gotta knife."

From the plastoskin sheath at her belt Jan pulls out a flat-bladed knife with a smoothed-off point. Together they search the closest block, find at last the thin welted seam where the two halves were heat-glued. Carefully, slowly, her tongue tucked into the corner of her mouth, Jan slides the blade into the seam, stops when it touches something solid, pulls it back a fine-judged bit, then runs it round the block from the bottom of one narrow side round to the bottom of the other. The foam creaks and splits with a waft of white powder.

"Turn it over?" Enrico says.

"Nah. I think, we just break it off now."

While Enrico holds the block steady on his side, Jan digs her fingers into the open seam and pulls. With a crack her half of the foam block splits at its base and comes away clean. Nestled in its white bed the horse gleams a silver grey with dappled flanks. Its white mane curls and tosses round the proud head with the flaring nostrils and dark deep eyes, the scarlet bridle, trimmed in gold.

"Oh she-it!" Enrico whispers. "Cool!"

"Yeah, sure is." Jan runs an admiring hand over the horse's smooth, cool flank. "Beautiful stuff, beautiful beautiful stuff."

Enrico nods, smiling, but Jan feels more than a little sad. All her life, since leaving school at sixteen the way most kids do these days, she's worked in construction and assembly, but in all those fifteen years or so, she's never had a job she liked as much as working on the carousel reconstruction. Soon this job will end, and it'll be back to the hiring hall, to scrimping pennies, to taking the first job that comes along, whether it's digging new cable housings or shingling roofs, because a woman with two kids to support can't be fussy.

"I betta call in," Enrico says. "Let 'em know the shipment, she okay."

He unhooks his callphone from his belt and punches in the number of the project office. Nothing happens. No squawks, no beeps, no answering voice. Just as he looks up, puzzled, the sound hits them. Jan can only think that the biggest quadro speaker in the world has sounded a note too low to hear but loud enough to feel. A vast pulse of energy booms soundlessly in the sky and shoves them with rushing air. Flecks of powdered foam, scraps of paper, dead leaves and twigs—all fly up from the ground and swirl round twice before they settle again. Silence drops from the sky like a shroud. Jan realizes that all the normal traffic noise just outside the park has stopped. She hears none of the normal white sound of a city—not one hiss or swish of an electric trolley or car, not one note of music or one word of a distant talk show on a distant TV.

"The Rapture." Trembling, Enrico sinks to his knees. "And we ain't been taken."

For one brief moment Jan thinks the same. Could it be true that Christ has come in all his glory to take away the faithful while she, miserable sinner that she is, has been left behind in the clutches of the Great Beast?

"Hell, no! That be some kind of bomb. Them pulse bombs, you see 'bout on the news. Oh my God, my kids!"

Without thinking she is running, knife still in hand. She sprints from the playground, then settles into a smooth-breathing jog on the concrete path that takes her past Hippie Hill and out the entrance to Stanyan Street, where two electrocars sit forlornly in the middle lane. *Ain't gonna be no buses.* On the sidewalk she stops, panting a little, and slips the knife back into its sheath. Both drivers sit inside their cars and stare straight ahead, hands clutching steering wheels as if in blind faith that the power will return, any minute now, to the grid beneath the surface and take them onward again. From the shops opposite, though, people are streaming out, looking up in the sky, starting to talk, to gabble, to point up as if there were something to see.

Jan jogs across the street and heads downhill while around her panic rises. She hears snatches of voices, snatches of news.

"Mine be off too. Everybody they got no power. Try the batteries, they work, nothing but static, no TV, nothing but static."

Jan trots past dead buses, keeps running. More people crowd out of houses and stand watching the sky. On the downhill slope she can run a long way, stops finally at Fillmore to pant for breath while she stares at a tangle of dead buses and pedestrians, standing around, talking always talking.

"Nothing but static. Last night on the news they said. Things in the sky. Shooting stars. I saw it, I tell you, on the news. Something in the sky. Orbits. One of them Chinese things, that's all. The government said. They lie. Nothing but static."

A man swears, a woman screams. Jan looks up when the screamer points at the sky. Far far up, a smooth grey wedge-shaped thing moves slowly from west to east, soundless in the blue, floating lower and lower as it curves over the city. A huge grey wedge-shaped plane of some kind, dotted with gleams of reflected light that must mean windows, scored and marked with lumps that must mean doors—it sinks toward the eastern horizon and disappears. Everyone in the street gawks after it without saying a word.

Jan threads her way across the street and takes out running again. Once she hits the flat at Market Street, where buses and streetcars stand mute in dead traffic, she's forced to slow down. She turns onto Dolores Street and heads toward her children's school, some thirty blocks away. As she hurries along, she joins a swelling crowd of women, some carrying infants or dragging toddlers, all walking fast, trotting when they can, saying nothing, saving their breath, heading for the school. Since cars can't run anyway, the women take over the street and spread out, hurrying past the row of ancient palms planted in the middle of the wide boulevard. Unencumbered, Jan can jog faster than most. A bit at a time she weaves her way to the head of the crowd, then leaves it behind, sprinting again when she crosses 24th and reaches the downslope.

Then stopping. Stopping and staring, simply staring. Hearing the crowd of women coming toward her, hearing screams as they too see. Jan, who never screams at anything, merely stares.

Coming down Dolores toward them march their children, clutching lunch boxes and paper bags. They march in tidy columns, three abreast, with their teachers walking along beside them. In front and in back are Others. Tall, so very tall, and all spindly arms and legs, but what Jan notices first are the wings, the big scaly blue and green wings, spread out as if to catch the warm sun. Behind a pair of these monsters she spots her two kids, right in front, both of them smiling and laughing. All of the kids are smiling, some skip along, swinging their lunch boxes. The teachers walk silently, their faces white or streaked with tears. As the procession comes close she can see that the creatures are smiling, too—or so she assumes, because their long slits of mouths and the folds of grey skin around them are all curved upward.

When the children see the crowd of women, the tidy lines break into a wave of running kids, dashing forward, calling out, laughing and dancing. Jan darts forward as Maradee, her older girl, hurries up, dragging little Amber behind her. Jan drops to one knee and folds the children into her arms. She can feel herself shaking on the edge of tears.

"Mom, Mom!" Maradee is laughing at her. "It be okay, Mom. Cool dudes, all of them."

Jan forces a smile, but she cannot stop shaking.

"Mom!" Maradee pulls away and points. "They got faces like us."

Jan looks up and finds one of the monsters hovering nearby.

Upon his grey and scaly face, a thing of horizontal slits and folds, she can comprehend, she can match up to some internal pattern and say to herself, "there, that makes sense," only one feature, his pair of blue eyes, perfectly round, shining like glass beads, but still eyes.

"They no look like us to me," Jan says.

Maradee considers the tall creature, who considers her in return. When the child smiles, it smiles.

"See?" Maradee says. "Faces like us."

L'Envoi, Without
the Roses

On top of Mt. Davidson in San Francisco there once stood an enormous concrete cross, visible from most of the city as it rose out of a grove of eucalyptus trees. During the Great Quake of 2047, it cracked at the base and fell, shattering into three enormous pieces and smashing the trees all round it. Even for an officially Christian government, money was too short to set it back up again. Over the years grass and oxalis grew up around it, then lost the struggle for sun when the eucalyptus trees reasserted their claim to the slopes. Now, some seventy years after the earthquake, although the earth below buckles and strains yet once again and new tension builds on the fault, the broken cross lies in a grove once more.

By positioning himself just right on the concrete stump, Nick Harrison can sit in the shade and look out between two trees to the western slope of the city below, edged with a high seawall and beyond that at the end of his view, a silver strip of ocean. He wears the sleek grey uniform of the pan-European occupying forces, currently operating under the direct command of the Masters, and of course, he's chosen the persona of a field-grade officer. Being a subordinate has never appealed to Nick. As he contemplates the view, he smiles, luxuriating in his victory.

"They all converted to Catholicism. Is that cool or what? There's millions of those scaly little bastards out there, all itching to hang a cross around their necks and believe. So they believe in God. Big deal. They also believe in *me.*"

With a crow of triumph he leaps to his feet.

"In me, they believe in me, I come with the deal, though the stupid bastards don't even know it yet! Jeez, louise, for a while there I was scared stiff, thinking their stupid church was gonna die on me." Nick hesitates, suddenly cold. "That's always the question, isn't it? Suppose no one believed in me. I mean, hey, what would happen to me? Am I immortal? Jeez, last thing I want is to get that answered the wrong way. Doesn't matter now, anyway. Millions of 'em, and they believe in *me.*"

Another crow, another strut.

"And hey, those Masters know how to whip people into shape. This is gonna be fun to watch. Lousy messy rotten human race gonna have to shape up fast now. But I dunno. What if the Masters get corrupted? I don't see how anyone can stay efficient on this crummy planet. I better think about that, or everything will start going wrong again. It's just not fair. It always cheats, you know."

"You're a fine one to talk, creature."

With a yelp Nick spins around to find Rabbi Akiba, standing in a patch of sun and smiling at him. Nick clenches both fists.

"What do you want, old man? Come to gloat, I'll bet, about your precious Israel. All safe and sound by order of the lousy Pope himself."

"So why shouldn't I be pleased? And I'll tell you something else. All the synagogues in America—they'll be open again."

"What? Why? The slimy little bastard! Wait a minute. You had something to do with this, didn't you? Didn't you?"

"And what could I do, one old man like me?"

With one last snarl Nick disappears. Rabbi Akiba smiles and addresses no one in particular.

"The galaxy needs Jews, you know. It really does."

And he disappears himself, leaving the sunlight standing alone between the trees.